D0282985

THE GRINGO
CHAMPION

Aura Xilonen

THE GRINGO CHAMPION

*Translated from the Spanish
by Andrea Rosenberg*

Europa
editions

Europa Editions
214 West 29th Street
New York, N.Y. 10001
www.europaeditions.com
info@europaeditions.com

D.R. © 2015 AURA XILONEN ARROYO OVIEDO
D.R. © 2015, Penguin Random House Grupo Editorial, S.A. de C.V.
First Publication 2017 by Europa Editions

Translation by Andrea Rosenberg
Original title: *Campeón gabacho*
Translation copyright © 2016 by Europa Editions

Library of Congress Cataloging in Publication Data is available
ISBN 978-1-60945-365-7

Xilonen, Aura
The Gringo Champion

Book design by Emanuele Ragnisco
www.mekkanografici.com

Cover photo © Ozgurdonmaz/iStock

Prepress by Grafica Punto Print – Rome

Printed in the USA

To my grandparents, my aunts and uncles, and my mother.

*To all the world's immigrants,
which, if we go back to our origins,
is all of us.*

Words, like ideas, are barbaric men's invention.
—LIBORIO

THE GRINGO
CHAMPION

And then it hits me, as the scruffs trail the gorgeous chickadee, hooting at her and talking dirty, that I can get myself another life by beating these pinches australs up. After all, I was born dead already and nothing fucking scares me. I could always prove it too, like I did a while back when I smashed in the teeth of a scruff who was making moves on the chickadee while she, silent, just stared down the street toward where the bus was supposed to be coming, all uncomfortable, especially when the prick pincered her ass with his esproncella-infested digits. At that, I cut the ties that bound me to the counter at the bookstore where I work; the dust vibrated around me, and I was off like a shot to drummel his snout with my fists—what did I have to lose, after all, since I've never had anything? And so I come up behind the guy and give him a sharp kick in the ankle, and he crumples over like a trivel running down a windowpane on a rainy day, all slow-like, and then I slam him in the cockles with all my might.

Pow! Bam! Wham! And I knock out his teeth till all I can see is his own ferrous swell there, red, whineous, and trembling, his body sprawling the length of the bench. By this point a little knot has gathered around me—street fights happen all the time, and the scruffs and yups hoggle around trying to get a better look.

One of his buddies says to me, "Fucking hell, cabrón, no sneak attacks. Bring it straight on, you fucking wetback, like a man."

And he lets me have it with a couple to the teeth, like those dogs that destroy everything they see, and just like that, instinctive-like, with the same foot I used on the first guy, I bazooka the second guy between the underpinnings and take him out. Before he went down I saw his eyes roll back; his balls must have been shoved right up his ass and into his brain. And he falls flat on his face on the ground.

Now nobody in the little knot wanted to get into it with me; they were just staring at me, bluish, dwarven, like they had crumpled under the weight of the air.

I tried to catch a glimpse of the chickadee or whatever, to see if she was O.K., but I didn't see her. There were so many scruffs, I didn't know if the bus had come or if maybe some yup had squirreled her off and dragged her back into the alleyways, where the houses are like rats' nests.

A black woman who'd seen the whole brawl comes up to me, grabs me by the arm, and pulls me out of the pack while some of the scruffs try to start something with the neutered negris on the bench; she drags me to the corner and says, "Sweet Jesus, kid, stop shakin' that wasp nest and get yo' scrawny ass out of here, or you ain't gonna last three seconds."

But I shrug her off and leave her there on the corner, muttering to herself, and cross the street to the bookstore to get back to helping the houseflies.

* * *

[Oh, I hadn't felt that good since that time I plunged into the Rio Grande and, with the strength of these emaciatious arms of mine, emerged again hours later, half dead, like I was breathing for the first time. I left behind all my squeams about harsh things there, at the edge of the water, on this side of the abyss.]

Back behind the counter at the store, Jefe comes at me like

a scythe and asks, "Sold anything yet, you fucking louse?" Then he goes up to the window that looks out on the street and spits out, "Shit, what the fuck is going on out there on the corner?"

I shrug my shoulders, a rag in my hand because I have to finish the dusting I left half-done when I took off to pound those scruffs in the chickadee's defense.

"Somebody ran over a dog," I say sulkily, or something like that, and insigh with exfuriation. Just then I look up and out the window and feel a shiver in the point of my tiepin, a pang in the pit of my stomach: the chickadee is crossing the street toward the bookstore.

Earth, swallow me up.

My balls shrivel from the shock. I can't even swallow my own spit.

I imagine myself evaporating into thin air with just a look from her; in the blink of an eye, I become fugitivious.

Jefe spots her too and calls me a moron.

"I'll take care of her, you odoriferous jackass," he says, and waves me off to the back of the store behind the bookcases so I can't embarrass him in front of the beautiful bird while he preens his goatee.

The chickadee enters the store, rumpling the air, ignoring the books piled up on the shelves and tables; she moves past and drills down in front of the counter. Jefe shriggles his eyebrows and rollicks his eyes as if he's trying not to stare at her chest.

I keep my eyes on the floor, feeling adrift on a paper sea among all those books.

My mouth's so dry, I start gargling the air.

She says who knows what—I've stopped listening. I only feel my temples fluttering a thousand miles an hour. Jefe waves me over and in a trinkly voice hisses in my ear, "What did you do, you louse-infested prick? She wants to talk to you."

Jefe moves away a few steps and pretends not to be watching, but I know he's got eyes in the back of his head and ears in his peepers. The chickadee looks me up, down, and right through, as if I were made of smoke, and just says, before turning and walking out, "Dude, gracias . . . but no thanks. I don't need a hero, sabes?"

She turns around and I feel all of her curves, her lips, her breasts, her scent, hit my craterized skin like a hurricane. Jefe ogles her pert ass as she heads out the door and crosses the street toward her building. I remain plastered to the tile floor, splattered with some sort of sticky substance or whatever. Jefe turns, frowning, and says, "You fucking shithead, what the fuck was that?"

I shrug my shoulders again and feel like gunning away right there, awash in the many gallons of ink it must have taken the printers to splatter all those books with letters. But it's not like I'm scared of his anger. In the brawl outside, my pulse had been cataleptic, mummified. Serene. I could have passed a camel through the eye of a needle while I was pulping those scruffs. No, it's chickadees, especially the beautiful ones, the flirtatious ones, that give me the shakes; I feel things leap in my belly just imagining I'm near one of them; I think I shouldn't even be breathing the same air they breathe; my marrow sizzles if I just brush their skin with my eyes. I can handle punch-ups, no problem. With those curves, though, I spin out and plunge into my deepest voids or whatever—but when the chickadee headed out of the bookstore I felt desolate, upside down, all saggy-like.

And me, not a peep, couldn't even make a peep around her.

"What the motherfuck was that?" Jefe yanks me out of my befogged quivering.

"Nothing, Jefe." I pull myself back together. "Chickadee wanted some kind of magazine we don't have," I say to the contusion so he'll stop poking around in the gaping fissure I can feel opening in my chest.

"Fucking Levitican cabrón, how's this store supposed to survive when you can't even sell a goddamn magazine, huh? Chingafuck."

And I stand there, dazed, nauseously engulfed in my own vomit.

I can't sleep; I just stare at the dull darkness that stings my iris, drills down into my pores and fills them with cold, up in the loft Jefe's letting me use here in the bookstore, crawling with mellifluous spiders, with bugs hunkered on the walls, ready to pounce on my flesh. Suicidal spiders. And no, I can't fall asleep. Instead I imagine the chickadee dangling from the bare bulb, and then she breaks all the windows and stabs me with her purple fingernails in the middle of the night. I even think I hear the fractured noise of her hands scraping my skin, tearing me to bits like when I rip up a newspaper to clean the windows, like the same noise glass makes when it shatters.

"Motherfucker. Shit. Fucking motherfucker. Fucking pyrolytic louse. Fuck, fuck, fuck!" he yells, louder and more deranged with every shout.

I don't want to get up.

I don't have the strength to do it on my own. I can feel the fever still clinging to my skin; a legatious turbulence is running in circles through my bowels. Just then, all of a sudden, as I'm watching the ray of sunlight fill with dust floating warm in its luminious bowels, Jefe shouts up at me from below, in the bookstore, like he's got a bullhorn attached to the back of his neck.

Cursing, I throw back the blankets and descend the little staircase from the loft with my eyes shattered, like I've been weeping ground glass all night or something. There, my eyes spiderwebbed from insomnia, I see a hell of a mess.

The bookstore's been turned upside down. Tossed. Jefe is

already righting a bookcase and gathering up the corpses of depaginated books. The bookstore looks like the path in Wells Park in autumn, strewn with tattered leaves, hundreds of them, carpeting the floor. A few books even seem to have been stabbed to death, or beaten, or ripped up with angry teeth. They lie amputated around us, as if they had a rocket shoved up their ass that blew out their guts. Jefe looks at me, holding a bunch of ragged pages in his hands, but instead of cursing at me, going for broke unleashing all his frustrations on me, I see how his eyes are shattering and he's collapsing onto his molten skin. I don't know what to do, so I don't do anything. I just shrug my shoulders again and start picking up whatever's closest to me. I adjust a broken table and drop a clamor of books onto it.

* * *

["Books bleed," Jefe told me when he met me that first day there, in the bookstore, because he needed someone young and super cheap to go into the nooks and crannies of the bookstore and clean it all, help him with everything: scale the walls like a scorpion to lift or lower textual petulancies; carry anacreontic boxes of volumes and take them to the storeroom to slow down their wormification, since all books fucking wormify; be wordaciously frasmodic to mop, shake, and tidy the shop.

"Tell me, kid, what do you know about books?" he asked me that first time when I asked him for a job.

"Nothing, sir," I said.

"What do you mean, nothing, kid? You're not a moron, are you?"

"No, sir."

"So what do you know about books?"

I remember I stood there staring at his weetzy shop crammed with bricks up to the ceiling, and just said the first thing that occurred to me in the moment:

"They're a real pain in the ass, sir."

For the first time, I heard him laugh with that laugh of his like an unhinged alebrije. He took off his glasses and buzzed like a bumblebee.

"Oh, shit, hoo-hoo-hoo! You're not just a moron, cabrón, hoo-hoo-hoo, you're a colossal dumbfuck!" He kept laughing a long while.

When he wheezed to a stop, he told me he wanted to see how I did washing the display cases for free.

"That way I can find out if maybe you're not as dumb as you seem, kid—maybe you'll leave my glass squeaky clean. Oh, and another thing—what's that smell? You smear your clothes with shit or something?"

I figured it would be a cakewalk; I'd leave his glass squeaky clean like the glass in a coffin when the corpse is no longer breathing and vamooses, to the other side of the air, impassive, nevermore, out of fucking breath. And I did: I scraped off the grime of centuries with my own fingernails like razor blades and my breath like glass cleaner.

Months later, Jefe would admit he hired me because I was the only kid who looked like he'd never steal a single book.

"What the hell would I want them for?" I answered, outbraided at having my honesty sullied. "I want to go to New York, not stay here just on the other side from everything I'm trying to escape. In the meantime, though, while I'm here, I'm just trying to put together a little dough so I can toss myself like a pebble into another pond."

But Jefe didn't hear that last part because I said it so quietly that maybe I only thought it.

So as the weeks passed, seeing I was ready for anything, he let me stay up in the loft in the bookstore. That way, in addition to working all day, I could keep an eye on the place at night while he went home to be with his missus and their little misters, and

*left me caged in there with padlocks on the outside and the little
window in the loft all boarded up.*

*"But if you need help, you ringuearme on that telephone.
Don't forget, you caustic little asshole, you call me, capisce?"*

*And he went off to the suburbs, pleased with himself, to cau-
terize his missus with his prick and produce more little misters.*

*After that, up in the loft, nervously, I started tossing eye
boogers at the books. First the ones with illustrations. I'd take
them upstairs. This was because sometimes an overdressed lady
would come in asking for books en español and ask me something I didn't know the first thing about. Jefe had noticed this
and yelled at me algorhythmically one afternoon:*

*"You brainless louse, you'd better start reading some god-
damn books, even if it's just the back covers, so you'll know what
the hell people are talking about and you can sell a fucking book
for once and stop being a goddamn moron."*

*And so, gun to my head, I inhaled a lot of bullshit written on
the books' back covers. Sweating bullets, because reading makes
your eyes hurt at first and your soul gradually fills up with lice.
At night I'd carry virgin books up to the loft and bring them back
down again in the morning, deflowered.*

*"Hey, dickhead, any idea why this fucking book is full of fin-
gerprints?"*

"No, Jefe, beats me."

"Don't play dumb, you simioid prick."

*And so I learned to put plastic bags on my hands so I wouldn't
leave marks in the books. I'd carry them up and carry them back
down again. I even learned to unwrap them and wrap them back
up in their original packaging to keep them pristine. Because Jefe
loved his books; for him, every time he sold a book it was like
selling a piece of his soul. That's the way puffed-up apes are: aged
by their own foibles.]*

"Go on, you purulent jackass, and tell my missus to get over here. Goddammit, I don't want to have to tell her about this and get her all worried and make things even worse," says Jefe, still kneeling in the upheaved bookstore once I've righted all the bookcases and started sweeping up the fallen leaves with a broom. I stand there staring at him. He looks so different, so on his knees, his dripping dampening the booksherds he's holding in his hands. He looks like a broken fountain; Jefe has become a bit of rain that's tethered to the clouds. In my eyes he's so nebuline, so unarmored, squealing like a fucking pig over the fragments of his torn-up books, that I leave the broom wobbling in midair and make a mad dash for the libidinous streets to clear my lungs or whatever, because there was still a tatter in my throat, clogging it like an avocado stone, a seismic vibration plugging my veins, I don't know, crouched in a vile pit. I inspel air through my nostrils.

"Hey, pissant, wasp sting yo' ass?" I hear the black woman shout toothlessly at me from the other side of the street, herding a little metal shopping cart full of junk. Then she moves off toward the corner and disappears around the chickadee's building. I keep standing there, malleted on the sidewalk, time rocking from side to side. I feel lost. I see a mob of yups walking by, tightly packed, cell phones glued to their ears; I see addos and scruffs wearing out their hands grabbing their balls; I see dudebros and chickadees crossing, coming and going, leaking carbon dioxide from every pore. I see the cars that stop and go, metallically spinning, weaving in and out. Horns, rumbles, the clanging of the sun striking the tops of the buildings, here all the birds are tangled in the wires. I see the high windows with flowerpots on their fire escapes, their cozy skylights. I see closed blinds and open blinds. The buildings brick-colored, gray, made of smoked glass. Sheveled trees and impeccable window boxes.

The barrio is like an appliances aisle.

A gussied-up lady with a micropooch wrapped in a bolt of fabric goes by. My eyes are really hurting. I slowly cross the street toward the bus stop, and a million horns bludgeon me from all sides.

"Fuck you, man," they yell at me. "Fuck, fuck, fuck. Go home, fucking wetback, get the fuck out of here, you piece of trash."

I get to the bus stop and crash out on the bench. From there I look up and see through its broken windows that the bookstore is rising up, lapidated, as if fatally wounded, buried. I sharpen my gaze and see Jefe still bent over, as if in prayer, before his crucified shop.

"Hey, puto," I suddenly hear behind me. "You like throwing down to defend asses that don't belong to you, huh?"

I crane my neck around to see who's touched my shoulder, just in time to see a coppery fist coming at my cheek at light speed. I don't even have a chance to helmet my eyes. Gobsmacked, I'm knocked from the bench onto my ass on the ground. I see little stars and feel blood start streaming out of my mouth and onto my chest.

"Fucking wetback!" continues the yup with the flowers, the chickadee's puppitonic one true love, the one who was hitting on her left and right. "You think you're real macho, fucking ass-robber. Who the fuckety-fuck gave you permission to go around defending culos that ain't yours, huh?"

"Oh, shit, motherfucker," a guerrilla scruff shouts, running up when he sees me sprawled on the pavement covered in mole sauce, "beat the shit out of that motherfucker."

I don't know how many of them are crowding around to kick the shit out of me, but I feel an army of prickly ants kicking me all over. I just shield my goods and curl up in the narrow space between their feet. From there I see the cars still rolling by, and for a moment the universe fills up with their blows. One, two, three, four, a thousand, eight thousand.

"Leave him alone, cabrones." A shout soars over the herd of dicks. The kicking suddenly ceases.

"If I ever see you near my pussy again, fucking wetback," the austral yup hisses at me, "I'll kick you in the balls so hard, you'll end up coughing them up." He gives me one last wallop and heads out of the knot that is gradually disappearing behind my lowering headlight covers. The scruffs slope off and scatter as quickly as they appeared.

"Are you all right, son?" asks a man with a gray beard as he hands me a handkerchief. He squats down next to me and stares at me as if trying to penetrate the river of blood flowing from my crown to my roots. "Madre santa, you look like a post-Passion Christ! They really gave you what for."

I take the cloth from his hands and start mopping up the blood mixed with sweat that's tattooed across my forehead.

"Are you hurt anywhere else besides your head?"

I say no with my noggin. I suck at my mouth, yes, my blossoming mouth, but I'm not missing any teeth. One of my ribs hurts, and one shin, my eyelids, my hair, under my fingernails, under my tongue, but I'll survive or whatever.

* * *

[My godmother always said to me when I'd show up with my headlights battered in, all brambled: "Bad weeds never die, you goddamn thug." Because down in Mexico the only way you survive is by fighting. That's why I came up here; I was sick and tired of wiping my nose with dirt and chewing on the earth's entrails.]

"Hold on, son, take your time getting up," the man says when the knot finally dissolves completely. I think they were even recording me with their fucking cell phones, fucking assholes, and I don't want to keep being a rug for their eyes. I stand up, and the man grabs my arm when I stagger as an oceanic surge of nausea laps at me. "You'd better sit down before you hurt yourself again." I obey and sprawl on the bus bench. My temples are still pounding at a hundred fifty miles an hour. "Do you have any family you can call?" I stare at him in a stupor, utterly temerical. I shake my head again. "Let's see," the man says, scrupulizing me. "You've just got some bruises and a few scratches. Take a couple of aspirin, apply some ointment and a couple of butterfly bandages, and you'll start looking like yourself again in a few days' time. Do you have a place to stay?" I shake my head for a third time, shrugging my shoulders. "Well then, why don't you come with me, son? You can stay at my place for a couple of days and we'll figure out what to do with you after that." I look at him with deep suspicion, hardened from all those brawls, tempered by the boiling oil I've been sizzling in. "Let's go," the man breaks in, noting in my eyes all the fear, all the rage, all the resentment tamped down at the bottom of my soul, ready to go off at any moment and blow everything to fucking hell. "Come now, son," he bleats, "the world isn't as bad as it seems. There's always hope, boy, there's always that, oh yes," he tells me passiflorally. He's quiet a moment, looking at me with his druilic eyes, and then holds out his hand to help me up. "I'm Mr. Abacuc," he says. "What's your name, kid?"

Yes, they've left me stratospherically muddled; my head-lights are burned out, racooned, straticated like a fucking panda. Black and blue. Turkeyfied. Back in my hometown they'd say I've got peeperitis, or what the fuck ever—like the green-eyed monster, shit. I can barely see where my peepers are reaching out their claws to touch things. My ears are asymmetrically buzzing, endecibelled by my ass-whuppative encounter with the addos. Out of the corner of my eye, I spot a red bus pulling up at the bus stop; part of the knot that watched me getting beaten up by the scruffs and the yup climbs on, and another knot of citizens gets off and scatters like fucking ants in a downpour.

The city's still moving. Everything revolves in its toothless, pointillated gears, like a huge wheel that crushes everything in its path.

"Liborio," I tell the man as I pass his handkerchief, smeared with a sheen of bloody snot, back toward his outstretched hand.

"Keep it, kid," he says pythagorously, his smile obtuse. "Crazy old fucker," I think, "who would help someone just for the hell of it?" There's always got to be something super shady, dirty, yeah, or whatever in people, something canned, filthy, and foul, where the flies are bigger than vultures, flies as huge as swine. "It's O.K., kid," Mr. Abacuc continues. "Here"—and he holds out a couple of ten-dollar bills. "Buy yourself some ibuprofen and some lidocaine cream and a box of Überkrauz butterfly bandages."

"What?" I'm dumbfounded.

"I'd better write it down for you—you're clearly out of it. And I'll give you my address too, in case you ever need a place to stay." He pulls a pen out of his coat, tears a small flyer off the telephone pole next to the bus stop, and scrawls on the back while asking me, "What were you fighting over—a girl?" and then waves it in front of my swollen nose along with the grubby bills.

"Are you loonytunes, Mr. Fruitcake?" I want to know whether I should kick him in the balls with my remaining strength and then take off running with my window shades only half open, even if I end up smacking right into a telephone pole.

"What?" He keeps smiling.

"Yeah, you old goat, are you fucking nuts?"

"Ha-ha-ha, oh, no, no, no. At my age, that would be crazy."

I look at him a moment, my eyes blurring. Then I grab the

bills and the slip of paper and stuff them in a secret place in my belt, next to my mother's locket.

"Perfect," he says. "Hope you feel better soon."

He turns and starts walking across the street.

"Hey," I yell, my voice cavernous from the pain in my ribs. "Do you believe in God?"

Mr. Abacuc stops, half turns toward me, and answers with an unwrinkled smile, "No, do you?" Then he keeps going and disappears around the chickadee's corner. I keep standing there, frazzled, as cars drive past. I don't want to move. I wish there were a leaf that would carry me into orbit where I could stay, nestled among the fucking stars.

* * *

["But dreams are just dreams," Jefe once told me when I said to him:

"Sure, why not, one day I'd like to have a family of little runts playing soldier together—yeah, munchkins all over the house and courtyard, if I ever manage to have a house—a wife and brats, and collect, my hands overflowing, all the fucking bullshit people spend their time with when they're trying to fend off boredom as they geriatrify."

"Hoo-hoo-hoo," chortled Jefe. "But you're hideous, you rancid pain-in-the-ass motherfucker. Who the hell's going to want to tap that ass?"

Rattled, I didn't say anything, morticated by the thought that other people see me as a loser. What if God doesn't actually exist and we're just shabby particles floating in time, destined only to destroy one another? I often wonder that, especially when trouble reaches out and shits my pants and my godmother, whom I always called auntie, used to box my ears to make me memorize the psalms.

"This way you can grow up to be an upstanding, respectable

*man without all this shady stuff," she'd say. And I'd blow her off;
the priest and his catatonic pretentiousness, that useless prude,
that perverted crotch-tickler, could kiss my . . .*

*Who the hell wants to become a clergyman and be chaste his
whole damn life?*

*I asked him that one day during catechism. "Father Terán,
how often do you manhandle your balls?"*

*He gave me an unholy smack upside the cranium. Then he
sent for my godmother, and the two of them blessed me with a
peppertree branch.*

*"I can't put up with you anymore; you scram right now or I'll
have them put you in jail," my aunt, who was not my aunt but my
godmother, told me not long after that. And so I was run off without a thing, to a life of filth, to skid row, to al fresco under-bridge
dwelling, to the hard place as a splintered rock. With my posse,
crammed in there among the stoners and losers and brawlers.*

*"You've gotta get out of here or you're not gonna wake up
tomorrow," I'd tell myself sometimes, in the shadow of the back-
stitched streetlights, staring at my bloody hands.]*

But what of it. I've made it through to the other side now.
That's all over. It's over? I raise the bloody handkerchief to my
nose again; luckily, I've always been made of concrete. Not
even mosquitoes could pierce my donkey flesh, or at least,
thanks to the elephant skin I wear fitted like a glove, I never
noticed when my blood became flying droplets inside their
buggy bellies. Just then a white truck slowly pulls up in front
of me and a lady in a hat and sunglasses calls to me in a con-
stipated voice from inside it:

"Hey, vato, get in." She opens the door. I'm not sure if she's
talking to me, so I ipsofacto as an ignoramus. "Come on, man,"
she says, "don't be scared."

I keep sitting there, mulish, because things go sideways
when you stick your foot in before your noodle. Seeing that

I'm not budging, she closes the door of her boat and yells, sounding like an influenzal firefly, "I saw how you took that beating without flinching." A few cars start honking wildly behind her. "Blow me, hijos de puta, if you can!" she yells at the drivers. Then she turns back to me: "You're a real fucker of a motherfucker, huh? How old are you, kidlet?"

"What the fucking shit do you care?" I finally answer to chill her out, wanting her to leave my life the same way she came into it.

"Fine, then, sassbucket, I'll come back later when you've calmed down and we can conversate. You work there, right?" She points at the bookstore. I ignore her. "All right, kidlet"— she takes out a camera and points it at me. Before the flash goes, I flip her the bird. "Hasta luego, güey," she says, and laughs screechily. "Bwa-ha-ha"—she snorts—"bwa-ha-ha-ha."

She starts up her truck and takes off, eventually blending into the horizon of speeding cars. I turn my head toward the bookstore and see Jefe, his back to me, staring down at the floor. He didn't notice a thing. I imagine in the face of his own tragedy, all other tragedies are minuscule to him.

Should I go see Jefe's missus, or should I go back and lick my balls in the bookstore? I get on a red bus that's just pulled up in front of me, pay my fare, and zoom like a rocket toward the back row, where brutes like me tend to go so we don't frighten the blacks and whites—because we're gray, and gray here is a sort of limbo cut off from both God and the Devil.

"What happened to you, kid?" the missus asks me the moment she opens the door to her casa.

"Nothing, ma'am," I say. "There's been an attack on the bookstore."

She hops back like a frog; she brings a hand up to her chest and starts falling to bits like a wobbly pile of rocks.

* * *

[*She wasn't mean to me. In fact, she would give me a little food sometimes when she was in the city. She even bought me some jeans and a shirt with the bookstore logo embroidered on it and a pair of low boots a few months back, not expensive ones, but more comfortable than my huaraches.*

"*Go on, take it, kid, we don't want you going around looking all tattyraggled!*"]

So before the missus hits the ground, I grab her by one wing and help her fall, like a plucked chicken. With her lying there in her sweats, her breath clucky, I roll her inside the house. Her little misters must be at school. What do I do? Like a moron, I grab a bottle from where they've got a little bar and an altar to the Virgin of Guadalupe. I unscrew the lid and start tipping the contents down the missus.

"I'm dying," she immediately crows, cramped coughs bouncing from her throat out to the backyard—the yard where Jefe grills his American-as-apple-pie hot dogs. "Vodka, you bird-brain? Are you trying to kill me?" the missus says when the coughing fit's over, and snatches the bottle from me. Yeah, well, what the fuck do I know about resuscitation, just that a dead man once got up and walked, with worms, I imagine, crawling in and out of his skin.

I help her up and a few minutes later we're in her truck, heading for the bookstore. "Why didn't you call my cell?" the missus asks once we're on the freeway. She keeps dialing Jefe's number. In the distance, the city looks glassily blue, lapis lazuli, drowsy from afar, its virous swarms hidden inside it. The tall buildings look like pillars—herculeonic, atlantidous—that hold up birds in flight, those birds I finally saw last autumn as they were leaving Wells Park, soaring high above me toward who knows where. "And did they point guns at you or what?

Did they beat you up? Is my husband badly hurt? How many were there? Did you call the police? Why didn't he call me? I'm going to call the kids' school. Oh, their godmother can go pick them up. Yes! What else happened? Do you know who they were? What time did it happen? Did anyone help you? And has anyone taken a look at those bruises of yours? How many attacked you? Holy Mother of God! Oh, kid, if anything's happened to my husband, I'll just die."

The missus isn't exaggerating—she truly loves him, loves him with every bit of her, as we could see, smell, and feel in her baskets of food, her hyperbolic caresses, and her pozole kisses.

* * *

[*"Look, you little prick,"* Jefe once told me at his house, at the second or third barbecue he invited me to, when tequila was already strangling his tongue, *"you see that old broad? That old broad is my lady, you greasy little prick—but you know that already, don't you? See her? And you know what? She loves me, she loves me; I know it, hand to God, here in my heart, I know it. And you know what? I love her too. Otherwise . . . For her, for her I'd, I'd do . . ."* And Jefe just stood there, rapt, agog, staring at his empty glass of tequila.

Later the crazy Argentine came up and sat down next to me. Jefe loves betting with him on all kinds of things and used to invite him to all his ragers.

"You're the guy who helps him out at the bookstore, right?"]

We cross over the last freeway and enter the city. The missus turns on the third cross street and heads toward downtown. We pass the shopping center overflowing with McDonald's, Starbucks, Walmart, Costco, Home Depot, 7-Eleven, Sam's Club, Domino's, a Cinemark movie theater, and ads for Coca-Cola, Western Union, FedEx, UPS, Apple, and Microsoft.

We bend left and skid onto the street where the bookstore is, burning rubber from sixty to zero in no time flat. She parks in a space out front and tumbles out in a frenzy, racing toward the store. I stagger after her.

The door of the bookstore is ajar, the books are still strewn around, and I see that the bookcases have been knocked over again. The lights are still on like fucking turn-of-the-century ghosts.

"Virgen María! Mi amor! Cariño!" The missus's shrieks scatter all over.

"Jefe! Jefe! Jefe!" I shout behind her, like an off-tempo echo.

"Where's my husband, kid?" the missus asks. I shrug my shoulders and stand there, fucking zombificated. "Did he tell you he was going to report it? Was he going to go to the police station? What did he say? You guys called the police, right?" she asks again. With every blink, her eyes are turning into red, swollen pools, into sharp, toadish lines under her neat eyebrows. "The loft!" She heads up the little staircase while I look for Jefe in the basement for the fourth or fifth time. Maybe he's wrapped up next to his fucking books of love poems like a goddamn cocoon, filling up with worms; or maybe he's in the bathroom, jammed in the drain by cowardly rage—because I know fear and bile change the way we smell; temper makes our phlegms oily, ambrous, viscous, bloody. But dogs can sense fear, and that's why they bite like crazy when your pores sprout feathers.

"No, there's no sign of him."

Jefe seems to have ghosted away.

I go out the bookstore's broken door, but there's nothing. I stop in its outline. The people are walking past like they always do, looking only at their feet with their eyes lowered or with their cell phones enmeshed between their heads and their hands. In that moment in the air, in the intemperance of the chaos of that awful day or whatever, my face starts prickling again like hundreds of little stingers going off; I sure am banged up, I think, but it'll pass.

Outside, evening is coming on in squally torrents. The sun's lowered its angles and is heading out, as it does every day, bouncing orange among the cirrus clouds. The cars are still going by. The scruffs are starting to emerge from their lairs. The chicas are swinging their behinds like pieces of expansive, miniskirtish waves. The bookstore's totally destroyed and no one's gawking? What's wrong with this goddamn world?

I go back inside and start picking up a few bookcases to put a bit of order to the fucking chaos. Just then the missus comes down from the loft with a pile of books I'd taken up to read and didn't have time to bring back down this morning. She doesn't say anything. What could she say when Jefe's vanished amid the shattered glass? She sets the books down on the counter, her trembling somewhat dissipated.

* * *

[Sometimes the missus would come to be with Jefe at the bookstore. She'd help him out by manning the cash register. Then she'd go pick up the little misters from school and I wouldn't see her again until a week later, when she'd bring him something to eat. When Jefe had a bit more trust in me, he'd leave me in charge of the bookstore and go wandering off with his wife at random times.

"Be back soon, you pigheaded prick! I'm off with the lady who owns my heart!" And he'd blast off, intrepid, like a besmitten astronaut into the fucking heavens.]

"We have to leave everything exactly how it is so the police will see how it's all been destroyed." The missus shreds the silence as her eyes prowl the bedlam of books and toppled bookcases.

I've never heard the missus say a single goddamn word in Spanglish. She either spoke Spanish or she spoke English, nothing in between. And she didn't curse, either, didn't use those rude words Jefe uses that aren't in the wordbook, the dictionary, that fucking dictionary I used to read because I didn't understand shit of what I was reading; incendiary words that are much clearer than all those muddled respectable words: those goddamn little ladies with sickly-sweet frills, language that is archaic, obsolete, old and priggish. I prefer whores, words that say everything in one fell shitkicker, not little by little. I don't know why the missus has always been respectable. I don't know. What I do know is I can't stay there till the police arrive, at least not till the trouble's over. The missus meets my eyes, realizing that if the police take me in to make a statement, they'll immediately launch me to the other side of the world, into the stratosphere, like a goddamn rocket.

"Here, kid," she says, her eyes red, and holds out a few bills she's pulled out of her sweatsuit. "I want you to take off for a few days till this all blows over. But don't disappear on us—we're going to need a lot of help putting this store back together. I'm going to call 911 now. Stay close by and make sure you have someone take a look at those injuries."

I take the money from her hands. It's three hundred-dollar bills.

"All right, ma'am. Jefe'll be back soon, you'll see."

I turn around and leave as she picks up her cell phone and dials 911.

And now what the fuck do I do? Cramps clutch my shins. They're like little windmills whipping hot chocolate in my arteries, atole drained from my veins. My face looks like I've been attacked by a giant wasp.

I cross the street. The cars have started to turn on their headlights. The streetlamps bloom at night. I've never seen a star here. In the cities, the trembling stars have been killed by the law of mercury. I look up at the blue sky and try with all my might to inhale the oxygen I'm lacking.

I'm in an unfamiliar city.

I don't have a single fucking friend.

I used to think the future meant moving forward without lingering on the individual days, on their poisonous hours, their cadaverous seconds that are inexorably destroyed as they accumulate, forming suicidal blocs of sixty. I cross the other street and head toward Wells Park. Before I turn the corner at the chickadee's building, I hear the ululation of police cars racing toward me. I stick my hands in the pockets of my jeans and hunch forward.

It's getting colder, and there's no loft or spiders to warm up the night.

W ells Park isn't ginormous; it's a medium-sized park with trees and stone benches ringed by a little gravel path. It has three fountains that the grown-ups use to sail little boats with their offal on their days off, after they come out of their various churches—Presbyterian, evangelical, Baptist, Christian, Muslim, Buddhist, Zoroastrian, Scientologist, androgynist, bluesist, jazzist, soulist, Arabesque, Jupitertian thermopile, poltergeistal, Orthodox, heterodox, and pedodox Catholics, with reverends, pastors, priests, monks, vicars, doctors, philosophers, musicians, barbiturate cascalytes, jovial, jivial, ojival atheists, lonely atheists, unbelievers, aderenalined intoners, reciters, and hustling charlatans.

Wells Park was also frequented by scruffs, yups, chickadees, dudebros, and kids. Whites, blacks, yellows, pinks, punks, old apes and young apes. Some people used a fenced-off area at the edge of the park to walk their housepets, carrying little plastic bags to pick up their caramels. Others went jogging in the morning or in the evening, enveloped in their iPods, dangling shackles pressed to their ears so they can swathe themselves in solitude like a shield; the music in their ears, I think, is a mask they use so they can go around without being bothered—and there were a lot of masks in the park.

* * *

[*The first time I went to Wells Park was on one of the first*

Sundays off Jefe gave me so I'd have something to do instead of sitting around tormenting ants once I'd finished with my doodies at the bookstore.

"Get out of here, you goddamn idiot, go get some exercise at Wells Park!"

"And what the hell am I supposed to do there, when I'm skinnier than your fucking mother?"

"What did you say, asshole?"

"Be back soon, boss."

That day I went out to the park and sat there all day watching the squirrels, watching the children splashing in the fountain to retrieve a sunken sailboat. Watching the dogs pad across the granite slabs and watching the other people who were sitting and watching without watching anything in particular.

Over the next few Sundays, I would seize the opportunity to smuggle a book out of the bookstore and read under a tree up on a hill where people would lock up their bikes and from which you could see the entire park, east to west, north to south. There I saw a few rollerbladers, a few rockatonics dancing with their boomboxes turned all the way up like snakes coiling in the air; there were also other street musicians—trombonated, violinitious, guitarified—across the battlefield.

I imagine a park as an intranquil pyramid where everybody gathers but they never mix.

That was where I saw the chickadee for the first time. She was walking by with a German shepherd on a leash, wearing black leggings and a sleeveless jumper. Her hair was pulled back in a simple ponytail, linear, like a Greek column, Doric, its capital unvoluted, like a Venus, yes, beautiful. Her nose narrow and her eyes as wide as the sky. I saw her and was stupefied, struck dumb, my heart trickling out of my pores. I couldn't breathe— right there, airless, dancing, tremulous waves shaking my body. I've never known whether fucking love at first sight or whatever, I don't know, actually exists, but that chickadee drove my peepers wild from the first moment I looked up from the book I was reading. She seared my retinas. I forgot everything I was reading and couldn't look back down at the fucking book. Standing there like that—bestially, savagely beautiful—she filled the entire park with her astonishing self.

I imagine she looked at me too as she passed, because I assume chickadees look at everything and see everything, even if they aren't going apeshit about it and it seems like they're not looking at anything. I sat gored there, cromalitic, under the tree full of squirrels and caterpillars.

Ravaged.

She took two more turns around the park and then crossed the street with the German shepherd on its leash. She disappeared into a crush of cars and people. I was still sitting there, ashen, bruised; the air I was breathing wasn't entering my body, my despotic, agitated cells.

I went back the following Sunday, hoping to see her again, my pulse precipitous, but I didn't see her.

And the following Sunday, but no dice.

I should have followed her, I kept kicking myself, beating myself, thinking: yes, if I'd followed her and then what—I'm too cluckatillic to talk to pretty chickadees. My hands sweat, my feet sweat, my ass sweats just thinking about it. And then what, I follow her and what? She notices and calls the police and they throw me in the clink as a murderous sicko who's violated the chickadee's personal space; they give me a thrashing and toss me in a hole. But I wouldn't have cared—so what, I would've been happy just to see her. I imagine that love too can be admired as a work of art might be—from afar, without touching it, without belonging to any space, any physical dimension, with the eyes alone, with all the senses that come together to produce butterflies in a person's fucking guts. Though I don't know if anyone's ever fallen in love with a statue; I think they have, pygmalionically I think they have.

And so no, she didn't show up at the park, and I didn't see her again until months later, as I was up in the window of new releases arranging several horrible Spanish novels and saw her walk past in sneakers and a suit, heading toward the bus stop across the street.

"Watch out, you moron, careful with the damn libros—they don't grow on trees! I'll take them out of your paycheck, you tub-blubber!"

I was pressed up against the glass, feeling the same old pang in my fucking butterflies. She smoothed her hair with one hand. A car passed and honked at her, another passed and honked at her too, five or six more horns until the red bus pulled up and she got on and sat in one of the front rows. The bus pulled out. Without thinking, I jumped to the floor and ran out to the street to watch the bus move off.

"Again"—and I started running after the bus.

I caught up with it two streets later and spotted her once more. She was looking straight ahead, beautiful, the most won-drous vision my eyes had ever beheld. When the green light hit us, the bus started off. "Again," I said, and started running, dodg-ing the people who rose up like befuddled telephone poles in my path. And I followed her for many more streets until they pulled onto the freeway and my breathing was a swarm of trampled and suffocated butterflies. I watched the bus become a fucking crim-son blotch of lost love or whatever, carajo. I lost sight of her amid the firmament of vehicles.

When I got back to the bookstore, Jefe was waiting for me at the door.

"You piece of shit, you really gave me a scare! I thought you'd been rounded up in a raid by la puta migra or something. You squeezed my soul bone-dry. What the fuckety-fuck happened?"

"Nada, Jefe."

"What do you mean, nothing? Nobody takes off like that for no reason! What happened?"

"*Nada, Jefe.*"

"*Out with it, you fucking prick!*"

"*O.K., Jefe. My bad, I thought I spotted your goddamn mother herding donkeys.*"

"*My ass you did, cocksucker. I'll show you.*"

"*Yes, Jefe, it won't happen again.*"

But I was brimming over on the inside. If the chickadee caught the bus right here across the street, that must mean she lives or works nearby.

Most likely she lives nearby because she was walking a dog, but why was she dressed all fancy like she was going to work outside the city? Was she heading home and only works around here?

I spent the next few days washing all the bookstore's plate-glass windows again and again, trying to keep one eye on the streaks and the other on the street in case she walked by. I organized the entire stock of Latin American novels, from prickly-pear to penguin. All the damn Spanish novels and the fucking gringo ones translated into Espanish. I organized the books in alphabetical order, from front to back, by title and then by author name, from a to z; then it occurred to me to organize them from back to front, from z to a. I also organized them by color, by size, by number of pages. I organized them by font. Then by subject. Almost all of the books were dull novels I'd already read up in my loft or in Wells Park; they were fettered by the superficial task of effectuating sentence after sentence, soulless, lifeless, simply tossing out pretty words right and left. That's how I imagined writers thread their novels together, wormy, airless, disemvoweled. But even though I kept my eyes peeled, the chickadee was nowhere to be seen, damn it.

When I was running out of ideas for rearranging the novels, I started organizing them by the authors' photos: the ones who seemed like the surliest, most disagreeable scruffs went in the first row so that the few lost souls who strayed into the bookstore would see them first, and the fucking scribblers who looked all

prettified and shiny, just like their goddamn respectable words—
wearing neckties in the photos, posing like candy-ass intellectu-
aloid yups—I left in the last row, piled on top of one another, the
wimps, so not even their mothers would spot them in the hades
of books down below.

On the third day of the last week of summer, I finally saw her
again. She was wearing Bermuda shorts and sandals with purple
flowers on them and a tank top. Her hair was up in another
ponytail, and she wasn't wearing a trace of makeup.

In an instant, my heartbeat took off like buzzing flies.

The chickadee went up the gray stone steps of the brick build-
ing across the way and passed through its gleaming wooden door.

"Please be true, please be true, please be true," I said to
myself. I don't know if I was whispering or not, but I think not
because Jefe yelled at me from behind the counter.

"You fucking dolt, lay off that praying and let me read the
fucking newspaper in peace."

I stopped dribbling words and started watching everything
that was going on outside, determined not to miss a thing.

"Jefe, can I go outside for a minute?"

"No, why?"

"I'm going to clean the outside of the glass."

"Didn't you just do that?"

"I'm going to get a soda."

"Didn't you say you were going to wash the windows?"

"I'm thirsty."

"We've got water right here."

"No, I want something bubbly."

"Well, whisk a goddamn fork in a fucking glass of water and
drink that, you parched parakeet."

"Jefe."

"What?"

"Up yours."

"What!"

"I said do you want me to bring you a soda."

"I heard you, you fucking prick. Go on, go get your damn soda."

Before Jefe was finished speaking, I was already out the door and crossing the street to the brick building. I raced up the stone steps two at a time, ready for anything. Fuck. Anything—well, I was here now, I thought, sweating bullets, might as well keep going. When I opened the fucking door to go inside the building, she was on her way back out. I looked into her eyes and she looked at me—I know she did because I felt a powerful hammering in my peepers. It was a fraction of a second, a giant explosion, as if the universe had been shattered in an instant.

My throat seized up.

I opened the door a little, moved aside, bent my head toward the floor, and let her pass. "Thanks," she said. Just "thanks." She went down the stairs, her hips swaying, and I felt her expansive waves melting me, millimeter by millimeter, turning my fucking body into jelly. Uncertain what to do, and with my ass clenched up into my neck, I entered the building and closed the door behind me.]

"Big wasp sting yo' ass," says the black woman as she walks past me.

I'm still slumped on the bench in Wells Park. Night has fallen. I'm feeling listless. The scruffs who overtake the wee hours haven't shown up yet. At night the park becomes a hotbed of hustlers like me. Shit yes, inexistent howlers from the shadowed margins. The woman guides her shopping cart a little closer to the small fountain, where there are some bushes and the grass is thicker. She pulls a couple of flattened cardboard boxes out from her odds and ends, spreads them on the ground, and then lies down on top of them. She tugs at a threadbare blanket with one hand and covers herself with it.

"Ass-face," she repeats, "wasp sting yo' ass." She lets out a wild laugh and then grunts, "Sweet dreams." She closes her eyes.

As if I could fucking sleep, I think to myself, when I've got my soul pendling from my nads.

I look at a few others who are coming toward me, nodding the night. Tattered. Vagabondious.

During the daytime, the city's drowsies are overshadowed by the kilometric frieze of ads, by shiny cars and beautiful people. At night, when only noises remain, the rest of us—druggies, junkies, illegals, scruffs, kids, and yups—materialize like demons crushed by our gaunt impecuniousness.

"Puta madre, and me busting my ass trying to keep my head above water."

I hunch down when a gust of wind rushes through the trees and tweaks my pores.

"Wassup, vato? This is our bench!" four little snotnose punks inform me. If I were in the mood, I'd be forced to beat the shit out of them to make them show me some respect, but my fucking face is enough of a mess already. I get up and let them crow over their bench. "That's right, faggot, go screw your mom!" they yell at my retreating back.

I wozzle along the flagstone path till I spot the tree where I've sat reading on so many Sundays. At the base of the trunk, I collapse on the roots. From there I survey the whole park. There are some dudebros rollerblading eastward under the orange glow of the streetlights, which are full of gargoylish moths. You can hear their laughter and their fucks when they fall down and get covered in mud, leaving behind shreds of skin as they pirouette across the earth. Then they get up like nothing happened and race off again. Off in the other direction, where the lights are burned out, are the Spenglerian papasitos, junkies, pot dealers. Cars go by, pause for a few moments to buy dime bags of weed, or eight balls of coke, or methamfuckingphetamines of crack, and then plow into the streets again with speed whetting their nostrils.

Nah, sí, fucking misery abides everywhere or what the fuck ever—from the mad-dash yuppies down to the threadbare impoverished, it's a fucking waterfall of shit. Just then I see a grungehead carrying a bag of glue, which he's inhuffing and exhuffing above his slack jaws.

If I fall asleep, I'm fucked, I think, because it's like sliding right down into hell. I nestle into myself. I hug my legs with my hairless arms; all I need is a fucking cowboy hat and a poncho to turn into a raggedy statue.

I only half close my eyes since they're already nearly swollen shut from the brawl and the lack of sleep. Here you have to sleep with your eyes open so nothing happens—but I can't think, don't need to think anymore. And the more I close my eyes, the more I see the chickadee.

Is love always a goddamn cascade of mirrors showing us the reflection of our own emptiness?

I want to become invisible so the chickadee will get out of my head, to dissolve so I can dissolve her. I can't bear the weight of her in my thoughts any longer. I see her smiling, penetrating every fiber of my brain and flaying me from within. Oh, and what I'm feeling soaks through me. I breathe deeply and gradually relax. The night grows more and more tyrannical, its fog overpowering me; I fall slowly, tangled, circumflex into its outstretched arms. I'll go. I'm going. I'm gone.

I feel a rap on my shoulder. It's still dark and the night is rolling on. Now I'm definitely shattered. I feel another jab, harder this time. The swelling in my headlights has given way to fucking crusties of steel. My lashes are stuck together with gobs of glue. I can't open my eyes. A third blow runs down from my shoulder to my wrist and splatters my clavicle.

"Hey, hey, tú, no esleep in el parque."

I hear it in the distance between dreams. It's like I'm blind, like I'm a dim-witted marionette that's missing its strings.

"Hey, hey, hey." They bash me in the shoulder for the fourth or fifth time.

"He death?" I hear a Latinoid accent.

"Yeah, mira, seems like he's not breathing," someone else answers.

"He got dinero?"

"I don't know. Hang on, yo chequeo."

Feeling his paws running over my bones, I writhe like an earthworm in a shower of salt.

"Fuck off, motherfuckers, let me sleep!" But my ocular chains are broken and my eyes flop open like quesadillas. They stop patting me down.

"Oh, shit!" yells the handsy Latinoid one. "He's alive."

"Hey, hey, hey, boy, boy, boy. You can't sleep in the park."

I blearily open my eyes a bit more and see two security guards or police officers, I can't really tell. "Chingada madre, just what I needed," I think. Before the goon hits me, I decide to stand up to them—in any event, things can't get any worse.

"You've got to be shitting me. What about all those fucking gueys passed out down there?" I say, ignoring the sharp nightsticks they've been prodding me with. They take a step back, hesitant, security guys feeling insecuritous. They're wearing their uniforms and their fucking helmets. They've got radios on their belts and shiny boots. They look like Martians.

"You have dinero?"

"What?"

"You've got to pay to sleep here, vato de mierda."

"What?"

"Dinero"—and he rubs his thumb with his index finger.

"Look, assholes, I've had a rough day. Fuck off. I'm not going anywhere," I tell them. I see them take another step back all skittery, like they're scared. "That's right, motherfuckers, fuck right off, I'm fucking exhausted."

They take another step back and look into each other's eyes like a pair of fucking lovebirds.

"Fuck," says one.

"Fuck," says the other.

"Fuck, fuck"—and then, a cantabrian glint in their eyes, they raise their spears, their banderillas, as if I were a fucking bull in a bullfight. They raise their crushing clubs and give me a few tastes, one after another, on my back, shoulders, and braincase. One precise blow on the back of the skullery knocks me out. They clobber me artistically, lovingly to sleep like a fucking baby at the foot of the tree in the melancholy night.

Fuuuuuuck!

Yes, you don't realize it, you never realize it, but you can always go lower; there's always farther to fall. There's a low that's deeper, cavernous, like a grave full of worms.

"Am I dead?" I ask groggily, lying belly up, when I see the chickadee's face leaning over me. My neck hurts, my arms hurt, my feet and ass hurt. It's day now, no idea what time, and the world is alight.

"Look, it's Ass-Face," says the black woman. "Yo' head must be made of concrete."

Just then I feel a massive tongue slobber across my forehead, as if a fucking angel were licking my wounds. I look up and see a large German shepherd sniffing at me.

"Candy, no," the chickadee tells it, standing up and yanking on the dog's leash.

"Am I dead?" I ask again.

"Ha!" the black woman says. "You's hardheaded, boy. Wasps stingin' yo' ass and you still alive." She grimaces with the three or four teeth she's got left, grabs her shopping cart full of junk, and starts dragging it toward the path the cyclists take. Chuckling to herself, she mumbles, "Ha! You's like a weed—cain't get rid o' you. Ha!"

I half close my eyes. Maybe it's all a dream, a psychedelic dream, or maybe yes, I'm actually dead and at any moment I'll be dissolved like a pyrrhic spoonful of salt into the vast pond of the universe.

"I was going to call 911, but that woman told me not to. She said it would be worse for you," I hear the girl's voice say. I open my eyes and see her again—she's looking at me. She looks at me. Yes, I'm dead. I must be dead; there's no other possibility. "It doesn't seem like you've got any broken bones."

"Huh?" I say with difficulty, as if I were quivering inside, I don't know why, but I say it at ground level. I can't find any other words in my vocabulary—they've all scrammed, and there's not even a stray letter wandering around my tongue.

"I shouldn't . . . Well, ya sabes. I was really rude to you the other day. Disculpa. I'm so sorry."

I'm out of focus. Not understanding anything. I look at her, beautiful, bending the space around her; if this is what death's like, I want all angels to be like her.

"I have to go," she says after a moment of silence in which I hear only the noise of her wings in the park, the chirping of her feathers rustling in the treetops, mingled with the noises of passersby, like the rumble of the shopping cart the black woman is pulling, which gradually disappears down the stone walkway, and the distant clamor of the cars whirling past.

"What day is today?" I ask her, my voice embarritiously breaking. She's wearing tight-fitting athletic clothing, her hair's pulled back, she's got gleaming little earrings, and for the first time I spot a tiny tattoo beneath her ear when she turns to look at the German shepherd. It's a feather.

"Jueves."

"Mmmm . . . what?"

"Today's Thursday, dude," she says.

I swallow with difficulty. I feel the grass tangling between my fingers. My reading tree is swaying above us. The sky is blue and cloudless.

"I saw you once. It was Sunday, a beautiful Sunday, the most beautiful Sunday," I babble at her, my mouth bruised.

She clearly has no idea what I'm talking about, because she answers:

"I've got to go. I'm going to be late." She tugs the dog's leash. "Ven, Candy, come on."

Before she walks off, she turns back to me:

"Hey, man, you got money for some food?" I nod. "O.K. Bueno, bye."

She heads back to the path and quickly moves away, the German shepherd dragging her to the edge of the park. Every fucking bone in my body hurts, but even so I sit up and watch her cross the street next to the park and keep going until she disappears from view. My body hurts, yeah, it hurts a lot, but something inside me starts to do I don't know what. I don't know. I lie down again, my face to the sky. I don't know what to think about, so I don't think about anything. I just let the roots of the grass settle all my bones in their place.

Moments later I turn onto my left side before the sun becomes a ball of ruthless splendor.

I gingerly prod myself to make sure I'm all there. Yep, nothing missing. Three beatdowns in a row and I've made it out unharmed. Just a few aching lumps, but not too bad: with familiarity, carajo, pain's gotten pretty cheap.

I stumble to my feet. I put one hand on the tree and try to regain control of my vertical. I think I must not be hungry because my stomach's crammed with fucking killer butterflies. That's what I read somewhere—those love bugs rub our entrails with their wings and stab hunger to death. I stick my hand in the pocket of my jeans, which are smeared with blood and dirt. Rotten fucking polypathetic crooks, carajo, fuck me:

those asshole policemen nicked my fucking money. I check the secret spot in my belt, where I was also carrying Mr. Abacuc's two ten-dollar bills, but it's all gone. They really screwed me; the only thing they left behind was the damn note he wrote me. I search a little more thoroughly and my mother's little locket appears; I put it back, fold Mr. Abacuc's slip of paper as a memento of the lost bills. "Oh wells," I tell myself as usual to keep from feeling like I'm always losing out.

I hobble to the sailboat fountain. Nobody's there; today's not Sunday, it's Thursday, and I've never been to the park on a Thursday before. It's not Sunday, and there are only a few faded amblers, ramaged, inscrutable, amid the lawn and the swollen trees. Two or three cyclists cruise along the dog-walking path. A few benches are occupied by couples who are oblivious to me. I cup water in my hand and splash it on my face. A little decoagulated blood drips into the fountain, and the drops just dissolve, the way the entire fucking universe can dissolve like a grain of salt. I watch the water stillen and see my reflection.

"Puta madre. Fuck. Fuck. Fuck."

My mind a blank, I plunge into the water, into the fountain, to end this once and for all, to let go of the only thing that belongs to me. The water covers me and I sink; I want to drown, merge with the fucking fishes.

"The world's a goddamn pile of shit. Vermin should be exterminated in a public fountain so people can see it's possible to go out as clean as you arrived."

The water in the fountain starts to get murky, filthy—the dirt from my clothing and the blood turn into gray atoms. When I run out of air, I poke my head out. I float splayed, flayed. I close my eyes and let myself jell. I'm sluicing away all my perspirations; I feel buoyant, transaquatic.

The water is freezing.

Inexplicably, I start to feel better. I don't know in the morning,

I don't know anything. The cold water purges my skin. I hang on to the edge and, scraps of water streaming off me, clamber up and out of the fountain. The lovers on the benches glance at me when I go by, dripping on the grass, and stop sucking each other's tonsils. I walk back to my tree and, as the sun macerates the granite with its fire, spread myself out to dry like a fucking dirty rag. My eyes don't hurt so much anymore; seems like nothing hurts forever. I sit down under the tree, my back pressed against its trunk. I look around. Cars over there, couples over here, two more cyclists come up and lock up their bikes. I feel fricasseed, letting my agitation flow down into the tree's roots; I'm weightless, miles away, dazed by the water and the fire.

"What happened to you this time, dude? You're soaked!"

A shudder suddenly runs through me, polyhedral, hematomous; it climbs from my ears down into my heart and back again. I turn my head to the left and see the chivata once more, this time holding a cup of instant soup behind me.

"Where's your dog?" is the only thing I can think to answer in my tremblishness.

"Candy? Oh, ya sabes, I went to take her back to her owner." She pauses between the tree, us, and the sky. Her curved lips envelop my pupils. "I think you don't actually have any dinero, dude, so I brought you soup; it's not much, just chicken soup."

She holds out the boiling styrofoam cup.

"Weren't you going to be late?" I ask bluntly as I take the soup, almost brushing against her beautiful fingers.

"I just barely made it. My boss leaves at ten and I can't bring Candy after that because I'd have to keep her till nighttime. I had to run to get there in time, sabes."

I blow on the soup a little and then take a sip, trying to keep my hands busy so she won't see how they're shaking. The soup's still hot and burns my tongue. I haven't eaten since the day before yesterday, and my belly's bluffing. The butterflies slowly come alive again, hot, and flutter around my intestinal labyrinth, which has now been asperged with instant soup.

"What happened to you, man, and what happened to the Spanish Bookstore?" She bends down and watches me suck down the bits of rehydrated chicken, peas, corn, and carrot. "The bookstore was all shut up this morning," she continues, "with that yellow tape, sabes, like when something awful happens."

I finish the soup with a slurp, scalding my small intestine, which I'm breathing from in order to heat every millimeter of the rest of my body. I'd actually been dying of hunger and I hadn't even realized it.

"My Jefe disappeared yesterday," I tell the chickadee, holding the empty cup in my hands after gulping down the last bit of soup and rubbing my rattletrap with my forearm to wipe away the pearls of broth.

"Oh . . ." She's pensive a moment and then, as if she were coming back to earth, exclaims, "Now I really do have to go, sabes. Seriously, thanks for defending me. I don't know, man, I'm not used to that sort of thing. The world is full of I don't know what—it's impossible to know what to think. Gracias. Adiós."

She straightens up and walks past me and heads toward the gravel path to the park fountains. I leap to my feet in an instant. My legs have become bouncy springs, cocked slingshots.

"Hey," I call wildly, pilgrimated with the airs of a stoic, a silent lover. I shout after her, endemically content, juxtaposed with whatever is afire in my chest. "It was no big deal," I say.

The chickadee stops, turns to look at me, and smiles.

"Take care, dude. Hope your clothes dry soon." Then she quickly turns back to the gravel path and heads down the little slope of the bike parking. I watch until she disappears from view among the trees, but even then I can still see her—I picture her as a flower, a beautiful flower clinging to the tendrils of the air, planted in the center of the universe. She reaches the edge of the park, crosses the street; I hear the horns in the distance honking at her; I hear the engines revving, the sloshing of the scruffs and addos unfurling their slobbery tongues and whistling at her in an effort to suffocate her circumferences, to scour every cranny of her lovely lattice. Then the light says go and the cars dart about again, euphoric, like dogs in heat.

I realize then how strong she is, how powerful with all that fucking world around her, and pipsqueak me defending her. All covered in patches.

"Fuck. Fuck. Fuck."

So, with my boots bepooled, my jean jacket steaming, and my bookstore shirt all wet, I plunge into the void among the trees in the park. I have no idea what I'm going to do, but I've got to do something. "Something. Something. Something, god-dammit." I crush the styrofoam cup in my hand. My brain aches like it did when I first started reading those fucking cheesy, fake, vomitous novels in the bookstore. All of them with their alphabeticated song and dance, all hat and no catacombs. Almost all of them were out of this world, out of this life.

Their clutches blown out from all those hollow words.

My brain makes me lose all my senses. I have to do some-thing; I feel caged like a fucking swine with panic attacks. I pace in circles on the grass, around the trees; I kick the ground, kick the air; I have to move because if I don't the fucking worms will eat me; I feel them moving through my flesh and swallowing each of my cells, my retrammeled vital follicles, with their soupy jaws. "What do I do? What do I do?" I don't know, but suddenly, without thinking, I start running like a lunatic, coco loco.

I race to the edge of the park. I don't have time to wait for the light to change; my heart is noisily escaping out from under my fingernails. I start dashing through the stream of cars speeding by. The cars whistle at me too; they yell at me. They honk at me. They rev their engines as I cross the crowded street. They curse me, insult me:

"Fuuuuck yooou!"

Two cars squeal their tires and skid to keep from pancaking me on the asphalt. I don't have time to look back, time is short; time is killing me with every second they've excised my heart.

On the corner I barrel into a careless yup in a suit who's talking on his cell phone and carrying a black briefcase; I blow him down and keep running.

There are more people up ahead. I try to plow into them as little as possible, zigzagging between them; I can feel their expressions, first surprised and then irritatedly pissed off, fuming, as if running for your life were inappropriate in the civilized world.

A little kid with a lollipop in his mouth wanders out in front of me; he's blond with long curls. I leap over him and leave him behind. His mother yells after me, "Fuuuuuck you, asshole."

I don't have time; life's getting away from me.

I whistle like a short fuse.

I turn the corner where the bookstore is and head toward the chickadee's redbrick building. I don't have any idea what I'm going to do or what to say, but I figure something'll come out. I climb the stone steps in a single bound and open the door. I'm panting, the water from the fountain now mingling with my sweat. The corridor leads to a winding staircase. It's dimly lit. I take the stairs two and three at a time and arrive at the chickadee's door, where I've wanted to knock so many times and where I've always chickened out and retreated, my knuckles burning with viral cowardice.

So I reach her door, a yellowish wooden door, the bottom half ragged. There's a faded bienvenido—welcome mat in front of it. I stop to gulp air and wipe the sweat from my forehead. I jump up and down a few times until my breathing starts to slow. I knock hard, my knuckles now like powerful harpoons.

"It's open." I hear the voice of an antediluvian man on the other side of the door. I push on it and step inside. The first thing I see is a vase with no flowers but full of peacock feathers perched on a chair. The room is illuminated with the sunlight streaming in through a large, half-open window with plain curtains tied back at the sides. There are two lusterless armchairs and a coffee table made of reddish, cholerical wood topped with a piece of smoky glass; on it is a runner made of hemp and decorated with sequins. To the left is a little table with a computer and a rolly chair. On the wall beside it hangs a large painting with lots of lines and splatters like colorful loogies, as if a consumptive had inhaled a few quarts of paint and blown out all his snot across the canvas. The floor is wooden, like the floors in all old buildings. The apartment has high ceilings and isn't very elegant, though it feels palatial. I move farther inside, and all the ribs of its floorboards creak.

"So your rooster came through for you today, huh?" the same voice suddenly says, sitting near the window in a highback chair.

"What rooster?" I ask.

"Pardon?" the man answers from his chair.

"I don't have a rooster!" I say.

"Who are you?" he asks.

I take another two steps toward the window. From there I can see a bit of the bus stop.

"I'm looking for . . ."—and in that moment I realize I don't know the chickadee's name. I've never known it. I'd never even given her one. Never. In the street, everything's so generic, multiplied, added, subtracted, and divided because everything is equal, like a fucking globalization of names: addos, yups, scruffs, dudebros, chickadees, papasitos, raggies, and even the mortifying jackasses of the city's east side. Fat Spañoleros with cigars and berets, hairy all over like apes.

"Are you looking for my granddaughter?" he asks, turning slowly, very slowly, in his armchair.

"I don't know," I say, all in a muddle, uncertain whether she's his granddaughter, his daughter, his assistant, a young woman, an angel, my peace, my war, the housekeeper, the surgeon who cut out my heart just by looking at me, or maybe I've got the wrong door and it was actually the other one, the one across the hall. Now all bashed in, I ask him, "And who are you?"

"Ha!" He emits a three-tiered cackle that bounces all around the room and sails out the window. When it dies down, he muses to himself, "Oh, what a world, ha-ha-ha, and in my own home too, ha-ha-ha, have you ever seen anything like it." He finishes turning the chair toward me, and I see a grandfather with blue, glaucomated eyes, like jelly garnished with raisins in the middle. He's holding a cane with a silver-plated knob in both hands. His hair is long and his broad forehead shot through with lots of wrinkles. He has a long white beard. He's wearing pewtazure checked pajamas and brown slippers. "If I were your age," he tells me, still laughing, "I'd be beating you with my cane for barging in here and bothering an old man like this. Ha-ha! But getting old means you start letting a lot of things go that you didn't used to. You'd better help me up so I can really go after you with my cane."

"Shit," I say, "are you serious?"

"No, of course not. I have to go to the bathroom, and my granddaughter already left for work. I was waiting for the young man from Social Services, but since you're already here, you get to help me instead. Let's go, my bladder can't hold out much longer!"

I approach the old man warily, concerned he might thump me on the headpiece with his cane.

"What do you need me to do?"

"Just help me stand up, and if you see me tipping to one side, push me the other direction. A man's got to preserve his dignity—his vertical—as long as he's still alive." He holds out his hands, covered with age spots and angular veins. I haul him upright. "My, my, the world sure looks different from up here, doesn't it? Have you ever heard of the tall-men theory? They say that tall men get better jobs because their egos puff them up like popcorn so they look down at us mere mortals from on high. Pure natural selection."

I shrug, aspartamized. Yeah, the world is a crazy shitstorm or whatever.

"Now what?" I ask the scrawny reed, holding my hands out so I can try to catch him in case he falls over so he won't bang his head on the floor so hard that he busts through right down to the ground floor.

"Nothing. I'm going to walk straight ahead here and you're going to follow after me in case I tumble over."

He starts walking like an infirm, ambivaleyed tortoise, as if he were carrying the weight of a hundred elephants tied up in a bundle on his back. Slowly, as if he had all the time in the world. Un pasito para adelante, otro pasito para atrás, one step forward, one step back, one step . . .

"Hey," I say, "do you want me to carry you?"

"Over my dead body! Dignity before all else, featherbrain."

Three centuries later, we finally reach the bathroom. He opens the door and says to me, "I'll take it from here. But if I'm not out in a couple of hours, call the plumber."

"What!"

"All right, then, the funeral home."

"What!"

"Come on, kid, laugh."

"Why?"

"Because when somebody says something funny, people generally laugh."

"But I don't feel like laughing right now."

"Well, all right, don't laugh, then; you're within your rights. I won't be long."

He closes the door and I hear his slippers polishing the wooden floor. A couple minutes later I hear the flush and shortly after that the faucet.

An overflowing moment later, he opens the door.

"You still there? I thought I might have hallucinated you. As you get older, you find new travel companions just by staring at blank walls. Can you see all my friends?" He heads toward his armchair.

"Are you doolally?" I ask, crumple-browed.

"Ha!" he exclaims, "it's been ages since I've heard that word! But oh, no, I wish! The world's an unbearable place when you're in your right mind. Lunatics can handle the mayhem a lot better; the only good sanity'll do you is that you can hang yourself without any help."

An evermore later, moving at the speed of serenity, we reach the chair. He turns around and prepares to touch down on his buttocks.

"Give me your hands. The hard part is sitting down and standing up. If I sit wrong, I'll throw out my hip again."

I lace my hands in his like a crane. I act as a lever, gradually lowering him till he's anchored in his personal ocean.

"So," he says, adjusting his pajamas, picking up his cane again, and resting on it with both hands, "you came looking for my granddaughter Aireen?"

"Aireen?" I repeat her name and it reverberates with loneliless, eternitude, between my skull and my heart; her name thunders like an air cannon, water cannon, earth-and-fire cannon inside my chest. "I thought you were crazy and forgetting things," I tell the old dodderer, like an instantaneous reflection, like a glowering grumpus, frittered between my desire to see the girl and her parsimony, to breathe her in as a singular, life-giving aroma, to experience those amorous urgencies of the exterior world and the sluggishness of the interior world.

"Ah, no, plover-head, I still remember lots of things. Old age isn't synonymous with imbecility."

"Are you mocking me again, sir?"

"Not at all, young man. Plovers are a kind of bird that's chicken-brained and pigheaded."

"Oh, all right then."

"And check out that photo," the grandfather tells me. "That's Aireen on her third birthday. And the woman behind her is her mother, my daughter. My only daughter."

"But they don't look like you at all," I say, trying to make sense of things.

"Oh, that's because she's only her mother's daughter."

"What?"

"Oh, kid," he says. "Everybody's got a history, some longer than others. A gazillion years ago I met a gorgeous woman . . ." He falls silent; an enormous pause arises between us, as if he were searching the blank walls for his memories, his eyes blue, elderly, scarred by his slow eyelids. He stills his cane. Swallows. He is absorbed, amber, his wrinkles perpetuating his face. Just then someone knocks on the fucking door. "It's open," calls the grandfather, corking his thoughts. Then he speaks to me. "I'll just say that a father is not the man who spawns a child but the man who raises her. Do you understand?"

A white Latinoid warrior opens the door and walks toward us.

"Good morning," he says, sweeping me up and down with his glance as he heads for the old man's armchair.

"All right, son, it's time for my physical therapy."

I place the photos on the coffee table next to the sequined runner.

"How's my favorite patient doing this morning?" the warrior, dressed in a blue shirt, Nike running shoes, and a walkie-talkie on his belt, breaks in, invisibilizing me. I head for the door.

"Not great, Zubirat; I woke up starving and disheveled, my belly button sticking out."

The warrior Zubirat laughs loudly at the grandfather's wisecrack.

"You're a real wit, aren't you? And what about Aireen, sir, how's she doing?"

I step through the doorway, still listening.

"Well, you know, always running all over the place. She's working a lot. She wants to stay in college, but these days everyone has to work like a peasant to try to live like a king."

"Well, tell her to say yes to me and it's all set, we'll figure out her money problems," I hear the petulant, doggedly creaky voice of the Latinoid warrior say.

"If it were that easy, Zubirat," the grandfather replies, "she'd go looking for someone with more money than the king of Persia"—and he laughs uproariously as I close the door.

In the hallway the lamps flicker absently. I think about the chickadee and the photos of her, especially the one with the cake, where she's blowing out the three little candles, her cheeks round and chubby but already destined for the great beauty she'd become years later.

I descend the stone-and-wood spiral staircase to the ground floor. The light clobbers me when I open the door to the street. Time is different inside the old red building; it seems like the time that marks melancholy, the taciturnity that sickens sighs once happiness has taken a powder.

"Happiness, man—what the fuck is that anyway?"

I look over at the bookstore as I start down the stone steps. It's closed and garlanded with yellow ribbons like a bow on a fucking gift. I can see inside. The bookcases are still upended. The broken windows have been boarded up. I sit down on the steps of the chickadee's building. My clothing is almost dry now; only my underwear is still damp. The sun is beating down on the sidewalk, and I feel its heat in my rump. The bus stop is the only place that has any shade. Cars are milling about unrepentantly. Three or four vehicles are parked on the other side of the street, practically right in front of the bookstore, and there are two gorillas in tight black shirts perched on the hood of one of the boats. A chickadee goes by dragging a baby carriage with a newborn in it.

"I could try to get into the fucking bookstore and grab some stuff, even if it's just my blankets, since those belong to me," I think. "How would I get in, though? Oh, I can hang from the telephone pole over on that side and get my foot up on the cornice and lever myself up onto the roof above the loft, where there's that boarded-up window. I could kick it open and sneak inside. Nobody would know I'm in there. I could even sleep there and nobody would realize. I could use the storeroom door to go in and out. The one that leads out to the back alley. Jefe never uses it for anything, the one behind that bookcase full of cheesy, dreary, syrupy poetry, the kind that only brainless guts read. Behind that is the service door."

* * *

["See, before this it was a fucking *restaurante mexicano*, and that door was what they used to take out all the fucking *basura*; that's why there's grime cobwebbing the roof back here, you pornographic prick. Clean it good up there, where that black splotch is."

"What if I fall, Jefe?"

"You're not going to fall. The ladder's not going to break, and if you do fall, you won't go through the floor."

"And don't you think selling tacos would be a better business than selling books, boss?"

"Shut up, you meddling little queer, and make sure all the stains are gone or I'll smack you upside the head with a book."]

"Or I could go into the building next door and jump from the roof. Eyeballing it, though, it looks like it's got to be twenty feet—I'd crash into the wall. Or I could scrabble up the drainpipe and drop onto the railing of the fire escape, though from there I'd have to jump like six feet in midair; if I don't make it, that's like a fuckety-foot fall down to the street, and I'd be bread-puddinged by the impact. It would have to be a little later too, when there are fewer people out and the streetlight's the only thing around to see me."

A bus goes by, stops, lets off passengers, and picks up the chickadee with the baby carriage. She climbs aboard with difficulty, carrying the kid in one arm and the contraption in the other. The bus pulls away and turns down a side street. The black-clad gorillas start across the street as the bus moves off. I eye the bookstore. Maybe I could remove the board that seems to be propped up by one of the tables of new releases.

* * *

[That table of books where the gaggles from the fucking limp-dick transatlantic publishing houses ended up because of all their intransitable verbs—would have been, would have seen, would have fit—and their agamanthine baby-babble idiocies; their words neutral and empty, like pneumatic tires rather than solid rubber, utterly limp-dick, formal, flat, wlobalicidal word world anxiously sought by some fine-feathered filly.

I also remember the Latinoid loco with a pimply face, rectangular glasses, and minnowy muscles who came in every couple of weeks to ask about some literary prizewinner that had just been published. I once heard him tell Jefe that he wanted to be a famous writer and make it big.

"*Chingonametrically speaking, as big as the world.*" He had an amazing story about spaceships, he said, and he planned to sell it to Hollywood to have them turn it into a movie. "*Because spaceships sell, man, just like special effects do. Just imagine, a huge spaceship comes down to Earth but it doesn't have any brakes. What would happen? The Apocalypse!*"

"*No, well, sure. That's a pretty good story,*" Jefe rejoindered as he counted the money the Latinoid scribbler had just given him for the latest Pulitzer-winning novel.

I stood there watching them, a dopey look on my face, and tried to imagine what a damn spaceship looked like. I figured they must run on coal in little braziers, and you'd blow like the dickens to make them take off to anywhere in the universe.

"*Hey, Jefe, what's outside of our universe?*"

"*You nosy little squirt, stop eavesdropping on my conversations with customers and stick to picking your ass instead.*"

Once Jefe complained that they wanted to sell the bookstore out from under him and turn it into a posh café.

"*Sell it, then, what do I care? You'll make some money off it, and then you won't be able to go around complaining you don't have enough money anymore.*"

"*Stop bugging me, you fumigational louse! I'm selling! And if I ever give you any coffee, it'll be up your ass.*"]

In any event, I think now, if I were the owner, the bookstore's megamaster, I would put in a fucking café there across the street so I could spend the rest of my life looking at the chickadee. Maybe I could even win her heart: I'd have scratch to go with my sniff, greenbacks so I could wrap her in my arms and kiss her, kiss her like I've never kissed anybody before. Yeah, some tables on that side, and over here, if I wanted something like Jefe has, a bookshelf for the few books that make it through unscathed because they're actually alive; all the rest I'd shred into a million pieces. And I even know what

I'd call my popsicle stand: "Aireen." "Aireen's Love." Yeah, that's it. Where's Jefe now so he can see I can do something with his fucking bookstore?

And suddenly the little hairs on the back of my neck stand on end; they warn me, stiffening like cats' whiskers. I sense the two gorillas in black bearing down on me. I leap down the three or four steps to the sidewalk and take off running, but one of them, the tattooed bald guy with an earring, snags me by the arm and I stumble into the chest of the other guy, who's a little slimmer but solid, his pecs like two marble carapaces. "No way, not another beatdown." They're much taller and heavier than I am, but one thing I learned in my street fights back home is that I'm going to be scrapping with them, not picking them up, and the more massabolic they are, the more painful their rotten fall to earth will be.

In street fighting, it's not about martial arts or Confucian technicism; it's a cross-country brawl, a pitched battle, and anything goes.

I don't even have time to think before I knee the marble-chested guy with all my might and he doubles over; he can lift all the fucking weights in the world and steel up every muscle in his body, but even Superman's balls are still fragile.

The other gorilla tries to yell at me to stop, but I'm deafer than a post: all I can hear is the sound of my own breathing. I kick him in the shin while jabbing him hard in the ear, where his navigational system is. The gorilla snorts in bewilderment, his eyes bug out, and he tries to slap me in the face, but I'm faster than him and dodge, bending at the waist, and then, from below, give him a powerful blow in the coconuts that takes him out.

"Fuck," he says before he goes down.

Just then I feel a pair of huge arms wrapping around me like an octopus from behind and lifting me like a fucking feather.

"Fucker got me this time; I didn't even see this guy coming."

I flail around, but I only manage to give the fucking giant squid a few kicks in the shins. He squeezes me harder, and I start to lose my breath. I figure when the fucking brute squad gets their shit back together, they're going to stomp my ass.

"Chill, man. Tranquilo," the huggy giant says in my ear.

"Chinga tu madre," I reply, and head-butt him in the nose. He squeezes harder. I feel my skeleton being compressed just like my fucking styrofoam soup cup. If he squeezes any harder, I'm going to shit my pants.

"Tranquis, bro," he repeats, though his nose is now leaking sauce. The other two gorillas are just starting to show signs of life.

"Let go of me, motherfucker!" I yell at him in a rage, my whole body spangalanged. "Let go of me and you'll see where else you leak, asshole!"

"Take it easy," he says, "I just want to talk to you." He then addresses his thugs. "Hey, pendejos, this little fucker thrashed you good."

He loosens his grip a little and allows me to catch my breath.

"I'm going to let you go, but don't try to run away, got it?"

Yeah, right, I think. *As soon as my feet hit the ground, I'm out of here.*

He loosens the pressure on my arms a little more.

"I've got a business proposition for you, bro"—but there's no way I'm interested. I'm panting like a fucking dog. "Fuck, man, I know what's good for you."

"My ass," I answer.

"Hey, pendejo," he tells one of the docile limp-dicks, who's currently groping his bruised giblets. "Take out your damn iPhone so he can see it."

The earringed gorilla takes out an iPhone and shoves it in my face. I look at his reddened eyes. His nuts must look even worse. He presses a button, and a YouTube video starts to play.

I recognize the chickadee's building, then the bus stop. I see myself crossing the street. I see myself sitting down at the bus stop. I see the yup who's in love with the chickadee come up behind me and deck me. The camera gets out of the car and starts coming closer. I see me lying there, and then ten or twelve fucking scruffs and addos surround me excitedly and start kicking the shit out of me. Then they stop kicking and scatter as quickly as they appeared. The video stops when Mr. Abacuc squats down next to me and gives me a handkerchief. Then the title of the video appears on the screen, along with a photo of me flipping off the camera: "How long?"

"That you, bro?" the octopus asks me.

"No."

"What the fuck do you mean, no? You're even wearing the same fucking clothes."

"What the hell do you want?" I ask.

"Just to talkear, man," the octopus gorilla says. "I'm going to let go of you real careful-like now, hermano, so chill."

He slowly lowers me down and I place my feet on the stone stairs. A number of onlookers start to move away; the few scruffs also take off like cockroaches under rocks. The show's over, and they're probably still looking for their daily melee. I feel an overwhelming need to run, to get the fuck out of there. I'll take a skedaddling over a paddling any day. The gorillas notice, and the three of them surround me like a wall of flesh so I can't get away.

"You calmer now?" he says before letting go of me.

I nod, but I'm not calm. I haven't been calm since I got to this country. I haven't been calm one single day. I'm always hustling, being hustled, looking over my shoulder, evasive, paralyzed, with no sense of security.

"It's a simple business, bro. I need someone who can take a beating the way you can."

"Why me?"

"Because you obviously don't break easy. With the thrashing they gave you, you should be muerto now, man."

"There any money in it?"

"Sí."

"How much?" I ask.

"Not much, but if it goes well, maybe it'll even be enough for you to buy some new clothes."

"Were you guys the ones who trashed the bookstore?"

"What?"

"The one across the street." I nod toward it. They turn to look and stand gaping like idiots.

"Shit, man," says the earringed gorilla, "what's a bookstore, Chub?"

Oof! Maybe that punch in the nose loosened his screws a little—or maybe he was like me when I discovered the bookstore for the first time.

* * *

[*I was full of shit when I got to the city. Walking around, I saw there was work available. I didn't want to go back to picking fruits and vegetables, since Pepe and the others must have crossed over to the other side by then. I didn't know a fucking word of English, and then I came across a sign in Spanish taped up in the bookstore window: "Solicito ayudante." Help wanted.*]

"We can talkearlo, bro, discuss it more comfortable-like someplace else," the giant says, "in a bar or restaurant or diner or something. Is there somewhere around here where you feel comfortable? I'm Chuby Jon, and these two lardasses are Sakai Dark and Deamon Dean. What do you say, man, shall we head somewhere else to chatterize?"

"Hell no," I answer. "If we're going to talk, we'll do it here. We can wordify right here. Not like in fucking novels, where if they've got something to say they always go to a more comfortable place just to say what they could just say standing up and without wasting everybody's fucking time."

"That's cool," the octopus says, befuzzled. He's got a goatee, a shaved head and arms all tattooed with snakes or whatever, jeans, and motorcycle boots. His front teeth are gilded. With the back of his hand he wipes away the blood from a small cut on his nose from when I head-butted him. "I'll get right to the point, güey," he says. "I'm a lucha libre wrestler, but they kicked me out of the damn league in a fucking antidoping thing two years ago. I'm banned for life, but now I own this gym where I train a few guys, and I want to do things right and not half-assed. I'm looking to make a little cheddar with a vato who hits like a beast. I can't get involved in lucha libre anymore, but nobody in boxing knows anything about me. So there's no prob. And I don't have a sparring partner good enough to take on my campeón. I saw your video on YouTube. It was uploaded by *Chronica News,* tagged with the location where the fight went down. I saw you and a lightbulb went on, man."

"How much?" I interrupt him.

"I don't know," he says, flummoxed.

"What? You come here to offer me shit and a half, and you don't even know how much?"

"A hundred a week," he says hastily, like he's trying to test my idiocrity.

"A hundred a day or nothing."

"Ha!" he exclaims. "Not even if you were made of solid gold, bro!"

"See you around, you silverbacked yups." I move down one step, push them aside, and start to head off. A hundred measly dollars to let them pound me to a pulp? No way.

"Three hundred a week and no more," the mollusk suddenly blurts.

I turn back toward them. "But with meals included, and Thursdays and Sundays off, and an advance of a hundred bucks right here and now."

The gorilla eyes me, wrinkles his forehead like a giant seal, and strokes his goatee from top to bottom.

It would appear the ape's thinking.

"All right, you win, man. But just for now, while we're training our campeón."

"Whatever," I say. Ultimately, I think, what difference would a few more punches make, and I don't know when I'll manage to find another fucking job.

"Here's the address." He tosses me a card that windmills in the air along with five crumpled twenties. "We'll start tomorrow at eight—we have to be ready for this year's Golden Gloves Championship."

"That's cool, man. See you around."

I head off toward the corner while the gorillas cross the street, limping like fucking bowlegged cowboys, and get in their boat. Poor preemie-dicked bastards, they're gingerly cupping their balls. I watch them take off and fade away. Then I look up at the chickadee's window and sigh. Aireen must be working like a dog at this hour. I sigh again. The light turns red and the cars stop.

I cross and head toward the mall. I'm going to need groceries if I'm going to stay in the bookstore. Yes, it's a fucking plan that will keep me alive. And then, out of nowhere, I start smiling. I have a little cash and the possibility of being close to the chickadee. Now that I know which window is hers, I can nod off to sleep in her shadow. I pass the little alleyway behind the bookstore and keep going.

The 7-Eleven is two blocks away. I'm contemplating what to buy. Things that'll last. I think about cans of tuna, pickled chiles, corn, peas and carrots, and a few sodas. Some boxes of the cheapest crackers. I can survive like a camel with a gallon of water; I'm used to not eating or drinking much. I can survive on almost nothing: a crumb and a dribble, like I did after I emerged from the fucking Rio Grande, my black plastic bag tied across the back of my shoulders. Like that, without water or anything, just eating a few fucking plants here and there that I found along the way.

* * *

[*"It's tougher now than it used to be,"* the coyote had told me. *"Crossing over used to be a walk in the park, but now the motherfuckers even have laser rays, fucking pain-in-the-ass gringos, and they peer down at us from above with their pinches satellites. So now you can't even shit in peace out in the fucking desert, thinking they're photographing your ass from up in the stars. But if you want, for fifteen thousand pesabundos I can get you over to where you're home free, buddy."*

But I was totally skint. I'd just taken off, looking to save myself, without any plans. Just escape and dreams, the dream of being on the other side of what you're fucking escaping from. And when I was getting temerous after walking for hours in the desert, I drank my own sweat, and after more hours of walking, I even drank my own piss, because I crossed all by myself, reckless-like.

"Look," a wetback on the Mexican side told me. *"You go straight across right here and start swimming. The current's pretty strong out there where you see those whirlpools, so you're going to end up over there. When you see a tree trunk that's fallen over the water, make sure to grab on; if you don't, you'll head straight into the next life."*

And so I plunge into the water, bam!, carrying my clothes in a black nylon bag and wearing only my underwear. And I start swimming, just like that, slowly at first, because the guy'd warned me, "Don't wear yourself out or you'll drown." And the current kept getting faster, forming green foam on the green foam, greening my eyes. And it got so jittery that I saw the fallen tree approach and then go by and then be left behind. But I never even considered letting myself die; I'd gotten this far and wasn't about to be food for some goddamn fish. So I started sculling with my arms until my muscles screeched with pain, but there was no choice—"Fuck it, life doesn't grow in flowerpots." And after eons had passed, I saw a rock I could cling onto like a pinche iguana. And so, yeah, I hung on with all my claws and lay there like a dead man until after the sun had already set.

Then I felt like I was breathing for the first time, like I was a fucking sperm that had fertilized an egg. I got dressed and started walking oxically that direction, "where you see those hills"—that's what they'd told me. And I pulled so far left that I ended up who the hell knows where, but just when I was running on fumes, a highway appeared. My feet were in shreds from all the blasters; my throat was leaden, clogged with sawdust.

But I started taking off my clothes piece by piece, because now I felt hot from the inside, burning up like a huge bonfire; first I took off my coat, then my shirt, my pants, my underwear, everything, because I was so filled up with fire that I felt like a coal melting in a brazier.

A car raced by and disappeared into the trembling hot air manufactured by distance and sunlight on the highways. There, already wordlessly cursed, parched, naked, I collapsed to my knees, awaiting my death.]

I take out a twenty and stash the rest in the secret place—which is no longer so secret—in my waistband, next to the note from Mr. Abacuc and the card with the gym's address, and enter the 7-Eleven. "I need canned food, water, and snacks," I think, "things that don't go bad but fill you up." I wander down the aisles of the minimart. I try to seem normal.

* * *

[That's what they told me when I finished my shift at my first and only picking job:

"If you see a policeman, don't run—if you run, they'll nab you."

"Act totally normal. Even look them in the fucking eyes— they won't know what to make of you."

"They can smell fear. If they can tell you're scared, they'll nab you. And don't get too comfortable—always keep an eye out. You have to toe the line, or else they'll nab you, beat you up, gulp you down, and then shit you back out where you fucking came from."]

I pick up some cans and toss them into a little plastic basket. I go over and browse the snack-food aisle. Then I pick up a couple of votive candles for light and grab a gallon of plain water. You don't need much to survive. Though maybe you do to live.

* * *

[Once I walked through this city at night, past its restaurants with glittering windowpanes and palm trees and lights illuminating their sumptuous gardens, their facades and terraces; where valets parked gleaming vehicles. There I saw decked-out women in brand-new sneakers and glossy papasitos nibbling at cow-sized steaks. I saw restaurants with candles and without candles, with dimmed lights, almost dark; I also saw caves with lights like sparklers that shellacked the eye to the beat of a strident boom-boom-boom. La vida loca. There, outside a Latinatious fleapit, I heard a vato singing named Calle 13 y que me prendo.

"Hey, Jefe, have you heard those bands that rap in Spanish?"

"You russet-colored runt, I don't even listen to my santa madre sing. Music prevents a man from thinking clearly."

"Is that why you don't sell records or movies at the book-store?"

"That's right."

"And so what are you thinking about, then, when there's no music and it seems like you're lost in space?"

"Fuck off, you ecritical worm."]

I get to the register and lift up the little plastic basket. The cashier starts to swipe the items over the barcode reader and places them in bags. I ask for some matches so I can light the candles when I'm up in the loft. The total on the register comes to $19.80. The girl seems like she's Latina, but she speaks to me in English. I pay with the bill. She gives me the change. I take the bags and go out. Night isn't falling yet. I sit down on a bench next to a planter in front of the 7-Eleven, pull out a bag of potato chips, open it, and start eating. Then I uncap the gallon of water and drink straight from the jug. I chew slowly, as if I were waiting for the potatoes to dissolve like fucking sacred hosts instead of crunching. I chew slowly until little by little the sun begins to evaporate.

The streets begin to turn blue, and the streetlights slowly begin to come on. In the tallest buildings, the offices light up. Down below, the businesses turn on their signs and the shops light up. The cars turn on their headlights. People pass by me. A while back I noticed that the papasitos walk straight and tall; the rest of us, the polloi, from scruffs to addos and dude-bros, walk like apes, as if untouched by evolution. It's like we feel less fully ourselves and are still hunching our backs to brandish a mandrill's red rump. Like we've already been pre-vanquished by some divine, carontic clause of fucking unalter-able destiny.

I finish the bag of potato chips. I take a last sip of water and cap the jug. That'll be enough till tomorrow. I close the bags with a double knot and wait a while longer, still sitting on the bench. The lumps on my face have unhardened and gone down. My face is almost back to normal except for a small cut above my right eyebrow. I still ache a little from the blow to the neck they gave me in the park, but everything else is practically the same as ever.

When I feel night brewing, thickening in the air, I pick up the bags and head back toward the street where the bookstore is.

Before reaching the corner, I turn into the alleyway out back. It's unlit and smells like piss. There are a couple of dumpsters beside the service door of the next building over. I see the bookstore's door. It's tapestried with cobwebs and dust. It hasn't been opened in years. I walk to the end of the alley. I take off my belt and use it to tie the bags from my purchase together and sling them over my shoulder, like I'm getting ready to cross a river. I get a running start and leap like a monkey so I can clamber into the bookstore.

Sleep frazzles out and immediately I open my eyes, pauperized, sensing that it is now very late. Up in the loft, everything is dark. I put out my hand and knock over the votive candle holder. I hear it roll until it stops next to the edge of my blankets. I have no idea when I went lights out. After closing the window and stuffing the plastic from the bags into the frame to wedge it shut, I laid out the blankets on the floor, blew out the candle, and rolled myself up like a burrito, and I stayed like that all night, without moving, like a fucking caterpillar that's gone into its cocoon to wait for the moment of truth.

I disentangle myself from the blanket and bang on the little window. It opens and the rays of sunlight stream solidly in. It carries me away. I wander around and pull my boots on; they're totally shot, but they're the only shoes I have.

* * *

["So what are you spending your dinero on, you greedy prick?"

"With what you pay me, Jefe, air's the only thing I can afford."

"Don't worry, you diabolical mooch, I'll raise your wages soon so you can pay me the rent you owe me for that loft."]

I cautiously descend the stairs. The good thing about the fucking bookstore is that it's like a ghost, an empty space between buildings; it's as if it didn't exist, a useless rubbish heap, a black hole. Hardly anybody used to stop to look at the books in the display windows. Sometimes an absentminded sparrow or two would flutter in, but they always left without buying anything. I get down on my hands and knees and, dodging the fallen bookcases among the naked tomes, head back to the little storeroom. The bookcase of starchy poetry is blocking the door—those sappy fucking books full of caramelized garbage; lovey-dovey, like cow innards when they've eaten a lot of grass and deposit beautiful, sweet brown patties. That bookcase is blocking the service door that leads to the alley I need to leave by. I pull down the books and put them in the case where the horror books used to go before they ended up rolling on the floor laughing. I finish and tug hard on the bookcase. One of the sides rumbles, but I manage to yank it loose and lift it so I can rotate the case and shove it into the corner where Jefe used to keep his most prized volumes, the ones he read over and over again.

* * *

["You don't need to read a lot, just the essentials. And as the years pass, you go back to your first books, and eventually you *cut down on those till there's only one left, till death do you part, you fucking numbskull."*

"Now I get why people don't buy any of this crap, Jefe: a single fucking book is more than enough for your entire life."]

I pick up a fat, heavy volume of Spanish poetry and bang it against the lock. The lock gives, and I push it to one side to remove it completely. I set it down and try to push the door open. It's still stitched shut with cobwebs and dust, but there's nothing a few batterations can't fix.

When I ram into it with my shoulder for the third time, the door gives way and I almost fly out into the little alley. I spring backward. I look around. And now how the hell do I close the fucking thing? I pick up a little book of the hundred best love poems in Spanish and wedge one side of the door. I push hard, and it remains jammed. I jiggle it to make sure it's all right, and it doesn't budge. "Damn," I smile, "I finally found a fucking use for poetry."

* * *

[And it fucking figures, later on I picked up a book of poetry—when I was moving on from picture books and that sort of thing—because it was skinny and didn't have too many words, and I ended up having to read the soddamn massive fucking dictionary because I didn't understand a thing the pinche poet was saying.]

I come out of the alley and head toward 47th, where the gym is. I'm not about to spend a cent on the bus. So I start running to try to fill the gap in time I've just made. I dash past the chickadee's building, past Wells Park, past the Century Theater. I reach the Ford Foundation's university complex and keep going, and before the intersection that leads to the baseball stadium, I turn right and jog toward 39th. Once I pass 41st, it's like another world.

The houses ramshackle and garish. Torn chain-link fences, like the area's a war zone. Fucking dogs digging through the garbage. The passersby are practically levitating off the ground. I think they're more fucked than I am. I see some stoned addos smoking up and huffing Krakow ether out of little bags.

There's an overpass soaring above us with cars whizzing past, its columns covered with graffiti. There's no grass in the planters here; they're full of dry seeds. The trees are so stunted they don't even sway in the wind.

I head toward a row of close-set little warehouses by a large median strip across from a cluster of three- or four-story tenement houses that stink of bodies and poverty.

When I finally get to 47th, I'm dripping with sweat. I spot some small lettering printed on a partially unfurled awning: CHUBY BOX NG G M. The gorillas' mothership is parked outside. "Chingafuck," I say to myself, "this fucking molluscular scruff isn't gonna be able to pay me even half of what we agreed."

I enter the gym through a glass-and-aluminum door. Inside, the lights are off and the only illumination is filtering in through some skylights that make you lose all sense of lice. The ceiling is high, like a warehouse. There are a couple of racks with weights over to the left. Then there are some benches for weights and dumbbells. In the middle there's a boxing ring where a couple of scrawny kids like me are whaling on each other. Across the room are some lockers, and toward the back is a sign that says BATROOM. A door marked OFFICE is next to a window with closed blinds. Another couple of kids are punching a bag that's hanging from a chain, and an older dude is stroking a speed bag with his fists all wrapped up like a fucking mummy. A guy's doing crunches on a black incline board. The whole place is painted blue, and a huge luchador mask is peeling off in the middle of the wall, next to several posters of some really ripped white dudes. A few mirrors make the gym look bigger than it is. I pause at the entrance. I feel like bailing right then and there. "It's not too late, nobody's seen me yet." Yeah, fuck these fucking vatos. I didn't come here to screw around. I turn around and smack right into a shaved-headed addo who's just come in. He shoves me hard in the chest and moves off.

"Hey, asshole," I say, but he apparently doesn't understand Spanish.

He heads for the office and slams the door. I see him lift up a slat of the blinds and glare out at me. I flip him off, and he immediately disappears. "Fucking cunt-ass bastard," I muse, "he must think he's a super-gringo," one of those descendants of naturalized immigrants who make life difficult for their own fellow citizens, their own blood, their own people, rejecting any origin tattooed on their chromosomes.

I push the door open and spit on the ground outside the gym. I start walking toward the median and then feel the mollusk's clammy embrace again.

"Fuck you, güey," he says, "why so late?"

"I got lost," I tell him so he'll let go. I see he's got a white bandage on his nose where I head-butted him yesterday.

"Dónde you going?"

"To get some sun. It's cold as the fucking grave in there."

"I know the place is a little rough, but just you wait, güey, as soon as I turn out a champion campeón, it'll take off."

"The only thing you're going to turn out in that place is hemorrhoids," I say. He looks at me dumbly. Probably has no idea what the hell I'm talking about. "Hemorrhoids are little fishies you get in your tushie."

His expression doesn't change.

"Where are your gym clothes?" he asks, changing the subject.

"What?" I say.

"Well, you're not going to need them anyway—you're not going to be training. Like we talked about yesterday, you'll just be espareando a little."

"And are you going to pay me what we agreed?"

"Sí."

"All right," I tell him, and we go back into the gym. He's leading me by the arm—no, that's not fucking true, I've got his gelatinous arm around my neck; it feels sticky, like it's covered with suction pads. I guess the fatso takes up more eyespace than I do, because now everybody's looking at us; bland little morsels like me must not even make a mark.

"See, man, after falling into the fucking abyss, taking all the shit I could get my hands on to bulk up and ending up with nothing, man, little by little I'm getting by, making do. It's not much, but I learned my puto lesson, bro. I'm paying for it as I go," he says as he drags me toward the ring, where two guys are hopping around like little girls. "Look, Yorkie, here's a sparring partner for El Crazy Loco."

A black guy with graying hair, kalamatic from torrents of sun, sits up on a bench hidden behind the ring and yawns, grendling like a cat. "He skinny," he says. "Your Loco's gonna break 'im in two."

"Are you sleeping?" the octopus kaslurps.

"Naw, man. Jus' gettin' a wink."

"Stop fucking monkeying around!" says the gigantic mollusk.

"No, no monkey," the black guy says with a toothless cackle, "dormouse mebbe."

"Goddammit, York, instead of keeping an eye on the ring, you're back there snoozing. What happens if those kids end up killing each other and ripping each other's guts out and you don't even notice, huh?"

The black guy looks over to where the guys are feinting, bouncing, swinging wildly and missing, dancing back and forth. Yorkie smiles.

"Those fuckers don' even touch when they's kissin' each other's ass. Heh!"

I, too, abruptly break out in laughter, just like that, natural-like, winging it. The mollusk eyes me casuistically, his expression suddenly angry. In a cavernously ectopic voice, he says, "Get those two fags out of there and put this raggedy-ass prick in. That way he can learn to love God in a foreign country, and we'll see if he's got what it takes."

Grumbling, he strides off toward his lair.

Cheerfully, York says, "The fat lady has sang. I'll be prayin' fer ya, funny guy."

He gets up heavily from the bench, and I see his feet are more twisted than the fucking tree branches outside.

"Lez go," he says. "You got clothes?"

"Yeah," I tell him, "I'm wearing 'em, puto geezer."

He turns and looks me up and down and then emits another toothless cackle.

"You keep that up, you ain't even gonna make it to geezer."

He moves off, walking like his balls are dragging on the floor, and rummages in a crate under the ring. He pulls out a mask and some red gloves.

"Used this before?"

"Yeah," I tell him, "on my cock."

The black guy doesn't crack a smile. He tosses them at me.

"Put 'em on then, asshole."

I catch them. I have no idea which way the laces go, but I'm not a total idiot so I copy the ballerinas the black guy is shooing out of the ring:

"Hey, ladies, come on down from there 'fore I has a heart attack from all 'at sugar."

The dudes are sweatily reluctant, but they obey. They detach from the ring, wriggling between the ropes, and head over to plop down on one of the ringside benches, exhausted. They look like two fucking pigeons that have been electrocuted on a high-tension wire. They take off their head guards, and I see their hair's trimmed short with mazelike designs shaved into it, like a fade but way more intricate. I put on the mask and strap on the gloves. My fists ball up inside them. I feel like a goddamn cat in house slippers.

"Hey!" yells the black guy. "Ain' ya gonna take yer shirt off?"

"Nah." I shake my head. Anyway, I've been wearing it so many days and nights in a row, one more isn't going to make a difference.

* * *

[*"What are you doing, kid?" a paisa once asked me back in my picker days when he saw me putting on my underwear inside out.*

"Nothing, I'm just recycling my clothes."

Because it was the only underwear I had and there was no water to wash it with, let alone soap. And the same with my sockrags: I turned them inside out again and again so they could air out and not reek to high heaven of bubonic paw-pits.]

I finish adjusting my gloves and tug on the laces with my teeth to tighten them. "Now what?" The black guy goes over to the pigeons to take off the pads they're wearing and starts throwing them into the box of odds and ends under the ring. "All righty," I say to myself. I turn around and size myself up next to the posters of the buff gringos. "Shit, I'm scrawnier than my fucking mother, and with these big red gloves and this huge red mask, I look like a goddamn beet with its balls al fresco!"

Chuby comes out alongside the motherfucker I ran into in

the doorway, who's now swathed in a gold robe that covers his head; he's bouncing along like a diarrheal grasshopper and punching the air. I suppose in order to think you're a champion, you have to look like one. He's got a towel draped around his neck.

Behind him comes the earringed gorilla, who's filming him with his iPhone.

They reach the ring. The mollusk yells at the black guy, "Fuck you, Yorkie, I told you to get him ready. He's still wearing his shirt and he's got his fucking mask on upside down."

York gurgitates from behind me, "Beats me, he didn't let me near him. This kid's like a rabid dog, a bad seed."

The mollusk stands in front of me, takes off my mask, and puts it on the right way. I adjust it under my chin. I can't see a fucking thing. I feel like a horse with blinders on that can only see straight ahead. Then he ties my gloves, making a Gordian knot so they'll never come off.

"Did you bring a mouthguard?" the mollusk asks me.

"Qué?"

"It doesn't matter. You're just going to be a stand-in so we can see whether you'll work or not. Just don't stick out your tongue—you could bite it off if he clocks you one, sabes!"

"Qué!"

"Now get in the ring." He smacks me in the back of the head.

"See here, dickwad," I protest, but he doesn't hear me because the bald, be-earringed ape comes up with his iPhone and says, "Aren't you going to weigh them, Chub?"

"No," the octopus says. "Seems like the kid's right about the same size as our campeón." He walks away and goes up to his flashy rockstar, who's flexing, doing squats, shadowboxing.

Instead of walking over to where there's a little staircase up into the ring, I boost myself up and roll under the ropes. I stand up, shaking off the white powder that's stuck to my jeans and my bookstore shirt. I look around.

The earringed ape is still buzzing around like a bumblebee, filming everything. The dudes and scruffs approach the ring: the guy with the speed bag, the guys from the punching bag, the abs dude, one coming out of the bathroom that I didn't see earlier. I feel their eyes on me; it's like being in a display case in a fucking museum.

The fat mollusk comes up the stairs and stands in the middle of the ring. He doesn't know what to say, so he says the first thing that comes to mind, addressing me:

"Just don't ralph on the canvas or I'll kick your ass."

"What am I gonna chuck up," I think, "when all I've got in my guts is nothing?"

He waves the Crazy Loco over with one hand. The guy clambers into the ring, accompanied by the black guy and the earringed gorilla. Vato's still hopping; he looks like a possum with a lit match in its snatch. Yorkie takes off the guy's robe and hangs his towel around his own neck. "Oh, man," I think, "check that guy out: even his six-pack's got a six-pack." His muscles are like a racehorse's: you can see the veins in his arms, neck, and legs, and I could swear you can see his pulse if you get too close; those thick arteries must be making the air throb around him. He's got one tattoo on his shoulder and another on his back of a pair of goat horns—literally, the kind of goat that bleats. His shorts are blue with red trim. They've got "Crazy Loco" embroidered on one leg in golden letters, and on the back, emblazoned across his ass, it says, "American Champion." He clenches his jaw, glaring at me with hatred.

Yorkie puts Vaseline on the fighter's face so the salsa will just slide off.

The earringed gorilla wanders around, capturing it all with his iPhone. He records the people sitting down, the guys wandering around and staring. When they've finished primping El

Crazy Loco and putting in the noxious ape's mouthguard, Chuby signals to us to move to the center of the ring. With his tentacles, he takes the two of us by the shoulders, but he addresses his protégé first:

"Take it easy now, campeón, we're just softening him up a little; we want him to last longer than the others did. I don't want you causing any problems like you did last time. If I say estop, you estop: you back off immediately. None of this keeping-going lunatical-ass bullshit, got it, Crazy Loco?"

The crazy dude is still dancing, but he nods. He doesn't say boo. I see he's got several inches on me.

"And you, bro"—the mollusk's talking to me now—"hang in there, and may the Lord have mercy on your soul, sabes!"

I nod, because that's what you have to do in this shitty world, just nod: say yes until no comes about of its own accord.

The fatso slaps us on the back, pushes me toward my corner, and starts acting as the referee.

"Give him hell, fucking Loco," he tells his fighter, "we're going for gold, sabes."

He makes a signal to the ringside, and Yorkie bangs on a bell with a little mallet that goes ting or ding like a ricketish boat.

Immediately the Loco leaps at me in a mighty fury; I know it because I see his eyes inflamed with rage, burning to tear me apart however he can. I see him with his jaw clenched so tight that his teeth and the veins in his temples might explode at any moment. I see him so determined to kill me that my only instinct, before that pinche Loco takes another step toward me and tears me apart, is to kick him hard in the giblets to settle him down. Zooooom fuuuuuck! I give him a sharp kick between the legs and watch him drop like a leaf in autumn, a crispy, suicidal leaf tumbling down from the yellow trees, and spit out his mouthguard, which sails off past the ropes. He crumples forward and then, like an anesthetized sleepwalker, spills backward. He plunges down like a meteorite in the middle of the ocean, raising a billow of dust from the canvas.

"Motherfucker!" yells Chuby as he runs to help him. "You really fucked him up, puto! Chingafuck!"

"Well, they didn't fucking tell me anything, not a goddamn thing," I yell back.

Loco writhes on the ground, wailing about his nubbins. His eyes are rolled back. Yorkie and the earringed chrome-dome climb into the ring. I hear the guys down on the floor yelling at me, "Fucking asshole! Asshole! Asshoooole!"

They splash water on Crazy Loco's face and put a cloth around his neck. Chuby the mollusk starts flexing the fighter's legs to bring him back around. He's so worried that I almost expect him to stick his tentacle down the vato's shorts and fondle his precious golden eggs. Slowly the dude's color starts to come back; he goes from a retina-searing red to a feverish, beany, eye-snatching blue. All I can see is the commotion that's been stirred up.

"Pendejo!" Chuby shouts at me, kneeling next to his campeón, now fanning him with a little towel. "You box with your hands, pendejo, not with your feet, pendejo. This fucking business is with your fucking hands, not your fucking feet."

"And how's that my fault?" I retort. "Nobody told me that. But that's fine, let's call the whole thing off. We'll just leave things right here and I'll get the hell out of this place."

"No way," El Crazy Loco says for the first time, still lying on the ground. "You're not going fucking anywhere because I'm going to break you in motherfucking half," he says, his tongue out of place, fumbling, bile oozing at the corners of his mouth.

"Easy there, campeón," I say with my heart in my throat, "you find your balls first, and then we can get into it."

I take off my mask and drop it onto the canvas before turning to leave. That's enough; I've had more than enough today.

I'm fed up with this shit. I bite at the gloves' laces to untie them from my hands. I can't do it; the mollusk knotted them too tight. I'm still gnawing on the laces when I feel a colossical twinge in my back and hear a viceversal shout:

"Fuck you, goddamn pinche raggedy-ass Indian, I'm gonna kill you!"

Fucking Crazy Loco is on his feet and working me over with his fucking chloroformeous gloves again. Yeah, he hits hard, real hard, like I've never been hit before. I feel a numbification in my ribs that almost brings me to my knees. I spin on my axis and see that the vato's possessed; his eyes are the eyes of the devil himself.

Chuby and Yorkie are still kneeling on the canvas. If he clocks me again, he'll send me ass-over-teakettle to hell. If he clocks me, he'll send me to wonderland, where everything's out of whack—I intuit this before I can think it, because there's no time to think during a beatdown. During a beatdown, thoughts are like sparks—there's no time for anything, just intuiting what might hurt the most and focusing all your rage there as a precise target, focusing all the unruly strength inside you on a single point so you don't end up dead, because you have to survive at any cost.

Fucking Crazy Loco sails at me to hammer me again with what looks like another powerful, devastating blow; he comes at me like a nuclear missile, vaporizing all the air in his path. He's like a comet of light and heat. Automatically, utterly without thinking, my feet leap backward, and, as if my cells have turned into microscopic springs triggered by fire, I bash out, driving all my molecules into the exact center of his glove. Zooooooom!

Our two fists collide at the speed of light. Furious. Interwoven by fire. We explode because there's no tomorrow. Tomorrow doesn't exist in brawls. And there, in that precise instant, I feel his wrist, millimeter by millimeter, cell by cell, shatter like a chain that always breaks at the weakest link; I see the flesh at his wrist swell up like a balloon when it collides with my fist and then collapse as if it's been punctured. A splinter of bone pokes through the skin in his wrist, and his whole arm goes limp as if it were dead, stringless, demarrowed.

Immediately I'm back on guard, keeping a watchful eye in case El Crazy Loco tries to pull a knife on me the way they've done so many times before; but no, the vato stares at his fucked-up limb and lets out a howl that echoes up to the stratosphere, beyond the cosmos, where our cries are steadily accumulating and will one day tumble down on us like a rainshower of rancor.

Nobody says anything.

Everything seems to have come to a standstill.

Nobody moves.

There's only silence.

The vato lifts up his arm, but the glove, with the fist and wrist inside it, dangles like a red pendulum that stops time; his eyes roll back and in that moment, with the veins on his forehead all swollen, clogged with asterisks, he crashes backward.

"Shit," says the earringed gorilla after an eternity, still filming.

Then everything starts moving at a dizzying pace.

Yorkie races to the campeón's side. He takes the towel from around his neck and wraps the mangled forearm like a sausage.

Chuby raises his hands to his head and shouts, "You fucked him up now, you little bastard, you fucked him up, fuck, fuck, fuck! You fucked him up!"

The dudes swarm up and haul El Crazy Loco out of the ring.

"Get 'im to the hospital," Yorkie exclaims, his balls no longer dragging the floor in his haste.

They manage to lift El Crazy Loco up, pass him through the ropes, and hurry off, carrying him like a bullfighter who's been skewered by the bull.

The earringed gorilla trails after them, glued to them like a fucking paparazzo, while Chuby pulls out the keys of his boat to take him to the hospital.

I run after them, but instead of following them, once I'm out of the gym I speed off in the opposite direction. "Don't stir shit up, you asshole," I mutter to myself as I move away from where they're loading the guy into the car and everything's in turmoil, a string of mayhems battering my eyes and ears.

They all push and jumble; they elbow one another and shout. Several of them clamber in like flies and start up the boat. The tires squeal at top speed as they take off and disappear around the corner.

I move quickly off toward the freeway overpass with the graffiti and the dogs and the scruffs penetrating their veins with pipe dreams. "They're gonna come after you," I tell myself, punching myself in the forehead with my gloves. "And if they come after you, they'll beat you up and put a rocket in your ass to launch you into another galaxy." And if they launch me to another part of the universe, I'll die. I'll die, simple as that, I'll die—because I won't see the chickadee ever again, ever again Aireen. And if I don't see her, I'll die. I'll die.

I don't know why I start crying. I don't know. I don't bawl, I never bawl, but tears come leaking out on their own, as if my head belonged to somebody else, as if my eyes weren't my own. Tears spill out and run into my mouth and dribble uncertainly down to my heart, salty, flayed as the ocean. I can't even wipe them away because of the fat gloves I'm wearing. I'm a goddamn blotch wandering around Fuckedville. There's nothing worse than seeing the love of your life every day and not being able to touch her—yes, kiss her, yes. Yes, hug her, yes. Yes, pull her body on top of mine so she can do with me what she will.

I start walking slowly, very slowly, to bring it all to a halt, as if my steps marked the pace of all the world's clocks. I need time, time I no longer have, time I sense is going to run out on me soon. Once they nab me, there'll be nothing left; I'll plunge into a vortex of sorrow and drown there at the bottom, alone, dying of love outside myself.

The afternoon starts slipping away between my legs. I reach a bench somewhere, who knows, and collapse onto it. My tears start to go staccato, like ellipses between me and the wind; I smear them with my forearm and jaggedly breathe in, gulping envenomed saliva. I sit there staring at nothing, like it doesn't matter what I'm looking at. The world is turning and I'm not there. I'm a squatter exiled from everywhere. Across the street is a run-down house with a desiccated yard; I watch some flea-sized kids playing with a ball. They're so small they can hardly stay upright. One of them kicks the ball to the other, and it hits him in the belly. They laugh, they're laughing. They don't need anything else. They run after each other; they chase each other around and tangle and disentangle. I watch them with interest. They wallow in the leaden dust. They laugh again, softly, loudly, down low, up high—in every cranny of the dry blades of their dead grass. Who cares? Who cares! Life is also those little things that cannot be measured with the hands or grasped with the peepers, that cannot cling to roots and leaves.

I get up. Who cares! Who cares! If I hurry, I might still find salvation for the things I harbor fatedly inside me, before they hollow me out and leave me bearing a tomb wherever I go.

I move forward sybaritically, blotting my plump tears as I go like a striding amanuensis. I bound over bushes. I roll under cars. I leap up to the clouds to hasten the rain. I penetrate the city's megalithic walls. I race through parks and gardens. I hang from trees and lampposts, and by the skin of my teeth I arrive just in time to wait for the chickadee to come back from work in the wee hours, on that midnight bus that drops her off amid the swell of scruffs. I get there to wait for her, on my knees, and tell her how much I love her; how much I carry her inside me; how much I can't live without her, sí. Without you, Aireen, mi amor.

"Jesus, you shit-dribbling little twerp, you're a hard one to track down. Where the hell were you? I looked for you every-where! Pinche pain-in-the-ass kid. And what happened to your bookstore? Did it get totally trashed?"

The lady gets out of the white truck she's left parked with its headlights on in front of the steps where I've been waiting for the chickadee for a while now.

"Are you coming with me, then, or am I going to have to beat you up?" she says, braying with laughter like an indiges-tive donkey.

"If you touch me, señora," I say, pointing at her with the fucking gloves I still haven't been able to gnaw off, "I don't usually hit old ladies, but I'll take care of you good."

"Ha!" She emits a loud cackle, like a macaw at a rolling boil. "Tranquis, kid, I'm just messing with you. Mind if I take up some space there with you? I promise not to touch you, won't even brush you with a goddamn flower petal." She moves closer and tries to sit down next to me, but I don't budge so there's no room on the step. She's wearing baggy sailor pants, sandals, a cowboy hat, and a bandana around her forehead. "Scootch over or I'm going to sit on your lap, got it?" But before I can respond, she's already perched on top of me. "You're super-bony, kid!" I try to push her off, but my gloves are as useful as fucking crab pincers. "Hey," she says, "stop prodding my tits with those lumps." I lay off paw-ing at her and try to push with my pelvis to make her get up. "Come on now, little punk, don't you think we should at least introduce ourselves and make out a little first? Or do you want to just go for it?" I stop shaking her pelvis with my pelvis and remain motionless, withered, wavering between her body and my thoughts. I feel her ass crushing my willy and her back pressed against my chest. "What are you doing out here all by yourself?" I don't answer; I'm pissed. "Come on, papi, answer me!" she says, cheekily wriggling her ass on my balls.

"What the fuck do you care?" I say so she'll stop moving.

"All right, kid, just don't yell at me—you're acting like you're in love or something!"

I seethe with rage.

Seeing that, she starts chatterboxing, sounding like she's got a few quarts of glue in her throat.

"Come on, kid, you can't fool me—you're in love. Anyone could see it, you skinny as a shoelace and throwing down like you're some beefy buffer. Who's the lucky girl?"

She bounces on top of me and shifts her hectoliters of flesh to my abdomen.

"I can't breathe," I tell her.

"Don't play dumb," she says bluntly. "Love suffocates but it doesn't kill." She turns her face toward me and our noses almost touch. "Oh, kid," she shrieks suddenly, wrinkling her nostrils, "you stink." She immediately leaps to her feet and, now on the vertical, adjusts her cowboy hat and hikes up her pants. "I'm Wendoline." She holds out her hand to shake.

"Crazy old broad," I say.

"At least give me five, kid. You should never leave a lady with a dick in her mouth," she says, still holding out her hand. "One . . . two . . ." I bump her with my left glove. "That's the spirit, campeón." She guffaws. Then she gets serious again and starts yammering questions. "(1) Are you left-handed? (2) Have you started taking boxing clases so they don't pummel you again? (3) Why are you wearing boxing gloves this time of night? And (4) what's the name of the girl you're in love with?"

"What do you care?"

She looks at me as if I were a dustbuster.

"Well, we can work that out later! I want to conversate with you about a few things so I was going to invite you to get something to eat, but now I see where we'll be doing it."

She crickets in front of me and claps her hands, plock, plock, plock. The lady's completely bonkers, a total fruitcake.

"I'm busy!" I sulk like a dysfunctional pipe dream.

"Oh, are you? Doing what? Warming this stone with your rear end? All right, fine, that's cool." She hauls at my arm and pulls me to my feet, still laughing. "Look, devil's snot, if you're waiting for somebody, you'd best go get cleaned up first. Reeking like that, the only thing that's going to jump your bones is fleas. Go on, get in my truck. Nothing's going to happen to you."

Something rumbles inside me because yes, I must stink to high heaven.

* * *

[That's what Jefe used to tell me:
"Wash your fucking wingpits, you toxic prick—they can smell you all the way on the far corner of the last block in Patagonia! They should use your sweat to unclog plumbing—or, better yet, as fuel for weapons of mass destruction."]

I hesitate in front of the lady, because whenever someone says nothing's going to happen, something happens.

"Go on, jumbleputz, ugly and filthy ain't working for you." She drags me to the edge of the sidewalk and steers me in front of the passenger door of her truck. "Oh, pardon me, Your Highness," she says as she opens the door for me, "you can't even rub one out with those Q-tips on your hands."

She gives a sweeping bow and steps aside to let me pass. I get into the truck and she slams the door. She walks in front of the vehicle, and the headlights illuminate her belly. She's not very tall—quite the contrary, I'd say she's short. She opens the door and climbs in.

"Can you even reach the pedals?" I ask, aggravated after everything she's said.

"Ha-ha, you jerk." She lets out another impish laugh. "I love it. You're starting to feel comfortable." She starts up the truck and we head down the street to the first red light. "What kind of music do you like, vato?"

I'm looking all around, especially behind us, to make sure we're not being followed—maybe somebody's just having me picked up so they can blood-sausage me.

"Calle 13."

She leans forward and opens the glove compartment. She scrabbles around in the junk and pulls out a USB memory stick. Then she presses a button and a little screen comes out of nowhere, making a little noise like a fly: Bzzzzzzzz. She inserts the memory stick in the USB port, and the screen lights up. She searches and selects an album. The woofers and tweeters start rumbling like earthquakes, as if we were in one of those places I've only peered into from the outside; the only thing missing is the colored spotlights.

"Doesn't my system sound awesome?"

"What?" I say because I can't hear anything.

"Can't you hear anything?" she asks.

"No!" I shout.

"Great, I can call you a dick and you won't even realize."

"You're the dick!" I yell, since I did hear her.

Both of us sit there for a moment, looking at each other, our eyes half-closed as if we were about to bite each other, and for the first time in a long time, I smile while she lets out a peal of laughter and a few fervent howls. She laughs unbuttoned, uninhibited, hazatious, while Residente from Calle 13 pounds our Eustachian tubes at six thousand miles an hour.

She turns onto Sixth and heads toward the hills of Palatine

West. We pass the last strip mall, its parking lot crammed with cars. We take the exit and merge onto the freeway. She suddenly turns down the stereo, as if she needed silence to think, and her laughter now is only leaking out of the corners of her mouth like lava, afire from the dizzying blaze.

"I once went into your bookstore to buy some books, and the fat guy with glasses helped me; I assume he's your boss. He ordered you to go up a ladder to bring down a book by Dr. Spengler, you know, that one about the urban tribes of warriors that live in some cities here in the border states. I needed it to get a handle on the language you kids use because I was writing something for the *Sun*—of course, this was when I was working for the *Sun News*. You might not remember me, because I still had hair back then and I wore skintight clothing all year round. But when you brought that huge book down and put it in my hands, you went dead or something, I don't know, and you almost dropped it when your fingers brushed mine. You were so chiqui, you didn't even have feathers yet! And the fat guy started cussing you out. Oh, I was so serious about things back then, and I didn't do anything to stop him. I should have jumped in and volumetrically walloped that asshole, but what are you gonna do. A person never learns till she feels the yardstick she'll be measured with drawing near."

The truck keeps moving. Yes, now I remember, I'm thinking as she talks. But that chickadee didn't at all resemble the one who's now in the driver's seat and turning at the intersection. That one had fire swarming up her legs like ants. While this one seems to have been crushed by a nutcracker.

"I don't remember," I say finally. She looks at me and, without saying anything, turns the music back up till it overflows the truck cab.

We roll on, climbing through the hills to the first exit and then leaving the highway. We go a couple of miles farther, and she starts to slow down. We pass through a checkpoint with a chip that's attached to the truck. The place leaves me agape, iridescent: I've never seen anything like it except in the magazines I used to leaf through in the bookstore.

* * *

[There were a few magazines that Jefe bought reluctantly.
"Listen, you indigestible prick, that Reader's Digest you're flipping through is going to destroy the few brain cells you've got."
"So why do you order them, Jefe?"
"To destroy the brain cells of the rich ladies who come through here," he said, and laughed mockingly with that alebrije inside him.]

The houses up in the hills have yards lit by lanterns. Some of them have lounge chairs outside and little fountains; others have children's toys and teak bum-resters. If those decorative doodads were in my town on the other side, I think to myself, they'd have been nicked already and sold on the street.

We get to a house with flagstone paving and surrounded by a few tarred trees. There's a lantern illuminating a little path up to the entrance of an elegant stucco house. The lady parks the truck and shuts off the engine. The music stops blaring and the screen automatically retracts.

"We're here, man." I don't even try to open the little door. "Oh, I forgot!" the lady exclaims, spotting my gloves again. "You're a jackass, and those hooves of yours are no use for human things." She cackles into the windshield. "I'll open it for you, young sir." She reaches over me, jabbing her elbow into my stomach, and yanks on the door handle with her other hand. "Sorry if I crushed your pecker," she says. "I just wanted to feel it again."

"Qué!"

"Relax, kiddo, you're not my type, but I still had to investigate a little to make sure what I felt back there was true." She laughs even louder and dives to the ground.

I leap out onto the grass.

"This way." She leads me to the little path. She flits from subject to subject as we cross the yard. "Sometimes I'd like to have more time to take care of my plants—look at them, they're wilting with embarrassment. A plant is like a woman: it needs love. I could have made an amazing lesbian because I know what a woman needs too, but no, I always liked dick." She laughs dyslexically, like she's got the hiccups.

She opens the front door and turns on the lights in an enormous foyer; then she lights up a larger room. She's got tons of paintings on the wall, lots more than Jefe has at his house, and lots more than at the chickadee's house. I figure people hang up paintings so as not to impoverish their vistas with bare walls.

"This place looks like a museum!" I say.

"That's exactly what I told my ex-husband. So to get even with me for taking his house, that asshole left me all his crap. Even the cockroaches!"

"There are cockroaches here?"

The lady looks at me and smiles. "It's just a manner of speaking, kid. Sometimes you seem older than you are, with those weird words you use, but other times you're so naive."

She turns on all the lights. The house is a museum. It's huge but crowded with things: display cabinets here, paintings there; it has some side tables that look really old, made of carved wood. Toward the rear of the house there's a vast dining room with twelve chairs; off to one side is a large living room with four armchairs as big as beds. To the right of the grand piano is a display cabinet set with gilt-framed mirrors that contains glass figurines and, on a lower shelf, a sculpture of a fish-woman.

On the other side of the house is one of those massive kitchens with a stove in the center—well, that stove part is just an expression, because all you can see is a black glass panel with several circles painted on it and a bell-like thing up above it. Hanging nearby are frying pans, pots, ladles. To the left is a bar with two stools, and in the rear, behind some sheer, gauzy curtains, is another lit-up yard and what looks like a swimming pool.

The lady goes over to a drawer in the kitchen. "You'd better entrust your soul to the Lord now, sassbucket—you're about to learn all about Him." She waves a chef's knife and walks toward me, her eyes cold. Then she shrieks wildly, "Don't run away, it's a joke, sassbucket! I'm going to cut those gloves off you."

I don't know, I hesitate at the front door, trying vainly to grasp the goddamn knob. I keep hesitating even as my legs tell me to take off running. A person must always hesitate, I've always said. But there's no way, my hands are fast asleep at this point. They must be black and blue inside the boxing gloves. I slowly approach her and extend my hands. "I'm in God's hands," I think.

The lady looks at me.

"You're right to run, but there's no need for it today."

She puts the point of the blade between the glove's laces and tugs hard. The laces give way and bloom open. She puts the knife on a side table and removes my gloves. It's true, my fingers are shaking.

"Where did that bruise come from?" she asks, examining one of my hands.

"Nothing, just another fight."

She squeezes my swollen, crampic phalanges. I feel her warmth enveloping my fingers; the ache is gradually disappearing.

"You're a funny kid," she says half seriously. "It's like no one's ever touched your hands before."

I don't know where to look, so I stare at the floor, turning into a cockroach. She keeps stroking my hands till they come back to life.

"Come on," she says subjacently, and takes me by the hand; she leads me into a wide hallway and opens a door.

The light comes on automatically. It's an enormous bathroom. A mirror across an entire wall makes it seem even larger. The sink is on a wide, glass-doored vanity, and you can see white towels on the shelves inside it. There are two chrome-plated brackets with glass shelves that contain a few decorative objects. The crapper's covered with seashells, and the seat is made of wood. The shower is off to the left, enclosed in glass; on the other side of the room is a painting of some little fish in high relief. In the middle of it all is a round white bathtub with blue trim that could fit three cows, three donkeys, and maybe, if you really crammed them in there, three laying hens. Above it, hanging on the wall, is a flat-screen television as long as I am tall.

"The only peace I find is in the Jacuzzi," she says absently. "In there, the world just disappears and the only thing that exists is me."

She walks over to some switches at the base of the tub; she flips them and the tub starts to fill. After a few seconds, steam and hot water start pouring out of a number of holes.

"You go ahead and get undressed while I go look for some clothes for you. Those clothes you've got on are well past their prime. Absolutely foul."

She leaves the room, and I don't know what to do.

The water bubbles and the drops crash into one another; they're like icebergs of steam. I look at my hands, which are macerated from all that time they spent inside the gloves. They smell like ass, a bouquet of vinyl and leather. I don't know, maybe they smell like mules, those animals swaybacked under the weight of the knowledge that they'll never have a family.

"Didn't you strip, squirt?" she says, coming into the bathroom with a bundle of clothes. She puts it on the counter. "Come on, you're like a little kid!" she says.

Where can I run to? I'm shivering. Maybe if I dive into that ocean of bubbles I can fuck off down the drain, or leap in every drop till I'm torn to bits. The lady puts her hands on my waist and removes my belt; slowly, she unbuttons my bookstore shirt, which is filthy with blood, sweat, and dirt. She pulls it off my shoulders and lets it fall to the floor.

"You're a funny one, kid. Stop shaking, nothing's going to happen to you." But she runs her hands over my marimbic ribs, touches them; my skin shivers even more. I get goose bumps. "I thought you'd have a tattoo of some Latin gang, from one of those urban tribes or whatever—maybe even from the MS-13. But no, you're barer than my damn head. All you've got are these scars that look like sunburns."

* * *

[*It was true. I'd never wanted to etch anything on my body, only the scars of the desert. I felt different from everybody else in the evenings, thinking about strange things—like leaping up into the leaves and swinging off through the branches.*

"That's homo shit," a paisa once told me dismissively when I was still back in Mexico, under the bridges, exiled from my godmother, stabbing the air with the alleycat breathing of my homeland.

"Say that again and I'll put you on pain meds for life," I said.

"You look like a fag thinking that fag shit," the guy repeated, and uncautiously I laid into him, cursing a blue streak.

"Cocksucking motherfucker."

And he takes out his knife—a big one, with a torsion spring, the kind you'd use to flay hogs, and me all unfazed, surrounded by guys who are eager to see blood.

"Fight!" they howled.

"Either put that away and we'll throw down right, or I'm not responsible for what happens," I said.

And he doesn't put it away, because he's already had his snout all battered in by my fists before.

And he charges at me, trying to gore me with the blade, and balls, I fend him off with my right hand, and nuts, I smash him in the legs so he spins in the air like a pinwheel, and boom, the moron lets go of the icepick and it flies up into the air and falls on top of him.

I saw him land facedown, denutted. I flipped him over and he still had eyes to see me, but just barely, life was leaking out of him through the hole in his gut. And me all bloody trying to stop the flood. Because he was my compadre out on the street, but sometimes your compadres get stupid. After that he didn't see anything; his powered-down mouth starched up, full of lost tattoos.

"Scram, cabrón," the other guys in the gang told me.

"Get out of here or they'll nab you."

And so I ran till my feet ached, under the streetlights and bridges, my hands puddled with blood.]

Suddenly a tremor runs through me, from all my cardinal points to all the astral points of my epidermis, yanking me out of my memories. The lady pulls my belt from my jeans and tosses it next to my shirt.

"Take off your boots so we can get your pants off."

I teeter but manage to get out of them. Her hands rest on my hips and lower my pants down to the floor. I stand before her, naked, root-bare.

"Madre mía!" She lets out a little shriek. "That firehose of yours is terrifying," the lady laughs. "You're quite a find, papito."

Right then my gut starts screeching. I haven't eaten anything all day. Just the potato chips yesterday and the water. The noise of my bowels jolts her out of the place she'd gone in her

thoughts, and I see her blush suddenly; she falters and immediately stands up.

"All right, papi," she says acrobatically, "into the water,
duckling."

She pinches my butt and pushes me toward the bathtub. I
plunge in. I hold my breath under the water.

I don't want to come up. Yes, the sea, I've never seen it, I've
never been—I don't know what it's like. I've seen it through
books: blue, full of noises like murmurs full of sunshine, and
the waves, succumbing to the gulls that tangle in their sandy
fringes.

What does the sea in books smell like?

When I finally emerge from the water, the lady's not there
anymore. She's dissolved into a sudden absence. I see only that
the water's starting to foam and there's a loofah and a scrub
brush on a shelf by the tub. I sit up in the aquatic seat and
perch there still as the grave, like flowers after their petals have
fallen and the wind blows across them, like that, contrite as the
bubbles cling to my body.

I lean back, resting my head on the edge of the tub, and see
a transparent skylight in the ceiling overhead.

There are no stars visible out there, just a bluish glow, but I
know they're there, indomitable, forming constellations,
tumultuous, with their planets hitched to their suns. Yes, the
universe could well be a wonder, I don't know—a marvel in all
its caspiricious nooks and crannies, where the light becomes a
cradle for every nestling dewdrop or whatever. Why was that
pockmarked writer who came into the bookstore always looking for things outside of Earth when everything may be right
here?

My guts start groaning again. I press on my belly and manage to get them under control.

I'd better get out of the tub before my fingers get even more
wrinkly. I pick up the scrub brush and start scrubbing myself

as if I were a dog. I scrub hard, angrily, until my calluses are polished off and my hands no longer scratch like sandpaper. I scrub everywhere, especially to get rid of the filth inside me, sloughing it off my soul in little clumps.

I finish scrubbing, take one last dip, and then spring out of the tub to wring myself dry with the towel. I pick up a pair of sweatpants that's in the heap of clothing and a T-shirt that says I HEART NY. I pick up the belt and wrap it around my waist, because my belt is part of me, it's like my life jacket even when I don't have anything stashed in its secret hiding place; I've got the mollusk's eighty dollars in there, the card with the address of the gym, the pastor's medicine, and, at the bottom, my mother's locket, which they say she was wearing around her neck when she died.

I wad up my jeans and the bookstore shirt and stuff them under my arm; I pick up my boots and leave the bathroom with my belongings.

I don't see the lady. The lights are still on. I walk down the hallway and into the museum. She isn't in the living room or the dining room; I don't see her in the kitchen. I don't see her anywhere. Maybe she's squeezing out her madness in the swimming pool like they do in shoddy novels, smoking a cigarette, or kneeling down and staring into the water, or having a drink and spilling nostalgia into her glass by the jugful.

I go outside, but she's not there. The pool is carpeted with fallen leaves. The grass is overgrown, higher than my pubes. "Fuck." I go back to the front door and open it. Her truck is still there. I return to the middle of the living room and decide to shout:

"Ma'am! Ma'am!"

I hear a peal of laughter like a lunatic goat from somewhere in the house.

"Come here!" she says.

"Where?"

"Here, you nincompoop."

I retrace my steps toward the hall where the bathroom is; I walk past it and on the far side spot a hallway bending off next to a planter. I turn down it and discover an entrance with double doors that open onto another enormous, dimly lit room with a bed in the middle that would fit the same three cows, three donkeys, and three hens all at once with room to spare.

Across from the bed are two large floor-to-ceiling windows that look out on the backyard and the pool. The lady is glued to a laptop on a desk that's covered with piles of papers. She turns in her chair and looks at me.

On the rear wall is a bulletin board with lots of pinned-up business cards, Post-It notes, slips of paper, photos, and I don't know what else.

Next to it is a vanity and several wigs.

"What were you doing out in the yard?" she asks. I don't answer. She half closes her eyes and studies me. "I see my ex-husband's clothes fit you perfectly."

I walk over to the wigs, which are perched on round stands. I look at them in alarm.

"What are these for?"

"Sometimes I need them for work. But I can tell you're not listening." She smiles. "Everyone calls me Double-U. None of this 'ma'am' crap—that's not necessary, right, squirt? I can't be more than fifteen years older than you."

She notices I've got my clothing under my arm and my boots in my hand.

"Oh, no, not in here." She snatches them away from me and hurries out of the room. "We should really burn these, toss them in the fireplace and douse them in formaldehyde to kill off all the creepy-crawlies you've got, but I'm just going to wash them in case you need them later, because here . . ."

Her voice fades off into the distance.

The room is the color of marble. It's quite large. There are two fans on the ceiling, and at the far end of the room hangs another television much larger than the one in the bathroom. The floor is made of wood but there are thick rugs laid out on it. I walk along the wall to a door; I open it and find it leads to a dressing room. I close it again. I walk to the windows. From there you can see part of the city. We're perched up on a hill. The lights of the city twinkle like stars, yellow and white. You can see the skyscrapers crowned with their pulsing red beacons. Closer in are dark areas of night; they must be the trees of the small, unlit forest that spreads over the hills, and over there, tiny, you can see the headlights of the cars moving along what seems to be the highway.

"Do you like it?" I hear the lady's voice behind me.

"What?" I ask without looking at her.

"The view of the valley—do you like it?"

I shrug; I don't say anything. Sometimes we're so blind that all we see is shadows.

"Do you believe in God?" I ask without thinking.

She is quiet a moment; I watch her shadow reflected in the glass. I see her turn and go back to her seat in front of the computer. I keep looking out the window. The light from an airplane goes by in the distance like a bird carrying a firefly caged between its wheels; it must be heading toward the airport. I've never been on a plane. I once tried to imagine what the Earth looked like from the clouds when I read a book about a journey in a hot-air balloon, but all my imagination could conjure up was rooftops bedecked with water tanks and clotheslines filling with soot and rain.

"Come on, come over here, kid. I want to show you something."

I unglue my gaze from the horizon and herd myself over to the lady.

"You're a legend," she says once I'm standing beside her.

"Qué!" I say, disoriented, strident.

The lady gets up and pulls a stool over so I can sit next to her.

"That day they beat you up outside the bookstore, there at the bus stop, I was nearby—a total fluke. Anyway, I wasn't feeling real good since the medicine they're giving me hasn't been completely effective, but you probably didn't notice me because I was wearing sunglasses. I was parked there, well, you know how it goes, sniffling snot over some of the crap I've been going through lately—but that's another story. I saw you come out of the bookstore and stand there on the sidewalk like a zombie; you looked like you were having trouble breathing. I just watched you. Then you started to cross the street, totally ignoring the cars that were honking at you, yelling things, all insults and curses, and you looked like you wanted to die crushed under their wheels right there. I took out my cell phone and started recording. It was instinctive for me, you know? I used to be a reporter at the *Sun*. Now I work for the *Chronica News*, but that's another long story. I was about to turn off my cell once you were sitting on the bench, but suddenly they were all coming up behind you and then, without saying a word, that bunch of cocksuckers started beating you up. I leaped out of my truck and went over to film you surrounded by that gaggle of assholes. I kept filming all of it, even the passersby who gathered around to gape. I recorded it all. And you didn't make a peep, didn't say a word. You didn't say a word, can you believe it? You took that pounding and didn't make a peep. I never imagined someone could withstand a beating like that. You didn't say anything or scream or anything. Like you were made of steel or I don't know what, stone maybe. But you made me think about a lot of things. Anyway, I wanted to take you to a doctor that day but you told me to fuck off, remember? I got home and that same afternoon I wrote the story of what I'd seen and uploaded the video to YouTube with the link for a freelance gig I do for *Chronica*

News. I'd written a lot of articles, especially about immigrants and their rights and the kitchen sink, you know, in support of the immigration law, but never anything really eye-catching. Well, this article isn't eye-catching either, just the basic facts and a bit of a reflective conclusion; the really remarkable bit is the video. Look."

She points at the laptop screen. I still don't understand and keep staring and staring at the screen.

"Look at the numbers," she says with a goddamn twinkle in her eyes. "It's had 1.7 million views in less than four days. Can you believe it? Facebook, Twitter. The world went apeshit over my video. It was a hashtag around the globe. Some in favor, some against. Yesterday they broadcast a special on CBS about immigration reform and civil rights, and they used the video as background footage. Last night CNN contacted me to see if I could help them out since I'd recorded the video. They want an exclusive interview with you. It's a hot topic now, muy caliente, kid. Everybody wants to know who you are and where you're from. You could be a huge help to millions of people here. Can you believe it? Can you understand that? Do you understand the magnitude of what I'm telling you? You're famous now! You're a hero! So can I interview you?"

I don't understand a thing; I don't understand a bit of what the fucking lady's saying. I only feel madness swelling up inside me, and I get up from the stool in a fury, like someone's rammed a chile up my butt. All my words disappear; they're stuck in my throat. All I can do is shout at her with lacerated eyes, knockoutified, feeling suddenly used, betrayed, downtrodden by what I've just seen and heard.

"Fuck you!" I shout at her.

The highway is dark like a fucking serpent, enlivened only by the cumuli of the car headlights speeding through the forest. Their lights tattoo my eyes like a rabbit, like a stupid deer, frozen stiff: an imbecilically lampified deerbbit. The rocks dig into my feet—I took off from the damn crazy lady's house without putting any shoes on. The pain creeps in through the soles of my feet and up to my spine, and there the pebbles pile up like a haystack of needles on top of my nerves. In the distance I can see the city with its turpentine streetlights tracing the virulent outlines of the buildings and their illuminated offices. The red beacons, which not long ago had seemed like lighthouses for my vagabondage, now look like somber buttonholes in the night sky. "Fuck you," I keep roaring furiously into the air like a shower of hurricane-swept nights and, seething, I start walking to go look for her, as if my pilgrimage were an eternal return. "Fucking dumbass broad," I say to myself. "Everybody's always trying to take advantage of you, pinche pendejo," I repeat. "Everybody." And I keep walking, stumbling, on the edge of the air.

* * *

[Like when I collapsed to my knees on the highway after crossing the Rio Grande, seeing the lone car move off into the distance, chasing the hot vapor rising from the road, and me now without clothes, because the heat was boiling up from within me now, spewing from my pores, and little by little I'd ditched my clothing, discarding it along the way, leaving it behind; I ended up stripped bare, buck-naked, my shoulders now blistered with sunburn, blisters fatter than agave caterpillars, totally fucking tunisian. In despair, I fell flat on my face to bite the crucified dust, to sink in up to my neck and wait for the vultures to strip me of my flesh and the sun to bleach my bones there in the gringos' desert. "Fuck it," I said to myself, feeling the scorching weight of death on my bare shoulders, on my burnt-alabaster skin. "Fuck it," I repeated as I roasted by the side of the road after crossing the Rio Grande—there, like a tortoise without a *shell, my arms splayed out like a cross, silent, breathing in less and less air and more and more dust. "Fuck . . ."*

And when I opened my eyes I was already in a truck, like I'd been transported to another dimension, full of paisas staring at me.

"It's a miracle you're alive, güey," one of them yelled, aiming a stream of water from a small jug over my blackened, thirst-swollen lips.

"Watch out, kid, don't drink too fast." He pulled the canteen out of my hands, which were shaking, shredded with desperation. "You can die if you chug it all down in one go. Take little sips, like that, a bit at a time."

"Ay, cabrón, it's a miracle you're alive," another says.

"Your skin's going to hurt like hell, it's going to hurt a lot, but you're alive and that's thanks to God and His mother, our Virgencita de Guadalupe."

"And thanks to us too—we came by just in time, kid," said another.

"We saw you there, sprawled out."

"And we stopped and poked you with a stick to see if you were still alive, and yes, you moved one hand like a snake, so we lifted you up into our truck here."

"Ay, it's a fucking miracle, it really is, kid. If you knew how many bones there are scattered around out there from vatos like you who get lost and never come back . . ."

"It's like you've been resurrected. A dead man brought back to life."

"A lacerated miracle full of thorns."

They'd already put a blanket over me to cover my nudities. My skin was burning like I didn't have any at all.

"Paisa," said the man with the canteen, "we can take you and drop you off near a gringo checkpoint, and the cabrones will fix you up there, but then they'll send you back to the grave you crawled out of. Or you can stick with us and we'll take a look at

*you and all chip in to give you a hand. It's up to you, kid: you can
either die here with us, or die on the other side."]*

When I leave the reporter's house, there is no sun scorching me; instead, I am enfolded in the embrace of the night and
the highway shooing cars in both directions. I feel violated,
betrayed, beswarmed on all sides by the pain of having someone hold out a hand to you and then turn around and stab you.
That dagger is much more painful than a stranger's, and it cuts
you deeper. Because betrayal always comes from close by,
never from far away; betrayal is the lowest circle of hell, the
one that tightens like a noose around the condemned man's
neck and doesn't slacken until his tongue is lolling out and
there's no life left to asphyxiate.

The highway keeps going that direction. I'm heading down-
hill, dazed, pebbles poking my calluses. I'm thinking about the
chickadee, about Aireen coming back from work. "Will I still be
able to threadle my way and get there in time to wait for her at
the bus stop?" I'm not sure—maybe I should look up at the stars
to figure out whether I've got the direction and the time right.
But destiny is never in the heavens, up there above, enflatulated.

"Shit," I say to myself when I see a highway patrol car
approaching. They race past me, and me looking straight at
them, meeting their gaze.

I hear their tires squeal as they brake twenty or thirty yards
down the road.

"Puta madre, they saw me. They're going to nab me."
Never run, they used to tell me, but now there's no choice: run
for it, puto, or you'll spend the night in the slammer.

Instead of sticking to the highway, I plunge into a group of
trees on the hill like a fucking gazelle fleeing a pride of lions.

You're not going to catch me that easily, assholes.

You're going to have to drag me down kicking and screaming from the highest treetops.

Now the stones are searing the soles of my bare feet; I feel the damp of the grass and all of its pricklers. The trees become denser and start to fall into line like black soldiers on an utterly dark, moonless night, two by two.

I splash through a small stream, muddying my feet. Behind me I can see the blue and red lights of the patrol car shattering against the trees and two flashlights shining in my direction, trying to pick me out.

I scramble toward a rocky promontory and climb up one side. I'm breathing heavily. Take a deep breath. Slowly, like everything's fine. Like you're just out for a little air. "Think about Aireen again."

I've reached the top and start descending again on the other side of the rocks toward a little hollow. I can't see the patrol car's lights clearly anymore; it's as if the trees have put up a wall of twigs and foliage, as if I were another tree they were trying to protect.

I head down a trail that seems to be used by mountain bikers.

I race ahead a few hundred fast-flowing yards. Now the rocks are jammed between my toes like little flintstones giving off sparks.

Suddenly in the sky I see the red eye of a helicopter approaching from the city. A few minutes later it passes over me, its blades and motors going at full bore, and heads toward the darkest area of the forest. It's got a spotlight that shines down from above like a giant luminous keyhole that unlocks the night.

"Pinches cabrones, they've even got a helicopter after me."

I start running along the path to get far away from there as quickly as possible, and I end up sliding down a steep hill. Branches slap me all over.

I keep rolling down the slope until I fall into a little ditch of soil and weeds. I'm out of breath from the impact, but I leap out in a prickle, a crown of bruises encircling my cabeza.

I roll a bit farther and tumble to the left. I can no longer see or hear the helicopter's engine. I stand up and start running toward my pursuers' antipodes. I've got to get to the city as fast as I can; it's easier to disappear there.

* * *

[Jefe once told me:

"Hey, pissant, if the migra comes poking around here one day, I want you to roll up into a tiny ball and hide in a crack in the bookstore. Right up there is a loft that nobody ever uses. I use it to store a bunch of crap. You go up there and coil up like a snake and don't make a goddamn peep, because if they catch us, the bastards'll take the both of us away. Got it, you illegal cocksucker?"

And that's when he got the idea of having me look after the bookstore for him at night.]

I pass a clump of trees, and the intersection at the edge of the city appears. There's a Conoco gas station. It must be dawn, yes, because the dew has gotten misty, almost elastic, and fills the air with cobwebs. My feet are covered with mud, pebbles, and scratches.

There are no cars coming in either direction. I skitter across to the other side of the freeway and turn left to avoid the gas station, where there are several cars lined up and the 7-Eleven is open.

I reach a graffiticated overpass. I walk under it and enter the outskirts of the city.

The streetlights spread out in a mapped grid.

My feet are on fire, but what the hell do I care. Two or three nocturnal scruffs go by in the distance, the kind that are sparks in the dark, lighting up only at night. Bums are invisible in the city, which is why we can disappear. Then a yup wearing a trench coat walks by; he doesn't see or hear me—seems like he's in a hurry. He picks up his pace and disappears in the other direction.

Two addos are on a corner with their feet crossed and propped up on a wall. They're smoking joints. I walk past and they size me up.

"Psst, hey, man, wanna score?"

I keep going and spot the mall in the distance. It can't be far now, less than a mile and I'll be there. I head for the other side, avoiding walking through the parking lot because the security guards might see me and chase me off.

I walk three more blocks and then turn right, heading into the heart of the city.

The tall buildings are like pencils scribbling on the sky. Their windows reflect me as I pass. Some of them have fountains that turn the water different colors. They're still running, yes; the fountains in these elegant buildings are on forty-eight hours a day; they're like the buildings' blood bubbling at their feet.

The night is quiet, hardly anybody on the street. A few cars pass or come or go, swiftly, toward the intersections and disappear into the distance.

My guts growl. My belly's calling the shots. I scamper into a 7-Eleven like a frightened rat. The fucking cashier looks at me with his tubular eyes, ready to tubulate me at the least provocation. I pick up a Coke, a can of tuna, some crackers, and some potato chips. I pull a twenty-dollar bill out of the secret place in my belt and pay: $13.30. I've got $66.30 left. I tuck the money back in my belt and leave. I'm in no shape to wait till I get anywhere, so I crack open the Coca-Cola and take long gulps. I open the tuna and crackers and munch my way through the entire can before I get to the first stoplight; I open the chips as I walk toward the bookstore. I finish the Coca-Cola to wet my whistle, then crush the can and stash it in the pocket of the sweatpants the lady lent me.

* * *

[Back in Mexico I used to collect soda cans to sell as scrap metal. Five pesos a kilo, which had to be a ton because the fucking things don't weigh hardly anything. So it had to be a huge sack of them so they'd weigh something and you could get at least thirty pesos and be able to more or less scrape by. That's when I sewed the secret pouch on my belt. Using a piece of leather and a pocketknife, I bored a hole and attached a snap. My assets have always been what I've got on me. I am my house and nothing more. And the belt's the only thing I never take off, not even that time I got sunstroke.

"I'll stick with you guys," I told the paisa when I was feeling a little better. And so I went off to that job, to wear out my hands with fucking cotton. Picking out the seeds on a small farm because the big ones had machines that could do the work of more than ten horses or a hundred men or a thousand dogs. This farm was so small that it needed fewer than ten of us guys for the work. It belonged to a couple of old men from I don't know where, but they had lots of wrinkles on their faces. And they spoke in English, and I couldn't understand a thing they said. They had to talk to me in signs.

"I'm Pepe," said the man with the truck, the one with the canteen, the one who invited me to come along with them. "But don't ever call me Pepito or I'll kick you in the nuts."

And all the paisas burst out laughing around the dinner table. Most of them were strangers who'd met because they came from the same town, Tetela. And because distance turns shared customs into fraternity, they were like family. Yes, just like that, practically eating from the same plate.

"The work isn't too bad because they pay in greenbacks. But one thing's for sure, paisa," Pepe continued, "you have to save every penny so you'll have it when you go back or send it over there, because things are really expensive here, so you end up *spending everything you earn. It only does you any good if you save. Me, for example, I send my paycheck to my wife and kids to pay for the house and food because we've got absolutely nothing back there, not even bits of air, to build something out of. Things are pretty good here, but only if you don't spend it all. And if you ever want to give yourself a lift so you don't feel like life's deflating around you, sometimes we go to the city to fill our bellies with beer in some dive bar—but you have to be careful, because if the fucking gringo migra catches you, they'll dump you out in the street across the border. We toss back a few shotties and get smashed so we can keep on with our daily toil. Except for El Ramonete—he always carries a hip flask with him so he can stay in shape for the heat that pounds down as we strip those cotton plants, which are as scratchy as cats and tear your fingers up till you can't feel soft touches anymore. Isn't that right, Ramonete?"*

An older man looked at me over the plants we were picking and flipped us off, then pulled out his flask and took a quick nip at it, the way you would a bride you don't want to use up in the throes of your initial passion.]

I reach the alleyway behind the bookstore and head toward the service door. Immediately something seems off. Light shines through the crack of the door. The fucking book of poems I used to wedge the door shut has disappeared. Silently, I try to push it open—no luck. It's closed tight. "Fuck. Fuck. Fuck."

I press my ear to the door, but I can't hear anything. I push on it again, but it doesn't budge. "I'm screwed," I think. Something's not right. I slink out of the alleyway like a dark shadow and stealthily approach the corner. There's nobody there. Not even a fucking car parked outside. The bookstore's still girdled in yellow. I look in one of the windows and see that the storeroom light is on in the back. It looks like there's nobody there, but maybe they found the jimmied door and left the light on to disguise the darkness.

"And now what the fuck am I going to do?"

My feet hurt like hell, like my hooves are worn off completely. I don't feel like shimmying up the drainpipe to the bookstore roof again.

The street is empty. No cars go by. The traffic lights are still stuck on yellow. I sneak to the other side of the street. When I get to the chickadee's building, I climb the stone steps and, in a little alcove next to the entrance, let myself collapse like a dog with my back to the wall. I'm starting to feel the cold now, so I huddle into a ball. "As soon as it's light out, I'll take off," I think.

I can see the bookstore across the way. Its broken windows are still boarded up. Everything was going so well—why did it all have to go to shit? I can't wrap my head around it, can't process the gap between good and bad.

"Where the fuck did it all go?"

Before, I was happy just seeing the chickadee walk by, seeing her catch the bus and come back again on the bus. Just seeing her like that, from afar, without being able to touch her, the way you can't touch light no matter how much you chase after it. I was happy, and I was also happy arranging books and, now that I think about it, I also think I was happy a few times when I felt like I actually understood a few of those books after dragging my eyes across all of their words, just like that, in bunches, all jammed together; I was happy tramping up to the loft with them and returning them the next morning intact, as if they'd never been opened.

I was happy at Jefe's parties on Sundays, entwined there among his tequilated beers and his dirty puns.

* * *

[*"All right, you pernicious yokel, have a seat and I'll tell you a jokel. Do you know why a cock's a real gentleman? You don't know, you capering nanny goat? Because it stands up so the ladies can sit down, hoo-hoo-hoo. Cheeeers!"]*

"Where the hell is Jefe?"

I start to close my ocules, like that, like lowering blinds. As soon as it gets light, I'm out of here. I don't know, maybe I should go north, to Chicago or New York, far away, till I've gone all the way around the fucking world to flee from my demons, from all this bad luck that's towing me who knows where. Go to the North Pole, maybe. Though I once read that even if a person goes all the way to hell, he'll always take his fucking problems with him, dragging between his legs, tied to his tail, between his skull and his chest.

* * *

[One afternoon, after we'd been paid at the cotton-picking farm, we toad-hopped toward the city to watch a match between the Mexican and US soccer teams in a bar. El Pepe, El Ramonete, El Jíbaro, Piolín, El Arenuco, and La Toña Peluches—who'd used to be known as Toño, but because his nuts were so hairy you couldn't see his prick, everybody called him La Toña Peluches—we all got into El Pepe's truck and headed off down the highway.

And so we were off, them looking for booze and fucking football, and me looking for soda pop, because alcohol gave me searing goddamn headaches like hammer blows.

We arrived at the Latinoid dive near State Highway 87 and spilled out of the truck.

It was a dismal joint lit by a couple of neon signs that said, "Open, cabrones."

A US and a Mexican flag were draped across the entrance. It was darker inside than it was outside. Wooden tables and chairs and a television for watching the game. The place didn't look dirty, though it stank of beer and sweat. The bartender was an ossified geezer with an arm full of tattoos distorted by wrinkles.

We sat down wherever we could find a spot; the place was awash with paisas. After all, when you're getting wasted, any hole is paradise, especially when there's a US–Mexico match involved.

El Pepe ordered the first round, dark, from the tap, to celebrate and have a laugh at life as the game began.

I was remembering when they'd brought me to the farm for
the first time. The three of them had lifted me down from the
truck and put me in a room all the way in the back of a barracks,
near a lean-to.

They placed compresses of cold water on my back, shoulders,
legs, head, and kept me crucified like that on a bed made of
planks. One vato injected me with an antibiotic whenever I
woke up, supposedly so my wounds wouldn't get infected.

"The sun, see," he'd say as he prepared the fucking needle he
was going to use to spear me in the backside, "same as it gives
life, also takes it away."

And they brought me serums to drink and to spread on my
arm, right there, roosted on a dunghill that seemed to me like the
most magnificent kingdom on Earth.

A couple of weeks later, I was able to stand. The scars on my
back had gotten less dramatic. Now there were just wrinkled
pieces of skin across my back, like trickles of honey running
down from the nape of my neck to my tailbone. An older man
would apply aloe vera, and another guy would squeeze lime juice
into abalone shells, telling me it was to "erase your scars, paisa,
because otherwise you're going to end up all lizardy, with scales
instead of pores. You really broiled yourself good, little squirt."

By the fifth week, it was as if it had all been a dream. I stood
up and managed to walk across the room and back without using
my crutch, which was a broom handle. So I started working with
them, like part of the family. First wrangling cables and then
hauling crates, until two weeks later I helped them harvest the
cotton flowers.

In the bar we had a few rounds. Me belching my Coca-Colas,
and them teasing me for being a pansy and not drinking beer,
and me just taking it and laughing and laughing as I watched
their eyes roll back every time they took a drink.

The match started after we all stood for the two anthems, the Mexican one and the gringo one.

"Viva México, cabrones!" came a shout from the other side of the bar, at another table packed with paisas.

And so the game starts without a fuss and things are pretty uneventful until, in a direct free kick by the Mexican team, the ball hits the crossbar and bounces off toward a gringo defender who can't get clear and, boom, an Aztec vato strikes it hard and, smackdiddly, it hits the net.

"Goooooooooal!" we all shout.

"Goooooooooal!" shouts the fucking announcer.

The whole crew euphoricates.

"Hell yeah. Hell yeah," shouts El Pepe.

El Ramonete keeps drinking.

"Hell yeah. One–nothing," says El Piolín. "Chili pepper's revenge. Sweet!"

"One more round."

And another.

Halftime arrives.

"One more, 'cause we're so damn happy," warbles El Jíbaro.

The second half of the match begins, and order seems to have the upper hand over chaos. A gringo player goes wide on the right, secures the ball, and swings it across the pitch.

"These guys don't make things personal, they don't try to be heroes. They want results," says El Ramonete.

The gringo kicks the ball down the center and it heads toward the box. The keeper leaps into the air, but the gringo's head reaches the ball first and, fuzzbuckets, it strikes the back of the net.

"Goal, motherfuckers!" yells a gringo behind us. "USA!"

"No worries, there's still time," says La Toña Peluches.

Two minutes later, another gringo passes it to number 10, who heads toward the middle. He passes to a holding midfielder, and the midfielder passes it back to number 10, who

kicks it backward with his heel toward a defender who's charg-
ing down the field like a freight train and wallops the ball like
a mule.

The ball arcs toward the goal, whistling like a fucking rocket.

The Mexican goalkeeper jumps and stretches sideways like a
batrachian, but his frog legs aren't strong enough and the ball
lands in the left corner, just like that, like a fucking ball of fire,
like a goddamn meteorite.

"Goddammit," says El Piolín.

"No big deal," says La Toña Peluches. "There's still time."

There are ten minutes left in the game.

"Things have turned on a dime," says the TV announcer.

"Mexico plays like never before and loses like always," says El
Ramonete.

"Come on, boys! We've got this! Two–one is nothing."

Then everything starts falling apart. The green team loses
focus and blurs into cowering blotches.

"Pinches ratones!" yells the paisa at the next table.

There's no offense or defense. The Mexican team tries to pressure the ball, but the gringos steal it halfway down the pitch and
one of them races toward the goal.

"Motherfucker," warbles El Pepe.

The gringo feints, cathematical, out of joint, and catches the
Mexican goalie off guard. The goalie crumples over, and the
gringo is setting up to shoot into the empty net when the goalie's
fist bastes him in the huevos.

"Hell yeah!" says El Ramonete, whose eyes are redder than a
rabbit's. "If you can't win clean, win dirty. After all, even the
strongest motherfucker's got fragile balls."

The gringo collapses and falls battered on the grass. They're
not real good at making a stink, don't have much of a flair for
histrionics, but this guy is rolling around like they've tattooed
his nuts.

The referee whistles and runs up to the Mexican goalie. He

gestures to the goalie to get up. When he does, the ref immedi-
ately gives him a red card. Ejected.

"Putoooooooo!" most of us paisas howl.

"Fucking bastard."

"Oh well," says the announcer. "Penalty."

"Motherfucker," El Pepe says again.

I get up, needing a piss, and head to the bathroom. I go in and
start peeing, drawing esses in the toilet with my piss. I even take
aim at a joint that's floating in the bottom of the bowl like a
nuclear submarine. I've almost managed to break it in two when
I hear a commotion.

"Puta madre!" they shout.

"Fuck! Fucking hell!"

"Goddammit!"

I hear crashes behind me and a massive scuffle spreads like a
wave from the entrance to the fucking exit.

"La migra, motherfuckers!"

"Run like hell, fucking cockroaches!" I hear what sounds like
a fucking stampede, and me there, with my dick in my hand, did-
dling around.]

"Dude," I hear as I lie sleeping. I cover my face with my
arms. I don't want to wake up; I don't want to open my eyes;
my eyelids are glued together with concrete. "Come on, wake
up, I'm going to be late, sabes!"

I deslumber in a flash when I recognize her voice, and open
my eyes.

The chickadee, beautifully awake, is squatting beside me.
She's holding a ceramic mug and a little plate.

"Here. It's not much, but . . ." She falls silent.

I don't know what to do. I feel scared. I've got long crusties
in my eyes like tomperil worms that are hanging down like
vines. I press back against the wall of the building like I'm facing an enemy army. I rub the crusties away with both hands.

"Come on, dude, it's getting late. Take this."

The chickadee looks at me with her enormous eyes, which are brown, honey-colored, greenish, yellow, blue, almost blue, gray, and black. Her nose is perfect. She's got her hair pulled back like always, with a purple ponytail holder. Her tattoo is peeking out from behind her ear. Now she's wearing little gold stud earrings. Her mouth has a slight gleam to it, buffed with the emery of a singular genetics.

I take the plate and the mug, my pulse juddering my body.

"I didn't want to wake you up, dude, but I'm on my way out, sabes, going to work."

I look past the girl, trying to break free of her magnetism. The sky has barely started to turn blue. It must be around six in the morning or earlier.

"What happened to your shoes?" she asks, standing up. I shrug. "Oh, dude, you just go from bad to worse, don't you?" She smiles at me for the first time, with a smile I suspect will remain tattooed on my retinas forever, because a person knows when something huge is happening right at the moment that it occurs. Her smile is the most beautiful cataclysm I've ever seen. "I have to go, but I'll be back later," she says as she starts down the steps garbed in black workout leggings, a gray sweatshirt, and sneakers.

"I love you." Did I say that or think it?

"Qué what?" She stops halfway down.

"Thank you," I say without thinking, lowering my voice till it's practically a papery whisper, a fucking murmur of a thank-you. She doesn't say anything; she turns back around and walks down to the sidewalk, and I hear her move quickly away as the few cars out at this hour start honking at her. At that moment, the cold grips me more firmly all over my body. The morning dew has coated the stone steps—the gray stone; my hair; my skin; my bare, blistered feet. I look at my clothing in the bluish-pink light of dawn. I'm covered with leaves and twigs. I have grass everywhere, bruises on my hands, dirt between my toes. My hair feels ashy, greasy between the follicles sticking up like thorns around my forehead.

"Fucking idiot, what the hell did I say to Aireen? Aireen!"

I sniff at the mug; it's black coffee. Without realizing it, I also start to smile. Aireen, beautiful Aireen! There's a tortilla on the plate covering a piece of meat and some white rice with chickpeas. A pewter fork. Love turns bread crusts into feasts. I take a sip of the coffee and feel restored; my belly grows warm. I put the mug down and start in on the meat and rice. I hadn't realized how much hunger could fit in my body.

I'm starving.

I finish the meat and rice wrapped in the tortilla in three gulps. I drink the coffee more slowly, nursing it as if it were the last bit of liquid on earth.

The streets are still deserted. There are very few people going by, their bodies bent forward to speed their steps. The scruffs have disappeared; now there are only yups heading to work. The addos have vanished off to school.

I salicate the coffee very slowly. I look over at the bookstore and notice that the light in the storeroom is no longer on.

"That's weird! It's fucking weird!"

I finish the coffee when the sun's already starting to cudgel the tops of the highest buildings. I place the mug on the plate with the fork. I don't know if it's my last supper, but it's definitely the best one I've ever had. I stretch out on the stone to watch the people start to emerge from their dens to earn a living.

Little by little the street fills up with footfalls. The avenues start to circulate. My eyes are still heavy. I haven't slept well the past few nights. To open them up and keep them from closing on me, I examine my feet. I've got huge blisters that have burst. A few tatters of filthy shredded skin are visible over my calluses. I yank them off.

Ouch. It burns.

And to think I swore I'd stay out of trouble on this side of the world.

* * *

["Run for it, dumbass, don't let them catch you!" El Pepe yells at me as I watch the Border Patrol agents corral him and drag him out of the bathroom.

I'm in front of the toilet, my dick still in my hand, and all there is is a little window like an air vent. Without finishing my piss, I tuck it away, soaking my hands and pants. I climb up on the toilet tank and smash the glass in with one hand.

Crash!

It's a good thing I'm skinny. I prop my foot up on the divider between the stalls and unfurl myself so I can squeeze through the window opening. I feel shark teeth of broken glass poking out of the frame and ripping my clothes.

I'm nearly halfway out the window. Almost free. Just a little bit more and I'm set. And then I feel someone hauling on my feet from inside, but I can't see anything, so I kick my feet wildly. I'm like a rat with its tail caught in a trap. In desperation, despite the pain in my shins, I strike out against everything, but my anaphylactic strength is no match for the people pulling on me.

They uncork me from the window with a sharp tug and I crash onto the toilet bowl, which shatters. All the shit inside it spatters across the floor. The Border Patrol agents are ranchers armed to the teeth with rifles and nunchucks, chains and tonfas. They're carrying walkie-shouties and are dressed like soldiers. They've got semiautomatics in their belts. Some of them are using night-vision goggles to hunt down illegals like rabbits and robots in the tunnels. Most of them are wearing wide-brimmed cowboy hats with braided leather cords. The real motherfuckers are wearing Kevlar helmets and gas masks and bulletproof vests; they're dressed as if they were going to space war against the Martians.

"Fuck you, you son-of-a-bitch, illegal beaner."

And they subtract me right there. They pistol-whip the air out of me. I double over and fall in the scattered shit. Piss soaks into my clothes. Shit stains my face. They drag me by the feet outside of the bar. My paisas are already there, roughed up, their hands bound with cable ties.

El Pepe's got a bloody cut above his eyebrow. El Piolín and El Jíbaro are leaking mole sauce from their snouts. La Toña Peluches's plaid shirt is torn, and lumps are already swelling on his cheek and temple. There are also a few other paisas, the ones from the table in the back. And the table in the middle. All of them badly beaten, staring at the floor. There must be a good twenty of us. They dump me next to El Pepe and try to bind my wrists, but since my hands are smeared with shit, they don't secure them tightly.

They think I'm disgusting.

The agent just puts the ties on my wrists and tugs, trying not to touch me to avoid getting crappified. He's got to keep his professional gloves spotless.

A vato at the other end gets up and takes off running down 87, trying to disappear into the thick scrub. He's got his hands tied behind his back; he looks like a dancing earthworm. Two agents chase after him, and a few minutes later shots ring out. El Pepe just closes his eyes and hangs his head even lower. Blood is now running out of his nose and dripping onto the ground, making tiny volcanoes in the loose earth. We have no words.

An agent goes up to the old man who was bartending and hands him a wad of bills. I don't understand English for shit, but I assume the money is compensation for the damage they've caused to his rathole.

Three civilian trucks arrive, and they herd us into them like cattle. They shove us into the back and toss us down like a flock of fish.

When I started working on the farm, El Pepe told me, "We're the

ones who clean up their shit, and they still treat us like crap. Not all of them, just some of them. Those fucking gringo bastards want us to lose the last of our dignity, but someday . . . someday . . ."
And he sat staring at the cotton plants. And I sat staring at him in bewilderment, and when he noticed he yelled at me, "Listen, chiquito, don't sit there gaping at me like a moron—go pick that shit. If we fall behind, we don't get paid this week."

And we worked there for hours, doubled over at the waist, wearing cotton-picking gloves and hats to shade our necks under the sultry sun.]

Here in the city, on the other hand, the sun is less catastrophic. Here it seems like the sunlight's been filtered by the windows of the skyscrapers. I scoot back closer to the chickadee's building and notice that there are lots of people on the street now. The blood on my feet has dried. I pick up the chickadee's dishes and clutch them as if they were part of her; I don't know, I think there are a few things in the universe that tell us about people. I close my eyes again to run away once more.

"What would I have wanted to be if I could have fucking been something else?"

Things work better inside my head than they do out there.

Here inside it's easier to live.

Out there it's a disaster zone.

* * *

["Fucking stupid brat," the aunt who was not my aunt but rather my godmother used to say, "you're always getting into trouble. Why don't you start sweeping and dusting so you can earn all that food you eat instead of sitting there watching the flies buzz past."

"If the shitters aren't spick-and-span, there won't be any dinner for you. You spend the whole day woolgathering."

"If your mother were alive, devil spawn, she'd up and die for a second time at seeing what a retard you are. You don't even know how to talk right."

"Yes, doctor, seems like he's retarded, though he does grunt occasionally."

"I don't know, doctor, mightn't he just be hardheaded like his mother, may she rest in peace? Because given the way she was, God rest her soul, she's got to be in the pits of hell now."

"Look, doctor, no matter how much I tell this pigheaded kid to do something, he gets more stubborn every day. Isn't there some shot you can give him to make him obey?"

"You can't get anything into that thick skull of his, not even with a whipping. The other day I beat him with the lamp cord, and he didn't even move. He's like a mule. Won't budge forward or back."

"Yes, doctor, the other day he stole the little locket that used to belong to his mother. But she left it to me because that was the right thing to do—it's no small task, after all, taking care of a little brat, and it's not cheap either. It was the right thing to give it to me, don't you think?"

"I don't know what he did with that locket, officer. I gave him a whupping but he didn't say boo."

"Nothing, he's worse than a mule. Yes, I'd rather you take him off to jail than have him here with me, because one day he's going to kill me in a fit of rage. He pounds the walls with his fists when he gets upset—what if he hits me one day?"

"No, no, I can't take it anymore, and after everything I've done for him."]

"Are you asleep again, dude?"

I open my eyes and there's Aireen. I'm still clutching the dishes; they're infused with my heat.

"Let's see if these fit you."

She puts some tennis shoes down in front of me. I'm afraid

to pick them up. She's done a lot for me already and I don't want to wear her out, I mustn't wear her out—it's so easy to wear people out.

"Come on, dude, take them—my boss gave them to me for you!"

"Qué?"

"Candy's owner. I told him a friend of mine had been assaulted and asked if he had any clothes he didn't need, and he gave me these. He's really good to me."

I pick up the tennis shoes, look at them. They're cool. The soles are wearing out, but they look like the kind they show on the big Nike billboards. I'm about to put them on when the chickadee yells and snatches them out of my hand.

"You can't put them on those filthy feet of yours! Come on."

She takes my arm and helps me up. The dishes almost slip out of my hands, but my reflexes are quick enough that I catch them in the air.

The floor hurts me.

I feel blisters ready to pop under the weight of my own fire.

She opens the door to her building and leads me by the arm.

I look like a combatant who's been wounded in some solitary war and is oozing shrapnel. And yes, everything on this side of the world seems to be against me, battling to exterminate me, using even insecticide and mosquito coils as its weapons.

"You opened the door for me one day," the chickadee suddenly says as she pushes it closed. "Do you remember?"

My knees are chattering. She's firmly buttressing me upright. I feel like a marionette and her fingers are the strings that keep me standing.

We reach a sliding door near the staircase, and she opens it. It's the building's maintenance room. We go in and she leads me to a sink behind two dilapidated washing machines. She picks up a bucket and starts to fill it with water.

"Lo siento, dude," she says. "Gas is really expensive and

the super doesn't turn on the main water heater till after ten, so the water's cold right now."

She pulls up a bench and sits me down. She picks up a bowl of powdered detergent and sets it on the floor; then she takes the dishes from me and places them in the sink.

She lowers the bucket of water and puts it in front of me.

"Vamos," she instructs me.

I roll up my pants to my knees and put my right foot in. Though the water is cold, it feels warm to me. The dried blood starts to dissolve along with the dirt and leaves. I stick in my other foot, and the searing sensation in my wounds starts to fade.

The chickadee takes a little of the powdered detergent and pours it into the bucket. She rolls up the sleeves of her sweat-shirt, squats down, and starts stirring up the water to form bubbles.

I look down at her hair, which smells of sunsets.

The tattoo behind her ear is beautiful, calligraphed in precise lines and curves.

One of her fingers brushes my ankle. I feel a shiver vibrating through me from my guts to my heart. I stammer frantically. I hate for her to see me like this, I don't know, beaten all to hell inside and out, and without meaning to, without being able to stop it, a fat fucking tear slips out of me, like that, and rolls down my cheek.

I don't want her to see me like this. But she looks up just then and sees me. I feel the way her eyes drill into me, down to my soul. I try to smile to avoid what I'm feeling just now, but I can't, and more fucking tears slide silently down my cheeks to my mouth. They're salty; they're hermit tears that have never left home before.

My heart is in tatters.

She doesn't say anything; she just looks into my eyes, and I, adrift in that bucket of water, feel like a castaway.

The chickadee reaches down to the bottom of the bucket, lifts my foot, and starts to wash it, still looking at me.

Her hands begin to heal all my wounds one by one as her gorgeous eyes open new ones.

My heart, I already know, hasn't belonged to me for a long time, since the first moment I saw her.

Aireen runs her fingers over my blisters, over my lancinated toes. I'm seized by childlike emotion and start to wheeze.

My nose is stuffed up. I gulp down oceans of saliva. My eyes keep squeezing out salty thumbtacks that leak into the corner of my mouth.

In all the fucking novels I read up in the loft or in Wells Park, love started another way—rationally, like a jigsaw puzzle assembled by the writer to create a fictitious yet lifelike construction in which, as soon as their feelings come to a boil, the lovers kiss. But literature isn't at all like fucking life—like here, in this boiling moment, as Aireen makes my pains disappear, my chest splits in half to take her words into my core when she says: "I think the two of us are going to be good friends, sabes."

And I don't care if we're just friends. For me, who was so far from her, on the other side of the world, on the other side of the street, in the antipodes of any encounter with the most beautiful woman on earth, invisible even to the air, having her as a friend is more than enough.

I don't need anything else.

Just looking at her, I feel as if the world is working more smoothly.

I smile at her, with a pure, natural smile, full of all my gratitude and all her kindness, because she makes me into something less huddled than I am.

"What's your name, dude?" she asks as she starts washing my other foot; her hands are fire. I look at her white, white teeth, straight like the idealization of the most perfect, exuberant ivory.

I smile even harder; the tears keep tumbling from my lashes.

As long as I can remember, they've always called me whatever they felt like calling me. Hardly anybody ever asked my name—they didn't need to know it. To the world, I'm the idiot kid, the goddamn putz, vato, pipsqueak, bastard, scruff, dude, barefoot Indian, negri warrior, boy, fucking punk, young man, illegal beaner—all names bestowed according to the circumstance. Here I want to tell her my name is Liborio, Liborio, Liborio, but suddenly I feel ashamed.

"I don't remember," I tell her, hanging my head and shrugging my shoulders, waterlogged with fucking tears.

"I'm Aireen, your new friend." And she smiles.

And me downcast, adrift, just like that, humble, immersed in beauty again. And she must understand what I'm feeling, because she smiles even more as she stands up.

"Oh, dude, one day you'll have a name that will fill your soul with pride."

She lopes out of the room, drying her hands on the hem of her sweatshirt.

I watch her leave.

My eyes are still wet, as if the earthen jugs inside me had cracked.

* * *

[In the truck, El Pepe told me about the Border Patrol as we turned off Highway 87 and headed down a dirt road toward the desert:

"We're not going back anywhere now, paisa. We'll be staying here. These fucking bastards aren't taking us to prison. They're going to murder us in the goddamn desert."

He gave a loud snort, full of bloody spittle, and expectorated, making a cavernitious noise.

"But we're already dead men, right? So the hell with it. They're not going to take me out without a fight."

His nose still clogged with blood, El Pepe prodded me with his foot, signaling to me to spring at the nearest agent like a rabid dog. At his urging, I leaped out of the truck.

Zoooom! Plop!

When I fell, the cable ties slipped off my wrists.

The air evacuated my body.

I couldn't see what happened next because of the dust, but I imagine Pepe must have been put down with a blow to the skull. The trucks kept going another thirty or forty yards, jolting along the dirt track.

Just then the last truck came to a stop, and again I told myself, all covered with dirt and shit, "Run, motherfucker."]

Aireen comes back with a towel.

I've already taken my feet out of the bucket and am dripping. The blisters have turned into white, wrinkly flaps of skin. She hands me the towel and I start drying my feet.

She unrolls some blue athletic socks with pink stripes and holds them out to me.

"I'm sorry," she says. "They're the only ones I had."

I don't say anything; I put on the socks and slip on the tennis shoes she holds out and suddenly, just like that, I feel as if I were not walking on land but instead floating in congested space. Skimming just above the earth.

I figure this is the weightlessness of paradise.

"They look good on you—a little big, but they'll do for now," the chickadee says, smiling. Then she turns away and starts gathering everything up—the bucket, the soap, the towel, the dishes—and says to me, "Let me see if I can find you a place to stay tonight. You don't have a place to stay, right?"

"I do have a place," I say without thinking, as if leaping to rescue the two of us—especially me—determined not to destroy everything I've achieved with her, because she's already done too much for me and everything has a limit.

I stare at the floor, and my eyes turn to horchata.

Aireen turns around and softly approaches me. With her right hand she lifts my chin and says, "Come on, dude, it's hard to find a friend these days. You can't throw it away before you even start. Sí? We're friends, amigos, no? So do you have a place to stay or not?"

And she looks into my eyes, straight into my eyes like a meteor, like that, a supernova that scorches my guts as it touches the most naked fibers of my soul.

My stomach twinges.

Suddenly I feel a shiver that runs from the base of my spine to my navel and back several times. I don't know how to describe it—it's something that has no words, and there's no dictionary to find them in. I feel caught between a rock and her beautiful eyes.

Her fingertips on my chin are a trident of fire.

I once read in Jefe's bookstore that love is incredibly difficult to find, so when you find it you should never let it go because it might never appear to you again.

"I do have somewhere to go," I say, so quietly that I have to repeat it to myself several times so the chickadee and I both realize what a load of crap I'm telling her. "I do have somewhere to go," I repeat.

* * *

[There are some branches nearby. I can barely see them. It's a moonless night and there are tricksy stars perspiring diamantine on high. On the horizon I can see the rocky mountains outlined in a tenuous aquamarine light. Without the cable ties around my wrists, I can wriggle among the rocks in the desert and the scrub. The trucks are driving in circles like spinning tops.

The agents are pissed. I see them get down and start pointing their rifles everywhere. They fire two or three rounds in different directions. Then one of them aims at something that's moving off in the other direction.

He shoots at it.

He walks toward what I think is a dead animal.

"Come over here!" the hunter shouts.

The others go up to him and examine what he's perforated. I don't know what it is, and while they pick up their rifles again to fire bullets into the thing that's lying there on the ground and barely moving, I scrabble through some brush until I find the hole of some fucking animal. It's not very big, so I cram myself in, twisting my bones in all different directions. With my right hand, I start throwing dirt on top of myself to cover the hole with me inside it. I take a breath and expel it like the cherry on top of my improvised tomb, that earthen womb from which I hope the goddamn migrant-hunting gringos won't manage to abort me.

Everything is darkness.

I don't know if it's a cramp, but suddenly I feel a tickling in my ankle, something that moves up my shin and starts to slither up my leg. Then it stops. Outside, the guards' footsteps are pacing back and forth like they're trying to trample every rock in the desert. Cold cramps crawl up and down my body. There are a number of them now. I feel a bit of fuzz rolling around in my ear. I have the urge to burst out of my hiding place and take off running. But I'd be leaving one hole only to enter another.]

Why the fuck did I do it? Why the hell did I tell her I've got a place to go? I don't know, maybe because I think I don't deserve her, that I don't deserve her or her friendship; that the laudatory epiphany of happiness is for the gods alone, and we fucking mortals are left to grind ourselves to bits with our own teeth—unremarkably to perish, bewallowed in the guts of everyday suffering, addled, delirious, without a goddamn shred of hope. But perhaps I also say it because, at bottom, I'm just a pendejo. And a pendejo doesn't think beyond his own head.

"All right, there you go, dude."

Hope is always there, in the distance, and though very few ever achieve what they desire, having it so close makes me want to inhale more deeply so I can expel the air in the form of sighs.

Aireen's friendly exclamation interrupts my thoughts. "God, now I really do have to get going. Sometimes I think the world isn't as bad as it seems, don't you think, dude?"

I watch her leave through the maintenance room door, carrying the dishes with her.

Without thinking, all bestumbled-like, I leap toward the door in my supersneakers and, confounded as a fly searching for freedom at a windowpane, race after her like a lapdog.

Emerging from the staircase on the top floor of Aireen's building, you can see part of the city and, beyond it, the hill where the bald lady Double-U lives. Down below is the street, the trees, and the bus stop. There's the bookstore's roof and the other buildings. Looking off toward the horizon, you can see the dome of the shopping mall and, in the other direction, the baseball stadium. A little closer, I see the trees in Wells Park. There are tall buildings that block the view west; they have reflective glass that mirrors the sky and the clouds as they pass, like they're wearing fucking polarized sunglasses. On the roof of the building where Aireen lives are several little rooms jam-packed with junk. To one side are the water tanks, in Indian file, and a jumble of galvanized pipes. Across from those are a stack of boards and some old, broken washing machines that look like they were built in the Stone Age; they're stained with rust and their copper pipes are green and black. Toward the back is another room secured with a heavy padlock. On its gray door is a sign that says HIGH VOLTAGE. Some plants with fat, very sharp thorns are growing out of a few cracks next to the wall around the perimeter of the rooftop. Fucking bastards.

* * *

["*Fucking bastards*," *my aunt over there on the other side used to call them.* "*Though some people call them 'pricklyburr.' They give you a rash if you touch them, see? What does that feel like? Itches like hell, right? Oh, stop whining—pain is for old ladies. It's for pussy girls, not strong men, you hear me, you runty moron?*"]

Off to the left there are some little windowboxes full of plastic plants that have been blistered by the sun. Mr. Hundred is up ahead. He's a man of about sixty with salt-and-pepper hair, scrotastically wrinkled; he has gray eyes and is wearing a beige vest that matches his canvas shoes; he walks with his legs bowed out at his knees. Behind him is the chickadee, and I'm trailing them.

"And don't even think about going into that room with the electric transformer—it'll fry you like a fish, got it?"

Aireen turns to look at me. She smiles.

I still feel like I'm in the clouds, literally, as if I were walking on cotton balls.

Aireen has skipped work because of me. Instead of going to work, she went straight to the building super:

"Mr. Hundred, my cousin just arrived and is looking for a place to stay."

"And why can't he stay with you and your grandfather?"

"He wants to be independent, right, cousin?" She looks at me. I nod, a hangdog look on my face. "And maybe you could give him some kind of job. He's a good worker."

"Your face looks familiar, boy. You aren't one of those young reprobates who swarm around out there in the street, are you?"

"Not at all, Mr. Hundred. You can give him a place to stay in one of the rooms on the roof, and in exchange he can clean the halls or whatever you need."

"I don't know, Miss Aireen. You and your grandfather are good people, but I don't know. This kid looks like a trouble-maker."

"Come on, you won't regret it. Say yes before he finds somewhere else and you lose this great opportunity."

"So what do you know how to do, boy?"

Aireen and Mr. Hundred both look at me. I don't know if my cheeks flush. I feel disoriented under their steady gaze. I attempt to clear my throat.

"I know how to read, sir."

Mr. Hundred lets out a guffaw.

"Well, that's a lucky thing. A real bonus. But do you know how to scrub floors? Pick up trash?" He looks at Aireen.

"Yes," the chickadee answers without taking her beautiful eyes off me. "He's also honorable . . . and very brave."

Mr. Hundred scratches his head.

"I don't know, miss . . . Hmm. But I can't pay you. I'll just let you stay in the room in exchange for work maintaining the building, understood? If you want money, go out and get a job."

* * *

[I don't know how much time has passed. I seem to be turn-ing into a reptile. I feel scales on my arms and legs and the back of my neck. I don't move so I don't disturb anybody. I no longer hear the border patrolmen's footsteps anywhere. Only the wind shoving across the ground, bouncing, as if its teeth were missing.

A while back I heard the trucks' engines start up and roar until they intertwined with the silent horizon.

I'm so tired. I don't know if the others are still alive or not. I haven't heard another gunshot, no sudden boom like rifles make. No pow!, ratatatatat!, bang!

Poor Pepe. His wife and kids won't have a grave to mourn him at. Their souls will never be at rest. Always hoping they might see him or at least his dollars every two weeks. There will be no tombstone pressing down on his bones.

"Look here, paisa," he told me one day, "these are my little ones and this is my wife. We're from Tetela, a village in Puebla. A beautiful spot beside a reservoir. Well, the water in the reservoir stinks from all the water lilies, and the water's as green as fuck, but I'd give anything to be there, wrapped up in their love, gossiping with the family. But there's no way—you've got to take care of the belly first, and then the heart. If you ever visit there, ask for El Pepe. Everybody knows me around there—you'll be welcomed into the family, and we'll toss back a couple of nice-cold cervezas, even though you don't drink, paisa, not even in self-defense."

And he tucked the rumpled, finger-smudged photo of his family back in his wallet.]

"And here's the room," Mr. Hundred continues, slowly opening the moth-eaten, louse-bitten wooden door. "As you can see, it's a mess at the moment, but you can get it cleaned up. Look, there's a bed over there. It doesn't have a mattress, but you can put those cushions on it while you save up for something better. You can gather up those metal rods and put them over there. There isn't any glass in the window, but you can use some plastic film and pieces of cardboard to seal it off. Early in the morning you'll need to sweep all the staircases and then dust the railings. I'll show you as you go along." He pauses. Scratches his head. "In the meantime, your cousin can help you clean up this mess. You can get it done quicker that way." Mr. Hundred glances around the hecatomb once more and then tosses me the keys to the padlock of the junk-filled room. "You'd better not be a troublemaker, boy." He turns around and heads out of the room toward the entrance to the building, opens the door, and disappears down the stairs.

"I think he liked you, 'cousin,'" Aireen says cheerily as she exhales, her lips spiraling the air in concentric circles that burst on my eardrums like alarconia petals on the pavement—those little flowers that look like dandelions and when they get touched by water or sunlight, they become transparent, weightless. "Can you handle this mess, 'cousin'?" And she laughs again, like that, seismically.

* * *

[If hell is underground, it must be infernally cold, an absinthic freezer. My arms and legs have gone numb. The effort of coiling myself up in my own rattle has dislocated me in my hole; the blood reaches my skin only in lackluster low-tide waves. Again I feel the fuzz strolling from my ear to my throat. It tickles me. My arms are pinioned so tight, I can't get one free to scratch myself. At that moment I hear a dull echo, muffled by the pile of earth, rocks, and sand that I've pulled over myself as if my own grave could be my salvation.

Bang!

I think of El Pepe and his family—but I think more about him and his crossing to the other side. Is it hard?

It's easy to die, I think, but is it hard to leap into that abyss?

Bang.

Carajo. Another gunshot.

The echo of the bullets bounces off the stones above me and dies out there, trembling, in the middle of the desert. From that

moment on, I think, the dead will have already forgotten every-
thing, even the fact that they're dead.]

Aireen leaves just like that, laughing, tied to her own waist.
I start to gather up all the pipes and place them in a corner,
strapping them together with a length of cord I removed from
some planks. I find a box of old magazines from the same pub-
lisher Jefe uses to fry the rich ladies' brain cells: *Reader's*
Digest. I place them on top of a stack of boards. There's a lot
of dust.

I have never been clean.

I once read in that book Double-U bought that poverty is
never clean—we poor people, it said, in addition to being
poor, are miserable and filthy. Only art can make filth beautiful, and the best asshole artists are those who make a fucking
work of art out of tragedy, poverty, neglect, like those pinches
photographers who swan into misfortune so they can take a
good photograph that'll win them a goddamn Pulitzer Prize;
but here, in everyday life, here, in this fucking country, poor
people are hunched, envious, vandalous, and only very occasionally solidary. We eat one another alive while wallowing in
our own shit, the gringo intellectual says. And there's no hope
of redemption. But today I don't know, seems like I'm trying
to beat the fuck out of this fucking dust. I lift the bed and drag
it toward one of the unpaned windows. I shove all the junk and
a few pipes under it. I lay the sheets of cardboard on top of it,
and in no time the room looks livable. I go outside and steal an
empty can and some plastic flowers. Then I lie down on the cot
to test it. The boards are hard and jab me in the ribs. I put one
hand under my head and stare up at the bare bulb in the ceiling. I don't know, damn it; yeah, I think, the world isn't as bad
as it seems after all, or what the hell ever.

I close my eyes and think about Aireen.

* * *

[*There in the shadows I feel the snake sliding across my cheeks. Its smooth scales sculpt the outline of my jaw and it slips through a gap to the world outside my hole. Another snake slithers up my calf and follows its companion. I have another one clinging to my back. It wriggles to my left and passes over the nape of my neck. Its tail slides along my ear and it dissolves into the gaps. Another one has encircled my stomach. It seems the odor of shit I'm steeped in has soothed them so they don't bite me, don't pierce my soul, my quivering body, with their fangs. Very slowly I free my right hand and start to move the soil away. My whole body's gone numb. As if the earth were about to give birth, I push hard, panting, and manage to extract my left arm. I exert force, yes, like that, and uncork myself outward, tensing my muscles. Yes, I'm a fucking fetus being born from the guts of hell. Brought back from the grave. The piles of earth and rock are darker now. The snakes emerge after me, in a group, rolled up into little balls, formed into rings. The night emaciates the stars, which pale above me, like a colander full of blackberries draining through white pinpricks. Dawn must be approaching: a blue or green wave is moving across the sidereal space, blurring it. The ants in my numb legs slowly disappear. I wiggle my fingers and toes. Slowly, heat comes back into my body. I exhale as if it were my life's last breath, and a second later I inhale, like that, cascalitic, filling my lungs with fucking life.*]

I descend the stairs of the red building. I dozed off on the plank cot and still have stripes perforating my back. My fucking eyes are drowsy, swollen, my hair standing on end. Outside the building, all the same things are swarming about; it's as if time has been petrified, and even in movement we have indecorously become mere decorations. Across the street, the bookstore looks exactly the same, dimmed, battered, mammillated at the edge of the sidewalk. I'd like to go in and swipe a few books so I can pass the time. I never thought I'd miss them one day. Jefe is a jerk but not a moron, greedy yet at the same time cavalierly clever. Where could he be now?

* * *

["Listen up, you erudite weasel. I see you're getting into the swing of things and have at least figured out where the fucking books are shelved. If you sell some more books, I might even give you a raise, hoo-hoo-hoo."
Asshole.]

I stand looking at the same streets for a while. I figured I'd come down from the roof to wait for Aireen at the bus stop, but then it occurred to me she might be annoyed with me since she's so strong on the inside, she doesn't need heroes defending her on the outside. I've also come down to the street because my stomach is squealing with hunger and I can't keep holding out on it. I eye the knot of scruffs splattered across the scene, whooping at the girls going by with their little shorts, their gorgeous gams; catcalling them, their fantasies tangled with hair and drool.

She won't be back for a few hours still. That's what she told me:

"I won't be long. I'll be back tonight, 'cousin.'"

That means I can leave for a while to try to scrounge up a little money, like Mr. Hundred said, and not be a loser and an outcast. I head left, looking for an opportunity that will let me carry my own weight. I know there are some gringos on the outskirts of the city who hire Latinos for under-the-table day labor.

* * *

[That's what I heard from a guy who was crazy in love and

came into the bookstore looking for a book of adventures and sex a while back:

"I want to give it to a babe who makes me wild—you know, man, something to help me bag her without having to spend so much money on flowers and get her real hot."

"Why don't you just take her to the movies, sir?"

"No, dude, I want to seduce her without even touching her. Plus, going to the movies is expensive, and since I'm married, it's better if I can do things without all the flowers and chocolates, you know, to cut down on the extravagances."

"You shouldn't be stingy, sir."

"I'm not stingy, just cautious. If she ends up rejecting me, I'll only have spent a few dollars and that's it."

"What if she says yes?"

"Then I'll have spent the same amount but I'll get to screw too, right? Ha-ha-ha."

Before leaving with his sex book full of illustrated asses and cocks in a paperback Kamasutra that cost $7.50, he winked at me.

"I like you, man. I'm a foreman, and sometimes I need cheap manpower. If you ever need work, come find me on Median Road. The pay's not great and it's hard work. But maybe one day you won't have the strength for this kind of intellectual labor and you'll be looking for a cement tombstone instead so you can go die out there the way fucking donkeys like me do. Ha-ha-ha!"]

I get to 92nd and head toward the highway that's known for the median strip where all the Latino laborers congregate. A red-light district where everybody looks the other way and migrants sell themselves to the highest bidder. There's hardly anybody now because it's late. It must be after noon—my impetuous shadow is right under my feet. The only person around is an old man with a gray beard who's sitting on a wooden crate next to a long gas can. Farther along, two guys are unloading some cardboard from a three-ton truck. They look at me out of the corners of their eyes as they keep working, panting like runaway buffalo.

"You're too late, kid. Everybody's gone," the old man says, still staring at the highway. The cars race by and move off into the distance. The sun is ergastulated under the rocks, kicking up burning dust, shards of insolar high tide. "The early bird catches the worm, that's for sure!" he continues absently, moving only his lips. He's got tanned skin and large ears with curly white hair sticking out of them. He's wearing a cowboy hat and huaraches made from old tires.

"Did you get here late too?"

The old man doesn't respond. Seems like he didn't hear me. The guys are still unloading the truck and piling the cardboard on wooden pallets that a forklift operator moves into a squalid warehouse.

"The only thing we old people are good for is storing worms. And we never get anywhere either early or late. Actually, we don't even get anywhere in the first place—not even death wants to carry me off. Yet here I still am, waiting but not anticipating anything," the old man grumbles, as if he's been suddenly been brought back from his daydreaming. He has just two or three teeth hanging from his gums like stalactites.

"Will anyone else be coming by?"

"Maybe, maybe not. Sometimes they've got night work and come looking for cheap labor to spread asphalt on the bridges or highways, but as far as I know, there hasn't been any work lately. Hardly anybody's working at night anymore because it's double the pay and the recession has hit people hard. Back in my salad days, when I was stronger than those two bozos put together"—he raises his eyebrows toward the two kids who are still unloading—"I thought I could drink the entire ocean in one gulp! But everything eventually wears out from use. The same way life slips out of our hands, in the end everything becomes useless."

The old man is quiet, his wrinkled eyes still gazing off at the horizon.

"Hey, are you drunk?"

The old man looks at me for the first time. His eyes are so wrinkled that his eyebrows tumble slantwise like white vines down to his cheeks. He grimaces and looks back at the highway.

"Everybody's already gone." And he sits there like a rock under the embers of the sky.

After hours of waiting here in the heat, it seems nobody's coming to hire. The old man stays tamped down there atop his crate, staring into the distance. I go reptilicate under a shabby Exxon billboard that's dribbling a bit of shade. I'm hungry, thirsty and hungry. The guys finished unloading the truck a while ago and have already sifted away through the cracks. The sun's so strong that it dissolves even my thoughts into a prolonged buzz.

"Hey," I say, my tongue like a necktie, "what time is it?"

At six in the evening I decide to go back to my provictional lair, my rooftop room. I haven't managed to get any work or achieved anything else except roasting my sudoriparous glands a bit more. It's true—just like the old man said, not even byzantine serpents would be coming by.

"If you want work, get here by six A.M. at the latest. And bring a couple of bucks to pay the fee."

"What fee?"

"What do you mean, what fee? The fee to be able to do business around here, chico! Don't you know anything?"

"And who do I pay it to?"

"Who do you think? The guy who charges it."

"And who's that?"

"Me, you botulistic buffoon."

"And what if I don't pay?"

"Then you don't work, period."

Aireen knocks on my door. I've been flipping through some of the old magazines in the room. I found a *Life* from 1964. It included a series of photos of Kennedy as he was being assassinated in Dallas. Yeah, that guy whose head they blew off. Unbelievable as it seems, without recognizing him by sight, I'd already heard of him in a fucking novel I'd read about his life and death, but it's never the same to see mummified words as it is to see the photo where they blast the guy in the bean. The photos were blurry and out of focus, but you could see his brains flying through the air and splattered on the trunk of his car.

"Door's open," I shout, but Aireen knocks again and I leap toward the doorknob like a spring-loaded gonad.

* * *

[But most of the books I'd read in the bookstore had only sprayed muddy garbage in my eye, full of buzzing wordflies like dull needles.

"Listen, Jefe, a while ago that fucking nutjob writer guy came by, the one with the spaceship with no brakes. He asked if we had anything by Pi 3.1415 Téllez. Something about a novel about tablets and social networks called Feisbuk Connection. Wondered if we could order a copy."

"So he isn't into narcofiction anymore?"

"He didn't ask for any Mexican authors this time."

"That prick changes his tastes as often as he changes his underwear. Pretty soon he'll even be a Coelho fan. Hoo-hoo-hoo."

"And that's bad, Jefe?"

"Goddamn right, you goddamn fuckwit! That's why it wouldn't surprise me if he liked that fucker, with all the crap he sucks in with those eyes of his."

"But Coelho's our number-one seller, Jefe."

"So what? A fucking toilet is a necessity in life since we all take a shit once a day, but we don't put it up on a pedestal in the middle of the room or give it prizes, do we?"

"I don't know what you mean, Jefe. You shit more than once a day."

"Jesus Christ, save me from this goddamn brain-dead chicken mite! Of course you don't get it, you cretinaceous dumbfuck. I'm giving you a fucking metaphor for capitalism."

"Asshole."

"What did you say, you fucking pothead?"

"Capitalism's a real bitch, huh, boss? Like you said the other day: fucking neoliberalism, right?"

"Don't get smart on me, you faggoty-ass motherfucker."

"Never, Jefe. Wouldn't dream of it!"]

"You've totally transformed this room!" Aireen says as she walks in. She's wearing a piece of fabric tied around her head and carrying a tray in her hands. The light from the bare bulb washes over her. I was going to wait for her at the bus stop when I got back from procuring no money at all and a light dose of heatstroke, but I decided not to, even though I'd been biting my nails this whole time. Instead I started reading those old magazines I found. By now it must be ten or eleven at night. Aireen sets down the tray with a glass of milk and a little casserole on one of the crates I set up as a coffee table. On it I placed the can with some plastic flowers I'd pulled from the planters outside. My hovel looks like a tidy little burrow. The bed's covered with the newspapers and magazines, and there's not a speck of dust anywhere. I've hidden the remaining crates out of sight under the bed.

"You like it?" I ask in reply, staring down at my druidic heartbeats.

Aireen's gaze flits around the room and stops on the flowers. She looks at them. For a moment I think she might say something like what I once read in a short story by some rusty old lech of a writer: "The advantage of plastic flowers," Popeye told his Popeyetta as he held her smitten hand, "is that they never die, just as what I feel for you today, oh, by-me-loved, will never die siempre." But Aireen doesn't say that. She just looks at the plastic flowers and smiles. She moves to the right around the crates and sits down on the planks of the bed. I don't know where to move to, so I don't; I just clasp my hands so they'll stop shaking.

"It's very peaceful here," Aireen says suddenly. She places her hands on the bed and arches her neck backward while closing her eyes. Neither of us speaks. There's not a sound—the silence has turned into foam that flows through the air.

Only sometimes, a very occasional sometimes, like an emetic rarity, does the noise of a passing car manage to scale the walls to reach us. Aireen starts turning her head like her neck hurts, like she's dancing to the beat of an invisible music. Just then Aireen opens her eyes and I am brought suddenly back from her lips, her exogenous smile, her perfect and neatly shaped eyebrows. She stops smiling, and I jostle the air around me with an estranged tremble, a shiver that runs up my spine from my tailbone to my noggin. I shrug and stiffen, a flush staining my face as if her eyes were piercing my cheeks.

"How old are you, dude?"

I'm still struck dumb, like a voyeur who's been caught peeping through a hole in a wall. I shrug my shoulders like a stabbed starling, a worm that's been dipped in salt.

"I don't know."

Aireen plunges into my eyes and starts swimming all through my innards.

"Qué! What do you mean you don't know, dude? Think back!"

I think back, trying to bring the remote past into the present. Aireen leans forward, still looking at me.

She's waiting for me to answer. My hands are now sweating so much, you could wring out my fingers one by one.

"I don't know . . . According to my aunt who wasn't my aunt but was actually my godmother, I must be about sixteen or seventeen, but I don't know. I think I'm seventeen, but I don't know. Maybe I'm actually older than that, or maybe younger."

Aireen half closes her eyes the way people do when they're thinking about deep things, when pondering penetrates deep into the gray matter, that territory where an idea can stretch into infinity and, with its serendipity, put asunder all the substance in the universe.

"So when's your birthday?" she says, her eyes still scuba diving, like spiral-bound saucers.

Immediately I look away, embarrassed. I feel uneasy. I don't know how to meet someone's eyes, how to endure having the things that hurt me be linked through our retinas the way a bridge connects two far-off lands. Slowly, as if pleading for forgiveness, scarlet with shame, I answer, my voice distorted, staring at her beautiful feet:

"I've never had a birthday before."

* * *

[*"Auntie . . ."*

"Goddammit, I told you not to call me auntie—I'm just your godmother, and I already regret being that. I curse the day I hired your mother as a housemaid. All it's brought me is pure misfortune and tragedy."

"Godmother, do you know what day I was born?"

"What difference does it make? You're never going to amount to anything anyway."

"Godmother . . . what was my mother like?"

"Your mother didn't have a mother herself. That's why she paid so dearly for all that sleeping around, to be frank."

"And did she see me when I was born? Did she hold me? Did she see what I looked like?"

"No, demon spawn. She was already dead and they had to cut her open to remove you from her belly, like at the fish market when they cut open the fish to remove the eggs. And if it hadn't been for me, you'd have ended up in a garbage can or an orphanage or something."

"Godmother . . ."

"What?"

"What was your fucking mother like?"]

Aireen reappears with a slice of bread spread with condensed milk, and her cell phone so she can take a photo of us, she says. She jumped up from the bed a little while ago and rushed off to her grandfather's apartment while I was polishing off the casserole and milk so my guts would stop growling.

"What!" she echoed, leaping gymnastically, and ran downstairs. I was left adrift, hollowed out when she moved past me. I never believed birthdays were important to other people, or that anyone would care about the years passing, celebrate them, affix them in memory, take a photo of them, and then let them go. "You can't have a birthday without candles," Aireen says cheerily as she tries to light one and stick it in the center of the slice of bread. Her fingers are slender, the nails painted with an iridescent bronze polish. "Now turn off the light, ahorita—you have to blow out the candle before midnight so you can have two birthdays: today and tomorrow."

I stretch toward the wall and flip the light switch. Night bursts into the room through all its open wounds while the lit candle, there, exposed, inflames me all over. Its tenuous, trembling light, as it burns down above the slice of bread, gives Aireen's eyes an endearing glow—her beautiful eyes like cheerful tacks, her chickadee eyes like an alabaster quarry. The chiaroscuro becomes real; our dark profiles, I imagine, are rembrandtified like works of art—at least Aireen's is, standing out from everything else on this night I wish would last forever, her staying awake for the rest of time, where any sleeplessness can be filled with fragments of eternal instants.

"Now blow!" she cries as she takes a photo with her cell phone. The flash blinks and goes out, bouncing around inside our peepers.

I blow so hard that the candle bends and the smoke spills across the bread and condensed milk and then we are left in darkness like an obsidian blaze.

"Blow again now—it's midnight."

I blow on another candle she's just lit while she takes a second photo. The flash of her cell phone rekindles and blinks out along with the candle's flame.

The pale smoke from the candles curls into our nostrils.

"Good," Aireen says there in the dark, "now you're nineteen and we're the same age," and she lets out a naughty giggle that I hear vibrating back and forth like a rubber band.

"Nineteen?" I immediately ask, like a georgic revelation, to make sure I've heard her age correctly, her beautiful age in which she is queen and princess of her empire.

"Yes," she responds, "but if you want to be older, no problem, we can light another candle and make you turn twenty just like that."

Without knowing how, without understanding its origin, I am overcome by a dactylic gale of laughter that runs from my stomach up to my face, and unexpectedly I hear myself for the first time, as if I were somebody else, maybe a hog, unfurled, laughing uproariously as if the mechanism of laughter were autonomous and I its unbrakeable conduit.

"Urrrr gra-ha-ha"—I sound like a grunting swine—"urrrha-ha-ha"—it's an attack of quarrelsome ants teeming in my throat—"urrrr gra-ha-ha-ha-ha-hai"—I can't stop; I'm a tangle of nerves that I'm expelling in the form of a grunty laugh. I try to explain it to the girl, stammering: "I-I-I ask ha-ha-ha-h-h-how old you aaaa-a-a-are ha-har-gur-gurg."

Aireen, hearing my stuttering pig squeals, I guess, starts laughing along with me, epidemic but clean, limpidous, sounding like a bewitched hummingbird, and within seconds both of us are a heap of helpless, dissonant laughter, our cacophony replicated by the walls of the little room where we've become infected.

And we laugh.

We laugh hard, loud, like a flawless burglary—punching holes in the walls to steal unimaginable treasures.

Consuming raucous oxygen, the kind that can gush only from a delirating throat.

"Shall I turn on the light?" I ask as we pause to catch our breath. My stomach is starting to hurt, and I'm weeping crackling tears.

"N-n-not yet, c-c-cousin."

And in an instant, when I hear her stammer the way I imagine sheep stammer when they give birth, I pick up my laughter again, uproarious, splattering it everywhere. My belly aches, but I can't stop the fit of laughter; I'm incontinent, and I laugh and moan, moan and laugh at the same time like Calchas.

* * *

["Go on and laugh, you anxiolytic asshole. Whenever I say something funny, you just stand there like an idiot, moronicated, looking like a sad pig."

"Why should I laugh, Jefe? You don't pay me enough."

"Don't be an idiot, you little shit, I'm not paying you to laugh. I'm paying you to wipe that trash-picking look off your snout and stop scaring the fucking customers."

"All right, Jefe, I'll laugh at your stupid jokes."]

We're reduced to hiccups. Worn out. The room is dark. I hear her breathing slowly grow quiet, unblooming, torpid, like chillic drops that nod off when they touch the planks of venetian oak.

Her body is no longer chipping laughter.

"Come on, let's go outside."

She gets up from the bed and goes out onto the rooftop. The city's mercurial light bounces back at us.

Aireen props one foot up on one of the wooden shutters that must be from the Quaternary Period and clambers up to the highest part of the roof, above the washing machines. I follow her on all fours, clinging to a railing. I don't say anything. It's as if we left all words behind in the room alongside our gales of laughter.

Up above, the wind blows gently in our faces from between the tall buildings with lit-up offices in the distance. There are hardly any cars out at this time of night. The traffic lights are all yellow. Aireen heads toward one corner of the building and sits on the edge of the roof. I follow her and sit next to her. Our feet dangle into the void. Below us, far below us, you can see the trees that line the streets. You can see the planters. The parked cars. A few yups coming or going. Neon signs blinking on or off. You can see the top of a garbage truck that's got its yellow light turned on. From this side of the building, I can see Wells Park better. It looks dark in some areas, but I can make out the main fountain, looking tiny. Beyond it is the baseball stadium, which is only dimly lit. And closer in, I see Aireen's eyes, which open and close rhythmically as she looks out at the city.

"Why did you defend me like a warrior that day?" she asks after a few minutes of incorruptible silence.

At her question, I turn to look at her. She's still staring at a point off in the distance, on that Yankee horizon. I shrug my shoulders and then turn back to watch a scruff who's riding a kick scooter along the bench down there.

"Anybody would," I say without giving it much thought.

We fall silent again. I look a little higher up and see a few clouds starched by some sort of white light from the city. The wind has become static, perhaps run aground on our invisibility.

"Not anybody. You did."

I don't say anything. What can I say? Aireen starts gently moving her legs back and forth, as if she were on a swing.

"I'm really sorry about your bookstore," she says after a bit.

"What?"

"You losing your job like that."

I try to turn my head to look at the bookstore, but it's on the other side of the building. That thought hadn't occurred to me. The missus, Jefe, the little misters. The bastard publishers. The fucking distributors. The customers—regular, irregular, occasional, unwitting. The books. The books of all sorts. The fucking poetry that was like a tongue-twister, like riddles I could hardly ever solve, even if I read every dictionary in the world.

* * *

[*"Does cold, too, succumb / to the heat of death?' What the hell's that supposed to mean, Jefe?"*

"It means, you evanescent elf, that you're a garden-variety moron, you frigid freak."]

Or the plays, too, and the doormat novels, the ones you can deflower in a quick lay. Or the photographs of ships in large, thick tomes. Or the book of American cities at night, illuminated by a shit-ton of royal-blue lights: Manhattan and Brooklyn, Dallas, Houston, San Francisco, Chicago, Los Angeles, all looking like cities on Mars and not like my hometown, which is illuminated only by perpetually lit candles.

I also think about all the illustrated children's books I leafed through up in the loft.

* * *

[*"Why do you think so little of children's books, when that's what sells the most, Jefe?"*

After all, Jefe himself used to buy them just to quench the wild beasts' thirst and, of course, earn a little money through the slaughter of the victims themselves, he'd always say.

"You bastardite dope, those adverbious idiots can diddle around with doodles all they want—what the hell do I care? Anyway, losers like you are perfectly happy with ignorance, right, you stratospheric little shit?"]

"I'll find another job," I tell Aireen.

Aireen closes her eyes and exhales noisily, her chest rising toward the firmament. She puts her hands by her sides and lies back on the edge of the roof, gazing up at the night sky.

"Did you like it?"

"Like what?"

"What do you mean, what? Your job. Whenever I saw you, you were always reading books or arranging them in the window. It must have been really boring, right?" She emits a giggle that sounds sarcastic, ironized by the ivory of her teeth.

"And where do you work?" I shoot back at her to avoid sitting there in silence like a super-sized idiot and turn the subject back to what's important: her breathing next to me.

But Aireen, instead of answering me, lets out an impromptu peal of laughter that takes off at light speed toward the far end of the galaxy, suddenly, amid the gray and black clouds that look like white ghosts.

When she stops laughing that laughter—which seems different from her laughter just a moment ago, or from down in the room earlier, because now her laughter is maybe more melancholy or whatever—she asks:

"Doesn't it scare you?"

"Does what scare me?"

"Being this high up, dude."

I lean forward and look down. My feet are floating some sixty-odd feet above the ground, next to hers, which are still swinging back and forth like butterflies' fluttering wings.

"Should it?"

Aireen half sits up, propping herself up on one elbow, and looks me in the eye.

"What about me? Do I scare you?"

Spellbound there, I swallow spit—or, rather, my fucking throat goes dry. I am atomized like a goddamn raw lump. I spritz the night with my tremoring. I don't know if Aireen notices or not, but suddenly, hopping to her feet without any fear of falling over the precipice, she says, "I'm kidding, 'cousin.'" She laughs. "Come on, let's go . . . It's late."

She holds out her hand to help me up.

For the first time I touch her hand with mine. For a moment I squeeze all of her fingerprints, all of her phalanges, all of her bronze fingernails; she feels labyrinthine. I stand up, but don't let her go. The buildings seethe around us. The wind picks up. We're aboard the roof, standing at its prow. One false step and we could plunge down like two meteorites onto the concrete, paving the street, the window boxes, the trees, the whole city, with our bones. But we don't fall. Aireen looks into my eyes. If eternity lasted as long as that moment, the entire universe would fit in the space of an atom. Her eyes, only her eyes, make a parabola that sets my own aflame. Everything in the city seems to have stopped: the cars, the traffic lights, the people coming or going, the dogs, the cats, the moths under the floodlights, the prowling of the rhinoceri and giraffes and airplanes. The murmur of the flowers and the rustling of the leaves of trees in love. The hiding places of Andromeda's dimming stars. Suddenly Aireen lets go of me and everything leaps into motion again. She turns around and starts climbing down the way we came.

"And what are you afraid of?" I shout, also for the first time.

Aireen lets out another guffaw similar to our first peals of laughter and jumps down from the shutter to the ground.

"See you tomorrow, dude. Sweet dreams . . . Happy birthday." She moves off, invertebrating the night, toward the stairs, where she tumultuously disappears in the blink of an eye.

It's still Sunday, I know.

I don't want to get up.

I can't get up.

I haven't slept well for almost a week, or I've slept really badly. Ever since my paleozoic pounding.

The planks of the bed are digging into my back like a cross.

I sense that the sun is well risen because even with my eyes closed I can see a bit of brightness, reddened by the translucence of my eyelids.

After Aireen left at dawn, leaving me like a kite crucified in the air above the rooftop, I collapsed on the boards and nails. I didn't even move the magazines before crash-landing on the bed. I was so tired, so homerically worn out, that for a moment I could have been fucking Catullus hating and loving at the same time, frenziedly, like those suicidal madmen who insist on adoring the thorns instead of the flowers.

* * *

[At the beginning of winter Jefe held out an old volume to me, like that, out of the blue.

"And where should I shelve this one, boss?"

"In your head, you empty-skulled cockatoo."

"What for? Are you going charge me afterward?"

"Hoo-hoo-hoo, you featheriffic pachyderm. Did you see the title?"

I read: Spanish Golden Age Poetry.

"Why this crap, Jefe? Are you making fun of me or something?"

"I made a bet with the Argentine about you, squirt," he said, putting on a fake conical accent.

"In my favor?"

"Why would you think that, you incorrigible pun? Of course not, I bet against you, hoo-hoo-hoo."

"Fuck your mother, boss."

"Don't get pissy, you trapezoidal tub. I made a bet with that dolterous blockhead, Che, that you've got shit for brains and won't understand a bit of that fucking book. That way we both win: you in ignorance and me in a little fucking solid cash."

"Go refuck your mother, boss."]

I clasp my hands behind my head like flesh pillows. Sleep is gradually shooed away as if my brain were leaky, a diamantine clepsydra whose water is running out.

A few minutes later I lower my feet to affix them to the floor. It's true, the light is at its bluest and most piercing. But I think it's probably later than it seems. I clamber down from the planks. It's Sunday. And I kneel stiffly on the floor. My whole body aches—from the laughter, from the cold, from the planks, from the fatigue. I look at my birthday bread lying there on the little plate with the scorch marks from the candles. I reach out my hand and pick it up. Hunger makes my eels bashful or something—I'm always hungry on the inside and thirsty on the outside. I take a bite, like that, like I'm registering its every contour until the last mouthful is tumbling around in the bottom of my stomach.

Ten minutes later I'm in front of Aireen's door with the

dishes. I already cleaned them with a rag so as not to give them back dirty. She opens the door. She's wearing a gray sweatshirt, gold lamé leggings, and little mesh tennis shoes.

"You washed them?"

"I just wiped off the crumbs," I say.

"Put them in the kitchen."

She invites me in. I follow her and close the door. The windows are open. There's another sequined tablecloth on the coffee table. The computer is off, the vases are still full of feathers, and I can hear a small television or radio in one of the back bedrooms.

"Are you hungry?" she asks as I put the plates in the dishwasher.

"I ate the bread and sugar a little while ago."

"That's not food. Help yourself!" she says, pointing to an aluminum pot on top of a white stove as she heads out into the hallway to the bedrooms.

I pick up one of the birthday dishes and serve myself a bit of stew. My eels start leaping again. I grab a spoon, put the plate on the kitchen table, and sit down on a wooden chair with a faded cushion. I look around and see a refrigerator with rusty hinges. There are little pans hanging on the walls and a few shelves with old knickknacks.

Aireen comes back when I'm almost finished.

"Was it good?" she asks. I nod my head, the spoon between my lips. "I'll make a good wife, right?" she says, and laughs with her white teeth.

I swallow and smile, bits of stew caught in my gums.

"The other day I came here to say thank you for the chicken soup but there was an old man sitting over there. Now I don't . . ."

"That was you who came on Thursday?" she interrupts. "My grandfather told me somebody came by looking for me, but he didn't know who. I thought it was someone else."

"It was after I talked to you in the park."

"That was Thursday. The man you saw sitting there is my grandfather." She lowers her voice suddenly. "He hasn't been feeling so good the past few months. Right now he's resting in his room."

"What's wrong with him?" I say, lowering my voice too.

"We don't know. His bones hurt. The doctor says it's his age."

"Is he going to get better?"

"Of course he's going to get better."

"He's a little cuckoo, right?" I say this even more quietly so there's no chance Aireen's grandfather will hear me.

"All artists are," she replies immediately.

"What? What does he do?"

"He doesn't do anything now. But those paintings on the walls—he did those. He was a painter many years ago, but he doesn't see well anymore. One day he said, 'I made it this far.' And then he put away his paintbrushes and started spending his time looking out that window, watching the days go by. He doesn't want to go anywhere anymore. If it weren't for the people from social services, my grandfather wouldn't have anybody to talk to but me."

I look at the paintings hanging on the walls. I think they're really ugly.

"Looks like your grandfather was angry when he painted them, huh?"

Aireen turns to follow my gaze and sees I'm looking at a painting with gobs of color splattered across it. A volumetric, expansive laugh like that of an insane nanny goat exalts her beautiful lips.

"Waaaaa-haaaaa!"

"What?" I look at her in confusion.

"I'm sorry, it just makes me laugh. I thought the same thing until he explained that those blotches were art, abstract art."

"Aireeeeen?" The grandfather's voice suddenly calls out from the end of the hall. "Are you all right?"

"Sí, abuelo, I'm fine," she calls toward the corridor. Then she turns to me and says quietly, "I do think he was angry when he painted his blotches, though he insists he wasn't."

"What if we take him out for a walk?" I say spontaneously, like that, feverish.

"You'd have an easier time taking a rock out for a walk. The people from social services have encouraged him to go outside, but he doesn't want to. He says the streets are a trash heap of drab surfaces."

"I can throw him over my shoulder like a pig and we can take him out for a walk against his will."

"We tried that, but he clung tooth and nail to the stair rail and we had to bring him back inside. You could hear the racket all through the building."

"We can knock him out."

"What?"

"You know, clock him. One blow to the head and we're set—he'll go down and we can take him to the park so he can enjoy a bit of life, look at the trees. Or the squirrels—there are loads of them."

"Ha-haaa!" she laughs again loudly, calambrically, her voice echoing through every nook and cranny of the kitchen out to the front door of the apartment.

"What?" I say, bowheaded.

"Dude, you're a laugh riot."

"Aireen, what's going on? What's so funny?" the old man shouts again.

"Nothing, abuelo. Hey, do you want to go out for a walk?"

"What for? Everything that's out there, I've already got here in my head."

"But you need to get some fresh air."

"There's nothing but smog out there. I'll stick with my personal pollutants in here, thanks."

"See?" she says, rolling her eyes and putting her hand on

mine. "My grandfather's never going to leave this house." Her eyes look sadder than any I've ever seen in my life, like that, huddled like Coatlicue wrapped in her own skirts of plaintive serpents.

* * *

[Boorish nonsense. Upright nonsense. Bedimmed nonsense. Why hadn't the bean-counting scribblers invented something new under the sun? Instead of just words that come prepackaged in the dictionary?

So Jefe had won a few bucks betting on my ignorance with the asshole Argentine. Despite my objections, I wanted to prove to myself that I could understand some dumb vato named Góngora and another fucking güey named Quevedo. It was a bust: seems whatever I took in floated right back out again through my ears. I couldn't understand half a strand, even after I'd already read the whole dictionary and the whole book of Spanish Golden Age Poetry, which had just made me feel leaden. Yes, I read an entire letter in the dictionary every three days, trying to become less stupid than I looked. But the stubborn poetry, cowled from head to foot, got away from me anyway—any way it could. They all seemed to be saying the same thing in different ways: "O how the plaintive muses / suffer and are afflicted / by all that distresses / faggoty-ass poets." Or that's how I saw it.

In midwinter Jefe asked me in front of his Argentine buddy, whom he'd started inviting to his cookouts at his house in the suburbs:

"Do you know what a hendecasyllable is, you wretched bastard?"

"Bite me, boss."

"Did you understand anything in that book?"

"Yes."

"All right, then. Tell me what a cowl is, you benighted twerp."

"I don't know."

"See, man? The boy's got a head full of feathers," he told the Argentine, who'd immigrated to the United States from Patagonia back in the Flintstones era. "You owe me a lot of money, dude."

The gaucho parvenu, who rode a bit low in the stern, pulled out a wad of bills but didn't hand them over, just said, waving them in Jefe's face, "You're a scrawl, che, you dim-witted son of a bitch. Let's go double or nothing on the Copa Libertadores soccer match, all right? Qué decís?"]

Aireen gets up and removes her hand from mine. Her warmth has melted me in a heart-shaped cauldron. She moves around the kitchen, tidying cooking utensils, making space to put away some cans in the back of a small, dilapidated cupboard, taking refuge in knives, forks, pots, bowls, mortars, nuclear warheads, stardust, suns and moons, shards of winter, of spring, idle hours, ants.

After bustling around for a while, Aireen sits down again across from me. She looks over my shoulder, behind me, where the kitchen window looks out at the wall of the neighbors' house. She sits there, seemingly miles away, like a bird in a cage that wishes with all its heart to go chirp in the branches outside. Who knows what's going on in her head right now.

* * *

[When I started reading books that didn't have illustrations, I enjoyed learning about the thoughts of the people who lived there, pressed between the pages, without even having to open their mouths. I was like a busybody snooping into everything that happened in those books. But then I realized that literature is nothing at all like day-to-day life. After all, I couldn't help noting that nobody knew what I was thinking when I lay down to

watch the squirrels, or the trees. Sometimes I'd try to find out what the people around me thought—Jefe or the bookstore customers, or the missus, or the Argentine, the scruffs, the dudettes, the vatos and vatas, the chickadee from the 7-Eleven, the cathetuses and hypotenuses. That's why the words in books sounded so fake to me, the thoughts so fake, all linear, bereft of the din of everything that befalls to us when we wander the streets, on foot, within ourselves; their shortcuts struck me as fake, the way everything was so tidy, the way nobody ever went out of the lines, either in word or in deed—but what the hell did I know about all that.]

Now I'm trying to figure out what Aireen is thinking, like some sort of morose psychic, a telekinetic freak able to penetrate her thoughts—but I can't: real life gives us only people's broad strokes, not the detailed contours you find in books that offer only entertainment. What is Aireen thinking as she gazes past my shoulder toward the window? Her irises are so still, they could freeze the molecules of time.

"Do you like fish?" she asks suddenly, restoring her gaze to me.

"The kind with scales?" I answer reflexively.

"No, moron, the kind with fur," she ripostes. Then she says, "Come with me to the Mall Center."

We go down the stairs and I leap in front of her to open the door for her as we exit her building.

"There's no need for that," she says, irritated. "I'm not crippled, dude."

I know that, but I don't say anything. I just wait for her to walk through and then I let the door close behind me. She's carrying a cloth tote bag that she pulled out of the oven where it was stored. Upstairs, in the apartment, she fixed her hair, went to tell her grandfather that she was going shopping, and then we left. Me behind and in front of her, like a bluebottle buzzing around her.

We go down the stone steps and cross the street to the corner where the bookstore is. The yellow caution tape is gone, and the glass in the display window has been replaced. The plywood from a few days ago where they broke in to ransack the place is gone. Nothing appears to be moving inside it. It's like a ghost ship that has repaired itself, the way a wounded animal licks its wounds to heal them. We leave the bookstore, turn the corner, and walk past the alleyway. The door is still closed.

"Sabes," she says when the alley is behind us, "I don't think it was revenge."

"Revenge?"

"Yeah, revenge on you and the bookstore for the other day, when you came to my defense and thrashed those scruffs and addos."

"What?"

"I don't know, it's just a hunch."

"Why do you say that?"

"I don't know, those addos can take a beating, and if they were looking for revenge they'd go after you, not your stuff or the place where you work."

I want to ask her about the yup who fucked with me for no reason and left me all mangled at the bus stop. But I just keep walking in silence.

"That bookstore owner is a real creep, isn't he?"

"Sometimes . . . Why?"

Aireen doesn't answer. I figure she's referring to the way Jefe is always going around ogling any girl who walks past the bookstore windows. All at once, like an obstacular ox, I realize that scruffs and yups are ocularaking Aireen up and down as we go by, but because I'm with her they move on past, pasturing their virility inside their erect pants.

* * *

["Look at that ass coming this way. Fuck, I'd like to sink my
teeth into that, you lubricious loser."
"What about your missus, Jefe?"
"What about her, you flailing bozo? Love is one thing and
desire's something else entirely! You can screw a filly without
kissing her! Of course, what would you know about this stuff—
you're all besmitten with the girl next door."]

Finally we reach the fucking Mall Center. It's a shopping
center with four thousand five hundred thirty-two LED lamps
and stores of all kinds: shops with lacustrine clothing for hypodermic horses; stores with athletic shoes, in the infinitive,
autarchical; stores with white sales, black sales, gray, iridescent
pink, and daltonic sales; bakeries that are epigastric, gourmet,
Italian, Chinese, French; car dealerships with sports cars,
Pontiacs, Mercedes, fucking BMWs; shitteriffic Western
Union and Adolac; UPS and FedEx carcamating their shoulders to shrug off their boxed customers; a travel agency for the
international airport: Traveler Quick, United Airlines, droopy-
winged American, Lufthansa and Air France, Aeroméxico and
Mexicana. There are two huge signs for banks: City Bank of
America and Chester Bank Inc. Along one side of the parking
lot are a McDonald's and a Border Onion, whose reek of
grease and French fries smacks us as soon as we enter their
viral orbit. It's Sunday, so lots of cars are coming in and out.
More toward the equator, you can see two large movie posters
for the 3-D cinemas surrounded by blisters of lights flashing to
a psychotronic beat. Aireen and I cross a wide bridge covered
with a chocolate-colored wooden pergola; planters and
lanterns are built into the floor and beams. When we reach the
main doors, they open automatically before us and we enter a
space station in another galaxy, beyond Taurus and asteroid

B-612. A number of stores—Cartier, Gucci, Tiffany, Louis Vuitton, Lazlwiu—are lined up across from a fountain spitting multicolored water and framed with natural vegetation. There's a glass waterfall, and under it you can see two large underwater screens projecting the images of fish and coral, dolphins and whales, rocks and diamonds. To the left is a three-level escalator, and a right-hand turn takes you to the three glass elevators that glide up toward the ceiling like transparent eggs. A little farther down is a Starbucks inside a Barnes and Noble, something called Hawaii Cup, and two or three high-end al fresco bars surrounded by palm trees and white decorative stones: Ollin Bear's, the Alone Dream, and Forever Young, where they play prehistoric music from the fucking nineties. Scattered about are benches occupied by couples sizzled by fatigue or, more eruptically, by love, kissing and hugging each other. There are also chairs where people are reading things on paper or luminous things on their cell phones. Aireen heads straight for the entrance to the Super Center, past the hypoallergenic tables where a bunch of gringo families are sitting strapped to their food, troglodyting anything edible with their eager teeth. Hanging above these tables is a large screen displaying ads for massive corporations: Coke, Apple, Google, Ford. We walk under it and keep walking a long ways till we reach the Super Center, where Aireen grabs a shopping cart with orange trim and we go inside.

"Here, I'll take that," I say so she'll let me push the shopping cart the way I used to for Jefe's missus when she needed me for a shopping spree.

"It's weird," she says after walking a few yards. "I almost always come by myself." And she lets go of the cart so I can push it.

The superstore has everything, infinitesimal, true: from bat wings to stoppers for plugging up oceanic whirlpools; from

elephant trunks to dinosaur teeth. It sells everything from rep-
tilian furniture to clothing in every style and fabric. Toys and
pharmaceuticals. Medicines and steaks. Canned and frozen
chickens. Bread, hot and cold. Tortillas and chiles. All kinds of
fruit. Sausage made from pig, swine, hog, porker. Three million products to meet every need. A person could live for two
hundred years off the stuff in the dairy and produce aisles
alone. They sell all sorts of alcohol, of every proof and in every
kind of champagne, wine, tequila, and vodka. They sell everything from car tires to post-hole diggers for the hanging gardens of Babylon. Tools for building pyramids or carving the
stone flowers that crown Precambrian Venuses. Aseptic, with
white light methodically illuminating all of the merchandise.
Our route takes us through the electronics section first: screens
in every size, computers, radios, home theaters, cell phones,
video games. The gringos are lording it up with all that technology at their fingertips. You can see it on their faces, in their
dreams, how badly they want it, how they're dying to have a
screen as vast as the Colossus of Rhodes so they can feel like
they're alive and their lives aren't a fucking waste.

* * *

*["Jefe, why did you accept the bet with that Argentine jerk-
wad when you don't like soccer and you don't watch television?"
"I don't care about the fucking reason for the bet, I'm just
interested in the bet itself. I've already taken that walking flatu-
lence for so much money that one of these days he's going to up
and have a heart attack—he always bets on fucking losers. Like
you, you pint-sized prophet, hoo-hoo-hoo!"]*

Aireen picks up a package of tilapia filets and checks the
price sticker. I try to calculate how much we've got so far with
the loaf of bread and a small jar of mayonnaise, but all Father

Terán taught me was how to use an abacus. I was slowly learning at the bookstore because Jefe left me on my own and I had to add things up to charge customers and subtract to give them their change.

"Hmm," Aireen muses to herself, "we'd better take this one instead." She trades it for a package of sea bass that has fewer filets and I think is cheaper. She tosses it in the cart and we move on to the produce section. She grabs a head of lettuce and a cucumber. Then she gets a clear plastic bag and fills it with six or seven carrots. "We can make a delicious cream soup. We need butter and cheese. You like cream soup, right?"

I nod as I push the cart.

We walk toward the giant refrigerators with creams, butters, yogurts, cheeses with holes, cheeses with green and blue mold, six-string cheese, Camembert, fresco, Gouda, cheddar, Parmesan. Aireen opens the glass door and grabs a quart of transgenic cream and four ounces of preterit cheese. She places them in the cart.

"Hmm. What else? Oh, yeah, wait here. Don't move."

Without saying anything else, she starts walking swiftly down the aisle. I don't know what to do, so I trail after her. I follow a little behind her to the pharmacy section. I see Aireen go up to the counter. I hover a couple of yards back. Aireen says to the clerk, "Clopidogrel 100, please." The employee looks at her and then goes to a shelf that contains a bunch of different medicines. He examines two or three and comes back with a small green-striped box and puts it on the counter.

"Anything else?"

"Oxitorine 500."

The employee moves off, and just then I see Aireen open up the box of Clopidogrel, remove one blister pack with pills while leaving the other in the box, and tuck the one she's removed in the front of her leggings. She turns her head and sees me watching her. She looks into my eyes for what seems like an infinitesimal eternity. Before I demagnetize our peepers, I see she's trying to smile at me, but I think a sudden wave of shame must inundate her, because her beautiful cheeks go pale around the edges, leaving an iridescent whorl in the center.

The employee returns.

"Sorry, miss, we're out of Oxitorine. Is there anything else I can help you with?"

Aireen shakes her head.

The employee swipes the medicine box over the optical scanner.

"That'll be five hundred twenty-nine dollars."

She stands thinking for a moment. I have no idea what. Finally, after a few seconds of inflexible uncertainty, she tries to take the initiative again and regain control of the situation. Her voice trembling and barely audible, she tells the employee:

"I'll come back later . . . because . . . uh . . . ummm . . . I'm sorry . . ." She turns around, and I see that her eyes have crystallized into a pair of burgeoning droplets. She walks rapidly past me toward the home appliances aisle, leaving the puzzled employee standing there with the plundered box in his hands.

Aireen walks so quickly that I can hardly catch up with her till we're almost to the line of cash registers.

"Aireen," I say to her for the first time. My voice sounds weird saying her name. I leave the cart with all our things in front of the registers. "Aireeeen!" I say again more loudly.

"Leave me alone!" she shouts, speeding up and pushing through the line of yups, chickadees, rubes, and gringa dudettes waiting to pay.

A hipster ape sticks his arm out in front of me, blocking my path.

"Are you harassing the young lady?" he says, showing his teeth. Aireen is already heading around the corner toward the exit and disappears from view. I see that several women are staring at me disapprovingly, knitting together their blond, black, blue, violet eyebrows.

"That Spic's bothering her!" shouts an obese normcore old bag.

"They should kick all the wetback good-for-nothings out of this country," shouts another ninnified, ballyhooing brouhaha.

I step back with my hands held high, not looking for any more trouble, and try to scuttle away via another cash register. There are so many people, it's hard for me to be intrepid. I finally break free of the clustered crowd of choleric flesh and move past register 22. I walk quickly, my heart wobbly and my breath steaming. I turn toward the exit and its automatic doors and run straight into a burly security guard who's clutching Aireen.

"Let's go see the manager at the pharmacy," the guard salivates, sulphorous with bile, trying to keep Aireen from reaching the exit.

Without thinking about it, like that, in the blink of an eye, I deliver a fucking epicrastic wallop to his jaw and the officer collapses as if a giant pair of scissors had suddenly severed all the strings keeping him upright. He tumbles down, smitten by my tenebrous clobber. I grab Aireen's arm and yank her toward the door.

"Run!"

We run, throwing off sparks, oregano seeds, volcanic exhalations, feathery diatribes. At that speed, I figure we're going to get a horseache pretty soon, the kind that squeezes your chest and makes your liver whinny. Aireen is running almost right next to me—sometimes she falls behind and at others she moves away or moves closer. I sail over a planter full of cacti while she swerves to one side, dodges a few large pots with a flying leap, and then straightens out again. I don't look back, but I can hear a lot of noise and shouting growing increasingly loud. Aireen and I look like jet-propelled rockets that are breaking the sound barrier, leaving only a murmur between their wings. Up ahead of us I see another security guy getting ready to grab us with his beefy hands. Aireen sees him too and slows down to reduce the impact of the collision—but I speed up, and a couple of yards before I reach his muscular arms, I drop to the ground and slide under him, giving him a massive punch in the stones with my right hand. The disjointed hulk doubles over toward the ground just as Aireen leaps over him. Having been in so many fights, I've got a sixth sense for keeping an eye out, as if I had a positronic radar system installed in my noggin. We sprint under the escalators and I catch a glimpse of the fountain of virtual fish. The shouts are still in hot pursuit, now deafeningly loud. I pass under one of the platforms supporting the screens of water. The shouts increase, multiply. Aireen gets ahead of me and in an instant has reached the exit to the trellised bridge. I once read the phrase *divide and conquer*—I don't know what that means, whether I should divide them or us, but to give Aireen a chance to escape I start dividing; I turn in the opposite direction from her. I hear the voices turn with me behind my back and remain in pursuit, hot on my heels. I lead them to the other end of the corridor, to the elevators that go down to the underground parking lot. I race down the indigo marble stairs, taking them two or three steps at a time. My breath is strangling me. My heart is leaping and diving like a kite. I reach the first level and charge out toward a line of parked cars. I zigzag between them to cross to the other side and, with a spring of my equine hooves, jump down to the first landing and manage to climb up onto a wall of the parking garage. I keep looping back on myself like a tangle of hair to elude them. I emerge at ground level near the edge of the mall parking lot. The voices palpitate behind me, echoing off my sweat-damp back. I take off running again until I reach the chain-link fence that separates the mall from the outside world. I grab on to it and leap over, scraping my hands and thighs. I crash down on the other side and keep running, crossing the main street, which is busy with cars whizzing in both directions. When I get to the other side, I'm gasping for air; I stop and put my hands on my knees to try to catch my breath and get more oxygen into my lungs. I turn my head to look back at my pursuers so I can figure out how much time I have to get myself together before I've got to take off running again, but my surprise swells and stumbles with an enormous clatter. There, with my own eyes, I see there's nobody on the other side of the chain-link fence. Nobody's chasing me. I must have lost them at some point. And then anguish drills into me right down into the marrow of my fucking bones: what about Aireen?

* * *

["Jefe, if you're an atheist, how come you believe in the Virgin of Guadalupe?"

"You tiresome tenderfoot, how the fuck do you know I'm an atheist and how the fuck do you know I believe in the Virgin of Guadalupe?"

"You take your missus to church every Sunday, don't you?"

"Going to church doesn't mean you believe in God, you heretical hieroglyph."

"So you don't believe in the Virgin of Guadalupe?"

"I don't just believe in her, I trust in her."

"So why are you always going around cursing God?"

"Because the Virgin's not to blame for the sins of the Father or the Son or the Holy Ghost, you iconoclastic midge."]

After my breathing eases to a less superlative level, I cautiously approach the other side of the bench near the main entrance to the bridge and chocolate pergola where I last saw

Aireen. From my vantage point, I don't spot any unusual movements at the Mall Center. Cars coming and going, entering through the access points of rising and lowering arms, yups and addos rattling the automatic doors with their movements. Nerds entering and leaving an Apple Store. Vagabond hipsters in their Ferragamo shoes and their rectangular Clark Kent Lacoste glasses. Geeks nesting on fricative technologies. Many, very many glued to their WhatsApp, to their intrauterine networks, as Jefe always used to call Facebook and Twitter.

* * *

[*"Boss, I want to buy a smartphone—which one do you recommend?"*

"Don't be a moron, you virtual dumbass; buy a book and read that instead. Smartphones! Ha-hoo-hoo-hoo! What do you want one for, little bastard?"

"Well, to talk."

"And who the hell are you going to talk to? You're more alone in this world than your goddamn mother! Go out and sweep the sidewalk, and when you're done with that, go pick your ass!"]

I don't see Aireen anywhere. A guard posted in the access booth turns to scan the area where I'm standing. I immediately hide, crouching behind a car, and wait, like a fugitive, for his straying eyes to roam elsewhere.

"Dude."

I turn my head and find myself inches from Aireen's face. I feel her boiling breath cut through my perspiration. She's dripping too, damp, beads of glass pearling her forehead. I look into her eyes, so close that I can see her iris full of green, yellow, brown flecks surrounded by a bluish gray, almost ocean, almost sky, almost water.

I blink, incandescent.

"Are you O.K.?" I ask to check that I haven't hallucinated her with all this fucking running around.

Aireen pulls back and I can see her chapped lips, which she's nibbling with her teeth. She's shaking—I know it because her eyelashes are fluttering.

"I'm sorry. I never . . ."—and without warning Aireen hugs me just like that, hard, like a typhoon, like a nuclear tsunami. Her arms embrace me and she buries her head in my neck. The scent of her hair dampens all my ganglions. I wrap my arms around her and perceive every bit of her. Eternity comes to a halt and, apocalyptic, I feel how, all around me, every object in the universe is racing past at an extraordinary speed, everything except her and me. I feel how the crepuscular light changes the humus color of the universe, how the Earth is spinning like a top and we're going from day to night, night to day in the blink of an eye, again and again, insistently. Everything around us seems sped up except Aireen and me, embracing there, squatting down, outside of time, hidden behind the cars in the middle of the fucking world.

Aireen lifts her head from my chest and I see her swollen eyes, which look like two doors trickling downward. I plunge into them in an effort to calm our nerves, which are crackling all over. Actually, I don't know about her for sure—it's just my intuition since I feel her chest sinuously trembling. I definitely know about me, though: I'm trembling at her nearness, at her embrace so frankly enveloping me, at her eyes looking at me.

When was the last time somebody hugged me? Was the mollusk's hug a hug? Was Aireen's grandfather's hug so he didn't totter sideways a hug? The Border Patrol agents' hug as they dragged me out of the shit in the bathroom? The black woman's hug so I wouldn't get stung by wasps? My godmother's hug when she used to hold me down so I'd keep still and she could beat my ass properly? Mr. Abacuc's hug? The hugs that all those vatos tried to give me when I was beating them up and they couldn't defend themselves from the pounding I was giving them? Jefe's hug to keep from falling down drunk?

And yes, or what the hell ever, I'm trembling.

Aireen's eyes blink again, generating a little breeze that suffocates me all the more acutely.

I lean in to kiss her.

"No dude, not like that!" She immediately turns her head and my kiss crashes into the corner of her mouth like a wish in a bottle that gets lost in the ocean, without a word, right there, sinking to the bottom. Engulfed, I pull away from Aireen, a stab in my throat as I feel everything spinning around me. I look at her and try to raise a hand toward her to cling to something solid and lean on it, but my legs have turned to glass. A hypodermic shudder in my buttocks presages the crisis and like that, dark as I am, I fall over, knocked out, at her feet.

The fever isn't breaking," I hear, sunk deep in dreams. The voices turn into the crashing of waves.

* * *

["*Do you know what the ocean's like, little beaner baby?*"
"*It's blue.*"
"*Really it's more like an earthquake crouched within its own white foam.*"
"*Jefe, why didn't you become a poet?*"
"*Why do you ask, you howling glowworm?*"
"*Because sometimes I have no idea what the hell you're talking about.*"]

I open my eyes a crack. All I can see is a blurry glow through a white slit. I'm soaking wet and cold. Someone puts something wet near my mouth and suddenly drips liquid, which I swallow eagerly into my parched throat.

Then I let myself go again.

* * *

["*Mamá, where are you? Are you dead? Why do I remember you alive? Why do I remember your brown eyes and that cloth with blue quetzals on it? Are we just a memory that we've been hauling around with us for centuries before our births? Mamá, why does it seem like everything my godmother told me is a lie? Huh? Why do I sometimes dream about you, and you have a strand of wool that my fingers are playing with? Those bits of blue, pink, orange, and purple yarn dangling from your hair— who do they belong to?"]*

I wake up sluggish. My eyes dance around until I manage to get them under control. I blink several times to get used to the darkness and return to consciousness, to reason, to the place where a person can make his own decisions. Everything is dark. A small window lets the light from outside trickle in. The curtains are see-through, and the night grays in through the glass. I have no idea where I am. My eyes are like two turds crushed under the weight of shadows. My head no longer hurts, and I feel only a slight pang in my temples that is gradually abating. I turn my head to loosen the muscles in my neck; the mattress on the bed is so soft that it's bruised every bone in my body. Laboriously, I sit up and perch on the edge of the bed, supporting myself with my feeble arms. My toes brush the floor. It feels like it's made of wood. The darkness slowly retreats until my eyes are able to snatch a few objects around me: a table with a clock marking the hours in tenuous fluorescent blue, a vanity, a dresser, a wardrobe, and a door.

I place my feet firmly on the floor and stand up, pushing off the bed. A long nightshirt hangs down to my knees. And my fucking belt? Motherfucker, my belt! Where's my belt? I tiptoe, barefoot. I keep the lights off so nobody will discover I'm alive. I grope around in the dark for my belt with my secret hiding place. There's nothing. It's nowhere to be found. I go over to the door and carefully turn the knob. Maybe outside. The latch gives; very slowly, I open it and go out.

* * *

[*"And why don't you like going to the movies, Jefe?"*
"Because the doors at the movie theater all fucking squeak when you try to open them quietly."
"But that happens with novels too, right?"
"You fucking twinkle-dicked bastard, have you been reading the books we're supposed to be selling and filling them up with fingerprints again?"]

Outside, a lamp mounted on the wall illuminates the long corridor with a dim yellow glow. Several wooden doors, all of them closed, are lined up one after the other. I don't recognize the place. An Eliason double door is at one end. I walk toward it on my tiptoes and push it open, revealing a large room with hardwood floors. Toward the back of the room, an incandescent spotlight is shining down on a basketball hoop. Dilapidated-looking bleachers rise up on either side. Above them are three or four large windows, two of them with broken panes. There's not a soul anywhere to be seen. I enter what seems to be a gymnasium or multipurpose space—there are blackboards and two desks with papers stacked up, jenga'd, like brick lollipops. Off to one side, where I hadn't seen it at first, is a small stage with an upright piano on it. I've never seen one in real life, only in photos: when a lady showed up at the bookstore asking for piano sheet music for Mexican music for her daughter and I hauled out a dictionary to look for composers who were riverine, antipodal, from the Nahuatl homeland.

Music has always fucking soothed the crickets inside me; it's like an oblique soporifying of my soul, oleaginous waves that soak into my hammer, anvil, and stirrup and cease to be part of me; music that rasps melodically in my soul's legs so it stops hopping about and settles down, drowsily fixed to the surface of my flesh.

I climb up on the stage and approach the fucking instrument. I place my fingertips on the wood and trace its edges with my index finger. Its mahogany is perfect despite the scratches that highlight all the battles it's experienced, all its wars. I sit down on the black lacquered bench, right in front of the place where the absent keys are supposed to be. I imagine they're sheltered beneath that wooden carapace. That piano, there in the middle of nowhere, of the perpetual void, velvety with silence, inspires me. I move my hands toward its body. I don't try to remove the cover from the keyboard: I wouldn't know what to do next, except maybe destroy the sounds in one fell swoop. I close my eyes so all I feel is the wood under my calluses, under the rough pads of my grooved fingers.

"Do you like it?" I hear a childish voice coming from somewhere in the gym.

"Who's there?" I ask, startled. The hairs on the back of my neck bristle like hedgehog quills.

"I'd like to learn to play the piano. It's really pretty when someone plays it."

"Who are you?"

"Who are you?" the voice replies.

"Come out here or I'll give you an ass-whupping," I insist.

"If you give me an ass-whupping, I'll report you to the human rights people."

"I don't care," I say, looking around wildly, trying to identify where the little voice is coming from.

"They can put you in jail," it replies.

"Come on, come out here."

"No."

"Why not?"

"Because you're going to give me an ass-whupping."

"That's not true. I'm not going to give you anything."

"Then why did you say it?"

"Because you startled me. It was a joke."

"Are you sure?"

"Yes, I'm sure."

"What's your name?" it asks.

"Promise you won't laugh?" I get up from the bench and walk over to one of the curtains and lift it up. Nobody's there.

"I promise."

"And you promise you're going to come out from wherever you are?" I climb down from the stage and look underneath. Nothing there either.

"I can't promise you that because I don't know you yet."

"All right. My name is Liborio. Now you know me. So now it's your turn."

"Your name's Liborio?"

"Yes. What's yours?"

"Why did you think I was going to laugh?"

"Because people always laugh at my name."

"Are you embarrassed by your name?"

"Are you coming out or not?"

Out of a gap in the bleachers, near some boxes of balls and rings, a little girl with tawny skin and ochrefied hair appears. Two ribboned braids wrap around her head. She's wearing a white blouse with colorful flowers embroidered across the chest. She moves toward me in a red wheelchair with yellow trim.

"I thought you were a boy!" I say in surprise.

"No, I'm a girl."

"And what are you doing here?"

"Same thing as you, dummy. I'm waiting for everybody else to finish dinner so I can go to bed."

"I'm not waiting for anybody to finish dinner. I've been lying over there for a while and . . . How old are you?"

"Why? How old are you?"

"Why do you always answer with a question?"

"You did too, just now."

"All right. You win. I'm nineteen."

"Nineteen? You look younger than that."

"What about you?"

"I'm eight, but I'm about to turn nine."

"You sound more grown-up than you are."

She comes closer, almost banging into my shins with her chair. She holds out her hand and says, "I'm Naomi." I look at her hand and hold out mine. "You've got really rough hands. Are you a bricklayer too?"

"Listen, where am I?" I interrupt.

Naomi's brow furrows. She purses her lips and I can see that she's missing a tooth.

"Well, you're here, right?"

"Yes, I know I'm here, but what is this place?"

"You don't know?"

"No."

"It's Bridge House."

"Bridge House? And how the fuck did I get here?"

"Mr. Shine doesn't like bad words."

I look at the little snotnose, who looks at me with her mouse eyes.

"Fuck, fuck, fuck," I say to her, babbling, chanting the word quickly and ever more loudly. "Fuck, fuck, fuck."

"I see you're awake now."

I turn to look at the Eliason doors. Walking toward us is the old man who gave me the handkerchief and the money to buy ointments and bandages when I got beaten up by that yup at the bus stop. I recognize him immediately by his gray beard. What was his name? Suddenly, there, right there, I feel fucking ashamed. I don't know why, but a flush of heat climbs up me, scale by scale, like a row of dominoes tumbling down. I look back at Naomi and see that she's smiling.

"Words aren't bad in and of themselves, Naomi," the old man says when he's a few yards away from the little girl. "It's the intent behind them that makes them harmful. Did you notice how quickly this young man can say four letters? If we enter him in a competition, he might even break a world record. Would you like that?"

"Yes!" Naomi cries with gap-toothed delight. "World record in bad words."

The old man pulls a little package out of his pants pocket and gives it to Naomi.

"I see you've already met our fine guest for tonight."

"Yes. His name is Liborio." She looks at me. "Liborio, this is Mr. Shine."

"Abacuc Shine," he says without looking at me. "But we'd better chat tomorrow, Naomi; it's time for bed now."

I interrupt their conversation. "How did I get here?"

Mr. Abacuc grabs Naomi's wheelchair and starts walking toward the door where he entered. I follow close after them.

"Leo brought you. Leo Zubirat," he says before pushing open the Eliason doors and leaving the gym. I stand there dumbstruck, dromedaried, bursting with caligulas. I push open the door.

"Who the fucking hell is Leo Zubirat?"

"You see, Naomi?" Mr. Abacuc Shine says placidly. "This boy could break any world record you set for him. No question."

* * *

[*"Let's see what you think of this, you perversified nonsensicator: 'I want to hide / my heart outside / tossed by your side / just to be snide.' Hey? What do you think?"*

"Oh, Jefe, all the big-ass books you've read in your fucking life, and you write that bullshit."

"Asshole."]

The dining room table is long and made of wood. I figure it

must sit twelve or fifteen men, or eighteen addos, or thirty kids. The benches are also made of solid, heavy wood. Along the walls of the large room are, in order of appearance, an old TV set mounted on a black stand and facing the table, two windows, two doors, and some framed diplomas, all of them in the name of Mr. Abacuc Shine. One of the doors is open and leads to the kitchen. The other leads to a bathroom with a sink. A bare light-bulb hangs from a black wire and swings gently in a draft of air that's gusting in from somewhere. A flock of moths is using it to toast their antennae, flinging themselves in kamikaze circles.

"It's not much, but it's something," Mr. Abacuc says as he puts a plate of vegetables, a small bowl of hot soup, and a spoon in front of me.

I sit staring at the soup, in a daze. It has little bits floating on top of it, something like grass. I'm hungry, but I don't know, I can't. Mr. Abacuc sits across from me and rests his elbows on the table.

"Naomi's an extraordinary girl," he says when he sees me sitting there stupefied. I come out of my tetrahedral introspection. "She wants to be a lawyer when she grows up . . . or something like that."

He props his chin up on his hands. His gray beard is pushed forward. I can see he's missing one or two front teeth because his mustache has rolled up and revealed a couple of splotches of darkness toward his palate and tongue.

"And you, how are you doing?" I feel him carefully scrutinizing me.

"What happened to my belt?" That's the only thing I can think of in response.

"Did you check in the wardrobe in the room where you were? All your belongings should be there—your clothing, your sweats, your belt, all your things. We may be poor here, but we're honest." And he lets out a light laugh that resembles the tumulus of a messenger pigeon.

"How long was I out?"

"Let's see . . . Yesterday, Sunday, Zubirat brought you here at about four or five in the afternoon, and right now it must be about eleven at night. So that would be . . ."—he holds out his wrinkled hands to count on his fingers—"four, five, six, seven, eight, nine, ten, eleven. Seven hours plus twenty-four. You were asleep almost thirty-one hours, give or take."

"Why didn't you wake me up?"

"Eat your soup. It tastes awful when it's cold, and we can't afford to heat it up again."

I pull the bowl toward me and dip the spoon into it.

"And did that Zubirat guy come by himself when he left me here?"

"He came by himself. You seemed like you were drunk. We had to carry you in between the two of us so you didn't collapse again." He pauses for a long moment while I keep stirring the fodder with my spoon. "I'm asking you this to see what we can do for you—are you taking any kind of drugs, young man?" I stare at him agape. "Crack, coke, pot, molly, special K, angel dust, krokodil, heroin, bennies, LSD, TNT, morphine, glue, solvents, crystal, kitchen sink, belladonna?"

"Are you a doctor or a drug dealer?"

"Neither," he says, and laughs a little harder, huffing on his mustache. "But it's good to be informed. I'm asking because you didn't even have alcohol on your breath. Do you have some sort of illness we should be aware of? Not even the doctor could figure out what was causing your fever."

* * *

["Go on, asshole, you write something if you think you're such hot shit, you trepeditious thermopile."

"Why me?"]

"Now then," he tells me back in the bedroom, "you can stay as long as you want, but in exchange you have to return the favor with a little work. Not for me, for the community."

"Listen, are you religious? Does this place belong to some sort of cult?"

"Oh, yes," he laughs, "the cult of the completely screwed."

Mr. Abacuc closes the door and I hear his footsteps moving away from the battered door. I go to the wardrobe and yes, there's my belt, hanging on a hook. I pick it up and put it back on like it's the only lifeline I can cling to to keep me floating above the world.

The first thing I see when I wake up is Naomi's face above me. Then I realize that a bunch of pipsqueaks are crowded around me, some on the bed and others standing.

"Yeah, I'm telling you, it's him," says a skinny, pot-bellied kid.

"But the other guy looks burlier."

"This guy's all wormy-looking."

"Wimpish."

"Scrawny."

"Is it really him?"

Unsettled, I sit up, and two or three of the kids slide off the blankets onto the floor.

"He's mad," one of them shouts.

"He's going to hit us!" shouts another.

The mob takes off running, yelling at the top of their lungs, and drains out the door like horned vermin.

"Ignore them," Naomi tells me. "They're still really little, and they don't know that there are laws that protect little kids."

"What the hell was that?"

Naomi spins around in her wheelchair, the front wheels raised in the air.

"They're kids—what don't you get, silly?"

"And what are you doing here?" I demand, scrubbing the sleep away from my eyes.

"Being nosy like everybody else."

"Well, go be nosy somewhere else."

Naomi spins on her axis in the wheelchair. It looks like fun behind my crusties. She's wearing the same blouse she had on last night and the same ribbons. The sun is beating through the sheer curtains. In the daylight, Naomi looks more like a girl than she did at night, when she could have passed for a boy. Her hair is a web of black wool, blue-black at the temples.

I see several little heads peeking through the door. Then I see the kids' eyes. I quickly grab my pillow and hurl it at them. The runts shriek again and dash off like a plague of leaping ants down the corridor.

"What's with those little monsters?"

Naomi rolls over to the door, picks up the pillow, and places it on her knees.

"Don't you know?"

"No. What?"

"You're like a hero for them, a legend. They admire you. Unless, of course, that wasn't you who was on TV . . ."

"Well, I don't know if I was on TV. But I don't think getting pounded into a pulp by a bunch of scruffs is any reason for a bunch of snot-nosed kids to think I'm special."

"What are you talking about?"

"Well, what are you talking about?"

"I'm talking about the video that was on TV where you destroyed a boxer's hand. They even showed it slow motion a bunch of times, like that, *zoom, pow!*"

* * *

["Look, Jefe, I wrote a paragraph to win that fucking bet from last week. Here—now you can't say I'm a fucking whiny-ass

bitch and that I lose by default. I worked my ass off writing it, but go fuck yourself."

"All right, let's have a listen to your bullshit, you ridiculous clown."

"'I saw her there for the first time, or what the hell ever, spinning serendipital through the trees of a Pleistocene paradise. But she, with the fucking sweetness produced by blindness, didn't see me till it was too late, mingled with a pagan night on a red bus, when we monsters sprout from the alveolar sewers of the city, under that hieroglyph that rains down ectoplasmic beatings on only a few, when amid the streets, amid the streetlights, amid the hanging gardens of the fucking stars, someone, in silence, falls in love.'"

"That's not yours—you can't have written that, you plagiaristic primate. Where did you copy that from? What book? Tell me, motherfucker!"

"It's mine, boss."

"It can't be—you can't write your own fucking name properly, and some of the words in there don't even exist! Plus, you're a fucking brainless reptile who couldn't even produce his own goddamn saliva, much less use that fucking vocabulary. So you lost the bet, you leperous dog testicle."

"It's mine. I wrote it."

"That's not true, motherfucker, fucking asshole, and don't you stubbornate with me. Since you're a fucking liar, I'm not going to pay you a fucking cent this week and you're going to work fucking double, you fucking mythomaniacal loser. Now get out of my sight—I don't want to see you again, fucking devil spawn!"]

"Qué!" I exclaim in surprise. The fucking mollusk and his stateless thugs must have uploaded the video of me and the fucking Crazy Loco to YouTube.

Poor vato, stripped down like a plucked Quetzalcoatl.

Naomi spins again like a fucking pinwheel. She stops suddenly.

"Ms. Webber doesn't like it when we mix languages. She says we should either speak English or speak Spanish. We take classes with her, and she says if we mix them up, after a while we won't know what we're saying and instead of enriching our languages we're impoverishing them."

"Qué!" I repeat.

"Didn't you know that?"

"Do you always talk like that, dandelion?"

"I'm not a dandelion, Liborio; I'm a little girl and my name is Naomi." She turns, her brow furrowed, and heads for the door. Some of the fucking dwarves move aside for her.

"Ooh, you're mad now?" I yell, but she keeps going and I watch the huddle of manikins trail after her like the rats of Hamelin. "Give me back my pillow!"

I lie back again in this incredibly soft bed. I've never spent so much time lolling about before, keeping bird lice warm between the blankets, under my wings, amid the nits.

I'm about to close my eyes again when Naomi comes back with a gaggle of children and plants herself directly in front of me. "I'm not mad at you—I'm upset, which is a big difference, and take your stupid pillow." She hits me on the head hard with the pillow and leaves again, herding the kids between her wheels.

* * *

[Jefe was pissed off at me for almost four weeks. He spoke to me only to curse at me, a fucking vicious circle.

"Clean, sweep, organize, put, take out, shake, wash, rinse, mop, bring, carry, scrub, carve, haul, fuck yourself, clean, sweep, organize, put, take out, shake, wash, rinse, mop, bring, carry, scrub, carve, haul, fuck yourself . . ."]

I leap lightly out of bed and spruce myself up like a fucking astronaut: my shirt, the sweatpants from Double-U, and the sneakers that Aireen gave me. I fold the nightshirt and leave it in the wardrobe. The doors in the hallway are open, and I can see that most of them are rooms with bunks. The beds are already made with gray-checked blankets. I move on toward the exit on the opposite side of the gym. I want to get out of there as soon as possible, like fleeing from wild beasts.

I get to the metal door and open it.

The street twists under the armor of the cars. The area seems run-down with age but not dirty. There isn't as much graffiti as in other parts of the city I've seen. There are even some little planters filled with green plants watered by the people from the shelter. I stop in the doorway and, to my surprise, smell food. Always with the fucking food, goddamn food harassing me day and night. The aroma is coming from the dining room to the left of the main entrance. I turn on my heel and plunge back into the jaws of the shelter, obeying the fucking hunger that always cuts trenches in my soul.

* * *

["You were right, Jefe, I copied that thing I wrote from a magazine."

Jefe removed his glasses and, smiling from ear to ear like a diabolical alebrije, pounded his fist on the counter. The sound echoed through the bookstore.

"Bingo! I knew it, you piratic plunderer! How were you going to write something like that? Maybe the fucking curse words were yours, but the rest of it, ha!"

"Well, I wanted to win the bet, whatever it took, boss."

"And you lost it anyway, you twittering pterodactyl."

"Yes, Jefe."

"Now bring me the magazine you pinched it from."]

"You must be the new boy," a stout woman says to me when I enter the dining room.

"And you must be the old lady, right?"

"Ha ha ha," she laughs. "I like your sense of humor, kid. Most people here are really serious. But what else can we expect? Life's not a bed of roses."

"My bed's really soft."

"Ha-ha-ha," she laughs again. "You can't have had it so bad in life, since you're still able to make jokes. Are you going to have breakfast now?"

"Yes, but I don't have any money."

"Don't worry about that. We've got plenty of dirty dishes to wash." She laughs, disappears into the kitchen, and returns with a tray with a roll on it. "This is all we've got left; breakfast starts at eight on the dot."

"But it smells like stew."

"Yes, that's right, but that's for lunch. If you want to get in on that, you need to be sitting down with your hands washed at two P.M. sharp."

I take the roll off the tray and start gnawing at it.

"It's really hard."

"Well, yeah, it's the bread we use to feed the animals."

"The animals?"

"Yes, the roosters and hens in the chicken coop we've got up on the roof."

I stop making faces and keep nibbling.

"And where is everybody?"

"Waiting in the gym for it to be lunchtime." And she heads back to the kitchen to keep banging the pots and pans around.

I finish jawing the roll. It's almost two, and the bit of bread has awakened my sense of time.

My timing.

I enter the gym, and suddenly everyone's staring at me. It

falls quiet. I'm not used to making heads turn wherever I go. I feel self-conscious. I walk toward one of the bleachers and lie down, curling up in an effort to turn myself into a clockwise zero. When I disappear, people go back to their conversations and the racket starts up again.

The bleachers in the shelter's gym are full of all kinds of kids. Only three people seem to be older: a beefy coach with a whistle, a lady sitting at one of the desks, and Mr. Abacuc, who's coming toward me. The rest all seem to be between the ages of four and twenty.

"You like fistfighting, right?" he asks, sitting down beside me. I've still got a bit of bread caught in my teeth.

I shrug. I don't know if the old man's looking for a fight, but I'm not interested. I could cram the few teeth he's got left right up into his skull.

A few kids are playing with a ball, trying to get it into a dwarf basket. They fumble it, and the ball gets away from all of them and rolls slowly off the court. The paunchy coach blows the whistle. He scoops the ball up and hands it to one of the kids, and the game resumes.

"Did you know sports are the best way to work through anger?" he remarks as one of the kids finally makes a basket and rolls around on the floor, ecstatic, in celebration of his miracle.

Naomi is on the other side of the gym, in front of the bleachers. She's holding some faded pennants and yelling at the kids. She cheers. She spins in her chair and yells again.

"What happened to her?" I ask, pointing to Naomi with my eyes. Mr. Abacuc looks at the girl.

"A tragedy," he replies tersely.

The giant coach blows loudly on his whistle, ending the game, and yells to the next team to take the court. He's sweating buckets trying to line some little kids up by height, but they're more interested in picking their noses than in following the big lug's instructions.

Mr. Abacuc strokes his gray beard. He's thinking. It looks painful. One of the blue veins in his forehead gets even bluer as he idly fiddles with a piece of paper. He looks at Naomi.

"One day her father lost control. They'd fired him from his job at the factory. He went home. He picked up a .22 and shot his wife, his daughter, and finally himself. Naomi didn't die, but the bullet broke her spine in two. This was years ago now."

I swallow hard. I look at Naomi's face. Can a person forget the past like that, quickly, as if certain things had never happened? Naomi keeps waving the little flags, two or three tots hanging onto her legs as if they were paper vines.

"Is she bitter about it?"

"I don't know, son. She's a smart girl, but I don't know. I don't know if she's holding on to something deep inside. I imagine she is, even if she doesn't want to be. Look at her— she's glowing, isn't she?"

"Why do you do all this?" I ask, looking around at the kids playing, the squirts cheering in the bleachers. They run, leap, crash into one another, laugh.

"What?"

"Go around giving charity to people."

"I often ask myself that very question. Especially when it's not enough. But look at them, the world isn't as bad as it seems and there's still hope—don't you think that's a good reason?"

"But if you don't believe in God, why? Why do all this?"

Mr. Abacuc smiles. He slowly closes his eyes and opens them again.

"It's true, son, I don't believe in God, but that doesn't mean I don't try to be a good person."

He puts a hand on my knee and gets up with some difficulty. He limps down the bleachers as if one of his legs were shorter than the other. He stops and turns around.

"Oh, I almost forgot . . . Somebody left a note for you—

that's what I came over to tell you." He holds out the piece of folded paper he'd been twiddling between his fingers.

"Why didn't you give it to me earlier?" I cry amid the din of whistles, dribbling, the shouts of children and circling flies.

"Because I'm old and I forget this sort of thing."

He descends another step and turns to look at me with compassionate eyes.

"It's very easy to lose control, son—what's hard is the opposite."

He continues down the bleachers and goes over to the lady at the desk. She's got a little boy next to her who's shrieking for some reason.

I hastily unfold the paper and start reading, my pulse spilling from my hands. Suddenly my blood freezes in my eyes, in my cheeks, and I feel a pang in my gut that pushes all the air out of my body. "I don't want to see you again. Aireen."

* * *

[*"We don't have that magazine anymore, Jefe. You sold it to that fucking fancy lady who wanted to know what a demiurge was."*

"The one in the rat-fur coat?"

"That's the one."

"But that magazine was about Mexican cooking."

"Well, I don't know, but you told her it had a recipe for demiurges in garlic sauce."

"Are you shitting me, you insolent ingrate?"]

I read Aireen's message three billion times in a matter of seconds, and her handwriting seems to get blurrier and blurrier. Those letters written in blue ink that proceed nervously, hastily, breathlessly down the page, as if they were fleeing toward the ice at top speed. Another improvised drop falls onto the paper and puddles it, like an ocean, like a river of scrambled words. Aireen, vestal of the sacred flame where a man will pay for any attempt at seduction with his own loutish life on a bonfire? With his heart ablaze? Fuck, fuck, fuck. And nothing grows in the darkness of despair, only those blooms of water, maybe, that make a person's peepers gleam with the ocean. Chingafuck.

"Why are you crying?" I look down and discover Naomi intersectioned below the bleachers. "Is it because our team's losing?"

"I'm not crying, you stupid kid. It's sweat."

"Sweat makes your eyes all red?"

"And black and blue if you don't shut up."

Naomi holds out a rumpled little pennant made of red paper.

"Stop sweating so much and start cheering for our team instead so we can win the world basketball championship."

I lift my head. Down on the floor is a cluster of the youngest kids. They can barely stand, and the ball is so large for them that it looks like a beach ball next to scrawny, potbellied ants.

"Cheer for those little twerps?"

"Yes, they're going to be our champions someday."

"And why should I cheer them on?"

"Well, we're all on the same team, aren't we?"

"But look at them—they can't even stand up on their own."

"That doesn't matter. They'll grow up one day."

I take the pennant from her and start waving it slowly, waterily, cancerously, until my epithelials are suddenly gripped by a fit of rage and I rise from my seat and start yelling like a madman, filled with fury, with bitterness, with the pain caused by Aireen's fucking note and her invisible presence rubbing against my waterlogged eyelashes.

"Fucking snot-nosed little brats, get the fucking ball in the goddamn fucking basket if you want to be fucking champions one day!"

The whole gym goes quiet, absolutely silent. The little kids stare at me, the devil in their faces. The enormous bewhistled coach lets his tweeter drop to his chest. The lady at the desk and Mr. Abacuc are aghast.

Without warning, just like that, like worn-out bells hurled by frenzied monkeys, the little kids all start wailing at once, in unison, like a fucking orchestra playing forte, fortissimo, howling like angels and devils.

"Now you made them cry," says Naomi at my feet beneath the bleachers.

I'm still shaking. However tough I seem, I feel smaller than the tiniest, shriekiest little child down there. Overpowered by powerlessness, I jump down to the floor and make for the exit. Just then, Mr. Abacuc grabs hold of me with a strength that's surprising in an old man.

"If you leave, you might never come back. But if you stay, you can do more good things than bad."

I push his arm away. I feel like taking off; my legs are cramping up with the urge to get out of there. To free myself of the whole goddamn world and smash it into fucking pieces. I start walking toward the double doors; I want to kick them down, but something stops me.

Something I can't really explain.

My own triumvirate conscience tells me *don't* and I don't know why.

Naomi wheels herself over to where I'm standing in front of the doors, panting so hard I can hear the horses in my veins galloping through my head like a spiderweb of clots.

Naomi takes my trembling hand.

"Stay!" That's all she says.

Nothing more.

Her hand is an ember that I can't distinguish in all that conflagration.

I know everyone's looking at me because I feel them hovering at my back like sharp knives. I can also see the shrieking children reflected in the round windows of the Eliason doors.

"Coach Truddy, please bring the therapy dummy," says Mr. Abacuc.

The massive whistler goes over to the box of balls and rings. He rummages around in the bottom and pulls out a cushion covered with tattered red and black vinyl.

"Get in position."

"Let's go!" says the giant, sweating like a pig as he secures the dummy to his chest with one foot in front of him and the other behind.

Mr. Abacuc shouts, "Punch that dummy with all your might, boy! You'll see, you'll feel better afterward."

Naomi squeezes my hand as if that might give me courage, and then lets go.

"Go on!" the girl says. "That's what we all do here when we're mad about something."

The truth is, I'm pissed at the whole world. I ache all over, as if every bit of me had been sent through a garbage disposal unit. I spin, spewing sulphur, and slowly move a couple of yards closer to the coach and his whistle. Then I turn into light, give a hypersonic leap, and unleash a furious punch, focusing all of my rage toward the center of the fucking vinyl cushion, like that, profaning the air with all my dark cells.

Fuuuuuuck!, whistles the wind around me, all of its molecules vibrating in the explosion.

Craaaaaack!, booms the dummy amid the total silence of the gym. And it doesn't just boom—it releases a huge cloud of dust as the vinyl splits under my blow and I send Coach Truddy flying on his ass like a felled tree in the middle of the floor.

The whole gym bursts into shouts.

"The boy's killed him!" screams the woman at the desk.

Mr. Abacuc rushes toward the sprawling hulk.

"Coach Truddy! Are you all right, Coach Truddy?"

The giant can't move. He's had the wind knocked out of him. All you can see is his chest struggling to inflate his lungs. His eyes are bugging out like a lemur's. His face goes from purple to red and then to blue. Immediately I go up to him and grab him by the legs, making him bend his knees so his diaphragm goes back to its normal position and he can get some air, just as I've done with so many guys during street fights so they could have the chance to leave the melee on their own two feet.

"You're right," I tell Mr. Abacuc as I dock Coach Truddy's legs to inflate him. "I do feel a little bit better."

* * *

["Jefe, the fucking distributor came by yesterday. He says you need to give him a check that won't bounce on him—otherwise he's going to take the new books somewhere else."]

Mr. Abacuc's office is on the other side of the foyer to the right, almost directly across from the dining room. We take Coach Truddy there. We settle him on a futon to recover in private and not under the watchful eyes of all the kids, who started crowding around him to find out whether he was dead or alive. The desk lady is clucking around the room in Spanish and English:

"Madre mía, oh God. Sweetheart, cariño, baby."

Naomi tugs on my arm. "That's his wife."

Slowly, the giant is regaining his shrimpish hue. The lady places another cottonball soaked in rubbing alcohol under his nostrils, and the hulk blanches backward.

The stout woman from the kitchen comes in carrying a plate and a spoon.

"Some nice chicken soup can revive even the dead," she says, placing it on a little table next to the paunchy coach.

"Thank you, Mrs. Merche," Mr. Abacuc says.

The cook leaves, skipping toward the dining room across the hall.

"How do you feel, coach?" Mr. Abacuc asks for the gazillionth time.

The tub nods weakly. His wife is interlacing her fingers with his.

She turns to look at me.

Her eyes are foaming.

"That boy is a menace."

"Ms. Webber, I am entirely and absolutely to blame here," Mr. Abacuc breaks in. "I didn't . . . I didn't foresee it."

"Let's hope he didn't turn my dear Truddy's guts inside out and dislocate his stomach."

"We'll take your husband to the doctor at once, Ms. Webber."

"I'm fine," Coach Truddy says at last.

"How can you be fine, darling? You can't even breathe! You turned all sorts of colors, oh God! You looked like you were dead. I almost died myself, of a heart attack!"

"He just knocked the wind out of me. It's nothing, woman."

"If you get the runs later, don't come crying to me!"

Naomi puts her hand to her mouth to cover a smile spreading across her face at Ms. Webber's commentary.

I smile too.

"And he's cynical too. Look, Mr. Shine, he's laughing."

"I'm sorry, I . . ." I say, and bow my head. Naomi looks at me and smiles at me from behind her hand.

"Ms. Webber. You're upset right now because of what just happened, but please remember you're a good person and we're here to help those who need it most, those who have the least. It's not the boy's fault."

Ms. Webber blushes. She takes her eyes off me and deposits them on her husband, who's already pulling himself together. He's sweating less, and he's now a healthy shade of pink.

"Jesus, kid," the coach says to me, his eyes wide and his breathing slow. "I was a mechanic on a battleship during my military service. We used to organize fights between the sailors and we'd bet dollar bills and cigarettes on the winner. In all my life, I swear, I've never seen anyone with a left like the one you just gave me."

"Neither have I, Coach Truddy," adds Mr. Abacuc, perching on the edge of his desk. Hanging on the wall behind him are more certificates with his name on them and some photos with a bunch of people I don't recognize. Everyone's smiling into the camera.

"You like boxing, son?" the giant asks me.

"Coach Truddy, are you thinking . . .?" interrupts Mr. Abacuc.

"It wouldn't hurt to give it a shot. What do you think, Mr. Shine?"

* * *

["Boss, the people from the bank called like five times. What should I tell them?"

"That I'm dead. Tell them that: I died yesterday and they buried me at ten this morning, so those fucking queer-ass merce-nary monkeys can lay the fuck off."]

"Look, son," Coach Truddy tells me in the middle of the gym floor. The other boys and girls already went off to the din-ing room to eat. I'm hungry, but the coach has to go to the doc-tor at his wife's insistence and he wants to get started immedi-ately. "We have to do this yesterday, Mr. Shine"—that's what he told Mr. Abacuc, wanting to have me debut at the exhibition championship for charity. "We need to raise money for the kids in the shelter, and quickly." "Look, son," he repeats, "these are called muscles, and we have to get them in shape. This is your sternocleidomastoid, these are your deltoids, then the triceps and biceps. Your latissimi dorsi run down your back. Here where your ribs are poking out should be some muscles called your obliques. And in front of them, your abdominals. Then come the glutes, and your thighs have your quadriceps, which are made up of four muscles: abductors, adductors, rectus femoris, and sartorius. There's also your biceps femoris and, down below, your calf muscles and your tibialis muscles. We have to transform them all into steel using crunches, push-ups, squats, and lots of other exercises. Got it?"

"Yes."

"Yes? So what did I say?"

"We have to fix me up from neck to shin, including guns, cheeks, and gut."

"Well, you've got the general idea, which is the most important thing. Tomorrow I want you to start off running for ten minutes, and every day you're going to add two more minutes. Jog first and then do ten- or twenty-meter sprints to work out your cardiovascular system." He looks at me meditatively. "Are you sure you've never trained in boxing or anything? You've got quite a fist."

"Never, Coach Truddy."

"All right, we'll see how things go. Tomorrow before five. And make sure to drink lots of water."

"And what's all this for?"

"Well, it's one thing to dish blows out, and something else altogether to take them."

"What?"

"Flex your stomach muscles. Ready?"

"Ready."

Without warning, he strikes out at me, and I instinctively move backward and to the right. He misses, his fist grazing my belly, and almost falls over from his own forward momentum.

"Let me punch you, son."

"What for?"

"To show you what I was just talking about."

"Can't you just show me with words?"

"No."

I remain still and tighten my abdomen.

His blow in the pit of my stomach makes me gag up my roll in the middle of the floor.

"And I didn't even hit you hard, boy," he says while I'm doubled over, out of breath, just lying there. "There are some monsters that are going to want to rip off your head with a single twist."

I wake up before dawn. The fluorescent blue clock says it's 4:45. I dress quickly and go down to the kitchen storeroom. I pull out a sack of feed, pick up a bowl, and fill it to the brim. I walk over to the spiral staircase that leads to the roof and climb up. There are several hens in a coop made of wood and wire. They're still sleeping on a crosswise pole. I pick up the tray and empty out the feed. Then I fill the waterer with the hose. I also water the wooden boxes that the shelter uses as a garden: basil, thyme, cilantro, parsley, mint, epazote, chamomile, rue, oregano, Mexican pepperleaf, greens, arnica, some cabbage, radishes, carrots, squash, cherry tomatoes, red chile, serrano, habanero, piquín, manzano, poblano, and jalapeño peppers. In some areas of soil, they've planted aloe and two little clusters of blue agave. A small avocado tree and a dwarf lime tree are planted separately. At a distance is a hydroponic tube for watercress, romaine lettuce, and some strange plants called "stars of the day" that look like grass for pasturing cows.

"Why aren't you growing any roses, carnations, or violets, Mrs. Merche?"

"You can't eat those."

"But it's food for the eyes, isn't it, at least that's what the poets say."

"Oh, kid, that's because poets are not of this world and they don't need to eat."

I finish stingily watering all the wooden garden planters up on the rooftop, just the way Mrs. Merche taught me, so I can earn my breakfast.

"Don't use a lot of water, or they'll rot."

I carry the container downstairs and leave it in the storeroom. I head toward the main entrance, open the door slowly so as not to disturb anyone, and go out to the street. The streetlights are still awake. I turn to the left and start walking. Nothing's open yet. Two or three people walk by, probably on their way to work at one of the factories on the edge of town. It's cold, so I start jogging slowly to warm up my muscles, as Coach Truddy instructed me.

When I get to Wells Park, I see there are a few other suckers who have also gotten up early to exercise. One is wearing a scarf, glasses, and headphones. Others are doing genuflections at the edge of the gravel path. The rest jog past me. I spot the black woman's battered shopping cart and a few people sleeping toward the center of the park. The air is cold. All I'm wearing is my sweatpants from Double-U, a sweatshirt Mr. Abacuc gave me, and the flying tennis shoes from Aireen.

What did he tell me to do first?

Oh, right.

I bend in half and feel my bones crunch at my waist, in the middle of my body. One, two, three. Then I straighten up and try to stretch my legs. I open my legs to either side and feel the pull in my groin.

It hurts.

I do a couple of squats, my knees creaking.

It's like I need oil or something.

I stretch my arms out in front of me and then try to stretch them behind me.

I move my head in various directions to warm up my neck.

I start walking down the running path. Then I pick up my pace and suddenly I'm running. It's a strange sensation to know that nobody's chasing me and I'm doing this of my own accord, not because someone's after me wanting to beat me up.

I take a couple of laps around Wells Park. My throat feels dry, and sometimes I get out of breath. I imagine the beginning must be like that. Nothing but pain.

Pure pain.

"And remember, son: no pain, no gain," Coach Truddy told me before leaving arm in arm with his old lady.

The sky starts to turn blue. Before I tire myself out completely, I lope out of the park and go straight to the chickadee's building. I look at its red bricks and feel as if a part of my life were slipping away from me there.

I used to be happy just watching her walk down the street, on the bus, in the park, so why do I feel this way now?

I stop and look up. At her window. Aireen must be sleeping right now. The sky is getting lighter by the second, and before it lightens completely, I start running as fast I can, hoping the physical pain will make me forget the enormous pain of knowing that she will never want to be with someone like me.

The sky is blue by the time I get back, though the sun is still nowhere to be seen. The shelter is wide open. Outside, a truck is unloading boxes and bags. Mr. Abacuc is carrying them inside along with Mrs. Merche. The oldest kids are lined up, passing the bags from hand to hand toward the interior of the building, where the middle kids are putting everything away. They're like ants passing twigs to one another in their jaws.

"What's all this?" I ask Mr. Abacuc as I help him carry a few boxes inside.

"Donations for winter," he replies, huffing a little.

I tote more large boxes until we've finished unloading everything from the truck.

"Let's see," says Mr. Abacuc. "Food goes in the kitchen

pantry. Clothing and blankets, in the storeroom in the back. Medicine, in my office."

"Is Coach Truddy here yet?" I ask when we've put away all the donations.

"He always arrives after breakfast, son."

"So what should I do in the meantime?"

"Come with me!"

We go into a room crammed with junk. There are filing cabinets, stacks of chairs. Lots of dust. Plastic containers in burlap sacks. Some beat-up lockers. Piled-up boxes. Musical instruments on shelves. A few dusty, forgotten books. Mr. Abacuc rummages around in some boxes and finally pulls out a bag that's covered with dust.

"Here they are. I hope they're still wearable and not completely moth-eaten." He passes it to me. "It's a boxing bag. It should contain some gloves, focus mitts, a mask, a speed bag, and I think even some mouthguards."

He unties the laces and yes, there inside is everything he said plus a jump rope, a jockstrap, and a cup to protect your balls.

"Tell Mrs. Merche to give you a little powdered detergent; wash these items in the laundry sink upstairs and hang them up to dry on the clothesline. Then come back down."

"What was this place used for?" I ask Mr. Abacuc.

He turns to look at the chaos around him.

"The only thing this room ever does is fill up with dust and useless junk."

Mrs. Merche gives me the soap and a nylon-bristled brush. I go up to the roof to wash the equipment. I dump everything out in the sink and start with the smallest items. I grab the mouthguard and wash it meticulously, as if I were cleaning the treasures in an Egyptian tomb. I rinse it and then look around. "This must go in your mouth." I put it in and confirm that, yes, it does go in your mouth, but the previous owner must have had crooked teeth, because mine don't fit into its grooves. I spit it out and wash it again. I move on to the gloves and see they're stained with dark blood. I scrub at them with the brush until all that's left is just a few scuffs that I can't get out. Then the focus mitts, mask, jockstrap, and cup. The cup is too small for my fucking package. I also wash the jump rope and finally the bag. It's coming unstitched along one seam, and a hole is forming. I wash it carefully until it's white instead of gray. The red and black trim gleams. I hang it up to dry on the clothesline. I can't see much of the city from there. Just some tall buildings, nearby trees, and somewhere out there, lost amid the ghostly zone and Wells Park, must be the chickadee's building.

* * *

["Jefe, why do you use so many bad words when you're by yourself and none at all when you're with customers?"

"What goddamn motherfucking bad words do I use, you fucking pinche interfering bastard?"

"Those ones."

"Those aren't fucking goddamn bad words; bad words are the ones you hear in soap operas coming from those pinches motherfucking respectable people with clean consciences and filthy asses, or from fucking Republican sons-of-bitches, goddamn limp-dicked pachyderms. Now those are bad words. Vote for me, I'll make things better, apply for a fucking mortgage, you're the king of your castle. Assholes. The way I talk is a way of expressing ideas without fucking dressing them up in pretty bullshit, you little prick."]

I finish hanging up the jump rope and go down to breakfast. The little runts move aside for me; it's like I'm in a glass bubble and it's pushing them out of the way with a gravitational force field. Only Naomi comes up to me in her wheelchair and sets her plate down next to mine.

"If you were a tree, what kind of tree would you be?"

I stick my spoon back in my oatmeal.

"Why are you so weird, kid?"

"You think I'm weird?"

"Really weird."

"And is that good or bad?"

I think for a moment.

"It's weird."

Naomi dips her spoon to her plate and scoops up some oatmeal.

"Did you really tell Mr. Shine you want to clean out that room and set up a library?"

"Who told you that?"

"Oh, Liborio, everyone always finds out about everything around here."

"Damn busybodies."

"Well? Did you?"

"No."

"Can I help?"

Coach Truddy arrives after nine in the morning. He's carrying a pair of boxing gloves under his arm and a large bowl of water. Ms. Webber takes the kids over to a corner of the gym where the blackboards are and starts teaching her English class. Naomi and the little squirts turn to look at us from time to time. Ms. Webber notices and raises her voice, and they immediately look back at the blackboard.

"Did you go running this morning?" Coach Truddy asks, dropping the gloves onto the wooden floor.

I nod.

"Well, at least you're not lazy," he says. "Let's see." He pulls a wrinkled sheet of paper from his sweatpants. He reads out loud: "Boxing is the world's most challenging, difficult, and demanding sport. Mastering it requires consistency and discipline. Plus a great deal of perseverance to transcend the limits of human effort . . ."

"Coach Truddy," I interrupt. "Have you ever trained anyone to box before?"

His pink cheeks flush even pinker. He's sweating like a pig.

"You're the first," the giant says, and then, to make up for his lack of expertise, adds, "But I did some boxing when I was younger and I know a little about it."

"How about not reading anymore and having me do some sparring instead?"

Coach Truddy crumples up the piece of paper and tucks it into his sweatsuit, bends over, and lies down heavily on the floor, faceup.

"You're quite right, my boy. But first we've got to get you in shape. Do a hundred sit-ups like this." He demonstrates with great difficulty. His breathing becomes oinkish. "When you go down, oof, and come up again, oof, exhale, ooof, hard."

I lie down next to him and start counting.

"1, 2, 3, 4, 5, 6, 7, 8, 9, 10, 11, 12, 13, 14, 15, 16, 17, 18, 19, 20, 21, 22, 23, 24, 25, 26, 27, 28, 29, 30, 31, 32, 33"—I start to feel a little tickle in my abs—"34, 35, 36, 37, 38, 39, 40, 41, 42, 43"—yeah, now it's getting hard to sit up, feels like my stomach's on fire—"44, 45, 46, 47, 48 . . ."

"Keep at it, son. Two more and you're halfway there."

". . . 49, 50." I collapse.

"Nobody said it was going to be easy. Now you've just got fifty left."

When I finish, he has me do a hundred squats until my ass cheeks feel as fiery as a mandrill's.

". . . 98, 99, 100." I'm sweating buckets, as if the seed of every river were boring through my forehead. I drink the water the coach holds out to me.

"Now give me ten push-ups. Like this, look: first you have to, oof, lower your whole chest, oof, oooof, until it almost touches the floor and then, ooooof, you push up again to, oooooof, work your biceps and triceps. Inhale, oooooof, at the top and exhale, uuuuuuh, at the bottom."

"But Coach, you're lowering your belly first."

"Shut up and get to it."

After another three sets of each exercise, the coach gets to his feet. My legs and arms are shaking. I don't know if I can stand.

"Now let's work on a little technique." He picks up the gloves and instructs me, "Hold out your arms so I can put these on you."

I hold out my arms, which are jellying all over the place. After twenty and a half push-ups, I'm beat. The coach puts the gloves on me and then lets go of them. They feel incredibly heavy, so heavy that I practically pitch forward onto my face.

"Don't fall," he says, grabbing me around the chest so I don't hit the floor. "You have to get used to carrying that weight on you like it's part of your own body."

"What do I do now?" I say, my arms hanging at my sides.

"Raise your gloves and get in a boxing stance, like this."

"I can't," I tell him.

"What do you mean, you can't?! All right then . . ."—and he throws a flying punch at my head. I immediately block it with my left glove. "Wait, didn't you say you couldn't do it?"

He keeps lashing out at me right and left for me to dodge or block with my gloves.

The little kids start shrieking.

"Miss, they're fighting."

Ms. Webber raises her voice to its maximum volume.

"Coach Truddy, would you be so kind as to not interrupt the education of these children with your savageries?"

Coach Truddy lowers his fists and, already bright red,

flushes even more deeply. He tries to calm down and regain his composure, though he's still grating copious cheese-like shreds of sweat all over his body.

"I'm sorry, Ms. Webber." He walks toward the bleachers and sits down. "We're done for today," he says as I, too, sit down. "We have to start slow or you could hurt yourself." He draws a deep breath. "Mr. Shine told me they found some boxing equipment and a jump rope. Tomorrow I want you to jump rope for half an hour, all right? That'll help you build up more speed and get a lot faster."

I nod, my whole body dazed, while he takes off my gloves. He sets them down on one of the risers.

"Here, kid, take this so you never forget what I told you." He takes the crumpled paper out of his pants pocket and holds it out to me.

He gets up and walks off, shuffling his feet. I feel a little bit sorry for the giant. He pushes open the Eliason doors and disappears. I look at the paper with shaking hands, then turn it over and over again and confirm, yes, to my surprise, that the paper is blank and there's nothing written on it.

At two in the afternoon I go to the dining room with the other boys and girls who've just finished their classes with Ms. Webber. Naomi settles down next to me.

"How was the training?"

"What, didn't you see it?"

"Occasionally."

"Well, it was brutal."

The cook comes up to us with a tray loaded with several plates with a scoop of rice and a chicken wing each.

"The coach told me you need to eat a lot of protein so you gain muscle mass, kidling, but we don't have a lot of that here, so you're going to have to eat what the rest of us eat, all right?"

"No problem," I tell her. "When in Rome, you've gotta

poop what you eat, cooo, cooo, cooo." I flap my sore arms like a chicken.

The kids around me and Mrs. Merche laugh at my outburst.

"Check this guy out—he makes them laugh," says the cook, smiling.

"They're afraid of him, but I think they like him," Naomi says.

The kids drop their glum eyes to the table and prop their elbows there like scraps of meat.

"And what about you, squirt—why are you sticking to this chimp like glue? Stay away from him—you don't want to fall in love and make things worse."

Naomi lets out a childish laugh, just like that, smooth, level, no furrows to blunt its innocence.

"You say the funniest things, Mrs. Merche! I'm going to study hard to be a great lawyer and defend every individual's human rights, and nothing's more important than that."

"My goodness. That's wonderful, sweetie. Study hard so you can fight the bad guys. But forewarned is forearmed, Little Ms. Lawyer." She guffaws and moves off to keep passing out plates to the other kids.

* * *

["And how did you meet your missus, boss?"

"What does that matter, you esoteric prick! That's between the two of us and nobody else!"

"Is it embarrassing?"

"Yes."]

I take out a dusty chair and sit in the middle of the room. I need to figure out where to start in cleaning up the fucking pigsty. I close my eyes to think for a minute.

"Don't go to sleep," says Naomi at my elbow.

I know, yes, I'm pooped.

I can't move without my eyelashes hurting.

I ache worse from the workout than if I'd been thrashed by a million policemen lined up Indian file. I hadn't realized I had muscles under my muscles. Even my teeth hurt. But no pain, no gain.

"Oh, my mandrill ass," I complain as I stand up from the chair so I don't pass out from exhaustion.

"Where should we start?" I ask Naomi, my thoughts jumbled from fatigue, holding a broom in one hand and a couple of buckets with rags in the other.

"We should choose a name first, right? This morning I was thinking we could call it the Liberty and Nature Library. What do you think? *Liberty* because of *L* for Liborio and *Nature* because of *N* for my name. We can hide our own names in the name of the library—isn't that great?"

"Or we can call it the We'll Fix It Up Later Library," I say, my eyes near to bursting with the strain of keeping them open.

"That name's no good, silly. But for now we could start by dusting off those books that are dumped over there in the back of that bookcase."

"These?" I pull them out of the sediment of centuries spent gathering lint, dust, and ancient cobwebs. "It's only four books!"

"That's the best way to start!" Naomi is practically hopping in her seat. "Just think, some libraries in the world probably started with even fewer books, maybe one or not even that—maybe there was one that started out with no books at all!" She laughs again, euphoric, her eyes full of delight and hope, showing her missing teeth. All the innocence of the air must be sneaking into her through the gaps.

It never rains, and when it rains everything shakes. Not a quaking of the fucking earth but of the sky. I didn't hear anything at first, not thunder or lightning, or even the fertile rain when it started to fall.

Once Naomi and I finished cleaning the whole room and dusting the shelves so we could set up our library's four books, corralling all the boxes in the back of the room, and hanging the instruments on some screws that were poking out of the wall, I went straight to my room and, without even having dinner, flopped onto the bed, like that, like a human smoothie that's dumped all its bones.

Deep in my dreams, I heard the voice of . . . Aireen?

"At least have some pan dulce."

I started chewing with my eyes closed until I finished it and then, boom, I was already on the other side, weightless, without any dreams that might disturb my rest; like that, empty, playing tricks on my subconscious so it would leave me alone.

And it did, because I didn't dream about anything.

A megalithic clap of thunder wakes me up, and I hear the water falling outside like a swarm of fucking broken glass. My ears are alert but I can't move, as if I've been buried alive and an intravenous catalepsy has robbed me of my will. I can't even shout. My voice has been abducted by a phantasmagorical opiape, a morbid acquiescence. I turn my head toward the fluorescent blue clock and feel thousands of little cramps in my muscle fibers, as if microscopic devils were pricking me with their tails and tridents.

The clock flashes 4:38.

In a few minutes I'll have to get up to start my second day of training, and I'm so dead tired, it feels as if my muscles are my own coffin. Why do we have to sacrifice in order to move forward in space? Why does my body hurt so much, as if a supernova has imploded inside my bones?

The clock grinds 4:49.

Fuck. Fuck. Fuck.

Chingafuck.

I wriggle on the bed. I stick out one foot and then the other, wincing with pain. Outside, the rain falls granitically. What if I stay here under the covers? I could give it all up, quit. After all, nobody can force me to get up and walk!

The clock wriggles too: 4:56.

Fuck.

No pain, no gain.

Does that go for love, too?

5:01.

Fuck.

I get moving, like I don't care about any of it, and leap out of bed. My muscles shriek, go numb; they shackle all my bones like bars made of invisible thread. The pain is strong, really strong, but my thirst is even stronger.

I get dressed and go out.

Outside the rain has soaked the chickens. I carry a wooden board that was in the library room up to the roof and arrange it so they can shelter themselves under it and not catch a cold or coryza or what the hell ever.

No need to water the garden now, just hope the roots don't rot from all the water falling on them.

I pull the soaked punching bag, gloves, focus mitts, mask, mouthguard, jockstrap, cup, and jump rope off the clothesline. I take them downstairs and hang them to dry in the foyer. Then I open the front door of the shelter.

The rain keeps falling.

There's nobody on the street, not a soul moving down any of the avenues, not a crack of dawn. The traffic lights change colors in streets empty of cars.

It's raining hard, shattering the sky.

Wells Park is empty too. I don't see the black woman's shopping cart or anyone sleeping there on the sodden grass. There are no runners or athletes wearing out the gravel path with their footsteps. I'm alone, desertedly alone among the trees and flowers that are feeding off the storm clouds. Cold water is running down my body, discoloring my fingernails. My breath is steaming. Today is Thursday, and I think maybe Aireen might show up somewhere later on, maybe amid the foliage, walking Candy on a leash, and I'll be able to look at her the way I did that first day I saw her. But that's impossible. The air is making me dizzy. With the cold fumbling through my guts, I start running along the rocky path until my muscles either kill me or make me stronger.

* * *

[*"If there were a fire, flood, or earthquake, which of these books would you save, Jefe?"*

"There aren't any floods here, you califragilistic prick, or earthquakes either."

"What about fires?"

"As far as I can remember, there's never been a fucking fire of any sort."

"Well, if you had to go to a desert island, what book would you take with you?"

"Why would I go to a fucking desert island, you blockheaded louse? And why would I take a fucking book with me and not a hot broad?"

"I don't know, Jefe, maybe because the banks are chasing you across heaven and earth like fucking pirates, looking to chop off your head."

"Stop inventing complete nonsense and get to mopping."]

"Good Lord! You're going to make yourself sick, you nitwit," Mrs. Merche tells me when she sees me go by the door. I'm a walking, dripping bowl of soup, unraveling rain on a wave-swept cliff. My body is literally giving off steam from under my arms, my chest, the back of my neck, my rump.

"What happened to the boxing equipment I left hanging up over there?" I ask as she hands me a shabby, threadbare towel so I can dry off.

"I put them next to the fireplace so they'd dry faster . . . I saw you covered up the chickens. Thank you very much—I was out like a light last night and didn't hear a thing."

"Do you know how to jump rope?" I ask out of the blue.

Mrs. Merche's eyes light up.

"Oh boy, centuries ago, yeah."

"Can you teach me?"

Mrs. Merche hesitates. She runs her fingers through her hair, which is shot through with gray and pulled back in a braid.

"But you can't tell anybody, O.K.?"

"Nobody, I promise."

* * *

[*"I've got another fantastic story in my head that'll sell millions in Hollywood," says the Latinoid writer, who's come into the store wanting to buy a book on cybernetic murder called* Cyber Gang Bang *written by a young Spanish woman, Jaira Droom, who just won the Medellín Fiction Prize. "Want to hear it?"*

"No," says Jefe categorically.

"What about you?" The pedantic praline has turned to me.

Jefe looks at me too and smiles mischievously.

"Oh, yeah, he's definitely interested."]

"No, no, no. Pay attention. For every turn of the rope, you have to count off the syllables. Watch." Mrs. Merche takes the jump rope again and starts jumping as she chants, 'White shoe, blue shoe, tell me, how old are you? Five! 1, 2, 3, 4, 5, out you go with a double-u.' Your turn."

I take the jump rope and start over.

"White shoe, blue shoe, tell me, how old are you? Five! 1, 2, 3, 4, 5, out you go with a double-u."

And finally, the million-and-fifth time, I make it through the entire song.

"Look," says Naomi at breakfast. "I got two more books for our library."

She puts them on the table, and I see that they're coloring books. One is called *Paint Your Rights*, and the other, *Bambi*.

I've already read *Bambi*, so I pick up the other one and read it in the blink of an eye.

"That's great, Naomi. They're just what we were looking for."

She smiles.

It hasn't stopped raining all day. The clouds are still clustered up there, and the noise in the gym is deafening because of the tin roof. A few spots are leaking, and we put out buckets to keep water from pooling on the floor. We cover the piano with blue plastic tarps. Ms. Webber has had to take the kids to our library, where, with the help of Mr. Abacuc, Coach Truddy, and me, she's set up a blackboard and the chairs.

"But what about the library?" Naomi asks Ms. Webber, clearly distressed.

"It'll still be a library too, young lady," Ms. Webber answers, looking at me from behind her cat's-eye glasses.

Coach Truddy and I are the only ones in the gym now. He's brought a drill and his toolbox so I can help him set up the speed bag, the punching bag, and the crazy bag, a ball that will be tied to the ceiling and floor with thick cords, all in the corner where Ms. Webber used to give classes.

I pass him items as he drills and screws.

"We have to get you checked out with a doctor to make sure you don't have any heart or head problems so we can apply for a boxing license," he says, settling the screwdriver against a screw and tightening the support for the speed bag. "Have you ever been to the doctor?"

"Yes."

"And what did he tell you?"

"That I had worms."

* * *

[*"And not just worms, ma'am—he's not getting enough calcium or any other vitamins and minerals. Just look at those blotches on his skin. The boy's so malnourished he's practically anemic. Are you sure you're feeding your son properly?"*

"He's not my son, doctor, and I give him lots of garlic for the worms."]

The shelter's showers are in a cement room at the back of the gym. There's hardly ever hot water. In fact, the two times I've showered it was with cold water. When I get out of the shower, it's still raining.

After installing the speed bags, Coach Truddy tells me amid the din of the raindrops on the tin roof, "The punching bag . . . with sand and sawdust . . . pieces of wood . . . get a . . . tomorrow. Do you know how to sew . . . ? It doesn't matter . . . help . . . daughter . . . I'll take . . . punching bag . . . in the end . . . installed . . . mount . . . tensors . . . hinges . . . ha-ha-ha . . ."

I can barely hear him. The noise of the rain on the roof is earsplitting. But I agree to everything he says, my donkey ears pricked up as if I were listening to it all.

* * *

[*"What the hell, boss, next time I'll kick you in the nuts!"*

"And why's that, greaseball?"

"You stuck me with that pompous ass."
"Calm down, ape-face. That vato just wants someone to talk to—he's lonely."]

I'm reading one of the library's six books when somebody knocks on the door of my room.

"I'm reading, Naomi. Did you already finish the book you checked out?"

"You have a visitor," says Mrs. Merche on the other side of the door.

My heart leaps wildly. But before I can even imagine that it might be Aireen who's come, pleading, to leap into my arms and cut off our breath with kisses, that lady Double-U bounds into the room wearing a platinum-blond wig, a minidress, and gold high heels and carrying a small gold purse bedazzled with little rhinestones.

"Oh, damn, I caught you dressed, papito, what a shame—I was hoping to see you naked again," she laughs.

Mrs. Merche peeks in and sees my startled face, and I see her disapproving one.

"Everything all right?" the cook asks in her sternest tone.

"Yeah, yeah, everything's fine," Double-U interrupts. "Could you just give us a few minutes so we can take care of a little business that doesn't concern you?"

Mrs. Merche interrogates me with a reproving look.

"I just want to chitchat with my nephew, who's harder to track down than a kilo of adamantium in firecracker country."

"I'll leave the door open in case you want to take off running, son," Mrs. Merche snarks. She looks Double-U up and down one last time and then goes off grumbling down the hall.

"What gives? You've found yourself a cranky mom now, kid? You should have let me know the position was open so I could apply—I'd be happy to breastfeed you!" She lets out the disheveled laugh of a boisterous chatterbox.

"What are you doing here?" I break in, my brow furrowed.

Double-U stops fluttering around my room, where she's already touched everything—the clock, the wardrobe, the table—and sits down on the bed.

"First of all"—she lowers her voice, as if she didn't want me to hear her—"I want to apologize for the other night. I shouldn't have . . . you know, I was very inconsiderate. See, I've always been really selfish. I didn't think about how I might be hurting you, and I did. I'm really sorry about that. Truly. I went out to look for you that night, but you zipped off faster than a snake. I even talked to some police officer friends of mine who patrol the area and asked them to look for you and make sure nothing happened to you, since you'd left your boots at my house. They told me they spotted you and you took off running like a shot, and you're so slippery, they couldn't catch you." She pauses to take a breath. "I'm truly sorry, kid, I didn't think you'd get so upset. I thought I was doing something big to change things in this fucking country, but I didn't know how to handle the situation. I was all dazzled from suddenly becoming famous overnight." She pauses again. She examines her fingernails and then looks up and meets my eyes with hers, which are shadowed in gold and blue and festooned with kilometric curly black eyelashes. "Do you forgive me, kid?"

I don't say either yes or no. In her masked eyes, like the shoulder of a wide highway traced by eyeliner and mascara, I see sadness—but it's a hard sadness, as if melancholy or whatever had solidified behind her peepers. Or maybe her sadness is a deceitful regret. I don't know.

"How did you find me?" I ask harshly.

She half smiles. In that moment, just in that moment, for a fraction of an instant, I see real melancholy, a faint spark behind all her makeup. Then it disappears and immediately the calcareous Double-U is back again.

"Oof, don't even ask. I went all over the place. I even met

your enormous friends from that video they uploaded to YouTube, which has overtaken mine in number of hits. Sniff. Over twelve million and still going up like a rocket . . . You sure gave that crazy vato quite a wallop. By the way, those big guys are looking for you too. But I'm getting ahead of myself. Day before yesterday I waited a long time in front of that building where I found you wearing those gloves, and I saw a really pretty girl arrive; superlative reporter that I am, I thought she might be able to give some hints as to your whereabouts. I asked her about you, and she was nervous at first, but then she told me she did know you but she didn't know where you were, but that I could ask a friend of hers who'd been there and helped her when you passed out on the street, offering to take you to the hospital in a taxi. Did you really pass out? Anyway, to make a long story short, she gave me the guy's number and this morning I went to visit him at the hospital and he gave me the address of this dump. That quack isn't very cooperative. What's his name? Hang on, I have it written down right here. Leonardo Zubirat? You know him? Is he a friend of yours? 'Cause if he is, oh man, nice bunch of friends you've got. But you know how I am. I told him I'd accuse him of kidnapping, attempted homicide, unlawful deprivation of liberty, slander, defamation, being ugly, faggotry, and any other bullshit I could think of in the moment. I'm an expert with that kind of accusation, you know—just ask my ex-husband. Anyway, I was going to come here earlier but the goddamn rain has been a real bitch . . . Oh, by the way, your new mom let me in and she thinks I'm your aunt, all right?" She pauses as a bolt of lightning cracks across the sky and we hear a long roll of thunder. "Is it true you're going to start boxing to win some money for this dump?"

"It's not a dump."

"Fine, then, sassbucket, I take it back."

She gets up from the bed and goes over to the window. She

pulls back the curtains and looks out at the shelter's courtyard, which is filled with puddles. The rain keeps running down the windowpanes, and the blue of twilight is fading.

"I have a plan! Don't you want to hear it?"

"No."

"It's so you'll forgive me, kid, and that way you win and I don't lose," says Double-U, still staring out the window. The streetlights are lit up with mercury needles like darts falling at random. "Come on! It's nothing too over the top." She bends her knee toward the ceiling to rest her feet from those stilts she's tottering around on, and her skirt scoots a couple of inches higher on her thighs. She's not wearing pantyhose, and I can almost sense she's not wearing any underwear either.

"Why are you doing this?"

"Doing what?"

"Coming looking for me. Trying to change the world. Making plans and more plans. What the fuck do you want from me? What are you looking for?! . . . I'm nothing . . . I'm a nobody, always have been, and you are somebody—look at yourself, you've got the whole future in front of you, or what the hell ever."

Double-U looks away from the window, as if she's suddenly lost interest in watching swampy puddles form in the courtyard, and stares at me instead. It seems like the rain has gotten stuck to her eyes through a transmutation of the elements, because a frail, minuscule, watery thread starts slowly, very slowly, cutting down her cheek till it reaches her fire-engine-red lips.

"You're wrong about that."

I don't know what to think. Other people's tears are outside my fucking wheelhouse, out of reach of my possibilities. I don't try to do anything because I don't know what to do. The lady dribbles a little as she readjusts her skirt to its original position.

"You're right, this is really dumb." She starts to leave but then pauses in the doorway and says, without looking at me, "Just do me one last favor, will you?"

"What?"

"Give me an interview about your fight and I'll promote it for you."

Double-U doesn't wait for my answer. She hurries out of the room and I hear her high heels disappear into the rain.

* * *

[*"Hey, boss, a guy from the bank really is out there looking for you right now. Should I tell him you died yesterday or the day before?"*

"Don't be a moron, you dodecaphonic shitwit. Tell him I'm traveling or out of the country or to go fuck himself and you don't know anything at all because you're a goddamn useless mental midget."

"Will do, Jefe. I hope they don't nab you the way they did El Tigre de Santa Julia."

"Shut up, you variegated varicella, and let me shit in peace."]

The sky is quiet; the only sound is the moon sucking at the sunken puddles. I thought I wasn't going to be able to sleep after Double-U's visit and everything she told me. I start going over it as I lie there in bed, especially the part about Aireen. But before I can get through the whole thing, I am delimbed under the covers like Coyolxauhqui's twin brother.

It's my third day of training, and I have to come back to life from the bottom of the rock, from the bottom of my own muscles that have turned into sarcophagi.

3:47.

I leap out of bed.

The sky is limpid, as if the curve of the Earth were a huge

retina and all obstacles had been swept away by a giant eye-lid.

I feed the chickens, which have contracted head colds.

The garden still has the ravages of the drowned; since there were no flowers to ruin, the downpour ruined many of the plants. I pick up the broom and start sweeping the water toward the drain. Then I keep going with the rest of the roof. I adjust some rotten planks from the planters and tie them in place with wire. Then I go downstairs and keep disheveling the puddles in the courtyard toward the drain. I never, not in a single one of the fucking novels from the bookstore, read about a fucking character working to sweep up the mess around him. Or washing the dishes or callusing his hands with everyday toil. Fucking loser-ass writers see life all clean, without any wrinkles to sully their goddamn white pages.

Wells Park starts to fill up with boys and girls. They come out of the woodwork. It's as if after the storm comes movement. Some gringas with muddy workout gear clinging to their curves are jogging together. Others are out in hats and sunglasses. Up ahead, people are bending and straightening up. A few chaneques are gamboling and leaping and crouching. I've already done one more lap around the park than I did yesterday. My shins are hurting less and less. My sneakers are still damp, even though I put them next to the fire to dry yesterday.

"That lady's not your aunt," Mrs. Merche said as soon as I went into the kitchen to drop off the sneakers and get something to eat.

"She's a friend."

"She's a hussy."

"No."

"I wasn't born yesterday, kid."

"She told me you act like my mother."

"If I were your mother, I'd have spanked you already."

"What for?"

"For being a troublemaking mongrel."

In the park, the birds start simmering in the trees. I leave the path, cross the street, and round the block. I climb up the stone steps and shove open the door. I race up the stairs and knock on her door.

I knock again, louder.

A light goes on inside.

I knock a third time.

"What's going on?"

I knock again.

Aireen opens the door. Her hair is a mess. She's wearing pajamas with little pink bears on them. She's surprised to see me standing there, sweaty, holding a little piece of paper.

"Is someone after you, dude?"

"Is this your handwriting?"

"What?"

I hold out the piece of paper and she takes it in her drowsy fingers. She rubs her eyes with her other hand. She reads it. She looks up. "No, dude. This isn't mine."

Without saying anything, just like that, out of the blue, I plant a kiss on her sleepy lips. Like that, swift, adolescent. Taking her face in my hands. A clean kiss, no tongue. Just my lips and hers.

Immediately I turn around and take off toward the street like a bat out of hell.

* * *

["Didn't you say you were going to the restaurant right now to eat with the love of your life, Jefe?"

"Yes indeedy, you pitted spermatozoid. You look after the fucking shop. Careful you don't fuck it up."

"Oh, that's great, boss, because your missus just called to tell you she's on her way with your little misters. Apparently one of them fell at school and broke his snout."]

I train harder today; my veins bulge from the effort. I deliver a few solid blows to the punching bag stuffed with sand and sawdust that Coach Truddy brought in, sewn by his daughter.

"You hit like the devil, boy, but that's not enough to win a fight. You also need brains and heart," the coach says, bracing the bag for me and getting redder with every kick. When he gets tired, he takes me over to the speed bag, panting his guts out. "The speed bag," he says in a strangled voice, getting in position, "is all about rhythm. Look. One with the right and one and two with the left. Then you change stance: one and two with the right and one with the left. Got it? Like that, slowly at first, really slowly, and then gradually pick up the pace."

"How's it going, Coach Truddy?" Mr. Abacuc is coming toward us, holding a few posters.

"Well, I don't know, Mr. Shine. The boy still hits the bag however and whenever he feels like it, and he still seems a bit too stubborn to learn. I'd say he's naturally hardheaded. Instructions go in one ear and I watch them sail out the other."

"Oh dear, Coach Truddy! Do you think he can be ready tomorrow?"

"What? Hadn't we agreed on the 17th?"

"There's a benefit fight tomorrow, and they need a competitor. Mrs. Marshall learned about it and asked if we might do them the favor . . . You know how Mrs. Marshall is. I tried to refuse, but she always works her charms on me."

"What charms would those be? She just uses her influence to beef up donations. The old harpy!" Coach Truddy objects, irritated.

"Don't be so hard on her, Coach. It's because of her and her marvelous proposals to the citizen board that we have those big, magnificent holes in our roof."

"Bah!" Coach Truddy glances up at the leaks, which are starting to look like stalactites.

"I want to fight." I interrupt their conversation and step in front of Mr. Abacuc.

"Do you feel ready, Liborio?"

I don't have to think about it long, so I answer with absolute sincerity:

"No."

"What are you smiling about?" Naomi asks me.

I ignore her and keep reading. The library has a new patron, a little squirt who spotted the *Bambi* book and is really going at it as he scribbles on the deer's horns.

"Is it because you're going to be boxing tomorrow?" Naomi continues, looking for the gazillionth time at the poster for Saturday's event that I tacked up on the wall beside the blackboard. "Even though your name isn't on the poster?"

The poster says in English and Spanish:

Saturday Boxing 6:00 P.M. Sábado de Box 18:00. Ford Foundation Center. Contribution: $1,000.00. Donativo: $1,000.00. For our children. Por nuestros niños. Poverty Association. John Pantos vs. Dulls Jara. Dwight Amir vs. Alanis Stanton. Jerry Knox vs. Will Servin. H. G. Flores vs. Anatoly Plinsk. Jim Vernon vs. Auden Reed. Cocktail dinner after the event. Cena coctel después del evento. Your strength inspires us. Tu fuerza nos ayuda.

The book I'm reading is called *1958-1959 Report on the Government Deficit*, and I haven't understood a word. But it seemed like the most appealing title out of all the ones we've managed to acquire for our library.

* * *

[In other words, as Jefe used to say, "When there isn't any bread, eat tortillas, you pugilistic pain-in-the-ass," though it's really hard to find cornmeal on this side of the border and even harder to find tortillas that aren't cold corn chips from Taco Grill or, in any event, books that touch my brainmeal with their ill-fitting words.]

My eyes keep automatically skimming over the words in English in this old book I don't actually understand, but I don't care—I'm thinking about other things. I suck on my upper lip; I touch it softly with the tip of my tongue.

I smile again.

"Or are you smiling like a slug because that book is really funny?" Naomi asks again from over next to the boy at the little table coloring Bambi's fur purple. She wheels herself over to me. "Could you loan it to me when you finish?"

"Uh-huh," I say absently, biting my lips, my mind far from my body.

Mr. Abacuc has an ancient Voyager van that he uses to transport supplies to keep the shelter going. He hardly ever drives it for personal use because he prefers walking; besides, he says the traffic in the city has gotten worse and worse since the seventh decade of the last century. "An old man can't go through life being cursed at for driving too slowly by all these neurotic people. It doesn't seem fair."

"Don't forget to take this case," Coach Truddy says as he anxiously places a black-and-yellow crate in the trunk of his own car, a 1981 automatic Ford Fairmont that he restored himself; it's in mint condition. We've packed the crate full of all the boxing equipment we've been able to find. I also stuck in a pair of red shorts and an ancient T-shirt with the name of some gringo vato that I found in the boxes of winter donations. Mrs. Merche gave me a pair of athletic socks. "After all, your socks, which I've never seen you wear, have more holes in them than a colander. And without sockrags, feet stink like Gruyere cheese, ugh."

Ms. Webber has an assignment too. With her arid eyes, she's responsible for assembling the boys and girls who are going to go with us to the boxing match—"because Mrs. Marshall needs to show us off for the press" to demonstrate that her charity cases are flesh-and-blood and not just figments of her imagination.

"Remember to jump the rope with each syllable, kid, and don't forget the other chants I taught you," Mrs. Merche tells me as she places a basket of food in the front seat of the van, "so you don't go around starving. Remember, as they say, 'Full belly, happy heart.'" She's going to stay behind and look after the shelter while the rest of us go to the Ford Foundation Center.

Naomi's coming too. She is, she claims, the official cheer captain of Bridge House's cheerleading squad. She's made some little paper flags from pieces of old newspaper and they've painted them red, green, and blue. She tells her subordinates, "We've got to shout a lot and make a lot of noise, all right?"

"Like this?" asks a little lieutenant of about four, and then emits such a piercing shriek that we all turn to stare. "Aaaaaaaaaah!"

"Just like that!" Naomi says after she takes her fingers out of her ears.

"We also need to take a cooler of water," the coach says.

"We don't have any coolers, coach," Mrs. Merche replies. "Let the rich people provide that." She pulls out a couple of large empty bottles. "And if you can, have them send along a sack of sugar too."

Mr. Abacuc goes into his office and comes out carrying a Kodak camera.

"Ms. Webber, do you think they still sell rolls of film for this camera?"

The teacher glances at the camera in Mr. Abacuc's hands and says sarcastically, "They don't even make that brand anymore." She makes a sour face. "I think your best bet is rolls of bandages to bury this relic." And she keeps giving the kids instructions. "Coach Truddy . . ." She calls to him and walks over to the Fairmont, where the coach is putting away the empty bottles of water.

I finish loading the cases into the rear of the van and settle down there. I take out the sheet of paper the trainer gave me this morning and read it again so I can memorize it: "No hitting below the waist. No head-butting. No kicking your opponent. No biting. No elbowing. No spitting. No hitting after the bell rings. No insults . . ." No, no, and no. "Fuck!" I say to myself again. "And I thought this was going to be easy."

"Is everything loaded up, son?"

"Yes," I tell the coach. "Though I don't know if we're missing something."

"How are you feeling? Are you nervous?"

"I don't know."

"What do you mean, you don't know? I was like jelly when I used to fight on the battleship."

"How many times did you fight, coach?"

"Enough."

"I don't know how I feel. This boxing business sure has a lot of rules. Why are there so many?"

"So what happened to me won't happen to you, son: debut and dismissal."

The Ford Foundation Center looks small from the road. Naomi points it out to me from the passenger seat.

"There's the Ford complex, Liborio." We've got her wheel-chair tied to the roof of the van.

Coach Truddy and the four oldest kids from the shelter are in the car in front of us. Mr. Abacuc is driving the Voyager, and there are eight of us in the back: three boys, four girls, and me.

The kid from the library looks at me as we turn at an intersection and continue onto a cobblestone drive with lights and splendid arches and decorated with neatly pruned trees. "Are you scared?"

"How can I be scared, Bambi, when nothing's happening yet?"

"Oh . . ." He sits there with his mouth open, drooling a little.

Naomi exclaims, "Look! It's the fountain of dancing lights!"

The kids stretch wildly and plaster themselves to the left-hand window. The fountain gets big and then little, and it has lights that make its guts glow: blue, purple, red, green, yellow, rose, oak, carnation, marmot. I, too, am amazed and nudge a kid to give me some room at the window until we reach the guardhouse of the complex.

We see Coach Truddy hand over his access pass to a guard, they give him instructions, and the automatic arm rises. He enters the complex. Then it's our turn.

"Where are you going?" the guard asks.

"Where do you think? We're from Bridge House and we're here to win!" says Naomi, not mincing her words.

Mr. Abacuc hands over the invitation and the guard reads it.

"Keep going straight, sir, and park in front of walkway B."

The arm goes up, and we go in.

The grounds are beautiful, full of green and lights. Large grassy lawns and planters filled with perennial flowers. Trees all in a row and ringed by white river stones and reddish bark.

The paving stones are octagonal and perfectly suited to the landscape. The large dome of the foundation's building looks huge now. Round and virginally white. We reach the parking area and Mr. Abacuc finds our assigned spot. There are already lots of cars, like at the mall.

He parks the van with a single movement of the wheel.

"Wow, we're here, can you believe it?" says Mr. Abacuc as he raises the power windows and shuts off the van.

"Don't open the doors till I get out," directs Ms. Webber.

She gets out and then, yes, she opens the doors for us and we spill out of the van.

Two spots over, Coach Truddy is emerging from his Fairmont.

Ms. Webber lines the kids up in single file and instructs them to hold hands. She leads them out of the parking lot toward the main terrace.

Mr. Abacuc opens the trunk while I untie Naomi's wheelchair and get it down from the roof, placing it on the ground next to the passenger door.

"Do you want me to help you, Naomi?" I ask.

"No thanks, Liborio, I can do it on my own."

Naomi grabs on to the handle hanging from the roof, gathers momentum, and swings her legs out of the van. With some effort, she stands up and hovers there for a moment, then twists her body in the air and, like a genuine miracle, lowers her rear end into the wheelchair. Then she takes each of her legs in her hands and lifts them onto the footrests.

I'm staring at her like a monkey.

"You're a force of nature," I tell her, agape.

Naomi leans back in her chair and turns toward me.

She smiles.

"I hope you are too and win this fight. I'm just your cheer captain, you know!" she says. Then she goes over to Mr. Abacuc, picks up her box with the little flags, and puts it on her knees. She wheels herself toward Ms. Webber and the flock of kids.

I grab another box and go to help Coach Truddy lower the box of whatsits we've brought. The coach has already dragged the kids over to the terrace. He leaves them there and comes back to the van. We pick up all our things and head over to the group.

"Follow me," says Mr. Abacuc, leading the procession.

Naomi has already passed out the little paper flags to the kids, who start horsing around. Ms. Webber is carrying a flag too, though she's waving it reluctantly. We move down the terrace until we reach a large passageway full of planters and fountains. Mr. Abacuc turns right, and we all follow him like a freight train being pulled by elephantious camellage.

We enter the ballroom, and my jaw drops. It's an apollonian space, almost tragic in its circular beauty. All around it are Roman columns and capitals above marble friezes, like a modern pantheon built of gold and silver to bury Doña Blanca, like in the children's song. The ceiling resembles the Sistine Chapel. Impressive windows sweep from the floor to the ceiling. The walls are hung with large portraits in gilded frames of prominent men and women who may all be dead, since they look really old and have lots of wrinkles around their eyes.

On the floor, which is paved with herculean slabs of stone, blue chairs are arranged around the ring, which rises, immense, in the middle of the splendid room. Some members of the cleaning crew, dressed in light-blue overalls and wearing name tags pinned to their chests, are putting the finishing touches on the floor, the air, and anything else that looks out of place.

I study the ring. It's got blue in one corner and red in the other; the rest of it is white. Its ropes are black, and it's skirted with swaths of blue, white, and red cloth with gold trim. In the middle, printed on the canvas, are a large ad for the Ford

Foundation and smaller ads for Montblanc, Google, and a few dozen other companies whose names I can't read because they're upside down.

Below the ring are the tables covered with blue cloth where, Coach Truddy tells me, the judges usually sit. "But because today is an exhibition match, there will probably just be some members of the press sitting there."

We keep walking until we reach a table with some dapper men in navy blue suits and red ties. Mr. Abacuc speaks to them. They tell him that we need to split up: the kids will go sit in a special area where the other children from the other shelters will be. The handicapped and retarded kids will be in front. The coach and I are supposed to go to one of the doors at the rear, they say, where you see those satin curtains with yellow lace. There, they continue, we'll find the maintenance staff's bathroom, which will serve as the dressing room today. Across the room are the tables where the dappers will eat dinner after the boxing event.

"If we get going," says Mr. Abacuc, "we'll make it on time." He looks at his wristwatch. "Two minutes to five. Ms. Webber, please get the children seated. Coach, go with Liborio and explain everything to him again to make sure nothing goes wrong." He turns to me. "Focus, son!" Then he speaks to the group. "In the meantime, I'll go find Mrs. Marshall to let her know we're here."

"Don't let that Medusa catch you off guard," says Coach Truddy, looking around the room. "Remember our leaky roof."

When I push open the bathroom door, I find three scruffs in shorts, a little taller than me, already jumping and stretching, rotating their wrists and opening and closing their jaws to warm up. Two old-timers are sitting in one corner, talking.

The fucking maintenance staff bathroom is bigger than Aireen's entire apartment. Almost as big as the fucking bookstore.

There are some gray lockers mounted on the wall and four wooden benches right in the middle. It has two showers, two toilets, and two urinals. One wall has a large, gleaming mirror above four sinks and a beige marble counter. Across the room are some large shelves stocked with cleaning equipment: brooms, squeegees, rags, mops, yellow wringer buckets, two huge vacuum cleaners, and two floor polishers. Beside them is a high counter with a table lamp, a bound notebook with a pen attached by a chain, and a black chair.

I keep walking and put down my box in a corner away from the others, Coach Truddy following me. He sets his box down on top of mine, his whole porkish bulk greasily steaming.

"Have you been here before?" he asks me, out of breath and gobstoppered.

"No, coach, this is the first time. What about you?"

He coughs to dislodge a bit of lint from his throat.

"I came here once, but I was only outside on the terrace, giving out food to people who'd been affected by Hurricane Katrina."

He slumps down on one of the benches and stares at the guys who are hopping around a few yards away. From here, the angular muscles that mark their arms, neck, and chest are clearly visible. Not to mention their shins—their legs look like horses'. The two older guys are still chitchatting in the back. One is wearing a brown flat cap and the other's hair is slicked back. I spot a black earring in his left ear.

"Are they going to be boxing too?" Coach Truddy blunders, like that, all of a sudden.

The younger vatos stare at him, baffled. To alleviate the tension, I attempt to make a joke out of what the coach has just said.

"No, coach, we're here to play marbles."

The vatos don't react, but the other men do.

"What circuit are you from, gentlemen?" the one in the flat cap asks.

"Circuit? What circuit?" the coach blunders again.

"What equestrian club do you belong to, you dolts?" the earringed one says mockingly.

They burst out laughing.

The coach decides to exit the conversation and says to me, "You go ahead and get changed, son," and then, more loudly so the others can hear him, "Just remember what I told you: I don't want you psyching out your opponents."

"What do you mean, coach? Didn't you say the opposite before?" Now I'm the one who sticks his foot in it.

"Never mind, forget it."

At that, the grape apes laugh openly at us.

As I'm taking off my shirt, three other scruffs about my size come in. Their greeting suggests they've all known one another for ages. They dump their bags on the ground.

Now shirtless, I don't even try to flex my muscles like Chinese ticks to impress the dudes. What point would there be in pretending to have what anyone can see from miles off I don't? I take out the T-shirt, which smells like creosote, and pull it on.

"Bill for Prez," the coach reads the lettering on my donated shirt and then exclaims, "Take that prehistoric thing off! Don't you have anything else, son?"

"What's wrong, coach? This was the only one in the clothes boxes that didn't have holes in it."

"They're going to destroy us." He starts sweating hard.

"Why?"

"Everyone around here is a Republican. Jesus! Let's see the shorts."

I take the shorts out of the bag and show them to him.

"They're red, like Mr. Abacuc told me to look for."

"'Sexy,'" he reads the pink embroidery across the ass of the fucking red shorts. "Shit, shit, shit." He gets even more flushed. "They're going to break us in half and then excommunicate us."

At that moment the scruffs start laughing—they haven't missed a bit of what the coach and I were saying. As they're chortling, the bathroom door opens and three or four more guys come in. This is starting to feel like a bus station.

"What's going on?" asks one of the newcomers, who's got a tattoo cascading from his cheek down to his neck. "What's the ruckus all about? Let us in on the joke, you fucking pandas."

The man with the earring answers, snortling, "Seems like the heavens decided to send down a couple of clownettes for our entertainment. May I present the 'Sexy Democrat' and her 'Fucking Mother.'" He guffaws again, even louder, viciously, excaustic. The others laugh uproariously at us.

Coach Truddy hangs his head like a beaten dog. His cheeks are contrite and livid. He's not much for conflict. I turn around to put on the red shorts, and one of the guys pinches my nipple.

"All right, mamacita, pull down those panties and suck my cock," says the scruff in a rough Cuban accent.

They all burst out laughing in unison, like a goddamn alebrije circus.

His hand still on my chest, I stretch back like a fucking slingshot.

"Nobody touches me." I don't have to say anything else. I drive my fist toward his face and clock him in the chin.

He drops like a fucking flower with its petals stripped off.

And as quick as they started laughing, now they all fall abruptly into a deep silence that cuts the air.

"What a jab!" the guy with the flat cap interjects, yanking the hat off.

"You shut up!" the guy with the earring tells him as he dives toward the scruff sprawling on the floor. "Jara! Jara!" He slaps his cheek. "Wake up, Jara! . . . Jara! . . . Get the doctor. Jara! . . . Jara! Wake up, goddammit. Get up, damn it, you're in the first fight!" He looks up at me and rakes my peepers with a murderous glance. "We're all screwed now, thanks to you, you fucking Indian."

* * *

[*"Have you ever cheated on your missus, Jefe?"*]

The doctor hurries in with a dapper in a red tie.

"What kind of trouble have you gotten yourselves into this time, warriors?"

He sees the guy sprawling on the floor and quickly bends down and starts checking his vital signs.

"Bring a stretcher. We need to get him to the hospital immediately."

"Is he going to be O.K.?" asks one of the scruffs.

"I don't know," says the doctor. "What happened here?"

"He slipped and fell," the earringed guy says before anyone else can speak.

"Is Mrs. Marshall going to call off the fight?" asks one of the other scruffs.

"Which fight was he supposed to be in?" the suit breaks in for the first time.

"The first one," says the older guy with the flat cap.

"Uh-oh. Troy's gonna burn," the dapper replies.

"They sent a sub for Knox. He can fight Pantos in the first match," the earringed guy says.

The suit stands there thinking for a moment while the doctor immobilizes the basted guy's neck.

"I don't know," says the necktie. "What about the Knox-Servin fight?"

"We can do repeats," argues the earring. "The point is to save the event, right? I don't want to even think about what Mrs. Marshall would do if her charity event got screwed up."

"But two fights in one day?" the dapper asks.

"We can do the first fight with just controlled shots, right, Pantos?"

"The show must go on," says John Pantos.

"And the second one too," says the earring. "Right, Will?"

"Sure," says another close-cropped muscular scruff with labyrinths in his hair.

"Hmmm," the dapper growls. He looks at the scruff all laid out on the floor, looks at the doctor, looks at all of us, looks at Coach Truddy, and looks back at the knockout. He breathes in and exhales sharply. "Oof! O.K., but pull those punches, got it? I don't want any more accidents. This event has got to come off without a hitch. Doctor, send for another ambulance and go to Central Hospital. Keep me updated as things develop. And you guys start warming up now—we're about to get started. Let's keep things moving!" The dapper strides out of the room just as the paramedics enter. They set up on one side of the room and start getting the vato ready to take him to the hospital.

Coach Truddy comes up to me and whispers, "Careful, son, they're really going to want to clean your clock now. I'm going to go right now and withdraw you from the event immediately."

"No, coach," I say, breathing onto his neck and urgently grabbing his arm. "If they want revenge, let them have it."

I don't want to be there. The air in the bathroom is like fucking concrete myrtling my spirit.

"I'm going to warm up out there, coach." I walk through the scruffs in my red shorts and antediluvian T-shirt. They don't react at all—it's as if I'm a ghost. The guy with the earring doesn't even turn to look at me when I open the door and leave, but I still feel his murderous gaze in the back of my eyes.

I take a deep breath and head toward a small hallway. The voices from the ballroom sound far away. I uncoil the jump rope and start hopping:

"One-e-le-phant-was-swing-ing-on-a-spi-der-web-see-ing-
that-it-held-they-called-a-no-ther-el-e-phant-two-e-le-phants-
were-swing-ing . . ."

I'm starting to feel hot by the time I get to the twenty-second
elephant. Sweat starts to flow. I jump the rope faster and faster,
my feet hardly leaving the floor, in a perfect union of gravity,
time, and space.

"Nice song."

I stop short. The jump rope smacks me in the shins.

A stout man wearing a cardigan and carrying a felt hat in his
hand is leaning with his back against a wall behind me, one
shoe propped up against the wall. When he lowers it to the
floor, he leaves a mark. He comes up to me.

"I haven't heard that in years. You're Mexican, right?"

"What?"

"I don't mean because of your skin color. Don't call me a
racist now that it's all the rage to go around tossing around
accusations at everybody."

"What?"

"I was saying you must be Mexican because the verb
'columpiar' is used only in Mexico. In other countries they're
more, shall we say, academic, if you'll permit me to use that
term, and they say 'balancear' instead, which in my view ruins
the rhythm if you sing it with the latter wording."

"My coach taught it to me," I say at last, having gotten over
my initial surprise.

"Your coach? A unique coach! I never would have guessed.
Again, though, you must be from Mexico—I can tell by your
accent, it's unmistakable. Though I think Mexicans do tend to
take on every accent—as long as it's with Spanish, of course,
and not other languages, such as English, for example . . . And
do you always sing when you jump rope?"

"It helps make the saltation less monochrome."

"Saltation? Monochrome? Well! You certainly do have an

odd way of talking. No, I take that back. To put it more accurately: you have a different way of using words. What grade did you go up to in school, young man?"

"See here, I'm trying to warm up and you're distracting me."

"I do apologize. I was just walking through here and got lost. I saw them taking somebody out on a stretcher. Do you happen to know what that was about?"

"No."

"All right, well, I'm just . . . how would they say it in your country? Sesame for every mole sauce? That's how you say it, right?"

I start jumping again, ignoring him.

"One-fly-lan-ded-on-the-wall-one-fly-lan-ded-on-the-wall . . ."

"One last question, and then I'll leave you alone with your fly on the wall. Why are you wearing those shorts on inside out, when you could read 'Sexy' more easily if you put them on right side in?" He shuffles off toward the ballroom at a turtle's pace. Then he turns back to me while putting on the felt hat. "Oh, and I also voted for Bill a million years ago."

"It's time," Coach Truddy tells me.

The bandages on my knuckles are squeezing me inside the gloves. I feel amputated, like a pig with just two hooves. My fists are compressed and I feel my pulse running through me from my wrists to my forehead. The crotch protector is uncomfortable too. It's squashing my balls and willy. "Are you sure it's necessary, coach?" "I'm sure." Then he puts the protective mask on me and tightens it so hard I can't breathe. "I can't see anything on either side of me, coach." Probably so he won't have to listen to me complain anymore, he tells me, "Open your mouth," and plugs it with the mouthguard. "Ow, dees ah by eeth," I say, but the coach can't understand a word.

"We don't use face masks anymore," the flat cap says behind us.

"What?" says Coach Truddy.

"They changed the rules for amateur fighters years ago."

"What?"

"They banned face masks because there were more injuries with them than without them, they said."

"That can't be right. This guy's pulling our leg. Those masks protect your head."

"All right, have at it then." He walks away.

"I'm telling you, they're trying to take you down, son. There's still time to pull out."

"Nnn, coeh," I say, shaking my head to make sure he understands me.

Another dapper in a red tie comes in. He's got a little metal name tag and an open folder.

"John Pantos?"

"Here."

"Dulls Jara?"

The earring jumps in. "In the hospital."

"I know," says dapper number two, "but we're keeping his name in the general announcement. Who's going to be subbing for him?"

"That guy over there." The yup points at me.

"What's your name, kid?"

"By dabe Ibodio," I say, the goddamn contraption blocking my tongue.

"I can barely understand you—you Cuban or something?"

"Uck."

"All right, Ibodio Uck, you're subbing in for Dulls Jara. You'll be fighting first."

He takes a few steps back.

"Dwight Amir?"

"Here."

"Alanis Stanton?"

"Here."

"You two are going second. O.K."

"Jerry Knox?"

"Right there." The earring points at me again.

"You again?"

"That's what Mr. Perl said," the earring says.

The dapper picks up his walkie-talkie.

"Yes, yes... yes... O.K." He hangs up. "All right, cowboy," he says to me. "You get changed into blue and go . . . Will Servin?"

"Here," says a bronzed macaguamo.

"You two are going third. Got it?"

"Yes."

He keeps going with the other scruffs until everything's all arranged on the paper he's carrying in that folder.

"All right, that's everything, warriors. Let the show begin."

We walk behind John Pantos and the earring. The coach is trailing a little behind me and seems more nervous than I am. I can't see much from behind my mask. They're really going to tenderize me, I think, but as we walk toward the ballroom, it seems like the blind man—that is, me—is leading the guide dog. A dapper stops us before we pass through the yellow lace curtains. A deep black voice is finishing the US national anthem. It goes high and then low at will. It stops singing, and the room explodes into cheers. I hear applause, whistles, noise-makers, rattles, jingle shakers, and little paper flags.

"Let's go, son. Go for it. You've got this, you can do it! Chin up! Put your heart into it! You've got this!" says Coach Truddy, his face bleached, slapping me on the back.

The microphone goes on and I hear a measured masculine voice, like a supermarket announcement amid the clamoring of the audience.

"Damas y caballeros, and now, the moment we've all been waiting for. The first fight in this extraordinary evening of charity and compassion. Fighting threeeeee rounds with youuuuu: Jooohn Pantooos from Chaaarityyy without Boooorders . . ." There's a racketous, caloritic, commotional din. John Pantos pushes through the curtain, leaping and punching the air, followed by the earring. ". . . against Duuulls Jaaara from Unity and Diiignity . . ."

Coach Truddy shoves me, and I pass through the curtain.

An explosion of lights beats down on me as I move forward. The roar echoes off the columns, sandwiching me between the dome and the floor. I'm agog and have to take mincing little steps on tiptoe so I don't fall flat on my face. People are whistling and applauding, making a ruckus and a half. The uproar trampolines from one seat to another.

I reach the little stairs to the ring and climb up.

I turn my whole body around to look back; I don't see Coach Truddy anywhere, but I do see a lot of men and women decked out in crisp, elegant clothing. Some of them are in tuxes and stoles. Lots of them are taking photos with and without flash, with their cell phones or tablets.

I duck under the ropes and enter the ring.

I've never stepped in one before. It feels watery under my feet, like walking in the sticky mud of my unpaved village.

An exuberant woman in short shorts, a bra, high heels, and a sash sweeping from her shoulder to her hip is in the ring holding a sign above her head that says in large, neat letters, "For me, for you, for them. Henry Ford."

The referee, a pudgy gringo with a light-blue short-sleeved shirt, a man-bun, and latex gloves, is weighing Pantos on the other side, in the blue corner.

The singer, a cadet in black with gold buttons, a sword in her belt, gleaming shoes, and a white military basin on her dome who's carrying a furled US flag, heads out of the ring.

Leaving by the other staircase are two older gray-haired men in tuxedos and a gussied-up lady with a little gold chain around her ankle that jingles when she raises her leg to get over the ropes and is helped by two younger men in red ties. There's also an old man in a gray blazer and white pants who helps the short-shorts lady down.

The man on the microphone keeps talking:

"Because the best causes are those that lead to victory . . ."

"No mask," the referee yells, coming up and yanking it off me. I take a deep breath as the man-bun tosses the protective mask out of the ring. "Gloves"—he tugs on my arms. He checks the laces, plucking at them. "Cup"—he fondles my crotch. "Mouthguard"—he pulls my lips open the way you do a horse.

He moves off toward the middle of the ring. The man with the microphone finishes yammering: ". . . and tonight is light. Thank you very much." He leaves the ring, waving his arm at the crowd.

"Get over here!" yells the referee, beckoning to us with his hands. I walk toward the middle. The scruff across from me moves forward too, not taking his eyes off me. I look past his shoulder at the guy with the earring, who flips me the bird and then leaves the ring. "All right. I already told you the rules in the dressing room. I want a clean fight at all times. No low blows. Fair play. Touch gloves."

The scruff pounds his gloves together and then punches mine, saying self-assuredly, seethingly, "Consider yourself dead, you fucking Indian. This one's for Jara."

The referee pushes us toward our corners.

The bell rings.

"Box!" yells the referee, putting his hands together like he's clapping.

The scruff leaps at me in a rage—I can smell his tense, jumbled musculature, scented with incendiary, maladous, murderous perspirations—but before he can tear me to shreds, I see him coming at me and just like that, palindromed, I leap to one side and bring my fist down on his right temple.

Immediately, the guy's legs twist and he delapiflates, unable to even catch a breath.

The referee grabs me by the arm and pushes me toward a neutral corner.

I hear all the people hollering. Their hoopla, their deep-throated raucousing.

The referee crouches over the slab, no longer attempting to do the countdown. He snatches the mouthguard out of the guy's mouth and puts his hand under his neck so he can breathe and his tongue doesn't knot up in his throat.

The doctor and the man in the white pants go up and start checking him over.

I spin around. Mr. Abacuc is down below, pale, his eyes bulging. I look toward the other side of the ring, where the kids are sitting, and I see them shrieking and hopping and wriggling in their seats. I don't see Ms. Webber looking after them. The handicapped kids are in front of them. Naomi's there, still waving the little flags, glowing with excitement, and shouting and shouting. I see she's given flags to some kids in wheelchairs whose heads are lolling; they don't seem to be aware of anything that's happening around them. I try to smile at Naomi, but I can't move my lips because of the mouthguard.

The man with the microphone comes up into the ring:

"Ladies and gentlemen, three seconds into the first round, the winner by knockout is Duuulls Jaraaaa."

They clap for me again. They cheer. The referee comes up and lifts my arm; he turns me toward the four sides of the ring while they keep packing up the swoony scruff.

The referee lets go of my arm.

"Now get out of here," he says stonily.

I exit from the white corner as the man with the micro-phone announces, "The next fight, which will be five rounds,

246 · AURA XILONEN

will begin shortly," and then approaches the knot of people
around the fallen boxer. I circle the ring and pass by the paramedics, who are just rushing in with the stretcher.

I go up to Mr. Abacuc.

"Wheb Coe Tuddy?"

He looks at me with silver eyes as he uncorks the mouthguard with his fingers and starts removing my gloves.

"He passed out back in the hallway."

Ms. Webber is stroking his hair. Her eyes are so red, they
could go blurry behind her pointy glasses. Coach Truddy is sitting on a bench in the hall we walked through earlier. He's still
pale and has beads of sweat on his forehead. Next to him is the
older guy with the flat cap.

"Are you O.K., coach?" I ask him there in the middle of
everyone.

"He was about to have a heart attack," the flat cap replies.
"Left arm fell asleep. His capillaries weren't filling up and he
said he couldn't breathe . . ."

"It was that boy's fault," Ms. Webber cries out, unable to
restrain herself. "He probably knocked his heart into another
part of his body."

I sneak a look at her and have the distinct impression she'd
like to whack my head off with a machete.

"Oh, son," says Coach Truddy with his eyes closed and his
lips parted, white stuff gathered in the corners of his mouth.
"I'd have liked to have been there with you, but when your
body says no, it means no." He leans his head back and rests it
against the wall. Then he asks, "How'd we do?"

"It's all over, but don't worry about that, coach, that's over
now," I tell him as if I were talking to a kid with a stuffed animal.

"I knew it." He opens his eyes and looks at me. His dilated
pupils are sweating.

"Your husband needs to go to the doctor right now before

anything else happens to him. It might have been just an arrhythmia or a fainting spell, but you should go now and not wait for an ambulance, which are swamped at the moment," the older guy tells Ms. Webber. "Do you have a car?"

"Yes," I say.

"Do you know how to drive, ma'am?"

"Yes," Ms. Webber answers plaintively, her voice thin.

"Go to the emergency room at the Central Hospital. Hey you, kid," he says to me, "you help him on that side and I'll get him on this side. How are you feeling?"

The coach opens his eyes again and blinks.

"I can walk on my own . . . I'm feeling better now . . ."

"All right," says the flat cap. "But we're going to help get you to the hospital. Understand?"

Coach Truddy nods his head.

"I'm going to ask you a few questions just to make sure we can take you in your car without making your condition worse. You go ahead and answer them, O.K.? What's your name?"

"Truddy, Benjamin Truddy," he says in a doughy voice.

"Where are you right now?"

"In the . . . the ballroom . . . at the Ford."

"How old are you?"

"Forty-eight . . . Yes, forty-eight."

"Where do you live?"

"On . . . on Avalon . . . 21 Avalon Street."

"O.K.," says the flat cap. "He's not disoriented, and his reactions are good. Let's lift him up!"

I grab Coach Truddy firmly under the armpit and we start towing him out of the hallway through an open door. Ms. Webber is up ahead of us and behind us, circling anxiously as we haul her husband along. She opens the door to the outside. We move among the planters and fountains. Coach Truddy's a heavy guy, leaves a dent in your bones. My legs are shaking in the middle. We round the corner toward the terrace.

"Oof!" the flat cap exhales with sweaty relief. Some distance away, there's a parked ambulance shining its red and white lights everywhere, its rear doors ajar, waiting for the paramedics to bring the felled boxer.

"Absalón!" yells the flat cap as we approach. "Absalón!"

The ambulance driver sees us through the window. He immediately gets out and speed-walks toward us.

"More trouble, cabrón?" he says.

"We need you to take him to the hospital—possible heart attack."

The driver climbs into the ambulance through the back door and unhooks a secondary stretcher. He hooks it to the supports.

"Lift him in," he says.

With an extra heave, we lift Coach Truddy's bulk into the ambulance. The driver sits him down on the stretcher and has him lie back. He deftly attaches some straps across his chest. Then he pulls out a neck brace and places it on the coach.

"My keys . . ." says Coach Truddy.

"What?" I ask, confused.

"To the Fairmont . . . In my pocket, son."

The flat cap sees I've still got my gloves on, so he climbs into the ambulance and reaches out while the driver finishes immobilizing the coach. He fishes the keys out of the coach's pants pocket.

Just then we hear a shout behind us. "Clear the way!"

The paramedics are wheeling the stretcher with the unconscious boxer toward us. The flat cap hops down to the ground as Ms. Webber and I move aside to let them through. The driver gets out to help the paramedics.

"One, two, three." They lift the stretcher up into the left side of the ambulance and engage the wheel locks. The driver closes the two doors and turns to face us.

"Who's coming along?" he asks.

"She is," the flat cap replies.

"Go on and get in front. There's no more room in the back."

Ms. Webber obeys immediately without objecting.

A knot of curious onlookers is already approaching the ambulance. The driver clambers into his seat. He turns on the siren and launches his unit at light speed down the road toward the gate till it turns into a meteorite and disappears past the guardhouse.

"You're oh for three," says the flat cap, grabbing my arm and placing Coach Truddy's keys in the middle of my glove. He turns around and heads inside the Ford Center.

"Hey, what's your name?" I yell through the bustle of people who are now also returning to the main hall.

"What's it to you?" he answers, turning his surly face toward me only slightly.

"Lend me some blue shorts, then," I shout at him, but he's already disappeared amid the planters and people.

* * *

["Never, you myopic moron. What gives? Are you going around spying on me or something?"]

Mr. Abacuc is looking after the kids, circling around them as they shriek exaphorically, galloping, howling at the two boxers beating each other up in the ring and moving back and forth—they weave, tangle, rise, float, land imaginary punches. It's the third round. The bell rings and the two fighters retreat to their corners, dripping foam.

The fourth round is coming up, says the announcer.

I keep going, shooting like a rifle toward the dressing room.

Everyone goes quiet as I enter.

The scruffs stop whispering. I don't see the guy with the

earring, but the other boxers are there, looking away from me as I walk past them toward the corner where I left my crap. I don't see the man with the flat cap either. I toss the keys to Coach Truddy's Fairmont into the bottom of the crate.

The dapper comes in:

"Jerry Knox and Will Servin, get ready."

"I don't have any blue clothes," I yell from the back.

The dapper looks at me and then at the others.

"Does anyone have some extra blues?" he asks the scruffs. Nobody says anything.

"Come on, somebody's got to have extras!"

"We don't have anything for that Indian bastard," Will Servin finally says.

"Come on, warriors! It was a clean fight. That's the way it goes," the dapper argues.

"He can kiss my ass!" yells a scruff with a square beard.

"We'll give you a hundred bucks, Will, if you break that prick in half. We'll take up a collection right now," says a caramel-colored guy who's wrapping his knuckles. "Right, guys?"

Affirmative echoes sweep through the room.

"All right," says the bronzed dude. "But you'd better get the money together!"

"Hey, there's no betting here," the dapper objects.

"Yeah?" says the guy with the beard. "Are you going to beat us up or something?"

"If I tell Mrs. Marshall . . ." the suit defends himself.

"There's no need to tell Mrs. Marshall," bewilders a guy who's sitting down tying the laces of his shoes. "She just came in asking about the idiot wearing the 'Bill for Prez' shirt. She was pissed, so we'd be doing her a favor. You're done for, you piece of shit!"

The dapper starts soaking the neck of his shirt. You can see his hair follicles writhing from across the room.

"Take that shirt off now!" he tells me. He yanks off his jacket and tie, unbuttons his shirt, takes it off, and then pulls his white undershirt over his head. He tosses it onto the bench for me and starts getting dressed again.

Then he helps me take off the shirt and put on his. It feels wet. It's huge on me because the dapper's three or four sizes larger than I am.

"What pants did you bring?" he asks once he's finished buttoning the shirt.

"These ones," I say, pointing to the sweatpants Double-U lent me.

The dapper comes over and picks them up. He takes them over to a corner of the washing machine platform and yanks hard. I hear the fabric give and then rip in two. He does the same with the other leg. He pulls at it and tears it off. Then he helps me put on my new shorts.

"I'll give you ten bucks if that guy doesn't make it past the first round!" he says loud enough for everyone to hear him.

* * *

["If you were a bird, what kind of bird would you be?"

"A rare bird, you sybaritic nunce. What kind of questions are these? Have you been manhandling the self-help books again, putito? I'm going to charge you for them, you stridentine pernacular."]

"They'll be fiiiiighting seven roooounds. In the blue corner, Jeeerry Knox, representing Hope Center Nooooorth."

I head out through the curtain again. I'm alone once more. My improvised shorts have got one leg longer than the other, so one comes down to my knee and the other halfway down my thigh. I walk quickly this time and climb the little stairs into the ring. I pass through the ropes and the referee starts fondling me immediately, while the man with the microphone announces Will Servin, who's representing Heaven, Earth, and Humanity in the third fight of the night.

The referee checks my gloves, makes sure I'm wearing a cup, and when he looks up at my face I see he's startled to recognize me, but he pulls himself together and says, unruffled, "Mouthguard."

I turn around and around until I spot Mr. Abacuc. I leap out of the ring and head toward him while the audience laughs at my nimble-footed exploit.

"I need the mouthguard."

"What happened to Coach Truddy? And Ms. Webber?" he replies.

"They went to the hospital," I shout above the deafening uproar. "But they left me the keys to his car."

His face goes grainy.

Tramplish.

He takes the mouthguard out of the front pocket of his coat and plugs it into my mouth. I feel little bits of lint between my teeth like the skin of woolly caterpillars.

"Ang," I say.

I go back to the ring and hop over the ropes. The audience whoops. They're seething. Unleashing their most basic instincts. In the din I hear Naomi's unmistakable voice: "Give me an O . . . What does that spell? Liborioooo!"

The man with the microphone finishes talking and leaves the ring.

"Come here!" the referee commands me, and I go up to him. I show him the mouthguard, pushing my lips back with my glove. "O.K." He gives me a nod of approval. Then he stultifyingly repeats his spiel, calling to the dude in the red corner. "I already told you the rules in the dressing room. I want a clean fight at all times. No low blows. Fair play. Touch gloves."

My opponent doesn't touch gloves with me—he just turns

around and goes to his corner. It's like being in the streets, where rage demolishes everything in its path, the way red ants demolish calendulas.

The audience roars.

It feeds off itself.

It idolizes its own essence.

The fucking bell rings.

"Box!" yells the referee.

The bronzed guy starts punching wildly right and left, trying to knock me out with one blow. His fists whiz past me, ephemeral, scabbing the air.

Just like with the jump rope, I start chanting, "Pretty little fish, come out and play. Come to the garden and we'll romp all day."

I dish out a right jab that shatters on one of his tentacles. I can tell it hurts because his pupils dilate. Immediately he shrinks back, on guard, like crabs when you touch their eyestalks.

"I live in the water and here I must stay; if I leave, I'll surely pass away."

Just then I release my left cross straight at his block, pushing every molecule of my being into a single atom. The collision is cataclysmic. Flushed. A nuclear chain. My proton hits his glove, his glove hits his face, and his face snaps backward, taking his body with it. Then his block stance opens up like a stupid flower waiting for the insolent rays of the chloroform. And right there, just like that, without giving him room to shield himself for a moment, I drive my right fist between his neck and his clavicle, between his carotid and his nape. People set off lightning bolts and trills in the room when I hit him.

The bronzed dude collapses to his knees as if he were supplicating before God.

And he stays there, as if he's been cut in half and has to repent in his soul to cleanse all the sins from his body.

The audience is aflame.

The bronzed dude, on his knees, has his head bowed. His arms fallen at his sides.

Then time returns and reunites with me and everything starts moving again. The bronzed dude's mouthguard falls out and he tumbles facedown on the floor. The referee shoves me hard, so I stop pounding the vato like an incubus strengthening his own bones with those of other people.

"Neutral corner," the referee orders me.

I head over to the white corner. I watch the referee turn the bronzed dude's body over.

"He's not breathing!" he yells, squatting down and prying the dude's mouth open with his gloved fingers. The medic rushes up with a can opener for throats, and they stick a long clear plastic tube in his mouth. Another knot forms around the prometheus chained to the floor.

The flat cap climbs up to my corner.

"Come on, kid, I'll get those gloves off you."

Without waiting for other instructions, I go over to him and he pulls some scissors out of his trench coat. The audience is still screaming, and some people are trying to scramble into the ring. A dapper climbs up, a cell phone glued to his ear, and two others try to block access to the little red staircase. I see the earring there, busy removing the wounded hercules's boxing boots.

"I swear," says the flat cap as he cuts the laces of my left glove, "either you're the luckiest dude in the world or"—now he's cutting the laces on my right glove—"you're a goddamn uberlucky bastard from hell." He takes off my gloves and tucks them under his arm. He pulls out one of the bottles he's got hidden in his trench coat and expertly removes my mouthguard. "Swallow!" I open my mouth and he pours some into my mouth.

I feel relief as the water spills down my throat and cools my innards.

"Thank you, sir," I say.

"Everybody calls me Bald."

"Thanks, Vald."

"Bald, not Vald."

"All right, Mr. Bald."

The man with the microphone ducks under the ropes and starts reading the card he's holding in his hand.

"Ladies and gentlemen, at sixteen seconds in the first round, the winner by knockout is Jeeeerry Knooox!"

The applause and cheers swell like waves that crash over our breakfronts, on the reefs of our ears. Naomi is clapping like a madwoman. The kids are going berserk.

The referee lifts my arm again and leads me back and forth through the knot of people that's already swarmed into the ring. When he lets go, I rush out of the ring and walk over to Naomi.

"Captain!" I say to Naomi, unable to contain my excitement. "We just won ten dollars for the library!"

* * *

[Sometime in the summer, another fat envelope arrived. When it came, I handed it over to Jefe. He looked at the sender and told me, "Throw it away, you deducified prick. Or burn it, or shove it up your ass, whatever, but I don't want to see it around anywhere. Got it?"

I went out of the bookstore and ducked into the back alley.

I set all the papers on fire.]

Mr. Abacuc comes up to us.

"You two are going to have to help me with the kids."

Behind us, the kids are leaping and cheering my name.

I flip them the bird and they laugh even harder.

They're irrepressible.

"Li-bu-rio, Li-bu-rio, Li-bu-rio!" they chant to their own beat, unleashed, blooming. Naomi's eyes are gleaming and you can almost see brown tears of joy. The little flags are tattered from being waved so energetically; they're hanging on by a thread.

"Well, well, dear Abacuc, who'd have guessed it! I didn't realize you'd brought in a professional for these amateur fights. You're making up for lost time, aren't you, you old fox?"

We all turn to see who's speaking.

I recognize the gussied-up lady with the little gold chain around her ankle. I look down at her legs and yes, the jingler is there above her shoe. She turns to me and holds out her hand, putting it in front of my face to make me look up from her legs. I don't know how to react, so I snap my teeth at her long, fragrant fingernails. Instead of drawing her hand back, she pushes it even closer and then turns it over and strokes my cheek with her slim fingers.

"My, my, and not a drop of perspiration on you, my dear. You're going to have to show me how you do it."

"Do what?" I yell amid the uproar as I feel her smooth skin on my cheeks.

"Turn the whole world upside down and not sweat an ounce of guilt."

"We just opened a library, Mrs. Marshall," says Naomi's voice, exultive, from her wheelchair. "Well, it was Liborio's idea, and we already have six books. But we're going to buy more, right, Liborio? Could you give us some books, Mrs. Marshall?"

Mrs. Marshall slowly pulls her hand back from my face, leans forward, and puts it on top of Naomi's hand.

"Of course, sweetheart. What a marvelous idea! Did you have fun tonight?"

"Lots," says Naomi, and waves the depilated flags.

"I'm glad to hear it, Naomi. Children's happiness is the most wonderful happiness in the world."

The dapper who gave me his T-shirt to fight in comes over, adjusts his red tie, and stations himself behind us.

Mrs. Marshall straightens up and looks back toward me. Her eyes are blue, outlined with shadows of iridium. She has a snub nose and is wearing igneous-looking earrings.

"You have a marvelous way of standing out, young man. Was it your idea or what?"

"What?"

"'Bill for Prez' . . . 'Sexy' . . . Goodness, I'm tempted to buy it off you myself." She smiles slightly.

"Mrs. Marshall," the dapper breaks in. "Congressman Warthon is looking for you."

"Well, he can keep looking," she tells him sweetly without turning to look at him. She winks at Naomi. "That way he can find out what it's like to play hide-and-seek outside of Congress, right, Naomi?"

Naomi smiles.

The dapper goes back to his place behind Mrs. Marshall and doesn't move a muscle.

"I was thinking we can do something with this young man, my dear Abacuc. What do you think?"

"Like what, my dear?" Mr. Abacuc asks.

"I don't know, darling, I'm still recovering from the astonishment. And when something astonishes you, my father used to say, you should always do something, because if you don't, the moment ends and never comes back."

"When it rains, a lot of water comes in through the holes in the gym roof at the shelter," I say just like that, without thinking, as the words enter my head.

Mrs. Marshall smiles at me. Her teeth are white and neatly aligned. Her lips gleam pink.

"You see, my dear Abacuc? Isn't he wonderful? And he has

a voice of his own too. We should all learn something from that—especially you, Naomi, since you have big dreams of being a prominent lawyer." She turns to the dapper behind her. "Dermont, make a mental note to send our contractor, Barnes, to meet with Mr. Abacuc on Monday and take a look at the leaks in the gym roof." Then she comes back to us. "Liborio, right?" She takes my face in her delicate hand again and strokes my chin. "I'm delighted to meet you, young man. You were the best part of the night."

"Thanks, Mrs. Marshall," I reply, calling her by her name.

"Well," she says, surprised, "I see I'm not the only person with an eidetic memory around here. Or have we met before?" She laughs.

"What's eidetic?" Naomi asks suddenly.

"It's a photographic memory," I tell her, recalling the example from the dictionary of a man with an incredible memory that I had to read several times to understand it. I quickly dart my dark eyes over to the blue eyes of Mrs. Marshall. "With a photographic memory, you remember everything that passes through your senses and never forget it."

"Goodness, you continue to surprise me." Mrs. Marshall smiles again. "Exuberant, darling, prodigial. If someone told me about it, I wouldn't believe them, especially not coming from a boxer." She takes a step backward. "Well, my dears, we'll see each other some other time—duty calls."

She turns around and starts walking alongside the ring, waving and blowing kisses and smiling left and right to a bunch of dappers with pipes and gloves. Mr. Abacuc turns to look after her as if he were hyptonized.

Suddenly, Dermont the dapper pulls me toward him and tucks a wad of bills into my hand, closing my fist around it.

"This is from us," he says swiftly, his forehead practically pressing against mine, "so you can replace those pants and because you shut those big talkers up." He winks at me and hurries after Mrs. Marshall, who's already reached the other side of the room. He catches up to her and they go out through one of the side doors that leads to where the tables are set up for the big charity dinner.

"Well, shoot!" exclaims Mr. Abacuc, still absorbed in his thoughts. "Now I understand why she never forgets anything."

I quickly enter the changing room to collect our things. I don't look at anybody. I head toward the corner where our bags and the crate are piled up. Naomi's waiting for me outside with the gaggle of little kids. We arrange them by height so we don't lose them on the way. Naomi counted them one by one after the last fight ended and, like a good captain, assigned them a section of her wheelchair to hang on to, and that's how we led them around, a cluster of boisterous children clinging to the chair. Mr. Abacuc, in the meantime, was over with some acquaintances, trying to find somebody to drive Coach Truddy's car.

"I put your gloves in your crate," says Mr. Bald, who's sitting in the shadows, almost behind the table with the unlit lamp and the pen with the metal chain. I hadn't noticed him. It seems like he's not looking at anything specific—it's dark on this side of the room, and all I can hear is him playing with his fingers, occasionally drumming on the Formica tabletop. "I also tossed your mouthguard in there."

"Thanks," I say. I unwrap my knuckles and drop the bandages to one side. I take the keys to the Fairmont out of the crate, then look for my belt and try to cram the wad of bills in it, but it doesn't fit. So I stuff it in one of the gloves and start getting ready. I take off the shirt and set it aside; I put on mine. Since my pants are torn, I stay like that, all bedraggled, one leg longer than the other.

"You know something?" he says like he's musing to himself. "In all the years I've been in this goddamn business, they've never ripped us to shreds the way you just did." He drums his fingers on the table more slowly. "Never. And I don't know what to think. Sergi's going crazy. We just lost the circuit contract for the rest of the year because we have three young men laid out in bed. Sergi rushed down to the hospital like a goddamn mother of ailing triplets to take care of them."

I just listen. I don't say anything. I keep cramming the bags down because I want everything to fit in the crate so I don't have to carry the bags on my back.

"It was all a mistake. A goddamn mistake. Sergi's always been stubborn, a goddamn mule. And he always ends up screwing everything up."

"Why don't you split up with him?" I ask when I'm almost done packing everything up and about to close the crate.

"Oh, kid." He lets out a lazy, tertulian, vinegary laugh. "Splitting up with family is a mission impossible, especially when your brother's your twin and your best bud."

I lift the crate up to my shoulder, like I used to do with the boxes of cotton I brought to El Pepe and the boxes of books I carried back and forth with Jefe, and start walking toward the exit.

"Hey," I say before opening the door, "how much money does a boxer make?"

Mr. Bald stops drumming his fingers.

"Millions if he's good, but if he's not he'll end up like me."

"What do you mean?" Just then Mr. Bald turns on the table lamp. His left eye is swollen almost shut and it's protemical, inflamed, purple from the irrepressible hematous lump that's practically split his eyebrow open. He sees me look at him carefully and I think he must feel bad because he tries to apologize.

"Sergi's my brother and I've never wanted to hurt him . . . Because I helped you, he . . ." He pauses and touches his black eye.

"Listen," I say, like that, suddenly, like the blow that purpled the rims of his socket—crude, like me, not like how Mrs. Marshall would say it, with her serene, assertive voice, never hesitating. "Do you want to work for me?"

"What?" He takes off his cap and I see the three hairs on his head.

"At the moment I don't have a pot to piss in," I say steadily, "but I want to be something more so I can do something good with myself and other people. And I need a trainer. What do you say?"

"And why me?"

I look at his cap for a second; he's twisting it in his fingers. It's clear he's utterly defeated by everything, everywhere—like me, by motherfucking life itself, Jefe would say. The light reflects off his cheeks, his bloodstained mouth, and his swollen eye, which is swelling larger all the time.

"And why not?" I reply.

I open the door and the kids start cheering for me again out in the hall:

"Li-bu-rio, Li-bu-rio, Li-bu-rio."

When we get back to the shelter, it's late at night. The kids are sleeping in the van like peeled chayote fruits. A trusted friend of Mr. Abacuc has brought the Fairmont back to Coach Truddy's house so it wouldn't be left parked outside the shelter and Coach wouldn't end up with his wheels being stolen or, worse, the whole damn car. Mr. Abacuc gets out of the van and heads up the walk to the house.

Naomi's slumbering. She fell asleep before we were even through the first intersection. She laid her head down on my shoulder and stayed like that the whole way home. Drooling.

"Naomi, we're here," I say, but she's out like a light. Mr. Abacuc has opened the front door, and suddenly I hear a little shriek.

"Oh, you startled me, sir," Mrs. Merche's voice says.

"Come help me with the children," he answers.

Mrs. Merche appears in a nightgown and sleeping bonnet.

"Take two of them," she tells me when I get out of the van. "Like this."

And she drapes them over her shoulders like sacks of flour.

I pick up a couple of kids around their middles like pigs and carry them to the bedrooms behind Mrs. Merche.

"This one goes here . . . this one goes there . . . this one here . . . this one there." We deal them like playing cards onto their bunks. I go out for two more little boys, and Mrs. Merche grabs two little girls. We deal again and go back out. She picks up the last two. Mr. Abacuc's trying to lift down Naomi's wheelchair. I help him, and between the two of us we manage to get it down to the sidewalk.

"Let's get Naomi into her chair," Mr. Abacuc says.

I stand on the running board of the van and lift Naomi in my arms. I pick her up by the armpits and carry her to the chair. I bend over to put her down, but she won't let go.

"Naomi, let go."

"No," she says drowsily. "Arry me inside."

Mrs. Merche comes back.

"Pass her to me," she tells me.

I place the girl in her arms, and she takes her inside.

Mr. Abacuc is already opening the back of the van. I take Naomi's wheelchair and load it up with the crate and the kids' bags. I push it to the gym and unload it there, grab my things, and then take the wheelchair to Naomi's room, where Mrs. Merche is already putting her in her nightclothes under the covers. I leave the chair next to her dresser and go out again. Mr. Abacuc closes the rear doors and locks the van.

"Are you tired, Liborio?" he asks, tucking the keys into his coat pocket.

"Not really," I say truthfully.

"I'm pooped," he says. "Let's go inside."

"I'll be there in a minute."

Mr. Abacuc stops and turns to me. He pauses for a moment before speaking.

"Liborio," he says to me. "I'm really sorry, son. I never intended . . . you know . . . I think we're all here on this earth to serve others, not to take advantage of them."

"You've always been very kind to me, Mr. Abacuc. Don't worry . . . Do you remember when you prescribed me those ointments for my bruises?"

"Ha!" He gives a sigh of relief, as if the memory has some-how alleviated the present. "How could I forget! They really clobbered you that time, son."

"See here, do you know other stuff about medicine?"

"Not as much as I'd like."

"Do you know what Clopidogrel is used for?"

"What-grel?"

"Clopidogrel."

Mr. Abacuc lowers his chin and strokes his gray beard.

"They prescribe that to old people to prevent heart attacks. It's a blood thinner, kid. Why?"

"Do you think Coach Truddy will need that?"

"I don't know, son. By the way, I'm going to try to get in touch with Ms. Webber to see how he's doing. I hope it's not too late at night. Don't be too long, Liborio!" He goes inside the shelter. I hear him open his office door and walk across the room.

I breathe hard, deep, scourging all my alveoli, sweeping a gale toward my internal roots. The oxygen revives me inside, like a homeric rhapsode. The air tastes different on this side of the city. I leaf through the street one last time and disappear through the door.

It's almost noon and it's raining again. The sky is gray but the rain is light, drenchative only on the surface. I turn toward the chickadee's building and discover they've demolished the front wall of the fucking bookstore. And the entrance is nowhere to be found. It looks like an old, dismembered shell. There's only a metal mesh containing it, like a straitjacket, from one side to the other. There are also a few wooden boards nailed up at the edges. I wait for a car to pass by, its wipers going, and cross the street to get a closer look. There isn't anything or anyone inside the bookstore. No bookcases, no books, no counter, just damp dust and some mountains of rubble piled up in the corners. The electrical cables seem to have been ripped out by the roots. The light fixtures have no bulbs, and the loft staircase is splintered. The shadows of the now-absent bookcases are traced on the walls, as if a nuclear bomb had vaporized everything in the joint. The tile floor has been pulled up, and the storeroom door has been yanked off its hinges and tossed aside. In the right-hand corner, where the shelves of American novels translated into Spanish used to be, there is now a metal structure that resembles a scaffold, or a tower, or a square ladder. On it are a few boards with some buckets perched on top of them.

"Jefeeee?" I shout loudly, the veins in my neck popping out. But its naked walls return only my echo, lacquered with dust. "Booooss!" I repeat.

"Duuuudee!" I hear Aireen's voice far off. Among the clouds, like an accordion of raindrops.

I quickly turn around.

I look all over for her, look toward one street corner, then the other, but I can't find her.

"Up here!"

Aireen is hanging out the window of her apartment.

"I'm coming up!" I yell to her from the sidewalk across the street.

"No, I'm coming down. Hang on a minute."

I cross the street again to wait for her on the stone steps. From there, the bookstore looks like a big cranium, a skull in the middle of the street. The upstairs windows have been removed too, and their empty holes gape out, staring at nothing.

"Did you find a job?" is the first thing the chickadee says when she comes out of the building. I look at her; she's wearing a little purple jacket and boots. We start walking toward the corner.

"Why?"

"Because you're wearing new clothes. And that sweater looks nice on you."

"It's a hand-me-down," I say without thinking.

"Oh." She's quiet. We turn toward the park.

"I brought you something," I say to break that silence that forms when a person has so much to say that he just keeps quiet. "I don't know what it is, but I think you need it. It's not much, but it's a present for you."

Aireen wrinkles her forehead. I think she probably doesn't like surprises. I take out a paper bag and hand it to her.

"What is it?"

"It's not chocolates, I can tell you that—they wouldn't fit in there. And it's not balloons or flowers either," I say, watching her profile as she bends over the bag. "Go on, open it."

Aireen rips open the bag and finds a box of Clopidogrel. She stops short.

I don't know if it's the rain, I don't know, but Aireen's face starts trickling too.

"Did you steal it?" she says without looking at me, staring at the little box of medicine.

"I got money."

"How? This stuff's really expensive."

I'm tempted to tell her they gave it to me for hitting some guys, but I don't.

"I got some work at the shelter where I'm staying."

"I used to be able to buy it," she says, downcast, pensive, as if seared by something intangible. "Now all I've got is Candy, and that's not enough."

"Did you lose your job?"

She looks at me. There are little droplets at the tips of her eyelashes.

"My grandfather thinks I'm still going to work. He doesn't know they fired all of us and took off, I don't know, to China or Russia or something."

We start walking again till we reach the traffic light. We cross the street and enter Wells Park.

There are hardly any people out. The rain is going chop, chop in the fountain water. The grass gleams with waterlogged clarity.

"Do you want to start a business?" I say as we walk down the gravel path toward the little palms and other trees.

"What kind of business?"

"I don't know, something you like."

"I wouldn't know how. Do you have any ideas?"

"I don't know." Truth is, nothing occurs to me. "What do you want to do?"

We reach a stone bench. It's wet, but Aireen sits down anyway. I do too. The water soaks through my pants and I feel a huge shiver.

"I want to travel!" she says.

She rests her hand on the stone.

I slowly

very slowly

put my hand on top of hers.

She doesn't pull it away.

The rain falls.

At this moment the grass must be blooming inside.

I hear it rustling.

Growing up around my feet.

"You know something?" Aireen says, asail in her own world, still not moving her hand. "Before my mom died last year, she made me promise to take care of my grandfather for as long as he has left on this earth. And I've tried, I swear—I've tried every way I can. Three jobs, because Mom's illness wiped out everything—our old house, our furniture, our dreams. I'm not complaining—my grandfather's a wonderful person, and I love him loads. He never made much money, but many years back when Mom was starting to get sick, he taught me to ride a bike. He would still leave the house back then and used to wander through the streets with his cane, and he'd take Mom and me to museums and concerts and art galleries. He'd take us swimming, and sometimes we'd go to the beach. Once, we went to Europe—yes, a marvelous trip with Big Ben, the Eiffel Tower, the Brandenburg Gate, the Colosseum, the Parthenon. I still remember it. He used to sell his paintings all over the place until he started losing his eyesight. I don't know . . ." She trails off. The rain wets her face. She doesn't blink. At that moment she looks fragile, crumpled under the raindrops. "If I die I want it to be fast, yeah, really fast, so I don't cause so much pain for so long to the people I love and who love me. It should be just like that, out of the blue, tumbling down like a little bird that's been struck by a bolt of lightning and lying there, lifeless, and that's it."

I don't know how to respond. The world seems so brand-new to me in this moment. At Jefe's bookstore I surreptitiously read Virgil and Dante, and I don't know what to do now because life isn't the way they describe it in books. I also read Catullus and Bécquer, and I don't know what to say. I read Boccaccio and Balzac, Homer and Tolstoy, in the park, and I don't know what to do. I read Cervantes and Dickens, Austen and Borges. Pylorus and Aesop. I read the Bible in an attempt to figure out what the hell Father Terán was going on about when he talked about hell, and here, in this moment, I don't know where to find an answer. I used to read because I didn't have any other life to build there in the bookstore, and now I don't know what I can draw on in order to say something, anything, that has any meaning. Life, fucking chingada madre, is not how they portray it in books. So all I can come up is this:

"Would you like to start a restaurant with me?"

Aireen turns her head and laughs, not a mocking laugh but with half a silhouette between us.

"Oh, dude . . ."—and unexpectedly, with her hand beneath mine, shivering on the stone, with the rain braiding our pores, Aireen moves closer to me and gently, unhurriedly, as the rain falls down, kisses me on the lips.

* * *

["Why is it there are hardly any women writers on the shelves, Jefe?"

"Good question, you deuteronomic dolt. I don't know, maybe because shes are better kissers than hes and they don't need fucking literature to work through their neuroses and all their other bullshit."]

Time is absorbed, primed on the canvas of the flowers, the wind, the leaves of the park garlanded with leaden raindrops. Aireen smiles, I can feel it in her lips kissing me. I open my eyes a little and see her beautiful cheeks, her damp eyelashes, her closed eyes, her brows dripping water, her skin. I shut them again and again all my molecules concentrate in my mouth. In the rivers flowing through the air, the clouds battering the atmospheres of the heavens, the lightning bristling the earth as luminous showers pour forth.

Aireen pulls back a little.

She opens her eyes.

I open mine too.

I feel her breathing so close and so deep.

We don't say anything, just sink into each other's eyes and make them enormous. Effulgent. Caramba. Interminable. I see the water trickling down her wet hair, down her cheeks, down her forehead, and runnelling toward her chest, toward the dactylic hexameters of her being the Helen of my life, the most beautiful woman in the universe.

She smiles.

She smiles fully.

She smiles with the indomitable clarity of another cosmos.

Without speaking, without saying anything. Without a word between us, she pulls her hand out from under mine and hugs me, clinging to my neck.

I feel her body through the fabric that separates us, inside the space that brings us together.

I feel her breasts against my sweater.

I hug her too.

I tighten my muscles around her and she presses herself to me.

I feel her shiver.

She shivers.

When it rains it shivers and the thunderclaps become climbing vines.

"Are you crying?" I murmur into her ear.

"No."

"What then?"

"It's the rain—it makes me sad sometimes."

Suddenly we're running east toward the restaurant on Park Street. We cross the street. The rain has intensified. A few moments ago the sky began pelting down again. Aireen got up and pulled me by the sleeve.

"Run!"

"Where to?"

"Crickets Family."

We barely see the puddles; I've already stepped in one and splashed everywhere, but then she stepped in another one and splashed me too. There's not a soul to be seen, just the two of us running, like deer, through the crossfire of the rain.

By the time we reach the restaurant awning, we're laughing after a car just raced past and lashed us with filthy water from the pavement. Aireen yelled at him, and so did I, but the car disappeared into the downpour and we started laughing right there.

I rub a hand through my hair, shaking water from it—I'm dripping. Aireen shakes her hair too and wrings it out. Then she expertly pulls it back and up in a ponytail, which she ties with an orange band she's got around her wrist. She takes off her jacket and shakes it out to get rid of all the leaves the car flung at us.

"Ha-ha," Aireen laughs when she turns and looks at me. "Your sweater shrank, ha-ha-ha."

It's true. The sleeves are halfway up my forearm, my absent musculature on display. I struggle free of the sweater and wring it till I can't get another drop out of it. I hold it out for a look and think it might be a perfect fit for one of the kids at the shelter, where I borrowed it from.

"That wouldn't even fit a baby!" She laughs again.

I throw it over my shoulder and open the restaurant door so Aireen can step through.

"Gracias, caballero." She curtsies and then enters.

The place is almost empty; only two tables by the window are occupied. At one is a couple eyeing the rain through the window from time to time; they turn to look at us when we come in. The other table has a woman and an older man along with a teenager. It seems like they must have gotten caught in the rain recently because there's a dripping umbrella beside their table. On the other end of the room is a bar where a woman in a hairnet is placing a plate on a tray.

"Bar or table?" Aireen asks me.

"You at the bar, me at a table." I giggle.

"Dumbass." She laughs as she heads to where there's another table behind the couple that'll give us a view of the street.

We sit down across from each other, still dripping.

"Are you hungry?" I ask.

"Starving," she says. She picks up a menu that's inside a clear plastic stand. "What about you?"

"Not really."

"Don't worry, dude. It's my treat. It's the least I can do for the gift you just gave me. It must have cost you a fortune.

"It's not that. I'm really not all that hungry."

"You should eat."

"I know, but something in my belly's really fluttering around."

"Are you sick?"

"No," I say, looking out at the street. "I think it's the butterflies."

"You're silly," she says, and takes my hand. She strokes it. Her fingers are so soft that it seems like just her spirit is touching me.

"What can I get you, Aireen?"

"Hi, Catherine," she says. "I'd like a slice of apple pie à la mode and a chocolate malt."

"How about you?" the waitress asks me.

"Do you have something with protein?"

She stares at me for a moment, holding the notepad where she's writing down our order.

"We have veal steak for $19, tuna cakes for $9.80, or scrambled eggs for $4.20."

"I'll have the eggs and a glass of water."

"We just have bottled."

"That's fine."

The waitress moves off.

"Is she angry?"

"She's always like that," Aireen says. "Though sometimes I suspect she doesn't like me. She has three kids to feed, and that always puts her in a bad mood."

"And how do you know her?"

Aireen picks up the salt shaker and tips out a tiny bit of salt onto her palm. She licks it.

"This is one of my boss's places," she confesses, leaning forward over the table.

"Candy's owner?"

Just then the aegis next to us says grumpily to the man, "I told you. This is going to last all night."

Aireen puts a hand to her mouth, smiles, and says quietly, "Yes. His name is Alexaindre."

The man moves his neck as if suppressing a reply. I'm looking at him because he's right in front of me.

"The one who gave me the shoes?"

"It's always the same with you. We should go out, we should stay in—you're never satisfied," the man says, his voice restrained by frustration.

"Are they fighting?" asks Aireen, who can't see the couple because she's got her back to them.

"I don't think so," I say. "Actually, they're about to kiss."

Aireen immediately turns her head to look and sees that I've lied.

"Dummy." When she turns her head back, her lips run right into mine. She swiftly pulls away, surprised. "Dummy," she says again.

I sit back down. I don't know what's happening to me. Something's making me act this way involuntarily, as if a mad destiny were controlling my movements.

"Do you know what happened to the bookstore?" I change the subject to force myself to stop thinking about her lips—they're driving me crazy now that I've felt them again.

"A lot of noise," Aireen says, flushing.

"I'm leaving," the woman says. She gets up and heads for the door.

"You're going to get soaked," the man yells after her.

The woman thinks about that, stops, and returns to her seat.

"When did it start?" I ask Aireen.

"Friday. A lot of workers came and started drilling with those machines that make a lot of noise. Yesterday, Saturday, they came with a truck to take away all the broken glass and piles of rubble." She pauses. "I'm going to miss you." She blushes deeper.

"What?"

"I used to be able to watch you from my window when you would wash the bookstore's front windows. You used to spend hours doing that. Are you always that conscientious in your work?"

The waitress arrives with a tray and sets down our order. She places some silverware beside our plates and leaves.

"Do you know what happened to the books and the other things that were there? Did they take them away?"

"I don't know."

The rain lets up for a minute.

The couple stands and quickly leaves. We've almost finished eating. Aireen gives me a little ice cream and I, in retribution, offer her some egg, which she rejects serically: "Yuck, eggs!"

I laugh.

"Have you ever been in love?" I ask her just like that, discordant, yammering.

She looks at me deeply as she eats one of the last spoonfuls of ice cream.

"Yes, once," she says.

"What's it like?"

"What do you mean, what's it like?"

"You know, what does it feel like?"

"You've never been in love?"

* * *

["We live off the world's scraps, you balding cypress. Atop the ash heap of history; we're what's been left behind, humanity's rubbish. Just think, you little prick, after all the wars that have been waged, what's left? Just garbage—billions of people rotting, swarming, starving, in the most awful misery we can imagine. The world's a piece of shit that we're condemned to inhabit. After the Leviathan, we'll never be able to return to the age of innocence, to the shelter of the womb. We're the worst species in the universe, always devouring everything in our path, like exultant plagues, like decrepitating insects. That's the way things are."

"Did you have another fight with your missus, Jefe?"

"Yes, you asshole."]

I feel my clothes disintegrating with the damp. Aireen asks for the check. I can't stop looking at her. I don't know, it's like I'm discovering new things with every step, new beautiful labyrinths to get lost in.

"What does your tattoo mean?" I ask her when she turns and I spot it again behind her ear.

"It's a promise," she says. "A feather. When I was younger, I wanted things to stop falling apart, but they didn't. So I promised myself, well, that if things got bad again, I'd take flight from the top of a building. But that's in the past now, the kind of thing you think when you have no idea where you're going. What about you—have you ever made a promise?"

"I once promised to help a friend's family."

"And have you kept that promise?"

"No. But I have a plan."

"It's always good to have a plan."

The waitress puts the check on the table.

"I'll pay," I say, and pull out a hundred-dollar bill from the thousand the dappers gave me.

"No, it's my treat," she says, and stops my hand. She pulls a little purse out of her jacket that contains her cell phone and the box of medicine, and counts out $16.90 in one-dollar bills and coins.

"Doesn't your boss give you a discount?"

Aireen looks up and seriously, very seriously, says, "What!"

"Sorry," I say, embarrassed, feeling like the world's biggest idiot. I try to take her hand, but she pulls away. "I'm really sorry. I didn't mean it like that," I say.

Aireen gets up and goes over to the bar to leave the bills and coins for the waitress.

I'm starting to get cold. Outside, the rain has picked back up. I realize in that moment that I don't feel like getting soaked again. Aireen comes back to the table.

"Shall we go?"

I walk beside her in silence. All I hear is the splashing of the storm drains. The looming sky makes it seem later than it really is. A large raindrop splats on top of my head and trickles behind my ears. I'm carrying the crumpled-up sweater in my hand. Aireen stops at the light. A car passes and honks, then accelerates and vanishes from view. We cross the street and head toward her apartment. She's walking with her arms crossed. She takes longer and longer steps, like she's itching to take off running. We turn at the corner and go up to the stone steps of her building. She climbs them quickly and opens the door.

"Thanks for the medicine," she says. She steps one foot over the threshold. "You know, dude, I'm not that kind of girl."

* * *

["What love doesn't kill, heartbreak destroys. That's God's honest truth."]

I wake up with a fever. Yesterday I got back to the shelter leaving a trail of puddles behind me. My whole body aches. I don't want to get up. I didn't go running. I don't want to do anything. Just stay in bed. I've lost Aireen over a stupid mistake—or maybe I never had her. But I'm sure I had her within arm's reach, and I let her get away. I feel anguished, wrung out by despair, which shatters every artery of my soul, enrages every cranny of my body. I sat there for hours last night, outside her door, silently calling to her. Waiting for her to look out and see me there, doing my penance, but no, there was nothing. Just rain and cars. And evening and night pooling around my bones. Once upon a time I asked for so little, just to look at her and nothing more, and then just for her to see me and nothing more, and just then for her to be my friend and nothing more—why now, when I know the touch of her lips, why do I feel like I have nothing? Why do I feel emptier than ever, when in fact I never had anything at all?

It was late when Mrs. Merche opened the door for me.

"Oh, monkey, you're either pigheaded or birdbrained. Why do you always show up soaking wet? Come on, I'll get you something to eat while you dry off."

She sat me down in front of a plate of chicken soup. I grimaced, but in the end I ate it to silence her scolding. I know there's no soup that can pull me from this ravine I'm drowning in.

Then, before sending me off to bed, she told me, "Your aunt came by, swinelet, and left a big box for you in your room."

Dragging the blanket, banging into the furniture, stumbling like a fucking drunk, I came up to my room to fill up with snot. And that's what I did. I spent hours snotting because of that goddamn seasonal flu like the kind pigs get. Lying in bed and sniffling snot mixed with ground glass.

"What did they bring you in the box?!" Naomi suddenly shouts, making my hairs stand on end.

"I don't want to talk to anybody." I burrow under the blankets, covering my head. I'm shivering.

I hear Naomi roll out of the room. I really don't want to talk to her or anybody else. I want to be alone, to be left alone.

Five minutes later she comes back with Mr. Abacuc. Wisely, she stays near the door.

"Are you not feeling well, Liborio?"

"Who told you that?"

"That's not important. You didn't go running today like Coach Truddy instructed you to. How are you feeling?"

"How's coach doing?"

"Still resting at the hospital. It was just a false alarm, but he needs to rest for now. How about you? What's the matter?"

"I'm sick. I've got a fever."

"Let's take a look." He pops a mercury thermometer into my mouth.

Naomi watches from the door, and I can hear the pipsqueak giggling.

A minute later he pulls the thermometer out and examines it.

"If I weren't seeing it with my own eyes, I wouldn't believe it," Mr. Abacuc says in a worried voice, sitting on the edge of the bed.

"What?" I ask, alarmed.

"See for yourself!" He holds out the thermometer. I don't know where to look, so I don't see anything. "Am I really sick?"

"Yes," says Mr. Abacuc, his brow furrowed. "You're really sick."

"What from?"

"Well, as it happens, you don't have anything at all—no fever, no cold. Your temperature's better than any of ours, I can assure you."

Mrs. Merche comes in, her eyebrows raised.

"You see, son? I told you you were going to get sick! Everything has its consequences. Every action has a head cold lurking outside the door." She turns to Mr. Abacuc. "Oh, I came here to tell you that contractor, Barnes, is finished. He's waiting for you in your office with the others." She spins around like a top and leaves, though not before telling Naomi, who's still hovering by the door, "Get out of here, squirt, you don't want to catch any of that monkey's bugs."

"Anyway"—Mr. Abacuc changes the subject—"if I hadn't seen it myself, I wouldn't have believed it. Mrs. Marshall sent the contractor and five men first thing in the morning to patch the holes in the roof. They changed out three sheets of tin that were beyond repair. That's a real miracle, why, yes, it is, and all thanks to you!"

He gets up and tucks the thermometer away in its plastic case.

"By the way, Liborio, there are some illnesses that don't have any symptoms."

When I open the box, I find a note. Naomi's hovering beside me; she keeps trying to get a look inside, but she can't reach from her wheelchair.

"Curiosity killed the cat," I tell her.

"Meow!" she answers.

I read the note: "Sassbucket: For the love of God I had to burn all the things you left at my house. So I'm replacing your filthy crap. Wendoline."

"What is it?" asks Naomi, her eyes bugging out of her head.

I pick up the box, place it at her feet, and say, "You can help, Naomi."

Naomi starts rummaging through the box. She pulls out a new pair of Everlast boxing gloves and sets them on the bed. Then some Nike sneakers with green stripes, some red-and-blue Adidas boxing boots, very shiny, and a brand-new mouth-guard in a case with instructions. Five pairs of shorts—one red, one blue, one white, one yellow, one green—all with hologram labels. A pair of blue-and-black Nike sweatpants with a match-ing jacket. A Ferrari coat with a hood for the snow. Some T-shirts made of a fabric so soft and stretchy, it could be the skin of a Mexican hairless dog. Five pairs of Wilson sports socks. Five athletic T-shirts for boxing. Five bandages and a book that Naomi hugs happily to her chest—"We have seven now," she jubilates—titled *Boxing for Beginners*. From the bottom, among the scraps of white paper that the things had been wrapped in, Naomi pulls out an iPod Touch still in its box.

It's got another note taped to it. "As you can see, I wasn't able to find a cup in your size, papito, ha-ha-ha. So I got you this instead, so you never have to run alone again, my dear champion."

"Wow!" says Naomi. "That's incredible!"

"Do you know how to use it?" I ask.

"Yes." She pulls it out of the box, removes the packaging, plugs in the earphones, and tells me, "Listen." She turns it on, we each place an earbud in one ear, and ta-da, Calle 13 starts blasting.

The first training sessions with my new trainer, Mr. Bald, were rough. On the morning of October 1st, he showed up at the shelter looking for me. I was furiously punching the sandbag. Without Coach Truddy, who was still in the hospital, I had started to train using Double-U's book as my instructor. I went running every morning without music—I'd given the iPod to Naomi so she could listen to whatever she wanted.

"If you keep hitting that bag like that, boy, you're going to end up injuring your wrists and elbows," Coach Bald told me when he entered the gym, followed by Mr. Abacuc. He was wearing his flat cap and a pair of black cotton pants.

"Mr. Bald!" I said in surprise. "I thought you weren't going to come."

"I wasn't sure myself, but here I am, boy."

"What about your brother?"

"I left him the entire family business and the boxers, who, by the way, are still out of it but should survive your assault."

"That's a good start," Mr. Abacuc said, smiling. "What do you think, Mr. Sixto?"

"Call me Bald, please," he said.

"What do you think, Coach Bald? Does he have potential?"

"More than anybody I've ever seen in my life, but we can't tell the boy that or he'll start thinking he's a big shot and end up losing everything."

"Did you hear the coach, Liborio?"

"I've never thought I was bigger than I am."

"Yeah, seems like he's got a golden fist." The coach puts on the mitts. "Let's see how you hit, son."

He plants himself on the floor, stepping forward with his left foot. He raises his mitts into position.

"Now punch me as hard as you can, like it's the final blow to win the world championship, boy."

I gauge the distance. I calculate my timing and launch my missile. But before my fist reaches the mitt, Coach Bald moves it away and my punch goes wide, pulling me forward with it; the coach takes advantage of my being off balance to smack me in the head with the mitt.

"Hey!" I say in a huff. "Don't move that thing away or I can't hit it, and don't smack me in the head."

Mr. Abacuc chuckles.

"So what have you learned today, boy?" the coach asks me.

"That you're a jerk?"

"Ha!" Mr. Abacuc laughs again.

"No, boy," the coach continues, "you learned that skill is more valuable than strength. All right, let's go again, hit me like your life depends on it."

"Are you going to move it away again?"

"That I don't know. Boxing is a matter of fate."

He puts the mitt right in front of my face and yes, people say only fools don't learn from their mistakes, so I gauge the distance but instead of launching my fist toward where the mitt is, I swing the other arm toward where I think the coach is going to move it, and yes, he moves it. I feint with my left arm, the coach moves the mitt to the right, I launch my right missile, and I punch the coach's mitt-covered palm smack-dab in the center. The blow sounds sharp on the vinyl. Thwack! Coach Bald immediately takes the mitt off and starts massaging his hand.

His palm is red.

"You see, boy?" he says, his hand numb. "You just learned

skill." Then he turns to Mr. Abacuc. "Mr. Abacuc, would you happen to have any ice you could give me?"

"How's the music?" I ask Naomi.

"Look at this," she tells me. She calls up a YouTube video of a music teacher giving a first piano lesson. "Do you think I could learn to play the piano?"

"You're way smarter than I am, so I can learn to pound on a speed bag, then you can certainly learn to pound on some keys."

"You can't achieve anything without sacrifice," Coach Bald tells me the next day, his hand wrapped in a bandage. "Whatever talents you have, boy, if you don't use them, you'll never get anywhere. So we're going to divide up your training into five simultaneous elements: physical training, technique, tactics, psychology, and theory. Each of these can be further divided into four elements: direction, volume, intensity, and recovery, and all of this in the pursuit of three fundamental elements: your athletic form, the maximum performance of all your abilities, and finally, boy, the optimum outcome. Understood?"

"Yeah," I say, hanging upside down from my balls like a vampire, trying to do the hundred-and-fiftieth of the sit-ups he's assigned me so that, he said, I'll develop a six-pack.

"Everything is about order and discipline. There's no other way to do it, boy."

Mrs. Merche started plucking more chickens.

"You eat like someone who's actually working hard, you baboon," she said one day after I scarfed down my food in a single gulp. Mr. Abacuc, on Coach Bald's recommendation, had given me a pill to kill all my worms. That's why my skin was blotchy, he said. He also gave me a bottle of vitamin pills so I could take full advantage of all the nutrients in my food and waste less when I went to the bathroom. It's going to make you really hungry, Coach Bald said. And it'll seem like you're never full. Drink lots of water.

This was my routine: Get up at 4:45. Feed the chickens. Go running for two hours. Come back, jump rope, and do physical training: sit-ups, squats, and push-ups of all sorts. Then eat breakfast and help out around the shelter: tidy clothes and bags, move boxes, herd kids like a flock of lambs to have breakfast and then go to Ms. Webber's classes, sweep the rooftops, fix anything that was broken or not working. After breakfast, at eleven, when Coach Bald arrived, start my technical training. He showed me the right way to hit the punching bag.

"If you hit it like that, you'll just get one blow in. But watch this now. A punch moving from your front leg is called a jab. Are you familiar with those?"

"Coach Truddy showed me."

"Good. You use it to maintain distance when your opponent is shorter than you. That's what you used when you knocked out Dulls Jara in the dressing room. It's not a very powerful punch, though you're an unusual case. Always jab with the arm you've got in front. If I put my left leg in front, it's a left jab; with my right, it's a right jab. Now, boy, a punch with the rear arm is called a cross. Look. See that? It can be up toward the face or down toward the pit of the stomach. If you go for the face, you can knock a guy out if you do it right. If you go for the stomach, your opponent will take a few seconds to go down. All right, now, this punch that you throw like a parabola above or below the shoulder is called a hook. You can aim it up at your opponent's head or down at his sides. Look, watch how I punch the bag. If you connect with the head, a hook can knock a guy out. Lower down, connecting with the liver or kidneys, it disables your opponent's legs. This is good for wearing down your adversary's resistance. You hit him right here, right where the liver is, and three or four good, well-aimed punches will make him curl up like an oyster when you throw salt on it. His legs'll go weak and he'll end up going down. Another punch is called an uppercut. This punch starts low and drives upward. If you aim it directly at the chin, you'll be sure to knock out whoever's unlucky enough to be standing in front of you. Look, you start down low and punch upward, like this. Try to throw your whole body forward and then up so all of your weight is pushing in that direction. Got it?"

"Yes, coach."

"Then let's get boxing."

After that came lunchtime, at about two in the afternoon, when I'd wolf everything down; even the pile of stones in the kitchen that Mrs. Merche set the pots on looked like chickens to me. Then I'd rest for a bit in the library, studying Double-U's book, which the coach said might do for now for a bit of theoretical training. It had instructions for how to wrap your knuckles without looking like a mummy. Or how to lace your boxing boots with a double L knot. Or how to clench your fist so as not to break the bones in your hand. Or how to do shadowboxing, imagining an invisible adversary. According to the book, there was a boxer back in Antiquity named Ars de Ilse who could box so fast that his own shadow, blistering there in the sun, couldn't keep up with him.

Then came Naomi, who almost always interrupted me and dragged me off to help her up to the piano on the gym stage. I'd lift her and place her on the piano bench.

"You're not going to fall?"

"I'll try not to," she told me the first time. "I used to fall a lot. See this scar? That's from when I fell down some stairs. I'd sat down there because I wanted to sit by myself, without anybody's help. And I pitched forward and didn't even stick my hands out to catch my fall."

When I lifted her down again, she would hang around my

neck like a medal as I carried her to her chair. After that, Mr. Abacuc would call me to help him unload or put away the daily supplies he picked up around town, or when needed I'd go with him in the van to pick up items that generous people were kind enough to donate to us.

At night after dinner, my eyes would shut of their own accord. And then, I think, my psychological training would begin: I would dream about Aireen.

The first time Double-U called me on the telephone, I was thinking about Aireen as I carried some boxes from the kitchen to a pile that was accumulating outside, which we were going to load up and take to the recycling center to trade them in for a few dollars since Mrs. Merche needed chocolate to make mole poblano for dinner.

"Your aunt's on the phone, monkey-pants," Mrs. Merche said, her eyes like pistols.

"Sassbucket," Double-U greeted me cheerfully on the other end of the line. "What's up? Did you like your crap?"

"Very much," I said enthusiastically. "Except I don't use it."

"Why?" she asked, faltering.

"I'll get beaten up on the street if I wear that stuff."

"Really?"

"No, I'm kidding. It's been really useful."

"Dumbass." She let out a loud laugh.

Then we started talking about how our various projects were going. She told me about the politics around immigration. That the state government wanted to toss all illegals in jail. That the right wing was more hazardous to life than the most toxic toxin on Earth. That she'd just gone back to the *Sun News* paper to do a report about the Minutemen group and she knew she'd done a good job because she'd received more than a hundred threatening e-mails from them. That she was reading a lot at night, especially romance novels, the pink kind with a lot of sex in them, because she needed to keep her mind clear of all the day-to-day garbage.

"And how are you doing, kid?"

"All right," I told her. "I've got my first tournament on the 17th. Coach Bald says it's not a big one but he wants to test me out with some guys who are better boxers than the ones I fought before—he says they were really green. It's a tournament that'll kick off the new boxing season."

"I'm going to promote your fight!" she said all in a rush, excited, without asking who the hell Coach Bald was or who the hell the green guys were.

"Why would you do that?"

"Remember, sassbucket, absence makes the heart grow fonder. I'll call you tomorrow."

"How's it going, Naomi?"

"Look," she told me. She was sitting on the piano bench, tethered there, because once she'd nearly tipped over backwards and if I hadn't been there and leaped to stop her, she'd have cracked her head open on the floor. She didn't want to use the wheelchair because it got in her way, so I'd decided, over her objections, to tie some ropes to her like guylines to make sure she'd be safe and keep her from toppling over. "I learned that that key, the one to the left of those two black ones, is called *do*. Did you know that music has names?"

"No, I didn't know that."

"Yes, all music is made from those same seven names: *do, re, mi, fa, sol, la, ti.*"

"Really?"

"Isn't it incredible?"

On the 16th I went to Aireen's house to give her a ticket to the tournament Coach Bald had signed me up for and to once again ask her forgiveness, as I had already tried to do so many times before. Nobody was home, so I slid the ticket under the door along with a note that said, "I hope you can make it." Then I went and sat down outside. The space where the bookstore used to be was changing. The wrought-iron windows upstairs were now a single large window with a wooden frame. The façade had been refaced with beige granite, and some men were installing LED lights above the door. The interior had been painted white, and some other men were installing what looked like display cases made of glass and wood. There was no more dirt or rubble. In the back I could see part of a new replacement staircase, larger and with an elaborate green railing. The floor of the bookstore was now wooden instead of tile like it used to be.

"Why isn't anybody home?" I wondered, since I knew Aireen's grandfather didn't like to leave the house or do anything outside. A red bus drove past. Without thinking, I dashed to the bus stop and hopped on.

"Kid." Jefe's missus's eyes shone. "Where have you been? We looked and looked for you everywhere. You had us with our hearts in our throats. It's so good to see you again!" She gave me a big hug. She led me out into the backyard, where Jefe was reading a book. He was wearing sandals, and there was a glass of soda on the table beside him. Their children were playing in the grass, building something. "Darling, look who's here."

Jefe lowered his book and glanced over at me.

"Well, look what the cat dragged in. Where've you been, you little shit?"

"I've been kind of busy."

"Well, well, well, a busy numbnuts. And with all those wonderful things keeping you busy, what brings you around here, then?"

"I've got a favor to ask you, Jefe."

"I'm not lending you any money, you beady-eyed little twerp."

"That's not it."

"What then?"

"I want to buy a box of books."

"My, my, what for? Are you going to start your own business?"

"No, Jefe, they're a gift."

"I see you're wearing brand-new, brand-name clothes. You a drug dealer now or something, pinche puto?"

"No, Jefe. I work in a shelter for homeless children."

"Well, fuck me. And to think I was going to offer you a job at my new business."

"Are you still at the bookstore?"

"Damn straight. But I'm remodeling."

"But how, Jefe? You were totally broke—you didn't even have enough to pay the light bill."

"Luck changes, you alopecious alligator. My insurance company paid for it all because the fucking bookstore was totally destroyed. I want to diversify my business so I can spend less time there. What do you say, asshole? Want to come back and work with me?"

"What insurance?"

"The policy I had the good fortune to set up a few weeks before the store was vandalized. What a stroke of luck, huh, you dravidian bastard?"

"Who vandalized it?"

"Oh, we'll never find that out, you meddlesome prick. What does it matter? It was an act of divine justice. I don't give a shit."

"And what are you going to put in there? The bookstore looks totally different now."

"It's going to be a coffeeshop, like Starbucks but with more cachet. I'll serve only the most distinguished customers. And I need someone to do the sweeping and cleaning. You'd get a real uniform this time. What do you say?"

"But you never liked coffee, or records, or the sound of music, or . . ."

"People change, you symphonic idget."

"No, Jefe, some people never change."

The October 17 flight was over pretty quickly. Only Mr. Abacuc, Naomi, and the coach went with me to the Dorvac Forum. Double-U was going to look for me there. She'd just published an article in the *Sun* about an unknown dark horse who was going to make the Latino community in the United States feel proud of its blood, its language, its skin color. She wrote such flattering things about me that I didn't recognize myself in the article. I passed it on to Naomi, who insisted on reading it.

"I'm already proud of you," she told me when she finished.

The dressing rooms were different from the luxurious ones at the Ford Foundation Center. This room was larger but much more crowded. It was like a mini-gym, and we were all crammed in like turkeys. Mr. Abacuc had gone to find seats in the front row for him and Naomi in her wheelchair. Coach Bald led me down the dark corridors. All we were carrying was a small suitcase.

"This is all you need," he said. "That's why we were making fun of you and Coach Truddy when you came in that day—you looked like you were moving house."

"Do you miss your brother?" I asked.

"Sometimes, but now that we don't work together we get along better."

"Have you ever been married, Coach Bald?"

"No, boy, I never have. I was with a lot of women, of course, when I was young. You know, I had a promising future, and when you've got victory by your side, you always have lots of friends of both sexes. But once you experience your first setbacks, everyone runs away from you like you're the plague."

I was going to be competing in the flyweight youth category, the lightest category, because of my malnourished weight, against a dark vato who was barely able grow a mustache and who was clearly very pissed off, pacing back and forth like a caged tiger.

"Watch out for that guy," Coach Bald told me. "He's been training since he was nine years old. He's Ruder Soch's son— do you know who that is?"

"No."

"He's a former professsional boxer who goes around promoting his son all over the place. He wants to make him a champion. He taught him lots of dirty tricks, so watch out, boy. I've seen that guy fight."

"Does he know who I am?"

"How could he, when this is your first fight on this amateur circuit?"

"So I've got the advantage, right, coach?"

We were the second fight of the night.

As soon as the bell rang, the guy tried to plant a fist in my face, but I quickly ducked it and then threw an uppercut, putting all the weight of my body behind it. I barely grazed the tip of his chin, I swear, but the kid writhed and fell back against the ropes like a rag on a clothesline and hung there even after the referee counted down the ten seconds. It took three guys to pull him down and take him off to the hospital with all of his teeth knocked out.

"Well done, boy," the coach told me as Naomi waved more paper pennants. She was wearing a wig she'd made out of newspaper to proudly represent the entire cheerleading squad, which hadn't been able to come. "First fight won less than twenty seconds into the first round."

They gave me a participation medal and a certificate, which Naomi hung up in our library. We now had twenty books, since I'd bought twelve—a hundred twenty dollars' worth—from Jefe.

Back in the dressing room, the coach started putting our equipment away.

"Your next fight is on November 9th, boy."

"Isn't there anything sooner?" I asked, wanting everything to happen faster.

"Don't be hasty, boy, we're just getting started here."

Naomi, Mr. Abacuc, and Double-U were waiting for us at the exit. Double-U was wearing a skirt and high heels under a leather jacket.

"Congrats, champion." Double-U leaped into my arms, kissed me on the cheek, then spun around. "Look who I found."

"That's right," says Mr. Abacuc.

"He's the one who helped you when those scruffs or whatever you call them beat you up."

"She's very generously donating more books to the library," Naomi says excitedly.

"And not just books, kid," says Double-U. "I'm also going to write an article about the work the shelter's doing. Hopefully someone important will read it and things will start looking up."

"You're very kind, Miss Wendoline," says Mr. Abacuc.

"Not at all, I see now that there are lots of us fighting on the same side, but we don't know each other so we could never help one another before."

"It's true," Mr. Abacuc says.

"Hey," I say to Double-U, "this is Coach Bald."

The coach takes off his flat cap and holds out his hand.

"Oh, I see why you call him that," Double-U giggles. "Pleased to meet you, Coach Shaggy."

Coach Bald and Double-U started seeing each other in early November, but I remained oblivious for a while till I put it all together.

"Tactical preparedness means being able to anticipate what's going to happen in the future," Coach Bald told me as I rested after a series of imaginary defenses and counterattacks. A couple of days earlier, the coach had brought me a sparring partner he'd borrowed from his brother Sergi's gym, and instead of telling the new guy to hit me gently "so you don't hurt the boxer," he said to me, "For the love of God, don't put him in the hospital." But I swear, I barely bumped his stomach with a cross and the guy doubled over at the waist as if I'd given him a case of the runs. Coach had to take him back to his brother and hastily promise never to bring me to the sparring sessions because I was laying out all Sergi's chickens. So Coach Bald himself started putting on the face mask, a baseball umpire's chest guard, and the gloves to make me dodge all kinds of punches.

At the end of the training, as we were drinking water, he asked, "So where's that lady jokester of yours from?"

"She lives on the other side of the city."

"Huh." And that was the end of it.

When Double-U called me up to tell me to read the article she'd just published in the *Sun* about the Dorvac Forum fight, she asked, "Is that bald guy really a coach? He looks more like a low-rent hobbit."

"Well, he knows a lot about boxing. I don't know if you need some kind of certificate for this boxing thing. Do you?"

"I don't know, papi. But I'm coming to the shelter tomorrow with a photographer for an interview."

"What time?"

"I'm not sure, we'll see. Whenever the photographer's free."

"All right, I'll let Mr. Abacuc know."

"O.K.," she said before hanging up. "Oh, and don't forget to read the article—I hope you like it."

I went to Naomi and asked her to use the iPod Touch to look on the *Sun*'s web page for Double-U's article: "Chronicle of the Birth of a Latino Hero" by Wendoline Wood.

When Double-U arrived, the coach and I were practicing some combinations on the crazy bag, a small bag that's attached to the ceiling and floor by a stretchy cord and that goes wherever it feels like when you punch it. The coach had told me, "Use your intuition, boy, not logic. Intuit where the crazy bag's going to go and throw it a jab and then a cross. Jab and cross. Then you smash it with a hook and finish it off with an uppercut. That way we'll increase your speed for offense and defense. You've got something in your genes that's been smiled on by the gods."

"That's what I like to see, papi!" Double-U shrieked as she strode into the gym. "Get a photo of him training."

The photographer comes up and points his camera at me and the coach.

"No, man, just get the kid. The other guy ruins the photo, and this is going on the front page."

Coach Bald steps to one side so the photographer can get photos just of me.

"Are you always this rude?" Coach Bald asks her.

Double-U spins around to look at him disdainfully.

"No, coach, sometimes I'm worse." She turns her attention to me. "Papi, act like you're punching that bag and flex all your muscles so the veins in your arms and neck pop out. That's it, like that, don't breathe."

I'm suffocating. The photographer gets a few more shots. Then he puts me on the bleachers and primps me like I'm a magazine model. He arranges my gloves in front and tidies my sweaty hair. He throws a little water on my chest and takes another photo.

"You look sick," Coach Bald tells Double-U.

"I do?" Double-U falters a bit for the first time and smooths her wig.

"You clearly need to go to bed."

"Bed?"

"Yes, so somebody can give you a good screw."

"Jerk."

"Witch."

"Did you read Miss Wendoline's article?"

"No, Naomi. Did it come out already?"

"Yes, she let Mr. Shine know just a little bit ago. He just told me."

"What does it say?"

"All good things. It says we're a shelter that's full of hope. That we have faith and goodwill. It says wonderful things about Mr. Shine. There's even a quote from Ms. Webber. Look: 'We're like a big family, and though my husband is still convalescing at home, we've tried to make this world a better place.' Mrs. Merche's in there too, and all of us. Look: '. . . and sitting in a wheelchair is Naomi, the little girl who wants to be a lawyer when she grows up and who, with Liborio, has been the driving force behind setting up the shelter's Liberty and Nature Library. She hopes to receive donations so that all the children will be able to read (coloring books accepted too) and improve themselves and achieve success.' It also talks about you, and there's a photo of you on the page. Look: ' . . . and, as we wrote in our previous article, this is where our humble hero is from, the young man who, through his hard work and initiative, has shown that heroes can be born anywhere on Earth and into any circumstances.'"

"Does it say anything about me?" Coach Bald asked when I showed him the article.

"No, coach. Not a word."

"I can't stand that hag."

"Come on, she's not that bad."

"No, no, she's not bad at all. She's just liver and onions."

The next day Naomi came in while I was straightening up the kids' room and fixing the shelf for their stuffed animals; it had fallen down when the little runts were playing Tarzan and dangling from it, paying for their fun with a lump and a scrape.

"Come on, hurry!" Naomi said, her face shiny.

Immediately I thought there'd been an accident, so I ran down to the entrance—but no, outside they were unloading two boxes from a truck.

"Is anything wrong, Mr. Abacuc?"

"Not at all, Liborio. They've come to drop off some books."

"They should have brought some bags of sugar instead," Mrs. Merche grumbles.

"Listen to the note, everybody: 'Sometimes it's good to give an imperfect memory a little nudge. Mrs. Dorothy Marshall. P.S. I read the article in the *Sun News* and I liked it.'" The kids, Naomi, and I jump for joy.

"Wahoo!" We all leap into the air, and even though the littlest kids don't know how to read, they join in with our celebration.

"Seeing is believing," says Ms. Webber.

"Let's put them inside," says Mr. Abacuc.

I grab one of the boxes, everybody gathers around to help push it because it's really heavy.

We make it to the library. Naomi can't wait any longer and opens it right up.

There are books of all kinds: for coloring, for beginning readers, for advanced readers, an encyclopedia. There are also games for kids. Some wooden jigsaw puzzles. Some boxes of colored pencils. Pens and markers. Watercolors. Boxes of paintbrushes. Sketchpads. Rulers and erasers.

"Let's open the other one," Naomi cries, and all the little girls and boys shriek with excitement.

We all go outside and bring it in—we look like laborers hauling on the final stone for the Tower of Babel.

Naomi opens it. We all stand there with our mouths open: Mr. Abacuc, Mrs. Merche, Ms. Webber, Naomi, the oldest kids, and, why not, the littlest kids too.

The box contains four sealed packages with apples on them that say, in large letters, "iMac."

"What are they?" Mrs. Merche asks anxiously.

"I have no idea," replies Mr. Abacuc. "But they look really beautiful."

"They're computers," says Naomi, practically drooling.

"Sweet Jesus, we're finally going to enter the twenty-first century," sighs Ms. Webber as she helps Naomi unpack one of the machines.

The library looked phenomenal when we were finished, all stentorian. We had, as Ms. Webber said, totally reengineered the room. I installed some shelves on the left-hand side all in a row so the books would be right there when you entered the library. Naomi counted up a total of five hundred twenty-one books including our original twenty volumes. I helped her decide how to organize them. "After all," I teased her, "who's the expert here, huh?"

We put the games, paints, and art supplies on the right-hand side. And under the shelves I used some boards left over from the chicken coops to build some little worktables for the kids. I made benches out of some of the leftover roofing materials and screwed them down so the kids could perch on them like birds on a wooden wire.

In the rear I built some tables that Ms. Webber requested for the computers. I made tabletops with part of a piece of furniture that was missing two of its legs that I turned upside down. I attached a crosspiece and then installed it, fastening it to the wall with some steel brackets I took from another piece of furniture that I used for parts for the computer desks.

"But you guys should set them up," I told Naomi. "I don't know anything about technology."

I plugged in an extension cord, and they started unpacking the monitors and keyboards.

"Where are the cables?"

"Oh, Liborio, these are wireless now."

"Well, the only one of these I ever used was the one in Jefe's office, and it had cables everywhere and its screen was green and the only thing on it was the list of the books we sold in the bookstore."

"That's so prehistoric!" She laughs loudly, showing her missing teeth.

After a few hours, the library has been transformed. Mr. Abacuc has brought the floor lamp from his office and made a formal donation to the largest and only library ever established at Sun Bridge House.

"Now we have to have the grand opening," says Naomi.

"She's right," chimes in Mrs. Merche, who also helped out earlier sanding the kids' little worktables ("Even though it's pointless," she said, "because they're going to end up even more scratched up than they were already").

Mr. Abacuc brings some string from his office and stretches it from a nail to one of the door handles at the entrance.

"Now all together we're going to pull on it to inaugurate our beautiful library."

"Wait, wait!" shouts Naomi through the uproar. "We have to take a photo with the iPod Touch."

She stands in front of the group to take a selfie. All of us are standing with our backs to the camera, our hands on the string. She says, "All right, on the count of three. One, two . . . three."

298 · AURA XILONEN

She takes the selfie with her in front, smiling, happy. And all of us behind her, breaking the string, looking into the camera.

Naomi and I made a deal. I would tell her what books I thought were the best ones so she could start reading as soon as possible, and she would show me how to peck at the keys on the computer.

"All right, Liborio, you type here and then you go there and open up a window so you can log in. O.K.?"

"And then what?"

"You put in your details and provide a password."

"A what?"

"A secret word that only you know."

"You're sure this is right?"

"Pshaw. You don't watch TV. Everybody has Facebook and Twitter now. This is what computers are like these days."

"We should read books and leave this stuff to the robots."

"Well, you can do that too. Look, you can use this link to download two million books. Which one do you want?"

"But that's not the same as having a paper copy that I can read in bed without having to plug it in."

"All right, fine, don't get agitated. Which book should I start with?"

"Well, you should start with the picture books at first, otherwise you'll just fall asleep."

"But I'm not a little kid."

"All right, fine, read *Don Quixote* if you want, that's your call."

"Hey, Liborio," Naomi said to me two days after starting *Don Quixote de la Mancha*. "What do encomium, visage, appertain, refulgent, sow-gelder, vouchsafe, redress, and vermilion mean?"

"I'll tell you if you tell me too, because I can't make heads or tails of this stuff. What's googling, re-tweeting, texting, hashtag, hyperlink, emoticon, and emoji?"

During the last week of October, as I was coming back from running in Wells Park and slipping another note under Aireen's door, I saw Coach Bald's car go by. He was driving like a bat out of hell.

"Hey, coach, I saw you driving by this morning on Seventh headed toward the highway junction. You were going pretty fast."

"I wasn't going. I was coming back from the hills. I went up to voice my complaints to the hag."

"Why?"

"Didn't you see what she wrote about me?"

"No."

"Here, look." He took a folded newspaper out of his bag and held it out to me.

". . . while some, like the dedicated people at Sun Bridge House, do honorable work and prove that not all hope for humanity is lost, other freeloaders try to figure out what benefit they can extract from the generosity of their betters . . ."

"See?" he said, irritated, the veins on his bald scalp popping out.

"But coach, it doesn't say it's you. It just says freeloaders."

"That's exactly what the hag said when I complained."

"And why do you think she's talking about you?"

"Because I went to her lousy newspaper to complain a few days ago. . ."

"What were you going to complain about that time?"

"I wanted to know why she hadn't written about me in her first article."

"Oh, coach."

At the end of October I noticed that the bookstore had turned into something else.

A large sign high on the front of the building said "Word's Coffee." The mesh had been removed and they'd installed some windowboxes in its place. The sidewalk in front had been set with paving stones; above the front entrance was a curved awning with a lantern on either side. The wooden doors were wide, with beveled glass. The large windows were covered with a dark film so you couldn't see the interior. A large Halloween decoration announced that the grand opening would be on the evening of October 31st.

"And what are we going to do that night?" Naomi asked Mr. Abacuc.

"Same thing as always, honey."

"What's the same thing as always?" I asked.

"Set up an altar for the dead."

I had the idea of inviting them separately.

"Invited to what, sassbucket?"

"A Halloween party."

"Is that Bald idiot going to be there?"

"No, he's going away with his wife."

"He's married?"

"Yes."

"Mr. Abacuc wants to know if you're coming to the Halloween party."

"Where is it going to be?"

"Here, coach."

"Did you invite that painted hag?"

"What painted hag?"

"Forget it. I'll see if I can make it."

I went to Aireen's apartment again. I knocked hard—no

answer. I wanted to invite her to the shelter's Halloween party. I needed to see her. I'd been dreaming about her for days. I dreamed about her everywhere: in the library, smiling; in the gym, sitting on the bleachers; in the bookstore, her behind the counter and me buying jugs of water; in the loft, crouching down because the light had gone out; I dreamed she was in the main hall at the Ford Foundation Center, decked out in beautiful dresses that turned into wings. I also dreamed that she was in Wells Park, swimming in the fountain in a downpour, and an enormous ship was approaching and I was trying desperately to stop the ship, and just as it was about to run her down, bam!, I woke up in a sweat. The clock said 3:40. I couldn't fall back asleep, so I got up and started writing an invitation to the party on October 31st.

The preparations for the Halloween party started on the day itself. Mr. Abacuc brought tissue paper to make little skulls.

"In Mexico people put out food for the dead on an altar so they can come and eat as much as they like."

"I know, that's what Father Terán used to do at church."

"Who's Father Terán?" Naomi asked.

"A really crazy vato," was all I answered.

"Well, here we're going to combine it with Halloween, because death shouldn't be so serious," Naomi replied. "Right, Mr. Shine?"

"That's right, Naomi. Death shouldn't be so serious."

I set up some cardboard boxes we had left over after unpacking our books, and we covered them with a white tablecloth that Mrs. Merche pulled out for us. On top of them we laid out the tissue paper in a variety of colors—purples, pinks, whites, greens, blues, yellows, reds—and then fruit that Mrs. Merche reluctantly contributed.

"That fruit is going to get all full of bugs," she said, "but if it's for the dead, all right, they shouldn't care if it's got a few extra worms. But if it's for the living, careful you don't make yourselves sick!" She snickered.

We put candleholders at each corner.

"Does this have anything to do with God, Mr. Abacuc?"

"Death is really more an affair of men and worms than of anyone else."

"So why do you set all this up? Do the ghosts come eat?"

"Just because I'm not religious doesn't mean I can't tell when to throw a party. Remember, even the worst party is still much better than the greatest war. Plus, I love sugar skulls."

"So do you celebrate Christmas too, even though you don't believe in God?"

"I do, son."

At five in the afternoon, everything was ready for the Halloween party. The altar was a thing to behold, the marigolds lit by votive candles. We were a bit rushed to get our costumes ready though. I'd told them we'd go out into the street to ask people for our calaverita, but Naomi stared at me with saucer eyes.

"What are you talking about, asking for our calaverita?"

"You know, asking people in the street to give you coins and then buying something with them."

"What planet are you from, Liborio?"

"That's how we did it in my village. I'd take a shoebox and poke holes in it for eyes and a mouth, put a lit candle inside it, and go out every Day of the Dead to collect pesos."

"Here we call that 'trick-or-treating,' but we go out as a group in costumes and knock on people's doors and then we sing them songs and they give us candy, not coins. Though since Coach Truddy isn't here, I don't know if they're going to let us go out."

"That's so boring! Just candy? Money's way better."

At six in the evening I was wearing horns. I'd decided to dress up as the devil and made some cones out of newspaper and tied them on my head like a hat.

"Ha," Naomi laughed. "You look more like a goat than a devil with those things on your head."

"You're a goat!" I poked her with one of my horns.

The other kids were dressed up in sheets, bandages, and paints, whatever we had: ghosts, mummies, ghouls, pumpkins, and two kids who we had no idea what they were but if you went near them they went, "Groaaar!"

Mrs. Merche had dressed up like a kitchen witch with her magic cauldron, which was actually one of the pots she used for cooking rice. Mr. Abacuc was wearing a tux with a bowler hat, patent leather shoes, and a gleaming black wooden cane.

"And who are you dressed up as, Mr. Abacuc? James Bond?"

"James Bond? Don't be ridiculous. I'm Chucho el Roto."

"But 'roto' means ragged—shouldn't your costume be the opposite? Holes in your shoes, holes in the knees of your pants, that sort of thing?"

"Back when Porfirio Díaz was president of Mexico, that was what they called the snobs, the dandies, the aristocrats. Chucho el Roto was a bandit who stole from the rich to give to the poor and had to pass himself off as a rich man to pull off his exploits."

"Like Robin Hood?" Naomi asked.

"Yes, exactly, like Robin Hood, except this was real and they sent him to the worst prison in the world: San Juan de Ulúa."

"Like Alcatraz?"

"Even worse. But he escaped and nobody knows where he died, if he actually died."

"What?" Naomi asked again, the kids swarming around her.

"When they opened his coffin, what do you think they found?" He paused dramatically. He raised his hands and cried, "It was full of rocks!" Then he leaped forward and scared the children who were wandering nearby. They fled into Mrs. Merche's arms in terror.

"And what's your costume going to be, Naomi?" Mr. Abacuc asked her.

"What else? I'm going as a princess."

At seven on the dot, Mr. Abacuc and I opened the main door of the shelter. We'd already strung up some streamers made from strips of orange and black plastic and drawn pumpkins on cardboard boxes we'd covered with orange paper. I'd cut some candles in half and arranged them in a little path to the gym. Naomi was dressed up like a princess now. She had a hat with feathers made of newspaper, her hair was braided with colored ribbons, and she was wearing a white dress.

"Which princess are you? A Disney princess?" Mrs. Merche asked her.

"No, I'm Princess Catrina."

"Who's that? What movie was she in?"

"None—she's the only real princess."

"But she's just bones," I said, recalling a book I'd flipped through that had an image of La Calavera Catrina.

"I don't care. She's really elegant," said Naomi. She grabbed Mr. Abacuc's arm so he could push her in the wheelchair. They paraded toward the exit like a king and queen.

A minute later some of Mr. Abacuc's guests started to arrive—his friends were older folks who tended to go to bed early, which was why they were on time. Mrs. Merche's sister and three of her children also arrived. She was dressed up as a crow with her little crowlings in tow.

At a little before seven fifteen, the Fairmont arrived with Ms. Webber at the wheel and Coach Truddy in the passenger seat. All the kids, Naomi, and I went out to greet them. We surrounded the car, shouting, "Trick or treat! Trick or treat! Trick or treat!" Coach Truddy rolled down the window and started passing out candy to every little boy and girl. When he finished giving out candy, he bent forward in his seat and suddenly reappeared with a mask with a pimply nose like a monster. The kids shrieked and took off running in fright, leaping everywhere. He got out of the car. I moved to help him, but he said, "I can do it, son, thank you. I'm not as old as I seem."

Ms. Webber was dressed up as a nurse; she had a white cap on her head, a stethoscope hanging around her neck, blood-red lipstick, and a prop syringe that she waved threateningly at the children. "Come here, little monster, I'm going to give you a shot."

They ran in terror, trying to protect their innocent buttocks.

Just then, Coach Bald and Double-U arrived at the same time. I think they didn't recognize each other at first—they kept walking through the knot of children running back and forth, pursued by the crazy nurse. Also, Coach Bald was wearing a long wig, a leather jacket and leather pants with chains hanging from them, tall boots, and white makeup all over his face, like a rock star from hell. Meanwhile, Double-U was sporting a pink wig, fake eyelashes, dark black eyeshadow, and black lipstick. She wore a black minidress and a garter belt that was visible even though she was standing up. She had on boots with really high heels.

"Papito," Double-U said to me, "don't you want to whip me?" She started laughing like a madwoman.

Mrs. Merche stared at me, her face fiendish.

"Uh . . . I . . ."

"Don't worry, papito," she said, finally putting me out of my misery. "It's a joke. Now you owe me some candy."

"Uh . . . I . . . okay . . . What kind?"

"I like a really traditional one that's typical in your part of the world."

"Which one's that?"

"I want a lollipop to suck!" She started laughing like a mad cow.

Then she skipped off inside the building.

"Who's that babe you were talking to?" Coach Bald asked me as music started drifting out from inside the gym.

We'd brought down one of the computers to play music on. I'd requested Calle 13. Naomi was our DJ, if only reluctantly because nobody else knew how to work the machine, and she came through for me—that was the first song she played.

"Let's dance!" I yelled euphorically, my horns twisting in the air around me.

And I started flailing around like a crazy person on the improvised dance floor. The kids followed me, and then Naomi pulled in Mr. Abacuc, who, one after another, pulled Mrs. Merche in, who pulled her sister in, who pulled her kids in. Coach Truddy joined in of his own accord and pulled his wife with him. Then I pulled in Coach Bald and Double-U. We all started dancing. The kids spun around everywhere, under our feet; they screamed and cheered and went crazy. Naomi whirled and whirled in her wheelchair. I was deeply contented, happy—I saw that Double-U and the coach, neither realizing who the other was, were getting along. Ms. Webber was smiling as she leaned against Coach Truddy's chest. Mrs. Merche snatched a piece of candy from one of the kids, roaring at him like a lioness. Mr. Abacuc did the danza de los viejitos, the folkloric dance of the old men, with a mob of children around him. Naomi pirouetted like a top in her wheelchair. Yes, I was happy, satisfied, but from time to time, when nobody was looking at me, I'd glance toward the door to see if maybe it was swinging open.

The training sessions for my second fight were more intense than the first ones had been. Now Coach Truddy had joined the team as Coach Bald's assistant. Between the two of them, they made me train like a champion. I had to do twice as many exercises in half the time, with four eyes sternly watching me. In the mornings I would go running after feeding the chickens, which to Mrs. Merche's dismay were greatly diminishing in quantity because the coaches had ordered a diet high in protein and carbohydrates for their scrawny athlete. Coach Bald found some cheap vitamin supplements at a sporting goods store, and they gave him some bottles of albumin so my puny muscles would turn to puny steel.

Coach Bald always insisted that discipline was the only way to achieve victory. "No slacking off. Slackers never get anywhere. Train, eat, sleep! The three pillars of success."

Coach Truddy agreed. "You see, son, that's what I've been telling you all along."

One morning Coach Bald showed up lugging a sack of cement.

"Sergi wouldn't let me bring over any weights, but I managed to grab this bag from the basement."

"What's that for?" asked Coach Truddy.

"You'll see, coach. Liborio, bring me those tubs of cream and those two buckets."

I brought them to him.

He cut the top of the bag of cement open and started emptying it into one of the buckets; then he asked me to bring him some of the sand left over from making the punching bag filled with sand and sawdust. Finally he added some gravel and started mixing in water with a metal trowel.

"Half a tortilla is better than none," he said. "We're going to make some weights out of concrete. There are some pipes over there."

Once the mixture was ready, he started filling up the tubs to the top and then, as if they were ice pops, stuck the pipes upright in the middle of them.

"We'll let those dry, and tomorrow we'll make the ones for the other side. Easy, right? Piece of cake."

We made a total of three dumbbells of different weights. And two barbells for doing bench presses, squats, and arm and back exercises.

After eating lunch and lifting weights like mad, which at first dried me out like a tree again so I couldn't bend in any direction, I would go to the library and start writing the letter that I left under Aireen's door each day after my runs. There, as I wrote those letters surrounded by Mrs. Marshall's donated books, things poured out of me that I hadn't even known I was carrying inside me. I remembered lots of things. I was like an ocean roiled by the pain of it all. An expiation of the marrow, of the flesh. I saw myself as being in exile from myself. And I started to write, I don't know why—to try to get Aireen to forgive me or so that I could gradually come to understand myself.

"What are you busy writing all the time?" Naomi asked me one afternoon.

"Things."

"What things?"

"None of your beeswax."

"Tsk, Liborio, that's super old-fashioned. Repeat after me: 'None of your business.' Tsk."

"Right."

"Can I see?"

"No!"

"Why not?"

"Because it's private."

"Is it a love letter?"

"No."

"I think it is—you just blushed."

"It's the heat."

"It's not hot in here, Liborio."

My second fight was on November 9th, this time in Gatbrick Palace. Thanks to Double-U's article, which had been picked up by several local outlets, including the *Chronica News* and the *Daily News Open*, some Latinos were expecting to see "the descendent of Montezuma, the Quetzalcoatl of the Sumerians, the Inca of the Babylonians, the Aztec Hercules," and any other description that occurred to that crazy broad as she was writing.

I was in the dressing room getting ready with Coach Truddy, who was putting on my gloves, when Coach Bald said to me, "Someone's looking for you outside."

I felt my temples do this: plop.

I imagined Aireen coming through the door and reassembling all the molecules here in this vacuum into solid, pure, beautiful matter.

"Who is it?" I asked Coach Bald eagerly.

"It's a man."

His answer brought my heart back down to earth; it stopped absinthifying me like a hypochondriac.

"Can't this wait till after the fight?" I asked, my mood suddenly shifting.

"That's just what I said, but he's a goddamn idiot, boy."

"Send him in."

Even before he entered, I recognized Jefe's musty odor.

"Well, well, little ass-tard, I suppose somebody'll want you someday! You see? You didn't focus on studying, you anemonous triglyceride, so now you're reduced to fucking people up with your fists."

"Your call, champ," Coach Bald said, blocking Jefe's way. "Should I kick this greaseball out?"

"I'll help!" growled Truddy, standing up and looming over Jefe.

I saw Jefe's Adam's apple rise up to the tip of his nose and plunge back down again.

"Hey now, hey." Jefe started perspiring ink.

"Boss!"

The coaches stepped aside.

Jefe moved toward me looking like he'd already been given a thrashing. "Um . . . I . . . well . . . uh . . ."

"It's all right, boss. They were just messing around."

Jefe attempted one of his alebrije laughs, but he only managed to cough out a few feathers.

"I . . . uh . . . I came because . . . uh . . . I saw they put up a mourning ribbon across from the coffeeshop, and your secret love, that super-hot chickadee, is wearing black . . . I thought you might want to know . . ."

"What!" I leaped at him and grabbed him by the lapels. Jefe went paler.

The coaches had to pull me off Jefe to keep him from shitting his pants.

"I'm sorry, kid, I'm really very sorry," he said.

My soul wouldn't fit inside my body.

"I have to get out of here right now," I told the coaches.

"You can't." Coach Bald blocked my path.

"What the fuck do you mean, I can't?" I glared menacingly, looking like I might beat them up.

"Well, all right, you can, but you shouldn't," Coach Truddy said a little more calmly.

"They're right, little bastard," Jefe chirped, observing the whole scene.

"See? Even this greaseball knows it!" Coach Bald shouted. "If you leave, things will all come crashing to a halt and then fall apart. There won't be any turning back."

I headed out to the ring, my eyes blurry. I could tell there were a lot of people, and some of them were chanting, "Indio, indio, indio," while others chanted the name of my opponent: "Murder, Murder, Murder." A man just as dark as me shouted at me, "I hope Murder kills you, fucking dark-ass indio." But I wasn't hearing anything at that point, or if I heard it I wasn't processing it. I was in a daze. What had happened at Aireen's house? Was that why she'd disappeared over the past few weeks? What if her grandfather had died? Aireen didn't have any more family. Would she try to keep her old promise and fulfill it from the roof of the building, leaping into flight?

Coach Bald shoved me into the ring. "Focus, boy. It's time to see what you're made of." He inserted my mouthguard and climbed down from the ring.

The referee called us over.

The boxer in front of me had a face like a dog. He had a lot of tattoos, like he'd been a fucking canvas in a previous life.

"Come on, hurry up, I don't have time to waste," I said as the referee gave us our final instructions.

The tattooed dogface showed his teeth.

The referee separated us, and as soon as the bell rang I sprang at my opponent. He put up a classic block. With no time to lose, I unleashed all my veins, all my blood, all my rage at that poor bastard, and before the dude could take a step backward, I threw a punch that smacked into his defending gloves, which smacked into his face. The impact was so powerful

312 · AURA XILONEN

that his feet remained glued to the floor even as his body tipped backward, bouncing his head against the ring. He didn't even put out his hands to catch himself as he fell, like a vermin, in the realm of the unknown.

I turned around and headed for my corner, spitting the mouthguard out into Coach Bald's hands.

"Let's go!"

Mr. Abacuc, Naomi, and Double-U had stayed out in the Gatbrick Palace parking lot.

"Calm down, son," Mr. Abacuc told me even after Coach Truddy told him what had happened.

Naomi and Double-U looked out at me through the window. "I'm sorry, kidlet. Sometimes things happen against your wishes, and other things, however much you wish for them, don't happen at all." Double-U looked at Coach Bald and then leaned out the window and gave me a kiss.

Naomi looked into my eyes and gave me a little flower made from newsprint.

"Come back soon," she said.

Coach Bald removed my gloves in Coach Truddy's Fairmont. Neither of them said boo about the fight.

Coach Bald toweled off my sweat and passed me the T-shirt for me to put on. Then I took off my boxing boots and put on my pants and tennis shoes.

"It's past Wells Park, right?" Coach Truddy asked.

Before the car had even come to a stop, I had already leaped out onto the curb. Yes, it was true, the ribbon hung there like a large black butterfly, making my eyesight even foggier.

"Run, we'll catch up with you in a minute," Coach Bald yelled at me.

I raced up the stone steps as if they didn't exist. I opened the door and ran up to her floor. I started to see strange people milling around. Suddenly a familiar face appeared.

"I'm so sorry about your grandfather, son." It was Mr. Hundred. He hugged me. "Whatever you and your cousin Aireen need, I'm here for you."

With that, my soul tumbled out of my body. My legs turned to jelly. I couldn't breathe. I walked slowly down the hallway toward the open door of Aireen's apartment. Everybody there was a stranger to me. When I reached the threshold, I saw chairs all lined up in rows; I got a little closer and spotted a metallic gray coffin covered with flowers. Some wreaths were arranged around it.

Without knowing why, without understanding, I started to cry. Gradually my eyes were flooded with salt. I felt a pressure in my chest that had turned me into a statue there in the doorway. Nothing. Death shouldn't be so serious, Mr. Abacuc would say—but what if it is? What if it's the last time we'll see the person we love? What if we'll never see the person who's left us again? I remembered Aireen's love for her grandfather. And I remembered when the old man had showed me the photos of her, her all happy, satisfied, proud. How could life be slipping away from us like this?

"Thanks for coming, dude," I heard behind me. It was Aireen's voice. I didn't have the courage to turn around. I couldn't look at her. No, because I should have been with her before all of this, helping her through everything. Embracing her as we consoled each other about the calamity that death brings with it. She came around in front of me and lifted my chin so I would look at her. "Thank you, dude, with all my heart." I opened my eyes and saw her. She'd been crying, but just then her tears blossomed again; they rolled slowly, lithographically, toward her mouth, lethargic. We looked into each other's eyes for an eternity, an eternity the size of all our lives. She smiled at me and gave me a kiss on the cheek.

"Is everything all right, Aireen?" A tall, blond, well-groomed man came up to us.

"Yes." She wiped away her tears with the back of her hand. "Look, Alexaindre, I'd like to introduce a great friend of mine, Liborio."

The man held out his hand and said, "I know these aren't the best circumstances under which we could meet, but . . . any friend of Aireen's is a friend of mine too. Thank you so much for coming to be with her in this time of such profound sorrow. Can I bring you anything, Liborio? A cup of coffee?"

Coach Bald came in first, followed by Coach Truddy. I was sitting in one of the back rows of the chairs that had been set up in Aireen's apartment. Her grandfather's coffin was there in front of us, gradually growing chiller. The coaches sat down on either side of me. I was falling apart. I couldn't process anything people were saying. All I knew was that everything seemed to be moving in slow motion. Aireen went to sit up front, Alexaindre beside her. Then a lot of people dressed in black and navy blue. Hanging behind the coffin was the painting Aireen's grandfather had done, the one that looked to me like colors had been spit at the canvas.

A little bell rang and an elderly man stood up. He was wearing a black suit with a white flower in his lapel. He leaned on his cane.

"Abraham Reinder painted to be happy, not to earn money. That is the difference between happy and unhappy men. And boy was he happy, but one day his body said no, and it was an everlasting no . . . Let's have a minute of applause for this great artist, father, and grandfather. May he rest in peace."

Everyone started clapping. Aireen bent her head forward and stood up. We all stood. The applause, I imagine, could be heard off beyond the hills.

As we were going down the stairs of the buiding, Aireen caught up to me.

"Dude!"

We stopped. The coaches looked at Aireen, then looked at me, and then looked at each other.

"We'll wait for you downstairs, champ," Coach Bald said, tugging on Coach Truddy's arm.

Aireen watched them leave. Then she rested her beautiful eyes on me.

"Thank you so much for coming, I mean it."

"I'd have liked to be there with you, by your side, in the hospital," I told her, placing my hands on the wooden bannister.

"You were there," she answered. "Your letters were beautiful. You have no idea how much they eased my pain and helped me think about other things while my grandfather was still with me. I thought about your past, about what you wrote about your godmother. About all the hardships you've lived through since you left Mexico, and your life here in the US About the border and the desert, and the way your paisas saved you, El Pepe, on that sunburned highway. About how you met me, and how you loved me from the first moment you saw me in Wells Park. I thought about that a lot, sabes?" She paused, still looking at me, and then continued. "My guess is the tall one's Coach Truddy and the one with the flat cap is Coach Bald, am I right?" She smiled, beautiful as always, forgetting for a moment all the pain she was feeling. Then she stopped—Alexaindre was calling for her to come back to the apartment to see to her visitors. "Remember this, dude: I'm never going to forget you. Not ever." She turned around and disappeared through the doorway.

We reached the shelter at dawn. Coach Bald and Coach Truddy made no effort to interfere with my silence. They just told me to take the day off, that we wouldn't be training the next day.

"Get some rest, champ," they said, and then left.

Mrs. Merche opened the door for me.

"Oh, son, you look like you've been horsewhipped. You need a nice bowl of chicken soup." She bustled into the kitchen, heated the soup in a pot, and served it to me.

She sat down across from me and silently watched me eat.

"Promise me something, monkey," she said suddenly as I strove to swallow the soup, which tasted to me like soggy pebbles. "Promise me you're never going to hurt Naomi."

"Why would I hurt her?"

"Don't pretend you don't know. Don't you see how she looks at you? She's still a little girl, but one day she'll grow up. If you ever hurt her, for whatever reason, I'll split your head open."

When I woke up, the first thing I saw was Naomi's face leaning over me.

"I brought you a muffin before they ran out. See, Liborio, we're always hungry here."

"Thanks, Naomi." I smiled at her over the black circles under my eyes, taking the muffin from her.

"I'm up to the windmills in *Don Quixote*."

"Oh? Do you like it?"

"I love it! I want to be Doña Quixota!" She hugged me.

"You will be, Naomi. I think you will be."

"And you'll be my Sancho Panza!"

Then she rolled backward and turned her wheelchair around.

Lying there in the middle of the bed, I watched her leave, her making that riotous, stratospheric hullabaloo I love so much.